P9-DFT-732

"If you have this under control, I should go."

Madeline glanced at her watch. "I have to be at work in an hour."

Jackson nodded, distracted. Even distracted he could make a woman take a second look.

"Could you stay, just until I figure this out?" Jackson's words stopped her as she started to turn away. "Please."

Reluctant, Madeline looked at the cowboy leaning against the door as if he needed it to hold him up.

He cleared his throat. She met his humor-filled gaze and managed a smile.

"I think it would be better if you called your family, Jackson." There, she'd been strong. She could walk away. He had people to help him.

But she couldn't walk away. Not from the teen girl dropped on his doorstep. Certainly not from the cowboy standing in front of her.

Brenda Minton lives in the Ozarks with her husband, children, cats, dogs and strays. She is a pastor's wife, Sunday-school teacher, coffee addict and is sleep-deprived. Not in that order. Her dream to be an author for Harlequin started somewhere in the pages of a romance novel about a young American woman stranded in a Spanish castle. Her dreams came true, and twenty-plus books later, she is an author hoping to inspire young girls to dream.

A *USA TODAY* bestselling and award-winning author of over thirty-five novels, **Roxanne Rustand** lives in the country with her husband and a menagerie of pets, including three horses, rescue dogs and cats. She has a master's in nutrition and is a clinical dietitian. *RT Book Reviews* nominated her for a Career Achievement Award, two of her books won their annual Reviewers' Choice Award and two others were nominees.

The Cowboy's Holiday Blessing

Brenda Minton

&

An Aspen Creek Christmas

USA TODAY Bestselling Author

Roxanne Rustand

LOVE INSPIRED

INSPIRATIONAL ROMANCE

If you purchased this book without a cover you should be aware that this book is stolen property. It was reported as "unsold and destroyed" to the publisher, and neither the author nor the publisher has received any payment for this "stripped book."

LOVE INSPIRED®
INSPIRATIONAL ROMANCE

Recycling programs for this product may not exist in your area.

ISBN-13: 978-1-335-42498-3

The Cowboy's Holiday Blessing and
An Aspen Creek Christmas

Copyright © 2021 by Harlequin Books S.A.

The Cowboy's Holiday Blessing
First published in 2011. This edition published in 2021.
Copyright © 2011 by Brenda Minton

An Aspen Creek Christmas
First published in 2016. This edition published in 2021.
Copyright © 2016 by Roxanne Rustand

All rights reserved. No part of this book may be used or reproduced in any manner whatsoever without written permission except in the case of brief quotations embodied in critical articles and reviews.

This is a work of fiction. Names, characters, places and incidents are either the product of the author's imagination or are used fictitiously. Any resemblance to actual persons, living or dead, businesses, companies, events or locales is entirely coincidental.

This edition published by arrangement with Harlequin Books S.A.

For questions and comments about the quality of this book, please contact us at CustomerService@Harlequin.com.

Love Inspired
22 Adelaide St. West, 40th Floor
Toronto, Ontario M5H 4E3, Canada
www.Harlequin.com

Printed in U.S.A.

CONTENTS

THE COWBOY'S
HOLIDAY BLESSING

Brenda Minton

Merry Christmas to all of you,
and a special thank-you to Stephanie Newton,
Nancy Ragain, Barbara Warren and Shirlee McCoy,
great friends who helped me so much
during the writing of this book.

To Bonnie, Ed and Willie,
for helping to carry the load at church.

To Mary, for a clean house.

To my family,
for always putting up with me
during the deadline crunch.

To my editor, Melissa Endlich,
for encouragement at just the right moment.

Come to me, all you who are weary and burdened, and I will give you rest.
—*Matthew* 11:28

Chapter One

The rapid-fire knock on the door shook the glass in the living room window. Jackson Cooper covered his face with the pillow he jerked out from under his head, and then tossed the thing because it smelled like the stinking dog that was now curled at his feet, taking up too much room on the couch.

The person at the front door found the doorbell. The chimes sounded through the house and the dog growled low, resting his head on Jackson's leg. The way his luck went, it was probably one of his siblings coming to check on him. This could go two ways. Either they'd give up, knowing he was alive and ignoring them, or they'd break the door down because they assumed the worst.

He opted for remaining quiet and taking his chances. Moving seemed pretty overrated at the moment. Three nights of sleeping on the couch after a horse decided to throw him into the wall of the arena, and this morning it felt like a truck had run over him.

The way he figured it, after another attempt or two they'd give up. Unless the "they" in question weren't his siblings, but instead someone with literature and an invitation to church. Or it could be that girl he dated last month, the one that wouldn't stop calling. He covered his face with his arm and groaned. The dog at his feet sat up.

The door rattled again and the dog barked. The next time they knocked harder. Jackson shot the dog a look and Bud cowered a little.

"Thanks, you mangy mutt."

He sat up, careful to breathe deep. Bruised kidneys, cracked ribs and a pulled muscle or two. Man, he was getting too old for this. He'd given up bull riding a few years back for the easier task of raising bulls and training horses. Every now and then a horse got the best of him, though.

He got to his feet and headed for the door, moving slowly and taking it easy. He buttoned his shirt as he walked. The dog ran ahead of him and sat down in front of the door.

When he got to the door he looked in the mirror on the wall and brushed his hands through his shaggy hair. He rubbed a palm across whiskers that should have seen a razor days ago.

"I'm coming already." He jerked the door open and the two people on his front porch stared like they'd just seen a man from Mars.

He glanced down. Yeah, his jeans were the same ones he'd worn yesterday and his shirt was pretty threadbare, but he was fully clothed and decent. He ran a hand through his hair again and tried to smooth it down a little.

"What?" If they were selling cookies or raffle tickets, he wasn't going to be happy. Take that back; he already wasn't happy.

The woman frowned and he remembered her. She'd moved into the old homestead a year or so back. She wore her typical long sweater, longer skirt and her hair in a ponytail. The glasses that framed big, brown eyes were sliding down her nose. He shook his head and focused on the girl next to her. A kid with blond hair and hazel-green eyes. Man, those eyes looked familiar.

"Mr. Cooper, we... I..." The schoolteacher stumbled over her words. He was on painkillers but he remembered her name: Madeline. Yesterday he'd barely remembered his own name, so that was definitely an improvement.

He grinned because the more he smiled, the more flustered she always got. At that moment she was pulling her heavy sweater a little tighter. A week or so back he'd helped her put groceries in her car and she'd nearly tripped trying to stay away from him.

"Ms. Patton."

"Mr. Cooper," she said, pushing her glasses back in place. She was cute, in a schoolmarm kind of way. "Mr. Cooper, this young lady was dropped off at my house."

"And this young lady is my problem why?" He shifted his attention from Madeline Patton to the girl at her side.

The girl glared at him. He guessed her to be about thirteen. But for all he knew she was sixteen. Or ten. Kids grew up too fast these days. And yeah, when had he started sounding like his parents? He'd kind of thought if he didn't get married and have kids it wouldn't happen.

Wrongo.

He leaned against the door frame. The dog had joined him and was sitting close to his legs, tongue lapping up cool air.

"Mr. Cooper, it is your problem…"

"Call me Jackson." He grinned and she turned three shades of red. He could do one shade better than that. "And I'll call you Maddie."

Yep, from rose to pure scarlet cheeks.

"Madeline." Her little chin raised a notch as she reminded him. "Please let me finish."

He nodded and kept his mouth shut. Time to stop teasing the teacher. But for the craziest reason, one he couldn't grab hold of at the moment, he couldn't stop smiling at her. Maybe he'd never noticed before that her smile was sweet and her eyes were soft brown.

Maybe it was the pain meds talking to his addled brain, scrambling his thoughts the way his insides were already scrambled. Something was causing random thoughts to keep running through his mind. Worse, to jump from his mouth.

"Mr. Cooper, this young lady was dropped off at my house by her aunt. She left the girl and drove away." She paused a long moment that felt pretty uncomfortable. He got the distinct impression that she was making a point, and he didn't get it.

"Why is that my problem?"

The girl stepped forward. A kid in a stained denim coat a size too small and tennis shoes that were worn and holey. She brushed back blond hair with bare hands red from the cold. When had it gotten this cold? A week ago it had been in the sixties.

The kid gave him a disgusted look. "What she's trying to tell you is that I'm your daughter."

"Excuse me?" He looked at her and then at the teacher. Madeline Patton shrugged slim shoulders.

"I'm your daughter."

He raised his hand to stop her. "Give me a minute, okay?"

Jackson rubbed his hand through his hair and took a deep breath. Deep as he could. He turned his attention back to the girl with the hazel-green eyes. He noticed then that the blond hair was sun-bleached, sandy brown more than blond.

The kid stared back at him, probably waiting for him to say or do something. Now, what in the world was he supposed to do?

"Aren't you going to say something?" She stepped close, a determined look on her face.

"Can you give me a minute? It isn't like I got a chance to prepare for this. It's early and I wasn't sitting around thinking a kid would show up on my door today, claiming to be mine."

"Mr. Cooper—" Madeline Patton stepped forward, a little cautiously "—I know this is awkward but we should probably be calm."

"Calm?" He laughed at the idea of the word. "I didn't plan on having the postal service deliver a package to my house today. I certainly didn't expect a special delivery that walks, talks and claims to be mine."

It really wasn't possible. But he could keep some random thoughts to himself. He could take a deep breath and deal with this.

"Why do you think I'm your dad?"

The girl gave him another disgusted look and then dug around in the old red backpack she pulled off her shoulder. She shoved past some clothing and a bag of makeup. Finally she pulled out a couple of papers and handed them to him.

"Yeah, so I guess you're the clueless type," she said.

Nice. He took the papers and looked at them. One was a birth certificate from Texas. He scanned the paper and nearly choked when he got to the father part—that would be the line where his name was listed. Her mother's name was listed as Gloria Baker. The date, he counted back, was a little over thirteen years ago. Add nine months to that and he could almost pinpoint where he'd been.

Fourteen years ago he'd been nineteen, a little crazy and riding bulls. At that age he'd been wild enough to do just about anything. Those were his running-from-God years. That's what his grandmother called them. His mom had cried and called him rebellious.

He handed the birth certificate back to the kid. Her name was Jade Baker. He wanted a good deep breath but it hurt like crazy to take one. He looked at the second paper, a letter addressed to him. Sweet sentiment from a mom who said Jade was his and he should take care of her now. The handwriting had the large, swirling scrawl of a teenager who still used hearts to dot the *i*.

The name of her mother brought back a landslide of memories, though. He looked at the kid and remembered back, remembered a face, a laugh, and then losing track of her.

"Where's your aunt?"

"Gone back to California. She said to tell you I'm your problem now."

"And Gloria?" Her mother. He kind of choked on the word, the name. He hadn't really known her. Madeline Patton gave him a teacher look.

"She died. She had cancer."

Now what? The kid stood in front of him, hazel eyes filling up with tears. He should do something, call someone, or take her home. Where was home? Did she have other family? He didn't know anything about Gloria Baker.

He looked at Madeline, hoping she had something to say, even a little advice. The only thing she had for him looked to be a good case of loathing. Nice. He'd add her name to the list. It was a long list.

"I'm sorry." He handed the papers back to Jade. "But kid, I'm pretty sure I'm not your dad."

Madeline Patton had pulled the girl into her soft embrace while giving him a look that clearly told him to do something about this situation. What was he supposed to do? Did she expect him to open his door to a teenage girl, welcome her in, buy her a pony?

He had known Gloria Baker briefly years ago. He'd never laid eyes on Jade. He wasn't anyone's dad. He was about the furthest thing from a dad that anyone could get.

This wasn't what he wanted. The kid standing in front of him probably wasn't too thrilled, either.

"We'll have to do something about this." He realized he didn't have a clue. What did a guy do about something like this, about a kid standing on his front porch claiming to be his?

First he had to take control. He pointed into the living room. "Go on in while I talk to Ms. Patton."

Jade hurried past him, probably relieved to get inside where it was warm. Madeline Patton stared over his shoulder, watching the girl hurry inside, the dog following behind her. He didn't know Madeline Patton, other than in passing, but he imagined that momentarily she'd have a few choice things to say to him.

Madeline watched Jade walk into the living room and then she turned her attention back to Jackson Cooper. He remained in the doorway, faded jeans and a button-up shirt, his hair going in all directions. Her heart seemed to be following the same path, but mostly was begging for a quick exit from this situation.

Although she didn't really know Jackson Cooper, she thought she knew him. He was the type of man that believed every woman in the world loved him. Well, maybe this would teach him a lesson.

The thought no more than tumbled through her mind and her conscience took a dig at her. This situation shouldn't be about a lesson learned. A child deserved more than this.

And Jackson Cooper wasn't the worst person in the world. He'd come to her rescue last week when a bag of groceries had broken, spilling canned goods across the parking lot of the store. He'd been fishing and was suntanned and smelled of the outdoors and clean soap and was on his way home, but he'd stopped to gather up her spilled groceries, holding them in his T-shirt as he carried them to her car.

Jade had disappeared into the living room. Time for Madeline to make her exit.

"If you have this under control, I should go." She glanced at her watch. "I have to be at work in an hour."

The wind blew, going straight through her. She pulled her sweater close and stomped her booted feet. Jackson nodded, distracted. Even distracted he could make a woman take a second look.

His suntanned face was angular but strong. Fine lines crinkled at the corners of his eyes, eyes that were nearly the same color as Jade's; a little more gray than green. His mouth, the mouth that often turned in an easy, *gotcha* smile, was now held in a serious line.

"I really need to go." Madeline didn't know what else to say, or how to remove herself from this situation, this moment.

"Could you stay, just until I figure this out?" Jackson's words stopped her as she started to turn away. "Please."

Softer, a little more pleading.

Reluctant, Madeline looked at the cowboy leaning against the door as if he needed it to hold him up. She'd heard the ambulance going down the road the other day when he got hurt. They had prayed for him at her Thursday Bible study.

A smile almost sneaked up on her because his grandmother prayed for him, too. The woman who had sold her little house to Madeline never failed to mention Jackson when prayer requests were made on Sunday mornings at the Dawson Community Church. Sometimes she even included fun little details about his social life.

Once or twice Madeline had heard a gasp from various members of the church.

He cleared his throat. She looked up, met his humor-filled gaze and managed a smile.

"I think it would be better if you called your family, Jackson." There, she'd been strong. She could walk away. He had people to help him.

"Right, that sounds like a great idea." He no longer smiled. "If I wanted them all over here in my business, that would be the perfect thing to do."

"They're probably going to find out about her anyway, since she stopped at the Mad Cow and asked for directions. Unfortunately she was one house off."

Madeline couldn't figure out how anyone could confuse her little house on two acres with this house on hundreds of acres. She felt tiny on the long front porch of the vast, white farmhouse that Jackson Cooper had remodeled. His grandparents had built this house after their marriage. But his grandfather had grown up in the little house Madeline bought from his grandmother.

The Coopers had a long history in Dawson, Oklahoma.

Her legacy was teaching at School District Ten, and building a home for herself in Dawson. And this time she planned on staying. She wouldn't run.

"Give us thirty minutes, Madeline." Jackson's voice didn't plead, but he sounded pretty unsure. It was that tone that took her by surprise, unsettled her.

She wondered how it felt to be him and have control stripped away by a thirteen-year-old girl. It was for that girl that she even considered staying.

She hadn't been much older than Jade when she'd

found herself in a new home and a new life. She would always remember how her sister had dragged her from bed, leading her through the dark, to safety.

"I'll come in for a moment, but I don't know how that will help."

"Me neither, but I don't think you should leave her here alone."

"She isn't *my*—" Madeline lowered her voice "—problem. I don't know her. She says she's your daughter."

"Right, I get that, but let's assume she isn't and play this safe."

Okay, maybe he wasn't as reckless as she had always imagined.

"So, are you a decent cook?" he asked as he led her into his expansive living room with polished hardwood floors and massive leather furniture. The dog and Jade were sitting on the couch, huddled together.

"I don't have time to cook." Madeline tried hard not to stare, but the house invited staring. It had the sparseness of a bachelor's home but surprising warmth.

"Just asking, sorry." He smiled at Jade then at her. "So, what are we going to do?"

"Do?" Better yet, "we"? He didn't need to include her in this problem.

"Yeah, do. I mean, we should probably call someone. Family services?"

"That's a decision you'll have to make."

"Right." He pointed for her to sit down.

Madeline sank into the luxurious softness of one of the two brown leather sofas. The one opposite had a blanket and pillow indicating he'd been sleeping there.

No Christmas tree. No decorations.

Jackson stood in the center of the living room. The light that filtered through the curtains caught bits and pieces of his expression as he stared at the young girl sitting on his sofa. They stared at each other and then both glanced away.

Madeline didn't know how to help. She could deal with children in a classroom. This seemed to be more of a family situation. And she had no experience with those.

"Maybe you should sit down?" She didn't know what else to say. It wasn't her home. Jackson stood in the center of the room, hands in his pockets. When she made the suggestion, he nodded once. Jade, sitting next to her, gave a disgusted snort.

Madeline sighed. She glanced around the big room, because the silence was uncomfortable and she wanted to head for the door. She glanced at her watch and then looked around the room again. A big stone fireplace took up the wall at the end of the room. The fire that crackled came from gas logs, not wood. A television hung over the fireplace. The walls were textured and painted a warm, natural color. If it hadn't been for the nervous energy of Jackson Cooper standing there staring at her, and then at the girl claiming to be his daughter, Madeline might have enjoyed being in this room.

Jackson moved a chair from the nearby rolltop desk and straddled it backward. He draped his arms over the back rest and sat there, staring at Jade. His legs were stretched out in front of him. His feet were bare.

Madeline picked up the throw pillow leaning against

the arm of the couch and held it in her lap. Next to her, Jade fiddled with her ragged little backpack.

Madeline did not belong in this little drama. She had to come up with something to move the action along so she could escape.

"Why did your aunt leave you here?" Jackson asked, zeroing in on the girl with a question Madeline had asked and not gotten an answer for.

Madeline shifted to look at the girl, who suddenly looked younger than her thirteen years. Jade shrugged and studied the backpack in her arms.

"Well?" Jackson might not have kids, but he had a dozen siblings and some were quite a bit younger. His parents had adopted a half dozen or so children to go along with the six biological Coopers. And then there had been Jeremy.

Next to her, Jade looked up, glaring at the man in front of them. She chewed on her bottom lip, not answering Jackson's question. This wasn't going to get them anywhere.

"Jade, we need to know what is going on. We might need to call the proper authorities." Madeline smiled to herself. The word *authorities* always did the trick. The girl's eyes widened and her mouth opened.

"My aunt can't take care of me. She doesn't have the money or a house for us."

Jackson rubbed the back of his neck and when he looked at Madeline, she didn't know what to say or do. She taught English at the local school. She wasn't a counselor. She no longer had siblings. The other foster children in the home where she'd spent a few years until she turned eighteen hadn't counted.

"Maybe we should have coffee." Madeline glanced at the man sitting across from her.

Jackson smiled that smile of his, the one he probably thought conquered every female heart. With good reason. There probably wasn't a single woman under seventy living in and around Dawson who didn't sigh when Jackson crossed her path. But she wasn't one of the women chasing after him. And she certainly wasn't the type he chased.

"You know, some coffee would be good. Do you have time?"

"I can make coffee, but then I have to go. School is out but it's a teacher work day." She glanced at her watch again, and not at Jackson. "You should call your parents."

Because this had nothing to do with her.

But years ago she'd been a kid like Jade, lost and alone, looking for someone to keep her safe. As much as she wanted to run from this situation, she couldn't leave Jade alone.

Chapter Two

The schoolteacher looked at her watch again and then she sighed. He nearly sighed in unison because he didn't know what to do with the kid sitting across from him. Madeline Patton taught school. She had to know more than him.

Jackson pushed himself up from the chair, groaning a little at the spasm in his back. He held the back of the chair and hoped it didn't roll away, because if it did, he'd be face-first on the floor in front of God and everyone.

Madeline stood, too. She faced him, looking him over as he stood trying to get his balance. His lower back clenched and he managed a smile to cover up the grimace.

"Are you okay?" Madeline faced him, her brown eyes narrowing as she watched him, her gaze settling on his white-knuckled grip on the back of the office chair.

"I'm good…" He was great. "I think I'll make that pot of coffee and try to sort this out."

Some kid had knocked on his door, claiming to be his. He had broken ribs and a messed-up back. He was wonderful. Every day should start this way. He managed a smile because it wasn't Madeline Patton's fault.

"Maybe she should go with you?" he offered, a little bit hopeful that he was right about her being worried.

"No, she shouldn't." Another little glance at her watch.

"I'm in the room." The girl slumped on the couch and Bud had curled up next to her. The dog raised its head and growled at him. Yeah, well, his hackles were raised, too.

Jackson shook his head and turned his attention back to Ms. Patton. "What do I do with her?"

"I'd start with feeding her."

He sat down, hard. The chair rolled a little. "Right, feed her. I think there's more to it than that."

"I know there is." She hefted her huge purse to her shoulder.

Concern flickered through those brown eyes. He hadn't meant to play her. He was long past games. In the words of his niece, *games were so last year*.

Yeah, he was going through a mid-life crisis, but Madeline didn't need to know that. She didn't need to know that he envied Wyatt Johnson for settling down with someone he'd wake up with every morning. Man, he was even jealous of Andie and Ryder Johnson's twin girls.

Jackson had two rocking chairs on the front porch, and at night he sat alone and watched the cattle graze in the field. He was as sick of being alone as a man could get. But most of the women his age, if they were still single, were listening to their biological clocks. They were ready for rings and babies.

Which brought him back to the problem at hand: Jade Baker.

"I'll get the coffee started, then you need to make a plan," Madeline offered.

"Thanks, that would be great." He smiled at her and she didn't even flinch. He was losing his touch or she was immune. Either way, he was a little baffled.

"Where's the kitchen?"

He pointed to the wide doorway that led to the dining room and from there to the kitchen and family room. Madeline nodded and away she went, that long skirt of hers swishing around her legs.

"Why don't you just give me a hundred bucks or something and I'll head on down the road." The kid, Jade, shot the comment at him.

Jackson turned the chair to face her. She was hugging his dog. She looked younger than thirteen, maybe because she looked sad and kind of lost. Wow, that took him back to Mia when she'd landed on their doorstep twenty years ago. Travis, nearly twenty-five years ago. Jesse when he'd been about twelve. Jesse had been an angry kid. Now he was a doctor.

Jade Baker, aka his kid. She'd asked for a hundred bucks to leave. Surely the little thing wasn't working him for money? Could it be she'd been dropped off by someone who knew she resembled their family? He rubbed his thumb across his chin and studied her. She just stared at him, with eyes that looked like his and Reece's. Eyes that looked like Heather's and Dylan's.

He could smell toast in the toaster. Jade glanced toward the door that led to the dining room and the kitchen. The dog perked up, too. The girl had pulled her blond hair into a ponytail. Her jeans were thread-bare and her T-shirt was stained. He didn't know a thing about her life or what she'd been through.

He hadn't really known Gloria. She'd been about his age and she'd liked hanging out at rodeos. Someone had told him she lived in the back of a van with her older sister. He hadn't believed it. He should have. The next time he'd gone through the Texas town where he'd met her, she wasn't there.

Fourteen years ago. He barely remembered her. But seeing Jade, the memories resurfaced. He hadn't loved Gloria. He let out a sigh. A kid should at least have that knowledge, that her parents loved each other.

He stood up, holding his breath to get through the pain.

"Sorry, kid, I'm not giving you money. We'll figure this out, but money isn't going to be part of the deal."

"Why not? You obviously don't want me here. With some money I can hit the road and find a place to live."

He admired her pluck. She had stood, and his stupid dog, Bud, stood next to her. "You're not even fourteen yet. You can't live by yourself or even take off on your own. And one hundred dollars? That wouldn't get you to Tulsa."

"I could get emancipated."

"Honey, at your age you can't spell that word and you can't even get a job. We'll try for plan B, okay? Let's go see what Ms. Patton is cooking up in there." He eased forward a couple of steps. Jade glared at him and started to walk away. He reached for her arm and stopped her.

"Let go of me." She turned, fire sparking in those hazel-green eyes of hers.

"I'll let go, but you're not going to blame me for not knowing about you." He'd made a lot of mistakes that he'd had to own up to. He sure wouldn't have walked out on a kid.

He would have claimed his kid if he'd known about her. If it was possible that she was his, he'd do everything he could for her. But she wasn't his. He was pretty sure of that.

"Yeah, well, you do kind of have something to do with my life and not being in it," she shot back at him, her chin hiking up a few notches and a spark in those eyes that dared him to tell her otherwise.

"I didn't know where your mother went to, and she never tried to get in touch." He had let go of her arm and they stood in the center of the living room, facing off.

"Yeah, well…" Jade stared at him, her eyes big in a little-girl face. Man, she was a tough kid. He didn't know what to do. He could hug her. Or he could just stand there and stare. He didn't think she'd want either.

"Well, what?"

"Well, you coulda tried." Her bottom lip started to tremble. "Haven't you heard of the internet?"

"If I'd known, I would have searched the whole world to find a kid of mine." He softened his tone and took a step forward.

"Yeah, right. My mom said you told her once that you never planned on having kids and so she didn't bother telling you that you had one."

"That was real nice of her to do that." He wasn't going to say anything against her mother. The kid had gone through enough, and he didn't know Gloria well enough to say much more.

She reached for his hand. "I didn't think you'd be so old."

"Well, thanks, Jade. Is Jade short for something?"

"Just Jade." She had hold of his hand. He looked at her hand in his, small and strong. Yeah, he would have been okay with having her for a kid.

The toast popped out of the toaster and coffee poured into a cup from the single-cup brewer on his counter. Jackson Cooper had the kitchen of her dreams. It didn't seem fair that he had her coffeemaker, the replica of a vintage stove and fridge she'd always dreamed of, granite countertops and light pine floors. But really, what was fair?

Life? Most often not. She'd learned that at an early age. She'd put away the baggage of her past years ago, when she realized carrying it around weighed a person down. If a person meant to let go of their burdens, they shouldn't pack them back up and heft them over their shoulder.

She pulled toast from the toaster and buttered it. From the dining room she could hear Jackson talking to the teenager who had knocked on her door just over an hour ago. A few minutes later they walked into the kitchen and their likeness floored Madeline. The two had the same strong cheekbones, the same strong mouth, and eyes that matched. Jade's hair was lighter.

Jackson walked to the sink and ran water into a glass. Madeline stood next to the counter, feeling out of place in this mess of his and even more out of place in his home. This wasn't where she'd expected to end up today, in Jackson Cooper's kitchen, in his life. When she woke up this morning, it had been like any other Friday. She'd been looking forward to the weekend and decorating her house for Christmas. Jackson hadn't figured into her plans. Ever.

She'd lived in Dawson for over a year, and even though it was a small town, she didn't run in the same circles as Jackson Cooper. Every now and then he flirted with her at the Mad Cow Café. But Jackson flirted with everyone.

"You made toast." Jackson set the glass down on the counter.

"I did, and the coffee is ready." She dried her hands and watched as he shook two pills into his hand, popped them into his mouth and washed them down with water.

"Are you eating?" He pushed a plate in her direction.

"I had a granola bar." She pushed it back. "You need something in your stomach."

"Right." He glanced at the girl that she'd delivered to his front door. "There's cinnamon and sugar in the cabinet if you want it for your toast. After we eat we'll figure this mess out."

Jade carried her plate to the table and sat down. "I don't know what you need to figure out. Fourteen years ago, you messed up." She shot him a look and flapped her arms like wings. "Your roosters have come home to roost."

"Great, she's a smart-mouth to boot," he grumbled as he picked up a slice of toast.

He took a bite and glanced out the window. He didn't sit down. Instead he stood next to Madeline, his hip against the counter. His arm brushed hers. Of course he would be comfortable in his own skin. He wouldn't feel the need for space.

She stepped away from him, picking up a pan that had been next to the sink. Not her pan. Not her mess. She grabbed a scrubber and turned on hot water. Jackson rinsed his plate and opened the dishwasher.

"You don't have to wash that." He touched her arm.

"I don't mind washing it." She rinsed the pan and stuck it in the dish drainer. She glanced out the window again. The land here rolled gently and was dotted with trees. Cattle grazed and a few horses were chasing each other in a circle, bucking and kicking as wind picked up leaves.

"Can she stay with you?"

"Excuse me?" Madeline glanced in Jade's direction and turned her attention back to Jackson.

"Look, Maddie..."

She lifted a hand to stop him. "My name is Madeline."

"Sure, okay, *Madeline*. I need to work this out and you can't leave a kid here with a single man, not when you aren't sure if that single man is her father. And I don't really want my family to know about this, not yet."

"So you want to hide her at my house?" She tapped her foot on the light pine floor and fought the urge to slug him.

"Not hide her. She needs to stay somewhere and she can't really stay here, not until we know exactly what's going on."

As much as she didn't want to, she got it. She also kind of admired him for thinking about the girl. They could call the police or family services, but then she'd end up in state custody. Jade definitely couldn't stay alone with him, a single man. What if she wasn't his? Even if she was, there were things to consider.

She glanced across the room at Jade and she remembered that first night, fourteen and alone in the Montana town she'd rarely visited as a kid. Frightened because she had fifty dollars and no one to turn to, she remembered flashing lights at a convenience store and being driven to a group home.

Fear knotted in her stomach, the way it had then, half a lifetime ago.

"Yes, she can stay with me for a little while."

Jackson watched her, his eyes narrowing. "You sure?"

"Yes, I'm sure."

"I'll pay you." His mouth shifted into a smile, revealing a dimple in his chin.

"Pay me?"

"For letting her stay with you. I can write you a check or pay you cash."

Madeline glanced at her watch. "I really have to go, and I don't want your money."

"There will be the expense of feeding her. She probably needs clothes. I need to pay you something."

Jade stood, the quick movement catching Madeline's attention, and from the jerk of his head in that direction, Jackson's also. The girl held her plate, trembling a little.

"Stop, okay? I'm a kid, not something you trade off or try to get rid of. I thought it would be different..." Jade bit down on her bottom lip and looked from Madeline to Jackson. "You were supposed to be different."

His smile dissolved. Madeline watched as he approached the girl who might possibly be his daughter.

He sat down at the table and pointed for her to sit back down. He was used to girls, used to kids. He had been raised in a house with eleven other children. Now he had nieces and nephews.

"Different than what?" he asked.

"Different, that's all."

"From?"

"From my mom. I thought it would be—" she looked away "—better here."

Jackson whistled. "So far we haven't made much of an impression, huh?"

Madeline wanted to correct him, to tell him *he* hadn't made a good impression. The girl claimed to be his. Madeline was just the unsuspecting stranger who had ended up with Jade on her doorstep. And she'd gotten tangled up in this.

"No, you haven't made a great impression." Jade rubbed her eyes hard. Madeline pulled tissues out of a box on the counter and handed them to her. Jade took them with a watery smile and rubbed her nose and then her eyes.

"Okay, let's start over. Jade, I'm Jackson Cooper and I don't know squat about raising teenage girls. Today one landed on my front porch and I'm trying like crazy to figure out what to do and to keep that from being a problem for both of us." He glanced at Madeline. "And this isn't *her* problem at all."

"I don't like being called a problem," the girl cried again.

"Right, okay, you're not a problem. But you are a situation that I need to figure out. And I need a little time to do that."

"Okay."

"So for now, you'll go with Ms. Patton because that's the best thing for us to do. And I'll work at figuring something out."

"She can't go with me yet," Madeline interrupted. "I have to be at work. Now!"

"Okay, so we'll work this out. She stays with me for now while you go to work and later we figure something out."

"Jade, I'll see you later." Madeline leaned in to hug the girl.

Jackson stood, probably to walk her to the door. She didn't need that. She didn't need any of this.

"I'll see myself out."

Jackson walked with her anyway. "You'll be back?"

"Yes, Jackson, I'll be back."

He must have read her mind.

"Thank you." He grinned as he opened the front door for her. "Sorry if I haven't been the best host. It isn't every day that I get a wake-up call like this one."

She didn't want to like Jackson Cooper. She didn't want to let her guard down. But he had a way of easing into a person's life, taking them by surprise.

"I think we've both been taken by surprise today."

Maybe she had been the most surprised. She had formed opinions about Jackson. Now she had to rethink those opinions.

Chapter Three

Jackson couldn't think of another reason to keep Madeline from leaving. He could think of several reasons why he wanted her to stay. She stood on his porch, brown hair, brown eyes, brown sweater and skirt. He couldn't quite figure her out, and he felt pretty sure that's what she planned when she camouflaged herself in brown. What she probably hadn't expected with her disguise was the fact that she intrigued him.

"I have to go." She stepped away from him, tripping over that crazy dog of his.

Jackson reached for her arm and steadied her. "Sorry about the dog. He can get in the way."

"Right, okay, I'll see you later."

"Madeline, thank you. I'm sure getting mixed up in this mess wasn't on your to-do list when you woke up this morning."

"No, it wasn't. And I'm still not sure how I feel about this. I think you should call family services."

"It's the right thing to do?" He smiled because he guessed she always went by the rules. "But then she's in the system and my hands are tied. I'd like to figure this out and then I'll make a phone call."

"She could be a runaway."

"I'm going to check into that. Don't worry, I'm not planning on harboring a juvenile."

Madeline's brows shot up. "I think you plan on letting me harbor said juvenile."

He grinned and shoved his hands into the front pockets of his jeans.

"If you go to jail, I'll bail you out."

"Thank you, that's very kind." She glanced at her watch. "I have to go. Please think about calling your parents."

The urge to lean down and kiss her cheek didn't come as a surprise. But today he had to think like Jackson the dad, not Jackson the guy who loved beautiful women. He smiled and promised her he'd think about calling his parents. But he'd already come to the conclusion that the last thing he needed was the entire Cooper clan descending on his house today.

Madeline hurried down the steps and across the lawn to her little sedan. He couldn't help but smile as she slammed the door, opened it and slammed it again before driving away. He remembered her doing that when he'd helped her pick up her groceries last week.

When he walked back inside he found Jade on the sofa, a throw blanket pulled over her body. She blinked, and offered a little smile.

"I guess you were up all night?" He eased down onto the desk chair he'd left in the middle of the room.

"Yeah, pretty much."

Jackson rolled the chair closer to her. "I'm going to

get some work done. You take a nap and later we'll figure out what to do next."

"What's next? I'm your kid and my mom is dead.
What are you going to do, dump me on the side of the
road somewhere?"

"No, I'm not going to dump you. I do want to check
all of the facts before we make any big plans."

"Fine." She looked a little pale and her eyes were
huge. "Do I have grandparents or something?"

"Yeah, you have grandparents."

She closed her eyes, a little-girl smile on her face.
After a few minutes he scooted in the other direction,
back to the desk and his laptop. He flipped the top up
and hit the power button, all the while watching a kid
who really thought he could be her dad.

He sighed and shook his head. First he checked his
email because a certain bull he'd been after for a year
had been put up for sale and he'd made an offer. Still
nothing on that front.

So where did he begin searching for Jade Baker's
story? And her mother's? Death records, obituaries and
telephone directories. Every search came up empty. He
had another connection, a friend who had gone into law
enforcement. He typed a short email asking for information on runaways—one specific runaway, actually.

He sat back, trying to think of other avenues for finding Gloria Baker. But it wasn't her name he typed in the
search engine of the internet. He found himself doing a
search for Madeline Patton.

She'd been in the area for a year. She'd moved to a
town where she didn't have family. She'd bought a house
connected to his land. The house had once belonged to

his great-grandparents. It had been their original home-stead, before oil and ranching paid off for the Coopers.

His grandmother had taken a liking to Madeline and sold that little house and two acres to the schoolteacher for almost nothing. Maybe his grandmother knew more about her than the rest of them.

Or maybe he was the only Cooper left out of the loop when it came to Madeline. That kind of bugged him.

His search of Madeline Patton turned up article after article, all from Montana newspapers. He leaned back in his chair and his finger hovered above the mouse. Her story, if she had one, should be private. But the brief sentence under the heading wouldn't let him back away. He clicked the link and started reading.

For a long time he sat there. He read newspaper arti-cles about a child named Madeline Patton. He searched for more articles. As he read he went from pain to rage. He had never wanted to hurt someone as badly as he did at that moment, thinking about that little girl.

Man, it made him want to drive to the school and hug her tight. It made him want to keep her safe. No one should ever be used the way Madeline had been used. Exploited. Hurt.

He closed down his computer because he knew these were her stories, her secrets. She had a right to her pri-vacy. She didn't trust him. She definitely wouldn't trust him with these secrets.

He stood, easing through the motion and then holding on to the desk as he took a deep breath. Jade remained curled in a ball on his sofa, sound asleep. He leaned over her, shaking her shoulders lightly. Eyes opened with a flutter and she pulled back.

"I have to get some work done in the barn. Are you going to be okay here by yourself?" He figured being by herself might be something she was used to. Just guessing.

"Yeah, I'm still tired."

"Sleep on. If you get hungry there's lunch meat in the fridge and a container of chili my mom brought over yesterday."

"Thanks." Her eyes closed.

Jackson slipped on his boots and pulled on a jacket. When he stepped outside he took a deep breath of cold, December air. It felt good to get out of the house. He never would have made it in the nine-to-five corporate world. Walls were not his cup of tea. He liked open spaces, horses in the field and bulls moving around their pens.

Blake, his older and less charming brother, could have the corporate gig. If someone had to count the money, it might as well be Blake.

Jackson whistled for the dog. He came running from the field, brown splotches on his back where he'd been rolling in the grass. When the dog got close enough, Jackson groaned.

"Bud, you stink. Get out of here."

Bud wagged his tail as if being stinky sounded like a compliment.

He shrugged down into his jacket and trudged down the driveway toward the barn. Horses whinnied and trotted along the fence line. Cattle started moving from across the field.

He flipped on lights in the barn and a few whinnies greeted him. He stopped in front of the stall of the little mare he'd bought last week. She stuck her velvety black nose over the door of the stall and he rubbed her face. She'd make some pretty foals. Her daddy had sired quite a few champion cutting horses. Her brother was a champion barrel horse. If people were concerned about pedigrees, hers topped the charts.

A minute later he walked on down the aisle to the feed room. As he unhooked the door he heard a truck easing down the driveway, the diesel engine humming, tires crunching on gravel. He stepped back to the center of the aisle and shook his head. Travis, late as usual.

As much as he loved his kid brother, Jackson missed Reese. They were closer in age and understood each other a little better. But Reese was deployed to Afghanistan and wouldn't be home for a year.

It was going to be a long year. He'd be doing a lot of praying during that time. He and God would be on pretty good terms by the time Reese came home.

Travis whistled a country song as he walked through the wide doors of the stable. He was tall and lanky, his light brown hair curled like it hadn't seen a brush in days. Nothing slowed Travis down. And nothing ever seemed to get him down.

"I didn't expect to see you up and around today." Travis pulled on leather work gloves.

"Is that why you waited until noon to feed?" Jackson blew out a breath, letting go of his irritation.

"Had a cow down and had to pull a calf. I knew everyone here had plenty of hay until I could get here. And I also know you well enough to know you can't stand staying down."

"Yeah, I feel better."

"Good, but let's not go crazy, right?" Crazy, as in give himself a chance to heal.

"Right." Jackson scooped grain into a bucket and headed for the first stall. There were only five horses in the stable; the rest were in the pasture. There were two stallions, a gelding he was training for a guy in Oklahoma City, a mare that had been brought over for an introduction to his stallion, Dandy, and the little black mare.

"You left your front door open." Travis stopped to pet the black mare. "You really think this mare is going to throw some nice foals? She's small."

"She's fast."

He didn't remember leaving the door open and wondered if Jade had woken up. Fortunately Travis let it go. He grabbed a bale of hay and tossed it in a wheelbarrow without asking more questions. He pushed the wheelbarrow down the aisle, whistling again, and Jackson knew he wasn't getting off the hook that easily. Travis didn't let go of anything. But for now he seemed to be content with a nonanswer. He shoved two flakes of hay into the feeders on the stalls. When he got to the stallion, Dandy, he pulled off three flakes.

"Don't overfeed him," Jackson warned.

Travis grinned. "He's a big guy doing a lot of work. He requires extra fuel."

"Not every feeding."

"I'm not five." Travis pushed the wheelbarrow back to the hay stacked in the open area between stalls. He piled on two bales for the horses outside.

"I know you're not." But it was hard to turn off "big

brother" mode. He'd been getting Travis out of scrapes for over twenty years.

"The charity bull ride for Samaritan House is next week. Do you think you'll be able to go?" Travis was a bull fighter, the guy responsible for distracting bulls as the bull rider made a clean getaway. Or distracting bulls when the getaway wasn't clean. Sometimes the bull fighter took a direct hit to keep the rider safe. That made him a hero. Travis had taken more than his share of hits.

Jackson slapped his little brother on the back. "I'm going to take a rain check."

Travis grinned. "Really? What's going on with you?"

The Russian accent was still noticeable, even after all his years in America, and being raised as a Cooper.

"Nothing, just not sure if I'll be able to make it. If you need me, though…"

"No, we should be fine."

They walked outside. The sun was bright and the sky a clear blue, not a cloud in sight. It hadn't warmed up much and didn't seem to be heading in that direction.

The corral held a few of their best bulls. Jackson walked up to the metal pipe enclosure and raised a foot to rest it on the lowest pipe of the six-foot-tall pen. He hadn't ridden bulls professionally for several years. He trained them, sometimes hauled them and then sold them. The Cooper bull breeding program was his baby. Gage, the brother between Reese and Travis, was the bull rider these days.

Raising bucking bulls had become a big business, bigger than they'd ever thought it would be.

Travis pointed to a rangy, Holstein mix bull. "Bottle Rocket is scheduled for the championship round in Oklahoma City?"

"He is." Not one of them had guessed that little bull calf they had bottle-fed would be a champion bucking bull. But there he was, pawing at the ground and looking for all the world like a top athlete and not the sickly calf they'd saved six years earlier.

A car rumbled up the drive. Jackson didn't turn as quickly as he would have a week ago. Travis beat him to the punch. And that meant a lot of explaining for Jackson to do.

"Isn't that Madeline Patton?" Travis crossed his arms over one of the poles of the fence but turned to watch as Madeline got out of the car and then the front door of the house opened.

What in the world was she doing here so early?

"Yeah, I guess it is." Jackson turned his back to the woman and kid heading their way. He needed to think fast and distract Travis.

But of course this would be the day that Travis was focused and sharp. He pulled dark-framed glasses out of his pocket and shoved them onto his handsome face. Somehow Travis always looked studious in those glasses. And serious.

Jackson kept his own attention focused on Bottle Rocket.

"So, Madeline Patton and a kid that looks like you. Something you want to tell me?" Travis stared straight ahead, his voice low.

Jackson wanted to clobber his younger brother. Travis was like the farm dog that kept chewing up shoes, but you kept it anyway. He didn't mean to cause trouble, he just naturally found it.

"No, I don't really have much to tell you."

"Well, there are rumors spreading through town about a kid that looks like you showing up at the Mad Cow asking for directions to Jackson Cooper's house."

Travis let out a sigh and shook his head. He stepped back from the fence and turned to face the woman and teenager heading their way.

"People in this town gossip more than they pray." Jackson walked away from his younger brother.

"Shoot, Jackson, what do you think a prayer chain is?"

Jackson didn't wait for Travis, but Travis caught up with him anyway. "Travis, I'd hope that a prayer chain is for prayer."

"Is she yours?"

Jackson glanced at Travis. "What do you think?"

"What are you going to do about it?"

Jackson shrugged. At this point he didn't have a clue. But it would help if he could find her mother. Since he'd discovered there wasn't a death certificate for Gloria Baker, he assumed she was still alive.

Chapter Four

Madeline didn't quite know what to say, not with Travis staring from Jackson to Jade and then to her. She wanted to lift her hands and back away. She wanted to explain to them all that this family drama didn't belong to her. But the girl standing next to her, what happened to her if Madeline took the quickest exit from the situation?

Common sense told her that someone else would step in. If she left, Jackson would have to turn to his family for help. She looked up, caught him watching her, probably wondering the same thing she'd caught herself wondering. Why in the world was she here? He grinned and winked.

Someday she'd regret this moment, the moment she decided not to walk away. But the past had to be conquered. She couldn't spend her life running from the fear. Standing there looking at Jackson Cooper, all of that fear, rational and irrational, rushed in, pummeling her heart.

She took a deep breath and Jade reached for her hand, holding her in that spot.

"Travis, maybe it's time for you to go." Jackson slapped his little brother on the back. "And if you can, keep your mouth shut."

Travis tipped his hat. "Will do, brother. If I can."

"Try. Real hard."

Travis laughed as he walked away. Madeline watched him go and then she couldn't ignore Jackson any longer. He stood in front of her, an imposing six feet of strength, muscle and charm.

She watched Jade's retreating back as she followed the dog into the stable. Madeline fought back the urge to run, because running was easy. Something had clicked in Sunday services a few weeks ago, about facing life with God's strength, not our own. If she couldn't be strong on her own, she could be strong, more than a conqueror, with God.

"Jackson, I know this isn't easy. I think the sooner you tell your family the better."

"I'm going to do that. It isn't as if I'm a kid who's afraid to go home and tell his dad he messed up. I've messed up plenty in my life, Madeline. I know exactly who and what I am."

That's good, because she didn't know him or what exactly he was. He could be charming and funny. He helped a woman pick up her spilled canned goods. He always showed up first when a neighbor needed help. The tornado last spring had been an example of that. He'd worked tirelessly on homes that were damaged. He'd hauled food and water to people trying to rebuild their lives.

She'd admired that about him. Admired him from a distance, of course. Distance kept a person safe.

"You're a good person, Jackson." The words slipped out, honest but ugh, so embarrassing once they were said. She looked away, seeking Jade, making sure the girl hadn't decided to climb on a bull or a wild horse.

Jackson stared at her for a long minute and then he smiled.

"Madeline, I think that's about the nicest thing anyone has ever said to me."

"I doubt that. But honestly, about Jade…"

He glanced at his watch. "What are you doing here so early?"

"We got out at noon today. I forgot to tell you that earlier."

"Right, a holiday?"

"For the kids. A planning day for teachers." She started toward the barn, drawn by the whinny of a horse and laughter. Jackson walked next to her. She glanced up at him. "What are you going to do?"

"I'm not sure. I can't find any information on her mother's death. And I emailed a friend in law enforcement. She hasn't been reported missing."

Madeline stopped walking. "So where do you think her mother is?"

He didn't have a clue. "Maybe she's the one that's missing? I might have to drive to Enid. I'm going to keep searching because I'm starting to think she's not actually from Enid."

"You think?"

"What, you came to that conclusion first?"

She smiled because the look on his face said he

clearly didn't think she could think of it first. "The thought had crossed my mind. I think there's far more to her story than she's telling."

"The guy is always the last to know." He motioned her inside the stable ahead of him.

Madeline loved barns of all kinds, but this one took the cake. Shadowy and smelling of hay and horses, it stretched from stalls to a wide aisle that led into the arena. Country music played softly and Jade stood in front of a stall petting a pretty black mare.

The girl smiled at Jackson, hazel eyes glittery and full of light. "She's a beautiful horse."

"I thought so." Jackson walked up next to the girl. "After she settles down I'll let you ride her."

"I've never ridden a horse." Jade's voice came out breathless and wistful.

"I guess that's something we'll take care of." Jackson turned to smile at Madeline and she felt a little wistful, too. "What about you, Ms. Patton?"

"I've ridden a few times with Andie Johnson."

Jade stepped back from the horse who had her head down, munching hay. "Why don't you have a Christmas tree?"

Jackson blinked at the rapid change of topics. Madeline nearly laughed because he clearly needed to adjust to how a teenage girl's brain worked. He didn't understand that a girl like Jade could have a dozen or more things going on in her mind at once.

"I guess 'cause I don't need one."

Jade's mouth opened at that revelation. "You have to have a Christmas tree. How can you have Christmas without a tree?"

Jackson shrugged. "Because I go to my parents' house and they have a tree."

Madeline didn't want to jump in but Jade turned, clearly intending to pull her in.

"Do you have a tree?" Jade asked, her attention now on Madeline.

"I have a little one." Pitiful, really. She had a pink tree with silver ornaments. It had seemed like a good idea at the time because it came pre-decorated.

Now a pink Christmas tree just seemed wrong.

"Christmas isn't about a tree." Jackson stepped in, almost defensive.

Jade blew out, obviously disgusted. "I think I know that. The tree isn't what Christmas is all about, but it kind of makes me think more about the holiday."

"We'll get a tree." Jackson herded them toward the door of the barn. "Tomorrow."

Madeline thought about tomorrow, the day she planned on baking bread, decorating her house and then working on finishing touches at the Dawson Community Center's living nativity. She also needed to run to town and buy ingredients for candy.

"We can drive my truck out to the back pasture and find a decent cedar. And if Madeline needs a tree, we can cut her one, too."

"I really don't." Madeline stiffened when his hand went to her back, lingered and then moved away. When she glanced at him his hands were in his pockets and his smile had disappeared.

"Of course you do." He looked down at her. "We'll cut down trees and then we'll come back here for hot chocolate and cookies."

Jade's face lit up. "Perfect."

Madeline wanted to disagree. Perfect would be how she'd describe her life before this morning, before being invaded by the two Coopers standing next to her. Perfect would be her little pink tree being left alone and her heart not hammering out the tune "Meet Me Under the Mistletoe."

She didn't want those thoughts, those dangerous-to-her-heart thoughts. She didn't want to be afraid. Of what, she asked herself. Afraid of rejection? Afraid he'd hurt her? Or worse.

Always worse.

God's strength. She reminded herself that she could do this, she could face her fears. She could be the strong person she sometimes knew existed inside her.

Tomorrow should be good enough to start on being strong. Today she had to deal with her emotions tumbling inside her, mocking her because she'd thought she had them locked up tight.

Jade and Jackson were still talking and laughing, discussing the plan for tomorrow. She wanted to explain that she already had plans. Instead she chose escape.

"I should go. I need to get some stuff done at my house before our big adventure tomorrow."

Jade walked away from the horse but her gaze lingered on the animal, and then turned to Jackson. Of course she wanted to stay with him. Madeline understood that. But Jade, like so many kids that Madeline knew who were used to disappointment, brushed it off. She raised her chin a notch, shrugged, and let it go.

Still, it had to hurt. Even if she knew how to pretend none of this bothered her, on the inside, where it counted, Madeline knew Jade had to be afraid.

Worse, she seemed to be counting on Madeline for strength and for guidance.

"What are you going to do for the rest of the day?" Jackson leaned against a stall door and she figured it had to be holding him up.

"Is there something you need?"

He grinned and winked. "A back rub would be good. Are you offering?"

"Do you ever stop?"

His smile faded. "Yeah, I do. I'm sorry for saying that. You might have to give me a few days to get the old Jackson under control."

"Right, of course."

"Do you think you'll be going to town today?" Jackson reached into his back pocket and pulled out his wallet.

"I had planned on picking up Christmas decorations in Grove. Why?"

"Because I thought I'd give you money for groceries since you've got another mouth to feed. And she might need some clothes and a warmer coat."

"I'm fine. You don't have to worry about me." Jade moved to stand next to Madeline, her shoulders squared and stiff. "I'm good at taking care of myself."

"I'm sure you are, Jade, but that isn't necessary. You came looking for a family and this is what family does." Jackson handed Madeline several bills and she folded the money and put it in her pocket.

"I can take her." Madeline smiled at the girl standing next to her. "We can have fun shopping."

Jade shrugged slim shoulders. "Okay, sure. So I'm leaving and I won't see you until tomorrow?"

After a long pause, Jackson eased closer, taking stiff steps that Madeline hadn't noticed earlier. She wondered if he was even supposed to be up, let alone doing chores.

"Jade, I want to spend time with you. We're going to figure this whole mess out and I'm going to do my best to help you..."

"I don't need help. I need a dad."

His features softened. "I know, and I'm going to do my best to help you with that. But honestly, kid, I need to crash. I think my ribs are about to snap in two and my back kind of feels like a truck is sitting on it. Now that isn't the toughest 'dad' kind of thing to admit. Especially in front of two women." He smiled a tight smile. "But that's the way it is."

"Fine." Jade stood on tiptoe and kissed his cheek.

And something about him changed. Madeline watched his eyes and face shift and suddenly, Jackson Cooper became a dad. Or at least what she always imagined a dad would be if she'd had a real one.

"We should go." Madeline reached for Jade. "What time tomorrow? And are you sure you don't want me to bring something over for dinner tonight?"

"I think by nine in the morning." Jackson winked at Jade before turning to smile at Madeline. "And don't worry about me. I'm going to crash, and food is the last thing I want."

They walked back to the house together, slowly. Jackson watched them get in the car and then he eased his way up the steps of the front porch and into the house.

Madeline waited until he stepped through the door before she shifted into Reverse.

"You think he's cute, don't you?"

Madeline blinked a few times at the crazy question the teenager sitting next to her had asked. Jade smiled at what Madeline had hoped would be a warning look. Maybe she needed to work on that.

"Jackson doesn't need for anyone to think he's cute. He thinks it enough about himself."

"Mmm-hmm."

Let it go, her wise inner voice said. *Let it go.* She drove on down the road, back to her house. When they reached her place she pulled up to the mailbox.

"Could you reach in and get my mail?" She pulled close and rolled the window down for Jade.

"Sure." Jade reached into the box and pulled out a few pieces of mail. Rather than handing it over she sifted through it. "Hey, a Christmas card from Marjorie Patton. Is that your sister or your mom?"

Madeline grabbed the mail and shoved it in her purse. "It's no one."

Jackson woke up in a dark living room, the dog at his feet growling. He groaned and tossed the pillow across the room. Twice in one day. In one long, long day. The doorbell chimed again and he pushed himself off the couch, groaning as he straightened, stretching the muscles in his back.

Things to do tonight: sleep in own bed.

"I'm coming, already."

He threw the door open and immediately backed down. "Sir."

His dad stood in the doorway, the look on his face a familiar one. At almost thirty-four, Jackson should be long past that look from anyone. But there it was, the "buddy, you're in big trouble" look.

"Come in, I'll put on a pot of coffee."

Tim Cooper stomped the mud off his boots and stepped inside the house. "Smells like dog in here."

"Yeah, the stupid dog refuses to sleep outside. Either he's worried about me, or he just doesn't like the cold. I'm going with the cold."

"Probably. You're walking like you're eighty years old."

"Yeah, well, I feel older than that."

"What spooked that horse? Did you ever figure it out?"

They reached the kitchen and Jackson motioned for his dad to sit down while he filled the water reservoir on the coffeemaker and pushed the power button.

"I think it was a loose door banging in the wind. We both know that isn't why you're here."

"I can be here for more than one reason. Your mom is worried because she tried to call and you didn't answer."

"I was dog-tired."

"I told her you were probably asleep."

Jackson reached for the bottle of painkillers on the counter and then he put them back. It wasn't so bad he couldn't walk it off. "And the other reason you're here?"

"Travis has a big mouth."

"Right, I figured as much. Something about the words 'Travis, keep your mouth shut' tends to loosen his mouth like an oiled hinge."

His dad kind of laughed. He took his hat off and sat it on the table. "She isn't yours?"

"Probably not." Jackson sat down next to his dad. He fiddled with the stack of mail he'd left on the table earlier that day. "But my name is on her birth certificate."

"Where's her mom?"

"Your guess is as good as mine." Jackson got up to make the coffee. He put a cup under the nozzle. "Black?"

"Yeah. Oh, your mom sent dinner. It's in the truck and I'll bring it in before I leave."

"Thanks. You know, I'll never learn to cook if she keeps feeding me."

"She isn't going to stop. I've tried. And she's itching to fix this situation for you, too."

Jackson set the two cups of coffee on the table. "I'll fix this myself. The fewer people involved the better."

"I don't think your mom thinks that she's one of the people who shouldn't be involved. She said to tell you she'll expect to see you tomorrow."

"Give me a few days. I'm trying to figure this out without hurting Jade."

"Is that her name?"

He nodded and took a sip of coffee. "Yeah, Jade Baker. I knew her mom. But you know…"

"Yeah. Might need to head to the doctor just to make sure."

"I will. I'm not turning her out in the cold. I'm not going to call the state yet. I'm not going to have her in the system at Christmas."

"Where is she?"

This is where it got tricky. He sipped his coffee

and gave himself a minute. His dad answered his own question.

"Travis said Madeline Patton was up here today."

"She was."

"Madeline, huh?" Tim grinned kind of big, the way a man did when he'd raised a bunch of sons. "Not your normal cup of tea."

"I've never been a tea person."

"No, you haven't." Tim lifted his cup and finished off his coffee. "Don't hurt her. If you don't want big trouble with your mother, remember that people think of lot of Madeline."

"I'm not chasing the schoolteacher, if that's what you think." He shook his head. "And I'm not eighteen years old. So thanks for the advice."

Tim stood. He put a hand on Jackson's shoulder. "She's the kind of woman a guy marries."

Yeah, that said it all. Put him in his place. Jackson, who had done his running around and then settled down on this farm with a dog and some livestock, had yet to outrun his reputation. It sure felt like he couldn't do enough good deeds to undo what the people around here thought of him.

He stood to follow his dad out of the kitchen, and he couldn't stop one last attempt at denial. "I'm not planning to marry Madeline Patton."

His dad laughed. "When do things ever go the way we plan?"

"This is different. She's helping with Jade."

"Right, of course." He slapped Jackson on the back. "Careful, son, the word *never* usually leads right where you never thought you'd go."

Jackson stood on the front porch, thinking of all the times he'd said never. It wasn't until his dad's taillights disappeared that he remembered his dinner in that truck.

Fortunately he'd lost his appetite.

Chapter Five

A light snow had fallen overnight, just enough to dust the grass and the trees. Madeline drove her car up the long driveway to Jackson Cooper's ranch. The old farmhouse with the wraparound porch looked pretty with the powdery white snow sprinkling down. In the field the cows stood tail to the wind, snow sticking to their thick winter coats.

"This sure ain't Oklahoma City," Jade whispered.

"What? And don't say 'ain't.'" Madeline pulled her car in at the side of the house.

"Nothing. And I'm sorry." Jade already had her door open. "I bet he's still sleeping."

"No, he isn't. I saw him walk out of the barn."

"Oh, okay." Jade slammed the door of the Buick and ran toward the big barn.

Madeline waited. And she worried. What happened to a girl when she thought she'd found a fairy-tale parent who would make everything right, and then found herself let down? Heartache? Madeline remembered a father, but he hadn't been her real father. She blocked the memory because too many other memories chased after it. Yesterday she'd gotten a card from her mother. Her mother always managed to find her. Madeline couldn't run far enough or fast enough to outrun Marjorie. She would never escape the past.

She never answered the cards or letters. Usually she moved and hoped it would be the last time. No matter how much Marjorie apologized or said she wouldn't hurt her, that she just wanted a chance to talk, Madeline couldn't believe.

The one person she wanted to see had disappeared off the face of the earth. She'd searched for her sister the way Jade had searched for Jackson. She hadn't found Sara. Maybe she had married. Or changed her name. Madeline had been given that option years ago, to change her name.

But she was Madeline Patton. She didn't know how to be anyone else. She'd always felt as if she had to face this life, not change her name and become someone else. Not that it hadn't occurred to her. Not that she didn't think a change of name would be a great way to start over.

"Come on!" Jade had raced ahead but she turned back, hugging her new coat to herself.

Madeline nodded and smiled. She followed at a slower pace, not quite as excited about spending the day with Jackson. Dealing with him. It exhausted her just thinking about it. He had too much energy and twice as much charm.

"You coming?" Jade headed her way. The dog ran out of the barn and caught up with her, nipping at her pant legs.

"I'm not going to run."

"You're walking too slow. We're going to get a Christmas tree." Jade reached for her hand.

"I know and it's twenty degrees out here."

"Right, that makes it more like Christmas."

Jackson walked out of the barn, smiling and waving when he saw them. "I have everything we need in the truck. I'll get it."

"Coffee?" Madeline shivered inside her coat. When she looked up, met his gaze, he smiled. And then he let his gaze drop.

"Where's the schoolteacher?" He winked at Jade.

"What does that mean?" Madeline looked down at herself and then up at him.

He moved his hands in circles. "You're in jeans. And you're not wearing your glasses."

Jade laughed, loud and silly. "I did it. I talked her into wearing jeans and putting in the contacts she never wears. You can't chop down a Christmas tree in a skirt."

"I see." Jackson took a step closer. "Not a bad change, Maddie. Not bad at all."

"It's jeans and contact lenses." She shot him a look and he raised both hands in surrender, his smile fading. She pulled her heavy coat a little closer. "And my name's Madeline."

"You're right, it's just jeans and a new coat. People change clothes every day."

Jade raced into the barn. A second later she ran back out, her face beaming. "It's a wagon, Madeline, a real wagon."

The pumpkin will be your coach, Cinderella. Make sure you're home by midnight.

She grimaced and pushed fairy tales from her mind

as she walked into the barn to see what had Jade jumping up and down this time. The girl went from defiant and strong-willed to giddy in the blink of an eye.

Maybe changing with the ease of a chameleon was a Cooper trait and the girl had gotten it from Jackson. Hazel eyes, blond hair and the ability to shake off pain and become someone else.

As they walked through the open double doors of the barn, Jackson touched her arm, his hand cupping her elbow. "It's a Cooper tradition. I know we aren't going with the family, but I thought we should do this the right way."

A buckboard wagon pulled by two honey-colored horses stood in the wide center aisle of the barn. The harness jangled as the two large animals nodded their heads up and down, chewing on the metal bits in their mouths.

"I told you." Jade ran to the back and started to climb in. The dog jumped around her feet, happy, it seemed, to have someone in his life who could be easily excited.

"Climb in." Jackson led her to the front of the wagon, indicating with a nod the little step and a handle on the side of the wagon.

"We're really going off into the field in a wagon."

"We really are." He put a hand on her waist.

Her hand froze in midair, inches short of the handle as his touch lingered. She closed her eyes and exhaled. Pleasure and fear mixed like some crazy concoction that made her brain fuzzy and her heart ache.

The woman in her wanted to know that someone could find her attractive, someone could see how special she was. Someone could want to love her. She wanted to believe someone could melt her heart and make her feel whole.

She wasn't sweet sixteen and never been kissed. She was twenty-eight, and in the arms of a man she'd never felt more than distance and the wild urge to escape.

The child in her, that little girl that had hidden in closets and tried to run, wanted to escape because this man shook her heart, and because another man had made her feel dirty to the depth of her soul.

And it had taken years of counseling to get past that pain.

It had taken a faith that renewed and taught forgiveness to get her past the hatred. She still needed to work on the part of the plan that said she could love herself.

She had never let a man inside her heart because she'd never wanted to feel that pain again. She never wanted to be betrayed again.

Jackson stood behind her, his hand still light on her waist. Jade laughed and played with the dog, unaware. Jackson stepped closer.

"I'm just helping you in the wagon, Maddie."

She nodded and his hand moved to her back as she stepped up and into the wagon. As she settled into the seat he led the horses from the barn. She ducked as they went through the door, but there wasn't really a need. In the back, Jade had settled under a blanket with Bud the dog.

Jackson, stern in a way she'd never seen him, tipped his hat to her and then walked around and climbed up next to her. They didn't speak as the wagon started on a worn trail toward an already open gate.

He had nothing to say and her heart seemed to be

tripping all over itself, trying to catch up with twenty-eight years of emotions and new revelations about herself.

She folded her hands in her lap as the wagon bumped and jostled along the trail. No cattle or horses grazed in the field they were traveling through. The winter morning was cold and quiet. Even Jade seemed to be too excited to talk. For once.

Madeline found herself wanting to talk nonstop. For once. Talking would be easier than the silence, easier than delving into that moment back in the barn. A moment when she'd wondered what it would be like to turn into his arms, to be held by him.

She nearly laughed at that thought. What would Jackson Cooper do if a church mouse like her threw herself at him? A smile crept across her face. He'd die of shock. He'd run for his life.

He surely wouldn't know what to do.

Not that women didn't pursue him. But Madeline Patton in pursuit would probably scare ten years off his life. It scared ten years off hers just thinking about it.

"Here we go." Jackson pulled the team up and set the handbrake on the wagon. Jade hurried to stand, wobbling and grabbing the back of the bench seat he and Madeline were sitting on.

"What are you two waiting for?" She hopped over the side, the dog, Bud, jumping after her.

"We're coming." Jackson glanced at the woman next to him. She'd been quiet the whole trip out. Not that fifteen minutes of silence was impossible for a woman, but he thought her silence said everything she wasn't willing to say.

He wasn't about to push his way into her life, to tell her she didn't have to be afraid, that he wouldn't hurt her.

He had hurt women, not intentionally, but because he hadn't ever been the guy that wanted to take a few dates and turn them into something more. Yeah, she was smart to keep her distance from someone like him.

But if he was going to have a cup of tea…

Crazy thought. He wasn't a tea-drinking man.

"We should get down." He said it smooth and easy, as if he hadn't just been having thoughts that shook him from his comfort zone.

Last summer he'd teased Wyatt Johnson about Rachel Waters, telling Wyatt that the woman would get under his skin. And he'd been right. They were married now and as happy as any two people could be.

He knew better than to let a woman get under his skin. Even one as sweet as Madeline Patton, with her quiet ways and soft smiles.

She looked up at him; her mouth opened as if she meant to say something. Probably something he didn't want to hear. He didn't think she would be the type to call a man names, but he'd been called a few in his life.

"Thank you."

That was it. And he didn't even know why she was thanking him. Before he could question her she hopped down out of the wagon and walked away. Her new coat was brick red. It was a crazy combination with her brown hair hanging loose and the wind blowing it around her face. Her boots left tiny prints in the light dusting of snow. She turned to look back at him, catching her hair back from her face with her hand.

"You going to join us?"

Yeah, he was joining them. He stepped down out of the wagon, landing with a jolt that shot through his pancreas or something. He took a deep breath and whistled as he exhaled.

"You okay?" Madeline called back.

"Yeah, I'm good." Great. Wonderful. Happy.

He grabbed the chain saw out of the back of the wagon and followed the two ladies on a merry chase for the "perfect" tree.

"You know there isn't a perfect tree, right?" He trudged along behind them, smiling a little as they circled a tree close to twelve feet high.

"What do you call this?" Jade turned and then she started singing, "Oh Christmas tree, oh Christmas tree."

"I call this too big for my house." He walked on and they followed after him.

"Scrooge," Madeline whispered as she moved past him.

"You'd better believe it." He snorted and she laughed. And he wondered if she realized how much fun she was having. "So how'd it go last night?"

She stopped and her gaze remained on Jade who had skipped away with the dog to survey a tree she'd seen and it had to be the one.

"She's a mess." Madeline smiled and started walking again. "And now my house is a mess. I think you need a turn at the trail of clothes, water on the bathroom floor and dishes on the counter."

"And deny you the pleasure?"

She sighed and didn't laugh. "Seriously, Jackson, her mom has to be out there somewhere. We can't keep her here forever."

"I know that. I've got someone working on it. I'll find her."

"And then what?" Madeline looked up at him, her brown eyes locking with his. "Send her back? What if it isn't a safe situation? What if…"

Jackson got it. "What if you get attached and can't stand to let her go?"

Madeline shrugged. "She's heading back."

"Right, of course. And you're very good at skipping out on answering questions."

"What, are you going to tell me you won't get attached? Or that you won't worry? I know relationships are easy for you. Are they that easy to walk away from?"

Jackson stopped, stunned, and more than a little mad. "That's a great assessment from someone who doesn't really know me."

"I'm sorry." She reached for his arm. "That was unfair."

"A little." Not too much. The old saying that the truth hurt might have worked for this situation. Not that he planned on telling her that bit of information.

"This is it!" Jade pointed to the biggest cedar on the place. It had to be twenty feet. "It's perfect."

"Really? Perfect for what, the White House? Let's see if we can't find something a little smaller."

She did the teenage eye roll and walked on. He didn't have a single parenting bone in his body. He was a fraud. The only thing he knew to do was mimic things he'd heard his dad say over the years.

"What about this one?" Madeline pointed to a medium-size tree.

"Hmm, yes, it's good. It isn't very full. It doesn't have huge open gaps." Jade walked around the tree. "Yes, this is good. And we need one for Madeline's."

"No, we don't have to do that." Madeline shot him a look.

He remembered his sister Mia, when someone would offer her something that she thought was too much and she didn't want to be a bother. He smiled at the memory.

"Of course you need a tree." A kid in his life for twenty-four hours and he'd suddenly turned into his dad.

Maybe he'd wake up and this would be a dream. Or a strange version of *It's a Wonderful Life*. This was his world invaded by domesticity. He could almost hear the angel, Clarence, telling him that his life would be better with a family. Without them his home was empty, quiet.

Now how was peace and quiet such a bad thing?

"I really don't need one." Madeline had already spotted one. He knew it the minute she smiled.

"That one, right there. The small one?"

She nodded and smiled at him. "Please."

"You got it, Maddie."

She didn't correct him this time.

He left the chain saw on the ground and picked up the handsaw he'd brought. It would take about five minutes to cut through the trunk of a little bitty cedar. The part he'd forgotten about was the kneeling down part. That meant him on the ground, cracked ribs and all, pushing a saw back and forth. Through one of the toughest little cedars he'd ever seen.

By the time he finished the second tree, standing up just about wasn't an option.

He backed up, on his hands and knees, inhaling through the sharp pain. Jade had hold of her tree and started dragging it toward the wagon. Madeline stood in front of him.

"Need help?" She didn't smile.

"I'm afraid to admit that I do." He sat back up, moving into a squatting position that proved to be pretty overrated.

She stood there a long moment and then she reached for his hands. He made it to his feet, holding on to her as he stretched and the muscles in his back relaxed. Briefly.

"Phew, that was fun."

She was still holding his hands. She looked up, her eyes wide and deep-down hurt, the kind that took years to heal. Inside those dark eyes of hers he saw the little girl she'd been. He wanted to wrap her in his arms and protect her. He wanted to promise no one would ever hurt her again.

He let go of her hands because he wouldn't be the guy that broke her heart. She needed someone safe and dependable. How was that for being the grown-up, responsible guy? He'd have to share this moment with his dad.

The day Jackson Cooper used self-control.

What in the world had happened to him? Had he grown a conscience? Changed? Maybe all of those prayers uttered at Dawson Community Church on his behalf were suddenly being answered.

He chuckled.

"What?" Madeline had backed away, as if she'd suddenly come to her senses.

"Nothing, just thinking about prayers said on my behalf."

"What does that mean?"

"Are you going to say you haven't heard my mother or grandmother stand up in church and spill their guts about my life and how I need to come back to God?"

"That isn't really something to joke about." Madeline's eyes narrowed and he felt very chastised, for a second.

"I'm not joking. I know what they say. I grew up in church."

"They don't gossip about you, if that's what you think. They love you and worry about you."

He smiled at her ruffled feathers. "I know. But I'm not so far from God as they all think. I pray. I read my Bible. I'm not dating a different woman every night of the week. I've hardly dated at all in the last six months." As if she really needed all this information.

They walked side by side back to the wagon. Jackson had pulled on his gloves and he dragged the bigger tree behind him. Madeline stopped him a short distance from the wagon. She put a hand on his arm.

"Why don't you go to church?"

He shrugged. "Got out of the habit, I guess. Years of running around, rodeoing, sowing those wild oats. God and I are working it out."

"I see. So when they ask for prayers for you on Sunday, should I tell them you're good?"

He grinned. "One of these days I'll show up and prove it myself."

"That would be nice. You know it breaks your mother's heart that you're not in church."

"I'm not the only one."

"I know. She wants all of her children in church with her."

"Have you always gone to church?" He lifted the cedar tree and tossed it into the back of the wagon. Jade had a stick and she tossed it for Bud to fetch. He watched her for a minute, wondering how much of her story was true. She didn't seem to be a heartbroken kid. Instead she acted as if she might be on the adventure of a lifetime.

"She's a cute kid."

"Yeah, she is." What in the world should he do with her? He couldn't just move a kid into his house and be her dad. He hadn't been sitting around his house thinking he wanted a kid cluttering up his bathroom, leaving dirty clothes on the floor and asking for money to go to the movies.

He watched her hug his dog when the heeler jumped up, front paws on her stomach. Truth time. He'd been thinking a lot lately about how empty his life had become.

"She's just looking for a family." Madeline's voice sounded wistful to him.

"I know."

"She admitted she researched your family when she found the birth certificate. A real family, that's what she wanted."

"So where is her mom?"

Madeline looked from the girl to him. "Try Oklahoma City."

"Gotcha." He whistled, and Bud came running back.

Jade loped after him, her cheeks red from running and playing in the cold.

"Time to go?" She looked in the back of the wagon. "Where do I ride?"

"Up here with us."

She grinned big and climbed into the seat. He stood behind Madeline and waited for her to get situated and then he climbed up, sitting next to her. They were pushed together by Jade on the end of the bench seat.

Madeline swallowed, he saw her throat bob, saw a flicker of a pulse in her neck. If ever a woman needed a man who would make her feel safe, it was this one.

She needed a Prince Charming, someone like his brother Blake. Yeah, Blake wouldn't hurt a woman. He'd set her up in a nice house at the edge of Dawson. He'd buy her a pretty diamond ring and bring her flowers. Blake was a cold fish, though. For good reasons, Jackson figured, but still, his big brother needed to learn how to let go.

He'd have to do one better than that for Madeline. She needed someone. He smiled down at her. But not him.

Chapter Six

The horses picked up the pace on the way back to the barn. Their easy trot jangled the harness. Madeline sat sandwiched between Jade and Jackson. She shivered, not because of the cold, but because of him. She closed her eyes and breathed in the cold air.

Jackson drove the team past the barn and to the front door of the house. "I'll unload the tree and take the horses back to the barn."

"Where are your decorations?" Jade nearly bounced from the seat as they pulled up to the house and the team came to a jarring halt.

Madeline grabbed the girl and held her in the seat.

Next to her, Jackson pushed his hat back a notch. "Well now, that's a good question. I guess I hadn't thought about decorations."

"You have to have decorations," Jade insisted, hopping down from the wagon and joining the dog who had already done the same.

"No, not really. I haven't put a tree up in years. Let's

take it inside and when I go to the barn I'll look in the storage shed."

Jackson eased himself down from the wagon, not as quickly as before. Madeline filed away that information about him, because it changed who he was in her mind. Jackson Cooper, selfless? Willing to put himself through all kinds of agony in order to ensure a child had a Christmas tree?

He was the man holding his hand out, offering help getting down from the wagon. She could refuse and do it herself, looking stubborn and a little silly. Or rude. She could take his hand and risk everything.

Risk what? She bit down on her bottom lip and his hand still reached for hers. She nodded and stepped over the side of the wagon. His hand touched her waist, her arm. She landed gently on the ground. When she looked up it was into hazel eyes that danced with laughter.

Smile, she told herself, make it easy. Jackson Cooper dated tall, leggy blondes and polished brunettes. He didn't date mousy schoolteachers. She knew the drill. She would always fit the role of person most likely to help. She had always been the one a guy called if he thought she could help him hook up with someone else. And she had always liked filling that spot, because it didn't hurt so much if expectations were low. It didn't hurt if you didn't get too close.

As she stood there gathering herself, he opened his mouth as if he meant to say something. But he didn't.

"We'll make hot chocolate." She stepped away, turning to go inside.

"I'll be right back." He walked to the front of the wagon and took hold of the first horse in the team. "If you want hot chocolate there's a mix in the cabinet. Mom makes it every winter."

"Thank you." *Say something smart and witty*, she pushed herself. But she'd never been the smart, witty type. She'd never been the flirty one, batting her eyelids or saying cute things. She'd been the bookworm, hiding behind glasses and her studies.

She'd been the one hiding from life, protecting herself.

How in the world had this become her life? Laughter and a barking dog reminded her. A mix-up had dropped a child in her life and somehow tied her to Jackson Cooper. She could have dropped Jade off yesterday and driven away, not looking back, not thinking she had an obligation of any kind. Somewhere out there Jade, more than likely, had a mother who wanted her back.

"Let's go inside." She motioned for Jade as she walked up the steps.

As she walked through the front door of the house she did what she knew to do. She put all of her crazy emotions in a box and shoved them to the back of her mind.

"Do you think he has any cookies?" Jade followed behind her with the dog, who left muddy paw prints on the wood floor.

"I think the dog should stay outside." Madeline pointed to the paw prints.

Jade had already moved on. "Where should we put the tree?"

"It isn't my tree or my house so I'm not going to make that decision."

Jade glanced at her but didn't seem to be too bothered. "He wouldn't have a tree if it wasn't for us."

"I'm not even sure why I'm here," Madeline said out loud.

That got Jade's attention. The girl turned quickly, her eyes widening and her smile dissolving. "I'm sorry. I mean, I guess you probably have other things to do?"

"No, not really." She would have been at home knitting another scarf. She might have been cleaning her kitchen or reorganizing her cabinets. "Jade, where's your mom?"

Deflecting. Always safe. Not always fair.

Jade's eyes got huge and the color drained from her face. She walked away, the dog right on her heels.

"Jade?"

"It's none of your business. Remember, you're the person who got stuck with me. I came here looking for my dad and instead I'm staying with a lady who sleeps with every light in the house on."

The front door closed. "Problem here?"

Jackson walked into the living room, carrying a rubber tub with a lid. He'd shed his jacket and was dressed in jeans and a button-up shirt. If he felt the tension, he didn't show it. He took off his hat and hung it on a hook.

"No, there's no problem." She offered Jade an apologetic smile but the girl walked away.

"Let her go." Jackson said it in an easy, relaxed voice. "She'll get over it. She's too excited about the tree to stay mad for long."

"I asked where her mother is," Madeline admitted. "I thought she might talk to me."

"Talking isn't always easy."

"No, it isn't."

He pulled the lid off the box. "We could get you a dog."

"Excuse me?"

"It can't be cheap to have all of your lights on all the time."

She pulled out a string of lights that looked as if they were from the last century. "What do you know about my lights?"

"I've driven by a few times and wondered."

"I'm fine."

He looked up, his hazel eyes asking questions she didn't want to answer.

"Are you really?"

The question made her wonder. Then she answered, and it didn't hurt, it wasn't a lie. "I really am."

Of course she had doubts. She did sleep with the lights on. But she'd come so far and she'd grown so much. But why did he ask? What did he know about her fear?

She didn't want his sympathy.

"We should go check on Jade." She backed away from him, but not fast enough. His hand shot out, stopping her escape.

"Jade's fine. She's rummaging through my cabinets and snooping through the kitchen. I'm getting you a dog."

She shook her head. "I don't need a dog."

"I'm either going to teach you to shoot a gun, or I'm getting you a dog."

"I don't really want either."

His hand still held her arm but he hadn't moved closer. "I know, but trust me on this. There's something kind of nice about coming home to a dog. It makes a house less lonely."

"I can get my own dog." It was her last attempt to hold on to independence and to take a stand against a man who had stormed her life as easily as Jade stormed his.

"I owe you for helping me out with Jade."

"I didn't have to help."

"No, you didn't." His hand slid down her arm to her hand. "But I'm glad you did."

"Jade," she whispered and glanced back over her shoulder.

"Right, Jade."

Jackson watched Madeline's retreat. He walked a little slower, giving her space, giving himself time to get his head together. What in the world was he thinking?

So she slept with the lights on. When had that become his problem? She'd been his neighbor for over a year. He said hello to her when they passed on the street or bumped into one another walking into the Mad Cow. He'd seen her lights on late at night, and he'd wondered about it. So now he knew and he thought he needed to buy her a dog to make her feel safe?

He needed his head examined.

Bachelor pad. That's what his house had been designed as. He walked into the kitchen and nearly groaned. The two females who had invaded his life were standing shoulder to shoulder mixing milk with his mother's cocoa mix. A plate of cookies had been set out on the counter. It smelled and looked like Sally Homemaker had moved in.

It smelled kind of nice, the combination of hot chocolate, cookies, popcorn and… Madeline's perfume. He leaned against the counter and watched the two of them have what looked like a mother-daughter moment.

"Did you find decorations?" Jade turned, a spoon in her hand. Her eyes sparkled and she smiled. Happy. And she wore it like new clothes, something she'd wanted and never had.

"Not much. I did find a couple of old tree stands. One for mine, one for the tree you're taking to Madeline's."

Madeline looked at her watch. "I have to go soon."

"We have to decorate his tree." Jade stirred the cocoa and then lifted the spoon to take a sip. Madeline took the spoon from her hand and tossed it in the sink. Jade's mouth opened. "Why'd you do that?"

"I don't want to share germs."

"Fine." Jade grabbed another spoon and turned to Jackson again. "We can string the popcorn if you have a sewing kit around here. And maybe make some snowflakes."

"Sure, why not," he grumbled as he pulled cups from the cabinet. "Would you like to crochet doilies for my tables?"

Jade laughed and pointed to Madeline. "She can do that."

Madeline looked away, her cheeks turning crimson. The hot chocolate steamed and she ladled the liquid into the cups he'd set next to the stove.

"I bet she can." He grinned at Madeline's back because she had turned away from him and was pretending to be busy with the cocoa.

"We need to hurry," she finally said. "I have practice tonight."

"Cool. Can I go?" Jade leaned close to Madeline.

"I tell you what, we'll go do something this evening. Madeline has to practice for her part in the nativity. We'll let her do that and you and I will go somewhere."

"Together?" Jade's eyes lit up and her smile radiated.

"Yeah, together."

Madeline turned with a cup in her hand. She held it out to him and said nothing. She didn't need to. She needed a break from Jade. She needed a break from him. He got that. Sometimes he needed a break from himself.

They migrated to the living room with a tray of hot chocolate and cookies. Jade carried the popcorn and the miniature sewing kit he'd found in the cabinet. As they settled down to the task of making decorations, Jackson pushed the tree into the stand and picked up the string of lights.

He unfolded the ladder and headed to the top with lights and a pulled muscle in his back. Madeline looked up from cutting into folded paper to make a snowflake for his tree.

"You okay?" she asked, her eyes narrowing as she watched him.

He looked at the scene below him. A woman and a child making Christmas decorations. His floor strewn with craft paper and ornaments. It looked like a picture from a Christmas card, not a picture from his life. Maybe the life he could have had?

"Yeah, I'm good."

Thirty minutes later, with the creative talents of Jade and Madeline, the tree changed from the sad Charlie

Brown tree they'd dragged in from the field into a real Christmas tree. Jade had even found a prize: a tiny bird's nest leftover from last year. She'd moved it from the inner branches and placed it front and center, filling it with tiny eggs made of colored paper.

"It looks good." He hadn't contributed much, just a star for the top and the string of lights. But it was a decent-looking tree, even with the big empty space on the side they'd pushed close to the wall.

"Now we have to decorate Madeline's tree," Jade proclaimed as she hung the last foil star. "She has real decorations."

"Hey, don't diss my tree." Jackson plugged in the lights. The strand of multicolored lights flickered and came on.

"I'm just saying." Jade smiled a cute kid smile. "Anyway, this is a good tree."

A knock on the door and they all froze. Madeline looked at him, then at Jade. Jackson shrugged and pointed at the dog who had decided to bark his fool head off. Bud sat down, tail wagging, but a menacing snarl still curled his lips.

"I'll be right back." Jackson touched Jade's head on the way to the door. "Stay in here."

When he opened the door a police officer stood on his front porch. Jackson stepped out the door and closed it behind him.

"Jackson, Douglas Clark called about the kid you have staying with you."

"She's not staying here. She's staying with Madeline Patton."

"I see. Can you tell me who she is and how she came to be here?"

"Well—" he paused because the only thing he had was Jade's birth certificate and her side of the story "—she's my daughter."

"Jackson, we need to clear this up. You have a minor who could be a runaway. That's not something we can turn our back on."

"I get that, Lance, but if she's my kid…"

"If she's not?"

"My name is on her birth certificate."

The officer started to get a grim look on his face. "Jackson, we need to try to contact her mother."

"Gotcha. What if I promise I'm trying to do that? Look, I don't want the kid in state custody. Not this close to the holidays."

"Find her mom."

"I will." Jackson stood his ground in the door but Lance didn't turn to leave.

"Jackson, I have to talk to her."

"We're decorating the Christmas tree."

Lance laughed at that. Why did everyone find it so amusing when he did anything slightly different? "That's pretty domestic."

Jackson motioned Lance inside. They'd met on occasion, usually at a fire or an accident that volunteer first responders were called to. That was the thing about a small town, a rural county; people knew each other. They knew stories. They knew where to find someone without getting a map or directions.

Sometimes that could be a good thing. Sometimes it got under a guy's skin.

They walked into the now-empty living room. Empty except the twinkling, pitiful tree and leftover decorations scattered across the floor.

"She must be in the kitchen."

Lance nodded and walked next to him through the living room and dining room. When they entered the kitchen Jade turned, her eyes going all glittery with tears. Madeline moved closer and shot Jackson an accusing look.

"You called the police?" Jade trembled, her face draining of color.

"No," Jackson said. "Not this one."

"Young lady, I need your full name and address." Lance stood in a relaxed pose but his eyes shifted, taking in the room, the setting. Cop training. Jackson could have told him to relax, no one would jump out from behind a door. But that training kept a guy safe on the job.

Jade hiccupped a little.

"Jade, honey, tell him." Madeline, soft-voiced and sweet but still shooting daggers at Jackson.

Jackson should do something. He should step forward, put an arm around her. He'd been raised in a close family with parents that were always there for them, holding it together during the worst times.

Jackson tried to grab hold of those experiences. He might not be Jade's dad, but he could step up and be who she needed him to be. Tim Cooper had been the best dad in the world. He still was a man whose example could be followed.

"Give her a minute, Lance. She's a kid." Jackson stepped closer to Jade. "Go ahead. Tell him what he needs to know."

She nodded and wiped at her eyes. He put an arm around her shoulder and pulled her close for just a second and then released her. She smiled up at him and sniffled.

"I'm Jade Baker. My mom is Gloria Baker. We live in Oklahoma City."

"Your mom is alive?" Jackson had known, but he'd been willing to believe her until he found out the whole story.

Jade didn't answer. She cried. Tears slid down her cheeks and she shrugged.

"We need to contact your mother." Lance pulled a pen from his pocket. "Do you have her number?"

"Yeah, but good luck finding her."

"What does that mean?" Jackson leaned back against the counter, watching Jade shift from foot to foot. She looked up at him, tears pooling in her hazel eyes.

Man, he hated tears. He glanced at Madeline and her eyes were overflowing. Though he'd grown up with emotional females, he'd never gotten good at handling tears.

"Jade?" Madeline had the soft touch, the gentle voice that the kid needed. He shot her a grateful smile.

"She's never at home. She leaves for days at a time. The reason I came here is because I found my birth certificate and decided I'd find you and see if you were any better than her."

"Did you leave her a note?" Lance wrote on the pad and barely glanced up.

"Yeah, I left her a note. But she doesn't care where I go as long as I'm out of her hair. She's high most of the time and that's what she cares about, her next score and how to pay for it."

"Let's try to call her." Lance waited and Jade recited a number. He pulled out his cell phone and held it to his ear. After a few tries he gave up. "No answer."

"I told you." Jade looked down at the floor, at the dog sleeping at her feet. "I wanted a real Christmas with a real family."

"You're truant from school. You're a runaway." Lance ticked the crimes off on his fingers.

"I'm with my dad," Jade insisted and Jackson couldn't get a word in to dispel that fact from her mind. "And I can go to school here."

Lance sighed and shook his head. "I have to call this in. I'm going to leave it up to you, Jackson, if you want to be responsible for taking her home."

"I'll take her home." He didn't look at the woman gasping in disbelief or the kid shedding tears that dripped down her cheeks. "Next weekend. I have to make a trip to Oklahoma City with a bull calf I've sold. I can take her then."

"Keep trying to make contact with her mom. And you might want to contact a lawyer to see what your legal rights are."

"I'll do that."

Lance put the pen back in this pocket. "Jackson, don't get me in trouble with the sheriff. I'm just doing my job and I can't afford to lose my career over this."

Jackson leaned forward and shook the other man's hand. "I'll walk you to the door."

Lance pointed a finger in Jade's direction. "Running away is serious. I could call a juvenile officer. If my boss tells me to, I'll have no choice. And let me warn you, if you're thinking of running again, don't. It's December. It's cold. There are people out there who would hurt you. You're just lucky that you ended up here, with one of the best families in the state. Think about that."

"I will." Jade's eyes overflowed again.

"Take it easy on her, Lance." Jackson growled the words as they walked out of the kitchen.

"I'd love to, Jackson. But I want her to know how dangerous this is. Some kids get in the habit of running and they never stop. They end up in serious trouble, sometimes in permanent custody of the state. I don't want that to happen to her."

"You're right, but she's scared enough."

"So, you have a kid."

Jackson shrugged. If he gave up too much information, Lance would probably haul Jade in. A simple shrug and let it go, that had to be his answer for now.

He couldn't let Jade go, not now, knowing her story. That Cooper DNA was catching up with him. Take in strays and fix people. His parents had a dozen kids and more foster children because of that trait.

After watching Lance's patrol car drive away, Jackson walked back in the house. Jade and Madeline were waiting in the living room. He glanced at his watch. "We should probably eat lunch."

Madeline looked at her watch. "I need to go. I have practice."

"Okay, gotcha. What about your tree?" Jackson smiled at Jade. Her eyes and nose were red.

"I can put it up later. Jade…"

"Can stay with me. We'll cook dinner and have a

nice meal waiting for you when you get home." Jackson stuttered over the words. "I mean, when you get back."

He felt itchy all over. His life didn't include a woman coming home and a kid hanging stockings on the fireplace mantel. It wasn't even a real, wood-burning fireplace.

"You don't have to do that." Madeline slipped into her coat. When she struggled to find the left sleeve, he pulled it out for her and held it as she slid her arm through.

She looked up, soft eyes and a soft smile. She smelled like hot cocoa and vanilla. He inhaled and stepped close, but then he backed off, remembering. But he couldn't let it go, not completely. He brushed a hand through her hair, pulling it loose from the collar of her coat, letting his fingers linger in the silken strands.

He took a deep breath and stepped away from her. "We'll see you later."

She nodded and hurried out the door.

Behind him Jade laughed. "I thought you were like some Casanova guy that knew all about women."

"I am and…" He grimaced. "I'm not. You know what, go clean up the kitchen."

He needed to get his act together, as his dad used to say. He needed to get his head on straight and think smart. His dad had said that too many times in his life. It had started when he dated Julia Hart. Two years older than him, and someone his mother didn't want him seen with. Julia hadn't lasted two weeks. His dad had made sure of that.

Jackson shook his head, remembering. And realizing his dad had been right most of the time.

Sometimes, though, a guy had to take a chance. He walked into the kitchen where Jade was busy putting away the dishes.

"I have an idea."

"I love ideas." She wiped at the few stray tears that rolled down her cheeks. "What is it?"

He didn't shake his head at the realization that she was just a kid, and she didn't really have anyone. But the thought hit him, broadsided him. A kid should always have someone.

Madeline had been a kid who needed someone. Probably still needed someone.

"It's a surprise for Madeline and you can help me."

Jade's eyes lit up and he only hoped that Madeline would be nearly as excited by his plan.

Chapter Seven

What Madeline loved most about Dawson was that everyone knew everyone else. What she loved least was that everyone knew everyone else's business. As she walked through the Dawson Community Center, formerly Back Street Church, she got the feeling that everyone knew. Or maybe they only thought they knew something.

She slipped past a group of teenagers who were preparing to be citizens of Bethlehem. She had a role as shepherdess, one of the few who were overwhelmed by the presence of angels in the sky on that first Christmas morning. She didn't see it as a lowly role, but as one of the most important.

It symbolized something to her, that the angels appeared to mere shepherds. Not to kings, to the wealthy or religious, but to poor shepherds watching their flocks by night. Thinking about it made her heart rush with love for the God who had loved her that much.

She hurried down the steps to the basement of the community center. Beth Hightree looked up when Madeline walked into the dressing room. Newly married, Beth smiled with a certain glow. She held out a robe. "There's my last shepherd."

"Sorry, I meant to be here earlier." Madeline took the robe.

"I'm sure you did. Tell Jackson you have to be here early tomorrow."

"I don't know…" Madeline stopped mid-denial and shook her head. "Beth, I…"

She didn't have a clue what to say. How in the world did these people spread information so quickly?

"You don't have to explain. He's cute. He's single. You're cute and single."

"It isn't like that."

What was it like? It was a shared secret. It was about helping a neighbor who, until yesterday, hadn't even been a friend. She looked up, making uneasy eye contact with Beth.

She wouldn't lie to her. She wouldn't lie to anyone, but Beth was more than a friend. Beth, Jenna McKenzie and Madeline had formed a support group in the last year. Each had gone through a difficult situation and survived. As survivors they knew being strong meant holding on to each other and lifting each other up. Staying strong.

Beth had survived an abusive marriage.

Jenna had survived injuries suffered in Iraq.

Madeline had survived her abusive nightmare of a childhood.

They had done more than survived. They had escaped. They had overcome. They were still overcoming.

"Madeline?"

She looked up, smiling at Beth. "It isn't what you think. I can't share what Jackson is going through. But I can tell you that I'm fine."

"Really?"

The two sat down on a little bench. Madeline held on to the rough cotton robe she still needed to change into.

"It's crazy, really. I've spent my life living in my little shell, protecting myself."

"And Jackson Cooper is cracking the shell?" Beth smiled big, her brown eyes sparkling with humor.

"No, I mean, I can't even call him a friend. I guess he's just a surprise. He's also a nice person."

Beth laughed at that. "Yes, he's a nice person. He's a flirt. He's dated more women than most of the Cooper men put together. But he's nice. He's actually sweet. And he's the last person you need to open yourself up to."

"Right. You're right." She stood and slipped the robe over her head. It hung to the floor and then some. "I think it's too long."

"I have a feeling you got the wrong robe. I saw Johnny Scott leave here in a robe about two feet too short."

"We can trade next time."

Beth handed her a long piece of rope. "Here's a belt. We can blouse it out over this and maybe you won't trip on your way up the stairs."

"That works for me." She wrapped the rope around her waist twice and then pulled to blouse the top of the robe. "Beth, I'm not going to get hurt. I'm just helping Jackson with something."

Beth nodded and reached for a box of safety pins. "I know, Madeline. The whole town knows."

Great. "There aren't any secrets in this town, are there?"

"Nope. Well, a few, but usually they get found out eventually."

Beth's words were innocent, teasing, but Madeline's mind went elsewhere, thinking about how things might change if everyone knew her secret.

"Madeline, are you okay?"

She nodded because words wouldn't come. Her throat tightened with emotion and she turned away. A hand touched her shoulder.

"Madeline, you have friends here who love you."

"I know." She hurried out of the room and up the stairs.

She knew she had friends who loved her. But suddenly she wanted more. Suddenly she wanted what she'd never wanted before. She wanted to be loved forever by a man who would walk next to her and never let her down. She wanted a man who could hear her story and not run or make her feel as if she'd done something wrong.

She didn't know if such a person existed. She remembered being little and looking up at a man she'd called Father, only to find he couldn't be trusted at all. He'd bought her ice cream and pretty dresses, and he'd taken her to the movies.

He'd taken everything from her and left her with nothing but nightmares, guilt and a heart that had closed itself off to the idea of ever being loved.

She walked outside, into bright sunlight, through the crowds of people who considered her a friend and neighbor. God had changed her life in the last few years. He'd brought her here. He'd taught her lessons about love and forgiveness.

Now it seemed as if she might be on the brink of learning another lesson, about God and about herself.

Someone touched her arm. She turned and smiled at Dixie Gordon. "Shepherds are over here. And it looks like you might have the wrong robe!"

"I think I might." As she followed Dixie her thoughts turned to Jade and Jackson, making it hard to concentrate on being a shepherd.

Out of the blue it hit her, she wanted to go home. She wanted time alone to think. She shook her head as she tripped over the robe. She wanted to be with Jade and Jackson, doing whatever it was they were doing.

She looked up, wondering how God could ask her to put her heart on the line this way. Of course she wanted to trust. But this felt like jumping into quicksand, knowing full well what it was before she jumped.

Who would do that?

The puppies barked and chased each other in the fenced-in yard. Jackson watched Jade run with them, then sit to let them crawl on her lap and lick her face. They were sable and black balls of fluff, wagging tails and sharp eyes.

Adam McKenzie shook his head and didn't say anything.

"I want a male." Jackson leaned on the fence. "They're nice-looking pups."

"Best German shepherd puppies in the state." Adam glanced his way before settling his attention back on Jade and the mother dog who had crawled up next to her for attention. "Not a mean bone in that mama dog's body. I found a male that was a good match."

"So a great pet as well as a great guard dog?"

Adam nodded. "Sure, they'll protect you. Why do you need a guard dog?"

"It isn't for me. It's for Madeline Patton."

"Oh, okay."

The tone said it all. Jackson waited for Adam to say more but Adam had turned his attention back to the girl inside the fence and the puppies. Jade picked up a puppy and it wriggled close to her, giving her face a crazy bath. She laughed and then rolled on the cold ground with the dog. "This one."

He nodded in agreement. Definitely that one. He still wanted to know what Adam McKenzie wasn't saying about him buying a dog for Madeline. What did he want Adam to do, talk him out of it? Tell him to back off before he got hooked into something he couldn't get out of.

Or better yet, tell him not to hurt her. That thought had run through his mind more times in two days than he could count.

Two days, and here he was buying a dog and remodeling her house. Yeah, big words telling Wyatt Johnson that Rachel would get under his skin. Big words, buddy.

"Talking to yourself?" Adam turned, a big grin on his face. Adam, ex-pro-football player, could squish him like a gnat.

"Not at all. We'll take that one."

Adam opened the gate for Jade to exit with the puppy.

"Fine by me, but he's a she."

Jade looked up, eyes big, pleading. But she didn't say anything. He'd learned something about her. She was pretty used to disappointment. When he'd announced that he'd have to take her home at the end of the week, she'd accepted with a quiet dignity unusual for a thirteen-year-old kid. She'd accepted it the way kids accepted when they were not ever getting what they wanted.

A home and a family shouldn't be one of the things a kid had to wish for. A kid shouldn't have to accept going back to abuse. And every time he thought about a hurting child, he shouldn't also connect dots to Madeline Patton.

He let out a long sigh and shook his head. His life was no longer his own. Not one but two females were getting under his skin.

"A girl puppy is fine." He touched the spiky, wet nose of the shepherd pup. "What do we call her?"

Jade held the puppy up, looking her in the face. "Angel."

"Angel?" He grimaced and shook his head. He should have known better than to let her name the dog. "Sure, why not. She's a guardian angel."

"Exactly." Jade pulled the puppy close again.

"How much?" Jackson pulled out his checkbook and Adam shook his head. "Adam, I'm buying the dog."

"Consider it a Christmas gift."

"I can't do that. I tell you what, I'll write you a check for Camp Hope."

"That's a deal." Adam took the check and slid it into his shirt pocket. "Have fun with that dog, Jade."

She smiled. "I will. But I have to go home next week. This is just a vacation."

A vacation from reality. Jackson put a hand on her

shoulder and guided her back to the truck. *Thanks for putting a knife in my heart, kid.*

"Jade, you and I have to do something on Monday." He opened the truck door for her and she looked up.

"What's that?"

"We're going to the doctor for a test. We need to make sure we know what's going on so we know how to fight."

"How to fight?"

"Yeah, for you to be able to stay here, we have to have proof that you're my daughter." Heat climbed up his cheeks.

Jade climbed into the truck. "Sure, okay. But I am your daughter."

Yeah, he kind of wished she was. When the test came back with the results he knew they'd get, what then? What happened to Jade when she learned the truth?

When he pulled into Madeline's drive, Jade and the puppy were sleeping in the passenger side of the truck. Wake them up or leave them? He decided to let them sleep. He could get his ladder set up, find the electric box and get his work done before Madeline got back.

In a perfect world.

As he set the ladder up, the truck door opened and the twin tornadoes scrambled out. The dog ran to the corner of the yard. Jade chased after her. Jackson climbed the ladder, smiling as he listened to Jade talk to Angel. The puppy yapped and ran in circles.

He'd bought motion lights for the front porch and the back. When Madeline came home, she'd have security lights that came on with any motion. Maybe this way she could sleep at night without being afraid.

It didn't feel great, climbing the ladder. But it felt

better than a few days ago. He reached for the old light, slipping it off the bracket and unscrewing the wire nuts that held the light to the light box. He wasn't an electrician, but he knew enough to hang a light.

In the yard Jade laughed and the puppy barked, yipping as the two of them raced around a tree. Every kid should have a dog. He let out a sigh, then froze as the ladder wobbled.

He looked down, the puppy stood on her hind legs, front legs on the first wrung of the ladder.

"Jade, could you get the dog?" He held the new light up to the wiring and twisted the correct wires together. He needed to connect them with the wire nut and then do the other set of wires.

Jade raced across the lawn to grab the puppy. "Sorry."

He let out a long breath and worked the other two wires together. "No problem."

The light fit into the box and he used the old screws to attach it. In a minute he'd flip the switch and make sure it worked.

The ladder wobbled again. He glanced down. That dog meant to kill him. He held tight and whistled to get Jade's attention. She'd gotten distracted, pulling Christmas lights out of the box he'd bought. She wanted Christmas lights on the front of Madeline's house.

The dog ran to the other side of the ladder. A ten-pound puppy shouldn't be able to push a ladder over. Jackson reassured himself with that bit of reality.

He grabbed the old light off the rafter of the front porch roof and slid the tools into his tool belt. He didn't want to make a scene, but he wasn't crazy about heights. A car came down the road and he knew Madeline would be home soon. It might be her now, catching him in the process of surprising her.

It wasn't.

"Here are the Christmas lights." Jade held them up, a strand of new lights.

"Sure, okay. Find the middle and I'll hook them here first."

She stretched them, pushing away the puppy who thought she'd found the best chew toy in the world. Finally she handed them up, bent where she'd found the center. He hooked them over a planter hook already in place.

Finished, he climbed down, more than a little relieved to be back on the ground. Good, solid earth. He stretched to relieve the tension in the middle of his back.

"You look a little weird," Jade announced as he moved the ladder to the end of the porch. "You okay?"

"Of course I am." He climbed the ladder and pulled the hammer from the tool belt around his waist. He pulled a nail out and made a makeshift hook for the end of the lights.

"Perfect. But hurry, she might be here in a few minutes."

"I'm hurrying. Is there even a place to plug these in?"

"Yeah, over by the door. You'll need an extension cord."

"Gotcha." He moved the ladder to the other end of the porch. The ground didn't look too level and the ladder wobbled as he climbed.

"Uh, be careful."

"You think? I'm recovering from cracked ribs and a

bruised kidney. If I go down, kid, I'm taking you with me."

She laughed and he shook his head. "No respect for old people," he grumbled.

"You're not that old."

"Thanks, I think." He hammered a nail into the wood trim of the porch roof. "There we go. She has a security light and Christmas lights."

"Isn't she too old to be afraid of the dark?" Jade moved close to the ladder.

"People are afraid of a lot of things, Jade."

"Yeah, I guess." She shook the ladder and he screamed. "Chicken."

"I'm going to get you, good."

She ran, laughing. The yapping puppy went with her. He saw another car. He turned and waved as Madeline came up the drive. Before he could make adjustments, the ladder swayed. He leaned, trying to push it back the right way. Slowly it fell backward, taking him with it.

Jade screamed. Madeline's car door slammed and she yelled.

As if he could answer as he jumped. He landed on his feet a short distance back from the ladder that crashed to the ground.

Madeline got to him before the dog. "Are you okay?"

He nodded because he couldn't really get the words out yet. These two women were determined to make him look like a weak little girl. He brushed a hand through his hair and inhaled sharply.

"Phew, that was close."

"You think?" Jade snickered and he reached for her. She moved quickly and got away.

Madeline looked up at her porch and then at him. "You put up Christmas lights."

"One better. You now have motion lights. Well, one motion light. I still have to put up the one for your back stoop."

"Jackson, you don't have to. I'm fine."

"You'll be able to sleep with the lights off." He didn't stay to discuss it with her. He picked up the ladder and headed around the side of the house, moving a little slower.

She appeared as he set up the ladder and pulled the second light out of the box. "You didn't have to do this."

"I know I didn't. I'm being a good neighbor. I should have thought of it sooner."

She stared at him, big eyes searching his face, questioning him. Probably questioning his motives, he guessed.

"Why? Why would you think of it sooner? For all you know I'm a night owl, an insomniac, addicted to computer games and coffee."

"You drink tea. Probably herbal. And you live out here by yourself."

It didn't sit right, knowing her story and her not knowing that he knew. He'd have to tell her. But how did he tell her, basically a stranger, that he knew her secrets?

"Jackson, whose puppy is that?"

He climbed the ladder and pretended to busy himself removing the old light, but he looked down at the woman standing close, holding the ladder. She didn't smile when she looked up. She didn't look away, either. He thought she had the sweetest face he'd ever seen. Pretty. She was definitely pretty. And he hadn't noticed till now because she hid behind those sweaters and big glasses.

"The puppy is yours, too. It's easier to be in the dark if you're not alone."

"I can't take a gift like that."

He hooked up the new light and twisted the wire nuts. "Yeah, you can. I've dragged you into my life and you've not asked for a thing in return. I wanted to do this for you."

"It wasn't necessary. I was helping a neighbor."

"That's what I'm doing." He climbed down. "And if you want to flip your breaker, we'll see if this works."

She nodded once and walked away. He watched her go, and he couldn't believe how much he wanted to go after her. But he stood his ground because he'd already warned himself that he wouldn't hurt her. She wasn't a woman he could casually date and then walk away from.

She had too much at stake. Too much to lose.

Madeline flipped the switch and stepped back outside to see if the light worked. Jackson stood nearby, looking up at the unlit light. He walked past and it flickered and came on. He stood beneath it in the gray light of early evening. She couldn't look away.

Jackson Cooper probably topped the list of eligible bachelors in Oklahoma. And he had just installed lights for her to sleep more securely at night. He stood in her yard, a cowboy in faded jeans and a dark blue flannel shirt. His blond hair spiked a little when he took off his hat. His slow, easy smile revealed a dimple in his chin.

Years ago she'd realized she could look at a man like Jackson and feel nothing. Which was better than the fight-or-flight instinct of her childhood. But feeling nothing had felt hollow.

Hollow but safe.

Jackson made her feel safe. But he wasn't. He could break her heart.

Because he made her feel.

"It works." He walked toward her, slow and easy, casual but she saw his grimace of pain.

"It does. Thank you."

Jade rounded the corner of the house, the puppy at her heels. "Hey, the lights on the porch work. Come and see."

Jackson reached for her hand. Madeline drew in a breath as his fingers clasped with hers and she allowed him to lead her around to the front of her house.

"Well, look at that, you have Christmas." He tugged her close, sliding her hand with his into the pocket of her heavy coat. His fingers curled around hers, around her emotions, her heart.

She needed space. She needed to breathe deep and clear her head. She moved a step away, focusing on the glittery lights that ran along her porch roof. It took a moment for her world to settle, for her thoughts to settle. The man standing next to her had done this. For her.

A sneaky thought poked at her, asking her why he'd done this. What did he want? She brushed the suspicions aside. Jackson Cooper had done something nice for her. *Let it go.*

"Thank you." She stepped closer to the house. The floodlight he'd installed came on, taking her by surprise, making her laugh. "That might be extreme."

"You'll have to get used to it, but it'll light up the yard

like it's daylight out here. And remember that every possum that crosses its path will probably set it off."

"I'll remember."

She would remember this Christmas, the year that a runaway girl pulled her into Jackson's life. The year her emotions had sprung free, totally out of control.

This moment equaled sneaking a peek at wrapped presents under the tree and then trying to shove them back into the paper, to make it the way it had been before.

An impossible task.

Jackson reached down to pet the puppy, groaning with the movement. "Jade, you need to take this dog in and feed it."

The girl turned from the lights and called the dog. The puppy ran to her new best friend and she scooped her up and headed into the house. The last thing Madeline needed in her life was a puppy. Close to the last thing she needed.

Jackson smiled down at her, his face shadowed by the brim of the cowboy hat he'd placed back on his head. "I should go."

"I could cook dinner. To pay you for all the work you've done and all the muscles you pulled jumping off the ladder." Madeline should have kept her mouth closed, let him leave.

"I'm good and we stopped at the Mad Cow. Vera cooked up fried chicken and the fixings. It's in the fridge."

"Thank you again." It sounded like a broken record now. His little kindnesses were taking her life in so many new directions she didn't know what else to say. "You can stay."

Common-sense Madeline had clearly left the building, to be replaced by out-of-control Madeline, her evil twin who obviously didn't think about broken hearts and the pain of the past.

"Thanks, but I'm going to clean up my mess and go home to crash." He picked up a few tools he'd left on the porch. "I'll get the ladder if you'll put this in the back of the truck for me."

"I can do that." She took the box, carefully avoiding eye contact with probably the most gorgeous man she'd ever met.

She walked to the back of his truck and set the box in the metal toolbox behind the cab. He returned carrying the ladder, walking a little slower. He grinned as he lifted the ladder and set it in the back of the truck.

Madeline brushed back her hair and shivered in her coat as a cold wind picked up, scattering dried leaves left over from autumn across her lawn. She looked up and he had moved closer, his hazel eyes settled on her face, watching her, touching her with a look.

When his hand touched her arm she closed her eyes, waiting, telling herself not to run from this, not to run from feeling too much. His fingers touched her chin, turning her to face him.

Grounded, she was grounded. Reality, not fear. She was in her yard. The earth was beneath her. The truck was close enough to touch. A car drove by. A neighbor honked. She opened her eyes, no longer afraid. Much.

His hand moved to her cheek, sweet and easy. His

fingers tangled in her hair and she looked up, wanting to know what it meant to be the woman in his arms.

When he pulled her close she froze for just an instant, then she exhaled and let go. He leaned in, soft breath and mint. The tangy scent of his cologne mixed with the winter air, a sharp breeze and wood smoke from the neighbor's fireplace. His hand slid to her waist and he held her for just a moment.

And as quick as that, he backed away, leaving her standing there in her driveway, unsure. Shaken.

He smiled and shook his head.

"Madeline, you're tempting, and self-control is not one of my strongest character traits. Some would say I have no control when it comes to beautiful women." His fingers touched her cheek, feather-soft. "But I always keep my word and I'm going to do that right now and walk away."

She backed away from him, not sure how to take this moment, this goodbye. Her heart raced and she breathed, trying to catch up. Jackson Cooper tipped his hat and got into his truck.

As she stood there trying to make sense of what had happened, he backed out of her drive and was gone. She had put her heart on the line, taken steps she'd never taken before. She'd been rejected.

Jackson Cooper, known for his many relationships, for having a constant string of women, had held her and walked away.

So what did that make her? Chopped liver?

For a long time she stood in her driveway, shivering in the cold wind and trying hard not to be hurt by his rejection. But it did hurt. Because she'd held her emotions in check for so many years and when she'd taken a step toward someone, the man had walked away.

It hurt because his daughter was in her house and she'd have to see him again tomorrow.

As she walked back into the house she told herself it didn't have to be him. He didn't have to be the man she took a chance with. She could find someone safe. Someone who wouldn't break her heart.

But she had a hard time convincing herself.

Chapter Eight

Jackson had to admit to a moment of real doubt as he walked up the steps of Dawson Community Church. Church, for the first time in… Well, he'd gone to funerals and weddings, but hadn't gone to church in ten years or more.

Except Christmas and Easter. He'd done the holidays for his mom.

Today he walked up the steps and through the door for… Himself? Jade? Or maybe for Madeline? Because last night he'd walked away from her, seconds short of a moment that he figured would have changed his life and hers in ways he couldn't take back.

His dad had warned him Madeline wasn't someone to play around with. Madeline had stories that he couldn't begin to fathom and pain that he wished he could take away. He wanted to hold on to her and promise no one would ever hurt her again. He was the last person to make that promise.

Church had already started. He walked through the double doors and into the vestibule. He stood there rethinking the impulse that had put him in church on a Sunday morning, dress boots and new jeans, a button-up shirt he'd actually ironed. He took off the black cowboy hat he'd shoved on his head as he got out of the truck and held it in his hand.

Someone stepped forward, reaching for his hand. Ryder Johnson. Not much more than a year ago Ryder had been single and he'd planned on staying that way. Now he had a wife and twin baby girls.

"Jackson, good to see you," Ryder whispered as he pulled him into a comfortable man hug and slapped him on the back. And then Ryder ruined things by whispering, "And look, the roof is still in one piece."

"Yeah, thanks." Jackson spotted a seat on the back pew. The piano played and the choir sang "I'll Fly Away."

"It really is good to have you here."

"Good to be here." Jackson sat down and Ryder went back to his seat next to his wife, Andie.

Jackson settled into the seat by himself in an empty pew. A few people looked back, wondering. His Gram sat near the front next to his dad. Her smile split her face and she nodded and looked up, thinking God had, at long last, answered prayers for the grandson gone astray.

He closed his eyes as the choir took their seats and Jenna McKenzie sang a solo. He felt someone move close, sit next to him. A body brushed past him. He opened his eyes and smiled at Jade, who'd taken her place to his left. And Madeline to his right.

Oh yeah, this wouldn't be a rumor starter. And a match on dry wood wouldn't start a fire. Right! By the end of the day everyone in town would be talking and they'd have a hard time deciding what to discuss first. Jackson Cooper had gone to church and the roof hadn't caved. Madeline and a girl that looked a lot like him had sat next to him in church. So much for slipping in unnoticed.

"You're here." Jade grabbed his hand. She peeked past him to Madeline. "I told you."

"Shhh," Madeline warned. "We're in church."

Jade nodded but she held on to his hand.

Somehow he managed to focus on the sermon about killing giants with faith. A decent twist on a story he'd heard all his life. Giants. He'd had a few that he'd faced in his life. He couldn't really say what had pushed him out of church. Maybe a lifetime of being told to get up, to clean up, to stop acting up? Maybe being busy, being gone on Sundays? Maybe shame for the things he'd done that he knew would make his mother blush and probably make God none too happy?

Today didn't really push him to the top of any spiritual mountains. Everyone in town knew him for what he was. Today they would think he was a dad. The kid sitting next to him, holding on to his hand like he was some kind of hero, thought he was her dad.

Maybe they'd think he was involved with everyone's favorite teacher. He had to admit, he didn't dislike the notion of people thinking he'd managed to snag someone who smelled like a spring morning.

Her arm touched his.

"Lunch at the Cooper Ranch after church," he whispered close to her ear.

She shivered and he moved his arm, settling it on the back of the pew behind her. Lunch with the family, a

Sunday tradition. Even when he didn't go to church he still had lunch with the family. Most of the time.

But he never took a woman with him. The word *date* slipped into his mind. He'd never taken a date to Sunday lunch. That hadn't seemed right. Not attending church hurt his mother enough without him adding a woman to the mix.

He settled his attention on the front of the church and something shifted in his heart. It happened when he saw his mother sitting next to his dad. Travis sat next to her. And Mia. And Lucky and his wife and kids.

Reese would have been there, but he'd joined the army and recently shipped out to Afghanistan.

Blake, probably busy with bank business, didn't attend church.

Heather went to church in Grove. She liked anonymity.

Jesse was probably on duty at the hospital.

Dylan had a load of bulls in Texas, and Gage was busy riding bulls.

Sophie did her own thing these days, and usually it had nothing to do with the family.

Everyone had lives, stories and places to be.

He should have been here sooner. If not for himself, for his mom. The look on her face when she turned at the end of the service drove that thought home. Yeah, he should be there for God, for himself, but his mom was the one looking right at him, with tears in her eyes.

After the closing prayer everyone stood, people moved and he had enough sense to know that most of them were heading his way. Jackson in church on a Sunday that wasn't a holiday? They'd all be wondering why.

"Hey, brother." Travis clasped his hand and shot a look from Madeline to Jade. "You coming out to the house for lunch?"

"I plan on it."

Travis leaned in close. "You bringing your little family?"

Jackson squeezed the hand that still held his. "Travis, don't make me have to take you out back."

Travis laughed and pulled away, a good-natured pup who needed a serious thump on the head. "Nothing wrong with settling down, brother. The three of you look kind of nice together."

Jackson reached but Travis moved a little quicker these days.

And then his parents stepped close. This had gone from a decent idea to one huge complication. Jade was in his mother's arms and his mom stared at him, eyes wide, lots of questions and answers.

Sooner or later he would have to talk to Jade, explain things to her. But looking at her in the middle of his big family, watching her smile and laugh, he knew it wouldn't be easy and it would break her heart. He could give the kid Christmas with his family. That's what she wanted, a family.

"Are you coming out to the house for lunch?" His mom still held on to Jade and with her free hand she reached for Madeline, pulling her close. And they were all looking at him.

Yeah, he'd planned on lunch with his family. Now that plan seemed to include the two females who were doing a lot to complicate his, up to now, uncomplicated life. Yesterday it had felt good to do something nice for

Madeline. It had felt pretty decent to spend an afternoon with Jade.

But taking them home to his family felt a little… He pulled at the collar of his shirt and wished it was not quite so hot.

"Jackson?" His dad shot him a look.

"Of course we're coming out for lunch." He avoided looking at Madeline but he couldn't miss the very pleased smile on his mother's face.

Sandwiched on the truck seat between Jade and Jackson, Madeline tried to make herself smaller. She sat up straight and kept her shoulders in. The truck turned and she slid a little toward Jackson in his new jeans, his dark cowboy hat covering blond hair that managed to look a little messy and made him a whole lot cute.

For the first time in her life, she felt young. She felt like a sixteen-year-old in a pickup on a Saturday night. It felt good. And frightening.

"Nervous?" Jackson smiled, eyes crinkling at the corners, and then shifted his attention back to the road. He reached to turn up the radio and an old Randy Travis song filled the cab of the truck. *Forever and ever, Amen.*

She'd never thought about loving someone forever. She'd always thought that being single meant being safe from being hurt. Safe now seemed to be a thing of the past.

"Of course not. Why would I be nervous?"

He laughed loud. "You and I both know that this isn't a simple lunch. The minute you sat down next to me, everyone in Dawson had us paired up and started wondering when we'd be announcing the big day."

She choked a little because she hadn't expected him to put it so bluntly. "Thanks."

His left hand firmly on the wheel, he moved his right arm and slipped it around her shoulder. His fingers tweaked her sleeve, and her arm buzzed beneath his touch.

"It's okay, Maddie, we'll get through this and in a week or two, people will realize you were the person rescuing me and Jade."

Why didn't that make her feel any better? Because he'd just let her know, in a sweet way, that she wasn't anything more than the person helping him out? Why did it suddenly, painfully, matter?

They pulled up the driveway that led to the main house of the Cooper ranch, the Circle C. Cooper Creek flowed through the field and circled back through the stand of trees farther on. The house, a big, brick, Georgian place, sat back from the main road. Trees lined the driveway.

The Coopers were everything a family should be. The Coopers were everything she'd ever wanted. Probably everything Jade had ever wanted. Not that they didn't have problems, but when they did, they drew together and held on to each other.

She'd never really had a family. Hers had been a group of people and it had never been safe or nurturing. Foster care had been a respite for a few years but she'd been too closed off at that time to get attached to her foster parents. She'd kept in touch for a few years but she'd finally stopped writing.

"They don't bite." Jackson leaned close as he pulled to a stop behind another car. Lucky's family piled out of an SUV. Jackson's hand rubbed her arm and he pulled her close for a brief instant.

"I know they don't." But her heart pounded hard, achingly hard. Not because of the prospect of lunch with the Coopers, but because Jackson's arm around her held her tight.

He held her tight and she wasn't afraid, not of him.

"You okay?"

"I'm good." Not good.

Her heart crumbled a little with the knowledge that it was this man who made her feel safe. It shouldn't be him. It didn't make sense that safety and fear should tangle together in her heart, pushing against each other.

Jade had already jumped out of the truck. Jackson reached for his door and settled one last look on her before pushing it open. "Time to face the music, Maddie."

"So sweetly put." She ignored the hand he held out. "I should have gone home. You could have spent this day with Jade and your family."

"My mother would have taken a switch to me if you hadn't come along."

"I doubt that."

He laughed and pulled her close. "Darlin', you have no idea. My mom is probably thinking you're one of the answers to her prayers. All our lives she's prayed for God to send the perfect person into our lives at the perfect moment. And she has no doubt that God will honor that prayer."

"But I'm not…"

"You won't be able to convince her of that." He leaned close, and she wondered if he meant to kiss her. He didn't. He flicked her chin with his finger and stepped away.

She obviously brought this new self-control out in him. *Way to go, Madeline.* For the first time she wanted to be held and for the first time in his life, Jackson Cooper had self-control.

Madeline took a deep breath and stood a little straighter. Time to face the music. She managed a smile and to not melt when Jackson held her hand and walked her up the steps of the big house, straight into the circle of trust that was the Coopers.

Jade didn't seem to have a problem. She stood in the middle of Jackson's very overwhelming family and allowed them to pull her in.

"What's for lunch, Mom?" Jackson's thumb brushed the top of Madeline's hand and he didn't let go.

Angie Cooper turned, smiling big, reaching for Madeline and forcing Jackson to let go. Madeline loved Angie Cooper. She was gracious, dignified and always kind.

"Madeline, thank you so much for helping Jackson with this…situation."

"It hasn't been a problem."

Angie's smile softened as did her expression. "Of course it hasn't. But it means so much to us."

Coopers were everywhere. They were laughing and talking, teasing each other. Angie Cooper continued to talk, not bothered at all by the constant commotion around her. Her family. Jackson's family.

Madeline nodded in answer to Angie's questions. In the blink of an eye Jackson stood next to her. She smiled up at him, pretending to be strong, because she'd pretended for a long time. But in the middle of this family she felt so much like a fraud, because she'd never had a family, not a real one.

She was strong. She'd spent the last fifteen years telling herself she was a survivor, not a victim. But survivors still had to deal with the past, with fear, with leftover anger and resentment.

With baggage that didn't unpack itself.

She'd done a lot of baggage unpacking. There were a few little things she still carried around with her, she knew that. But eventually she knew she'd let it all go. She'd trust enough to let it go.

She brushed a hand across her cheeks to wipe away stray tears that had trickled out before she could get control of her emotions.

"Let's walk." Jackson took her by the hand. "Mom, we'll be right in to help set the table."

Angie Cooper shot her son a narrow-eyed look. "Jackson."

"Five minutes." He winked at his mom.

Madeline thought about telling him no. But for Jackson, his charm seemed to come naturally. He could wink at his mom, smile and they all went along with his plans. At that moment she had no choice but to go with him. She either went or she fell apart in front of his family.

Somehow he knew that she needed a minute to gather herself. Later she would thank him for that little bit of intuition. Later she might even wonder how he knew her so well.

Hand in hand they walked out the front door, down the steps and across the lawn. Neither of them spoke, which was good. What would she say when they did speak? Sorry for being so ridiculous?

At a small gazebo at the edge of the lawn they finally stopped. Jackson smiled down at her, a gentle smile. No wink. No flirty grin. "I wanted to make sure you're okay. I thought a little fresh air might help."

She nodded, unsure. "I'm fine, really I am."

He stood in front of her, and she felt as if he saw everything about her. Including the things she didn't want him to see. He touched her cheek. "You're sure? Because I recognize that 'need to escape this family' look."

"I'm sure." She laughed a little because she had been thinking exactly that.

Was that part of Jackson's charm? He could read people and it made a woman think that he really cared, really understood? Of course that was it, and for that reason alone she should back away.

He shouldn't be the man she wanted to kiss. She moved closer and his brows arched. His hand moved from hers. He slid it around her back and held her close. But he didn't kiss her.

Okay, fine, she would make the first move. She could do this, even if she fainted in the process. She didn't plan on living her life in a box, afraid to feel. Braver than she'd ever been in her life, she stood on her tiptoes and rested a hand on his shoulder. Jackson whispered her name as he bent and drew her close. Telling herself she wouldn't regret it, she touched her lips to his, closing her eyes to the landslide of feelings that slammed her heart.

"Madeline." He pulled back first.

"I'm sorry." She didn't know what else to say. "I can't believe I did that."

"You don't have to apologize." He winked—a little of the old Jackson obviously still existed.

She had kissed Jackson Cooper and he had pulled away. Now she had to go back in the house with him, sit at the table with him, and pretend it didn't hurt to be rejected, to be the woman that Jackson Cooper could resist.

She blamed herself. She'd taken a single moment and turned it into something it hadn't been, ever. He had done a few sweet things for her and she'd obviously taken it wrong. Last night she'd thought he would kiss her and he hadn't. She should have learned then that he wasn't interested.

As she hurried up the steps he called her name. She didn't turn back. She wouldn't. She'd been humiliated enough. For years she'd been praying that God would help her move past her fear. This probably hadn't been His plan.

The front door of the house opened. Heather Cooper, blonde, petite, pretty, smiled. "Madeline, Mom told me you were here today. She said to find you and Jackson."

Heather peeked around her. "There he is." And then her attention refocused on Madeline, and Madeline wanted to melt into the concrete of the front porch. "Are you okay? What did he do?"

Nervousness turned to hysteria. Madeline giggled and then laughed. She turned to watch Jackson walk up the steps, still the gentleman, shrugging and saying nothing.

"Nothing happened." Madeline wouldn't let him take the fall for her mistake. "Nothing at all."

She hurried inside the house and left Jackson with his

sister. Nothing at all had happened. Nothing would ever happen. Jackson had given her the space she needed to come to her senses.

He had rejected her. That knowledge settled in her heart where it felt heavy and cold. And she had to go in to lunch with him, sit across the table from him and avoid looking his way.

Which she could do because she'd always avoided him. She needed to do that for a little longer, and then she would put distance between them. Jade could stay with his family. Madeline could go back to her life. Thanks to Jackson, she could walk away without regret.

At the moment, thanking him was the last thing she wanted to do.

Chapter Nine

After a pretty miserable lunch, Jackson loaded Madeline and Jade back into his truck and drove them to the church where they'd left Madeline's car a few hours earlier. A five-minute ride felt like five hours with neither of the women in his truck speaking. The younger one seemed to be talked out—finally.

The older one looked hurt and wounded. Exactly what he hadn't wanted to happen. He'd been doing his best to protect her and she'd messed that up royally.

Jackson pulled his truck into the church parking lot, stopping next to Madeline's sedan. Jade dozed in the seat next to him. Madeline had managed to sit near the door this time. He had thought long and hard about that kiss, about the hurt look on her face when she ran away.

He couldn't let her go home thinking this was about her. The woman who hid behind big sweaters and glasses needed to understand that he hadn't rejected her because of her.

But when would he tell her, and what would he say? Nothing for now, not in front of Jade. Not in the church parking lot when he would be driving home and she'd go back to her house.

"Jade, climb on in Madeline's car. I'll follow you back to your house." He nudged the sleeping teenager.

"We'll be fine." Madeline opened the truck door. "I'll bring Jade to your house in the morning before I go to work."

"I know I don't have to follow you, but I'm going to. We need to talk."

Madeline moved for Jade to get out of the truck. "We don't need to talk. Really, I don't want to talk. I think we've said it all."

"We actually haven't said a word and I want to explain."

"No, thank you." She got out and closed the door.

Jackson watched as she rummaged through her purse for her keys. She had reverted to glasses today and a big brown sweater with a denim skirt. He shook his head as she fumbled, dropped her purse and then opened the car door and tossed it in the back seat. Angry gestures. Mad at him or mad at herself?

After she drove away Jackson sat there in the parking lot, thinking about a lot of stuff, most of which didn't make sense. He didn't need this. His life was fine. He had his ranch. He had his family and friends.

This church that had always been in his life, he even had that, when he wanted.

When he wanted? On his schedule, his time?

Okay, he got that God might not like that idea. So this was all some "jerk you up by the seat of your pants" faith plan? He remembered the chorus of an old hymn his grandmother loved.

No turning back, no turning back.

He could argue all day that he kind of liked the old Jackson, the old life, but God was sending a pretty clear message. No turning back. It set him back on his heels a little, and he took a long time getting back on the road.

Tomorrow he'd move forward. He'd go to his doctor in Grove.

He'd try, again, to get hold of Gloria Baker.

And he'd fix things with Madeline.

Tonight, though, he'd find a way to get his mind off the crazy twists and turns his life had taken. First he drove past Madeline's, making sure she and Jade got in the house safely. The porch light burned bright. She'd parked her car under the carport.

He turned his truck around in her driveway and headed back to town, in the direction of Back Street. He had work to do on the living nativity. Since the horse had thrown him and then Jade showed up, he'd kind of neglected his job of building Bethlehem.

The front porch light of Dawson Community Center cast a wide arc of light across the front lawn of what had once been his family church. There were a lot of memories tied to this little building. Most were pleasant, some weren't.

One that he had mixed feelings about had to do with Jeremy Hightree, his half brother. They'd grown up together, not knowing that they shared the same father. Today they were probably closer than ever. But the relationship was still strained. It took a lot for a guy like Jeremy to let go of pride and resentment. Jackson figured Jeremy had done better than he would have.

After parking he grabbed tools out of the back of

his truck and walked across the lawn to the makeshift buildings. An inn, shops, and on the other side of the lawn, the manger scene. He needed to work on the inn. He strapped a tool belt around his waist and hooked the hammer into the loop.

"What are you doing here tonight?"

Jackson turned, smiled at Jeremy and pulled nails out of his mouth so he could talk. "Thought I'd get some work done. I've kind of fallen behind on the job."

"From what I heard, you fell off a horse. I didn't expect you for a few more days."

"We don't really have a few days, now do we?"

Jeremy shrugged and walked a little closer. "No, I guess we don't. Saw you at church today. A little advice?"

"I'd rather you not give me advice, if you don't mind. It wasn't that long ago that you were running hard and fast from anything that had to do with Dawson." Jackson grinned and avoided looking at Jeremy. "As a matter of fact, I remember a dozer aimed at this building."

"Right, I guess you've got a point."

"I guess I do." He placed a nail and lifted the board that needed to be attached. "What would you do without me, anyway?"

"Oh, we'd manage." Jeremy stepped closer and Jackson saw that his brother wasn't smiling. "I'm just going to go ahead and say this."

"Really?"

Jeremy nodded and for a second Jackson wondered if he was about to get punched. Jeremy smiled but his eyes were steel-hard in the evening light.

"Jackson, if that kid is yours, you'd better not leave her out in the cold."

When an old dog got riled, he bristled. Jackson felt a lot like an old dog but Jeremy looked a little ahead of him, more prepared for a fight. He put the hammer down and took a step away from Jeremy. He got it. He knew why Jeremy would say something like that to him. Jeremy had spent most of his life feeling like baggage that got left on the side of the road.

"I think you know me better than that." Jackson picked the hammer up again. He tapped the nail into place, and reached for another. "And you don't really know a thing about this situation."

"I know that everyone in town is talking about a kid showing up on your doorstep claiming to be yours and looking a lot like you."

"People assume a lot, don't they?"

"Maybe they do, but sometimes the facts point to the obvious answer."

Jackson pushed a tarp out of the way and pulled a piece of plywood across the opening. "I'm really not going to have this discussion with you."

Jeremy didn't budge. He didn't back down. "I guess it isn't any of my business. And I guess I'm making it my business because she's a kid and I know what it feels like to be that kid, wanting to be a part of a family."

Jackson exhaled a whole lot of frustration. He finally looked at Jeremy, shaking his head and wishing he'd gone on home. Instead he'd come here thinking he could work alone, get his thoughts together and figure out what to do.

That's what he got for thinking.

"She isn't mine."

Jeremy stared for a long minute and then looked up at the sky. When he zeroed in on Jackson, it felt pretty uncomfortable. Jackson's attention focused on a closed fist and then on the hard stare.

"Really?"

Jackson picked up another board and nailed it to the frame of what would soon be the inn that turned Mary and Joseph away. For all eternity it would be the inn that turned away a baby, the son of God, the savior.

But the story would have changed if Jesus hadn't been born in that manger, the humblest of circumstances. He might not go to church every Sunday but Jackson got that God always had a plan. Things came together for a reason.

A young girl had landed on his doorstep. For a reason?

"Jeremy, she isn't mine. I know that she looks a lot like a Cooper and my name is on the birth certificate. But I'm about one hundred percent certain she isn't mine."

"'About'?"

"I'm done with this conversation. I'm either going to finish the inn or knock you into the middle of next week. Which do you prefer, brother?"

Jeremy raised his hands and backed away. "You go right ahead and finish the inn."

"Thank you, I will." Jackson pounded another nail with Jeremy watching.

Of course he wouldn't be quiet for long. Finally he cleared his throat and stepped forward again.

"She's a cute kid and she seems pretty high on you."

Jeremy cleared his throat again. "As a matter of fact, she isn't the only one who seems to really like you these days. Two women, is that a record?"

"It isn't a record and you're a piece of..."

Jeremy slapped him on the back, laughing loud. "Jackson, I'm the best thing that ever happened to you. I'm your brother."

"I don't know how you think that's a good thing."

Jeremy backed toward the door. "Well, I haven't knocked you on your can yet. And I put up with you coming over here in the evening, making noise and bellowing like an angry bull."

"I put up with you on Sundays and holidays." More than that, but he wasn't in the mood to be congenial.

"I'm going to give you a sweet little niece or nephew in about eight months."

Jackson froze, holding the board, pretty amazed. "Seriously, you and Beth?"

"We're having a baby."

"Congratulations." Jackson meant it, but today it didn't come out as easily as it once would have. Today he could only think about the little girl who wasn't his and the woman who had kissed him this afternoon, unsettling him, and changing his mind about a lot of things.

"Thanks. It's going to be a big change for us." Jeremy grinned and snorted a laugh. "At least we get to work up to it. No *'surprise, it's a teenager'* for us."

"You're a laugh a minute."

"I try. Hey, it's getting late and Beth will wonder where I am. Why don't you head on home? We'll get some more work done here on Wednesday."

"Yeah, I think that's a good idea." He slipped the

hammer into the tool belt and stretched, groaning when the muscles between his shoulders protested. "I think it's time to go home and put my feet up."

"Let me know if I can do anything to help." Jeremy walked out the door ahead of him.

"Yeah, I'll do that."

A few minutes later Jackson drove down the road, slowing as he got close to Madeline's driveway. Every light in the house was on. A week ago he would have gone on by, wondering about her, maybe smiling.

Tonight he pulled in, parking behind her car.

It took her a few minutes to answer the door. He knocked a little louder, rethinking the decision to stop by. The puppy barked and Jade shouted, which meant he couldn't leave now. He had to stand there, not quite sure of himself. He pushed his hat back and waited.

Who was he kidding? His mom said he'd been sure of himself since he turned three and managed to kiss Annie Butler on the cheek in the church nursery. He grinned, not that he remembered, but he liked that story. Even if Annie hadn't ever dated him.

Commotion erupted inside the house. He peeked between the curtains and saw Jade race through the hall, the dog following her. Madeline yelled that she would get it and for Jade to get in the shower.

Wow, domestic. Family. Not at all what he had been thinking about. A book on the table and a coffee cup. Pictures on the walls. The smell of wood smoke filled the air. A cat hopped up on the porch and sat looking at him, licking its paw and blinking the way cats did.

The door opened a crack. Madeline peeked, sighed and opened the door the rest of the way.

"Why are you here?"

He shrugged. "Guess I felt like we have unfinished business."

"Really? I think it's all been said. Jackson, can't you let a woman crawl off and hide without you chasing her down and making her remember that she made a fool of herself?"

He moved a little into the door. "You didn't make a fool of yourself, so that isn't why I'm here. And I'm afraid I do like to be the one who chases the woman."

"So this is because…" Her cheeks turned pink. "Because *I* kissed *you*."

"And hurt my male ego?" He smiled and then laughed. "It isn't that at all. Why don't you invite me in for a cup of tea? It's cold out here."

And he wasn't a tea person. But he thought she probably was. He could hear water running and knew Jade would be out of the shower soon.

"Okay, tea." Madeline led the way through a house he'd been in hundreds of times in his life. His great-grandparents had lived here. His grandmother had grown up here.

Jackson took a seat at her tiny dining room table. A poinsettia graced the center. She'd put her Christmas tree in the corner of her little dining room. Jackson watched as she moved around the kitchen heating water, finding tea bags and placing cups on the counter.

After a minute he stood, because he couldn't sit and watch her. He had to stand near her, watch her expressions, her serious brown eyes. He knew her story, but he wanted to know everything about her. He wanted her to share her dreams with him. He wanted to hear her laugh.

He'd dated a lot of women who talked nonstop, whose constant stories about themselves grated on his nerves. This woman didn't talk enough.

"The other day when I was looking for information on Gloria Baker," he said, leaning against the counter. Madeline kept her back to him. She poured steaming water in the two cups. "I searched your name."

She nodded but still didn't turn to look at him. "Okay."

"I know what happened when you were a little girl."

She poured hot water in the cups and didn't look up. It took everything for him to stay in that spot, watching her, not moving toward her, not reaching for her hands that trembled, not putting an arm around her when she shivered.

He knew all the right moves. He'd spent his life studying women, figuring out how they ticked. He knew how to make them feel special. This time he didn't know. Or maybe he did. Maybe standing there, letting her pull herself together, not reaching for her was the best move.

It was just a new page in his life. A new game plan.

"Why are you telling me this?" Her voice trembled but there were no tears.

"I'm telling you to explain that I didn't pull away because of you. I pulled away because of who I am. I don't want to be another person that hurts you. And let me tell you, I'm the guy who could. I've had plenty of angry messages on my answering machine. I've dated a lot of women and most of them are no longer in my life. A few still send me Christmas cards. Thirteen years ago one of those women put my name on a birth certificate as the father of her child. I'm keeping my distance because I don't want to hurt you."

"What did you learn about me?" She turned, handing him a cup of tea before walking away. He watched her take a seat at the oak dinette.

When he'd searched her name he hadn't really expected to learn anything. He hadn't expected to learn information that would change his life. Maybe hers.

"I guess I learned everything. Or at least the facts available on the internet. But there's more to you than that story."

"It isn't something I share with many people, Jackson. It isn't a great opening line. Hi, I was born and raised in a cult. My mom worshipped a man who convinced her that all of the women owed him their little girls."

"You were a victim."

She shrugged. "It's my past. It changes how people think of you when they learn something like that. Doesn't it?"

He moved to the seat across from her, carrying the cup of steaming tea in a tiny little cup that represented the woman staring up at him with liquid brown eyes and a soft smile that trembled and faded.

"I'm sorry." What could he say? That he wanted to find that man and hurt him for what he'd done to her and countless other children. He didn't need for her to share the story of a man who used little girls as objects, dividing them amongst his disciples, marrying them off at young ages after their innocence was already stolen from them. He didn't want for her to have to tell him the story in her words. The story was on her face, in her eyes and hidden in her heart.

But she'd survived.

Her hands trembled as she sipped the tea. The cup clattered in the saucer when she set it on the table. He kept his hands on the porcelain cup of amber liquid, thinking it should make him calm, but it didn't.

"You don't have to be sorry." She smiled up at him, brave, amazing. Too good for him. "Unless you mean you're sorry for snooping."

He laughed a little, surprised by her smile, her soft laughter. "I am sorry about that. I'm sorry if anyone ever treats you differently because of what you've been through. You are more than what happened to you in that place."

"I know." She sniffled a little and reached for a napkin in the basket on the table. "I get caught feeling blessed because I escaped with fewer scars than so many of the children. And then I feel guilty because I escaped. I owe Sara everything."

"Your sister?"

Madeline nodded again. She held her cup of tea in both hands, not drinking it. He sipped his, waiting, not wanting to push.

"She took me to town. And then she disappeared. I haven't seen or heard from her since."

"Your parents?"

"I don't know who my real father is. My mother finds me and sends a Christmas or birthday card every year or so." She glanced toward the hall, toward the bathroom where water still poured from the shower.

"Your mother is out of prison?"

She nodded. "Jackson, I'm glad I can help you with

Jade, but you have to understand. I've spent years trying to convince myself that it wasn't my fault."

He held the cup of tea because he wanted to hit something. Or somebody.

"I've been numb. I've been afraid. And over the years, I've been happy with my life." Her brown eyes twinkled. "Even when I sleep with the lights on."

Jackson reached for her hands. He moved them from the cup and he held them in his. "I haven't had a lot of experience with this, but I think I make a pretty good friend."

She laughed at that. And laughed some more. When Jackson started to let go of her hands, she held tight until her laughter dissolved and she had to wipe her eyes.

"What's so funny?"

She laughed again. "You, being a girl's friend. The idea of it makes you turn a little red." She touched her neck. "From here up."

Footsteps in the hall meant they were about to have company. Laughter and the dog barking. Madeline smiled. "You have definitely unsettled my life. My neat little house is suddenly chaos, clutter and a Christmas movie come to life."

"I hope that's a good thing. I think we've both been a little unsettled this week."

"More than a little." Her eyes darted toward the door. Still no sign of Jade. "I think she's not as happy as she pretends to be."

"I think you're right about that. I think she's trying to pretend this is some great adventure."

"We can't run from life."

"No, we can't." He stood, leaving the nearly empty

tea cup on the table. Maybe he was a tea person after all. "I'll see you tomorrow."

She followed him to the door. He could still hear Jade and the dog. They were probably in the spare bedroom at the back of the house. It was probably better that she didn't crash in on this conversation.

He knew Madeline's story. She still didn't know his. He thought that one was better saved for after the doctor's appointment he'd made for the next day. A DNA test and a check-up.

"Jackson, thank you." She stood on the front porch, hugging her sweater around her thin frame. The full moon captured her features, her big eyes and sweet smile.

"You're welcome." He leaned in, kissing her goodbye. An easy kiss on the cheek. "I'm getting very good at this."

Her eyes narrowed. "At what?"

"Nothing."

He tipped his hat to her and walked down off the porch, whistling a song and thinking that maybe self-control wasn't such a bad thing. But she didn't need to know that.

They were friends. He could give her a simple kiss on the cheek to tell her good-night, or an easy hug. He could be there for her, make her feel safe. Friendship.

Yeah, simple, easy, friendship.

He'd keep telling himself that.

Chapter Ten

Mondays were always hard for Madeline. The kids were fresh from the weekend, lots of energy, homework not done and attitudes definitely not in check. This Monday proved to be even more difficult. She couldn't relax and the kids were bouncing off the walls. When she left at the end of the day she wanted nothing more than a long soak in the tub and a nice, easy dinner. Maybe takeout from the Mad Cow.

But halfway home she remembered Jade. She remembered Jackson. She remembered all the ways her life had changed in the last few days. And none of it had been her doing. A few weeks ago in their Sunday school class Clint Cameron had taught how God changed our lives to make more room for Him and His plan. She hadn't really thought about it before. She'd made her own changes, such as buying a home, forcing herself to stay and not run.

God had brought other changes. She hadn't thought about Jade or Jackson in that light. She'd thought about

Jade on her doorstep as a mistaken address and bad directions.

What did any of this have to do with her? Maybe God wanted to use this situation to show her that she could open up to people. More specifically, that she could trust a man. Of all the men she should be expected to trust, God picked Jackson Cooper? Why not someone like James Wilkins, the nice teacher who had asked her to lunch on occasion?

Why not the very handsome coach from the Tulsa school where she'd taught?

She pulled up to her mailbox and pulled the mail out, shuffling through the letters, junk mail and an electric bill. Another card from her mother. She tossed the mail, all of it, on the seat next to her.

Why another card? Wasn't one unopened card at Christmas enough? Didn't the lack of a response tell her mother what she needed to know, that Madeline had no interest in a relationship with her?

Madeline pulled up her driveway and parked. She sat for a long time, not wanting to move. She wanted to run again. But she wouldn't. She looked at her little house, now adorned with Christmas lights and two new motion lights.

People in Dawson cared. They wanted her in their lives. Jackson Cooper had installed security lights to make her feel safe. She had a church family and neighbors. She picked up her mother's card but she wouldn't open it, not yet.

Instead she forced herself out of the car into the cold December day that gusted and blew. The cold went right through her and she shivered down into her coat.

When she walked into her house she was slammed by more changes. Kid stuff. Jade had left dirty dishes on the counter. Madeline quickly washed them and put them away. A towel had been left on the bedroom floor. She tossed it in the hamper, wiped the sink and tub and then made the bed in the spare bedroom.

Neat and tidy, everything in its place. She turned to the sound of whimpering. They'd left the puppy on the screened-in back porch. Madeline groaned, knowing this wouldn't be pleasant.

The rug had been chewed to pieces, as had her slippers that she'd left on the floor. The stink of it made her gag and she backed away. The puppy whimpered and plopped down, resting her little head on big paws. Madeline glared at the little renegade.

"No messes in my house, puppy." She pushed the dog aside and reached in the cabinet for paper towels. "My house, my life, is neat and tidy, not messy."

The puppy did a little dance around her feet, barking and nipping at her boots.

"You really don't care, do you?" She leaned to pet the fluff ball. "Neither does he. He doesn't care that I don't want my world turned upside down. No, he brought you, and a child."

He'd pushed his way into her life, her thoughts, her dreams. No one belonged in those places. Dawson had been her safe place. Until last week.

She stomped into the kitchen for a spray bottle of the strongest cleaner she had. The puppy whined at the door.

"Oh, *now* you want to go outside?" She pushed the door open and watched the little dog race outside.

It chased blowing leaves, sniffed grass and then

found a stick to chew on. Madeline pulled on rubber gloves, held her breath and started to clean the mess that should have been Jackson Cooper's to clean. Yeah, she should call him and tell him to come down and clean up after his rotten puppy.

If it hadn't meant having him in her home, all male and smelling good, she would have. But she didn't want his faded jeans and cute grin cluttering up the place that way.

Tires squealed and she heard a horrible yelp. The puppy. She tossed the cleaner and paper towels and ran out the front door. A truck sat in the middle of the road and an older man had picked up the puppy.

Jade's puppy. Her puppy. The stupid, sweet, messy puppy.

"I think she's okay." The farmer, a neighbor named Clark, held the ball of fur. "I tried to stop but she was chasing something."

The puppy whimpered and stared with dark eyes. Her little body trembled. "I should take her to a vet."

"I think you probably should. I'm real sorry. She came out of nowhere."

Madeline closed her eyes to the surge of tears. "I let her out. I didn't think about her running across the road."

She didn't know a vet. She didn't know anything about dogs. Or cats. Or cows.

"Let me put her in your car." The farmer, in bib overalls and a straw cowboy hat, trudged through the ditch and up the hill. "Do you know where to take her?"

"I'll figure it out."

"Doc Marler is good. If you can catch him."

She nodded and her mind spun in crazy circles trying to think about dogs and vets and what to tell Jade.
A new batch of tears streamed down her cheeks. She'd
have to tell Jade.

"I think she'll be okay. And if you send me the vet
bill, I'd be happy to pay it."

Madeline rubbed the useless, silly tears from her
eyes. "No, I'm the one who let her out and didn't watch
her."

"Well, you let me know how she is. She's a cute little pup."

"She is, isn't she?" Madeline sighed and shook her
head. "I didn't know I wanted a dog."

The farmer left the dog in her car and headed back
down the driveway. Her cell phone rang. She pulled it
from her pocket and groaned when she saw the caller
ID. She didn't need this, not right now. And then, she
did. Because he would know what to do.

She answered her phone with a quick hello and then
said, "The puppy got hit by a car. I don't know what
to do."

Her body trembled the way the puppy trembled. The
poor little thing hunkered in her front seat, holding her
front leg out.

"I'll be right there." Jackson's voice over the cell
phone undid a little of the fear. He wouldn't leave her
alone to handle this. Of course he wouldn't. He helped
everyone. He rebuilt tornado-damaged homes and
searched for missing children.

When he pulled up a few minutes later, she breathed a
little easier. Jackson jumped out of his truck and headed

her way. His smile shot clean through her, tender and unexpected. And she started to cry.

"Hey now, what's this all about?" His voice had a huskiness that undid every last shred of calm. "The puppy is going to be fine. Look at her, she's getting all worried about you."

Madeline nodded but she couldn't stop the tears. Everything inside her broke loose and she couldn't shove it all back inside. The puppy whimpered and belly-crawled to the edge of her car seat.

"Shh, you're okay." Jackson pulled her to him and held her in strong arms. "Shh."

She sobbed against his shoulder and knew that the strange calm seeping into her body, into her heart, was from him. Safe. And suddenly, not so safe.

"I thought she was dead." Make it about the dog, much easier to make it about something other than the Grand Canyon splitting open inside her heart.

"A puppy against a truck. She beat the odds today." He still held her. His lips brushed her hair and he didn't let go.

"Jade will be so upset."

"She's fine. I called and she's going to stay the night with Heather. Doc is waiting for us."

"Thank you." Madeline moved from his arms, brushing her hand across her face. "I'm a mess. And I need to run inside and get my purse."

"You aren't a mess." He brushed hair from her face. "Get what you need and I'll put her in my truck."

She nodded and rushed back into the house for her purse. She turned off lights on her way out and locked the front door. When she got to the truck Jackson had the door open for her.

The puppy crawled close, head resting on Madeline's leg. She looked quickly at the man sitting next to her. A friend. He had said it himself. They were friends.

The local veterinarian had been in town most of Jackson's life. He had even delivered a baby once, years ago. It had been a stormy night and the woman, a dairy farmer's wife, had gone into labor while Doc had been there taking care of a sick cow. When things had moved a little too quickly, Doc delivered Jasmine Porter.

Jackson parked and got out. Madeline, still pale and shaken, held Angel in her lap. He'd heard her murmur a few prayers, even promise the dog that she did like her and was glad she had her. He smiled as he helped the two of them out of the truck.

"You know, you didn't do this to the dog."

"I was really angry that she chewed up my rug and made a mess in the utility room."

"So every time a dog's owner gets mad, God sends a truck to teach them a lesson?" He kind of chuckled, and she shot him a look that took the humor right out of the moment.

"It isn't funny."

"It kind of is, if you think about it. I don't think life works that way. I don't think God works that way. He doesn't get us back every time we have a thought He doesn't approve of."

"I know." She smiled a little. "I know it's a crazy thought. I'm a woman, we get at least three crazy thoughts a week."

"I'll try to remember that." He opened the door and she went through, still holding the puppy she hadn't really wanted. He smiled as he followed her inside. He couldn't stop smiling.

Something must have happened to him when he got tossed off that horse. Maybe he'd hit his head and they hadn't realized.

A door to the left of the desk opened. Doc walked out, slipping into a pale green jacket as he did. He nodded at Madeline and the dog before turning to Jackson.

"How old?"

"Eight weeks, Doc. Looks like her front leg."

Doc's bushy gray brows shot up. "You're a vet now?"

Jackson laughed. "Doc, you're more than a vet."

"Yeah, I'm the guy that…"

Ran Jackson off when he took Doc's daughter out a few times. But since Doc had the only veterinary clinic in Dawson, they'd worked past the resentment.

Doc took the puppy from Madeline.

"I'll take it back for X-rays. You two stay here."

Madeline stood in the center of the room, looking a lot like a woman letting go of a kid for the first time. Jackson looped his arm through hers. "I'll buy you a cupcake if you'll stop looking so guilty."

He led her to the vending machines at the end of the room.

"What kind?" He pulled a few ones out of his wallet.

"I love cinnamon rolls."

He fed the dollar into the machine and pushed the button. The package of cinnamon rolls dropped down and she reached in and grabbed them. "Thank you."

"Something to drink?"

Madeline shrugged. "Water. I'm so sorry that I dragged you over here. I know you're tired and still trying to heal up. And you have other things to do. You have a life."

Pink flooded her cheeks and he grinned at the rush of random words that spilled from her lips.

"I do have a life." He fed a dollar into the machine and pushed the button for a bottle of water.

"I mean, you know…"

He laughed. "You mean…women?"

"You know what I mean. Don't make me say it."

"Dating women is something I do enjoy. I'm a single man. That makes it okay."

"Right, I know that." She took her cinnamon rolls and the bottle of water back to one of the hard plastic chairs that lined the wall near the door. "I'm apologizing because I know this is keeping you from your life. I can't even, I don't know…"

He sat down next to her. "You can't, you don't what?"

"I could have called Jenna or Beth. I have friends. I do have a life." She glanced at her watch. "I have play practice in two hours."

"I know you have a life."

"I just panicked and when you called, I blurted it out."

"And I offered." He couldn't tell her the truth, that he liked being the person who came to her rescue. "Don't worry, she'll be fine and as soon as she's taken care of, we'll head over to Back Street."

"We?"

"I have some work to do over there."

"Oh, okay." She reached for her purse and pulled out a stack of mail. Her face paled a little and she looked away, shoving the letters back into the side pocket of her bag.

"Bad news?"

She shook her head and her shoulders slumped. "My mother sent me another card."

"What does it say?"

"I didn't open it. I don't open them."

"Why?"

She looked up at him, staring as if she thought he'd dropped off another planet. Okay, maybe he should get this, but he didn't. Women weren't the most understandable creatures in the world. Beautiful, nice to hold, but definitely not easy to understand.

"Why would I open it?" She held it in her hands and he wanted to take it from her, open it himself.

"Because you need to."

"That sounds easy." She smiled up at him. "So, just open this card and, 'tah-dah,' everything is better?"

"No, but I think it would be a beginning. Look, Maddie, I know that my family looks pretty great from the outside, but we've had our problems and we've learned that it's best to take care of situations from the get-go. Don't let it drag on. Don't let it take root."

"It's already rooted, Jackson. This is more like having to weed a garden that's been let go."

"I understand."

She put her hand on the edge of the card and tore just a little. "This isn't easy."

"No, I bet it isn't. But remember, the only thing in there are words, and if you don't like them, toss them in the trash, burn them, never open another card from her."

"Right." She slid her finger under the flap and pulled out a Christmas card.

Emotions flickered across her face as she read. Jackson watched, waiting, not pushing. She bit down on her bottom lip and then her eyes closed briefly. Finally she shrugged and handed him the card.

"She was pregnant, sixteen and living on the streets. She thought Rainbow Valley sounded peaceful, like a place to raise a baby."

"Are you glad you read the card?"

"It changes things." She took the card back, looked it over again and then slid it into the envelope. "But it doesn't change what happened. It doesn't answer the other questions. Now I have more questions. Why didn't she leave?"

"I guess those are questions only she can answer. But maybe not questions to answer in a card."

"Sara wasn't really my sister."

Jackson moved his arm, encircling her slim shoulders and pulling her close. Two weeks ago she'd been a neighbor, not even a friend.

"Maddie, did you ever think that the two of us would be sitting here together sharing huge events in each other's lives?"

"Never."

He laughed at her strong response. "You make it sound like the worst thing that could have happened to you."

She looked up and took him by surprise. Her hand touched his cheek, rested there and then moved to his shoulder. "It hasn't been the worst thing at all."

The door opened and Doc walked out, carrying the

injured puppy. His weathered gaze shot from Madeline to Jackson and he shook his head. "Some things never change. Here's the dog. And here's the bill."

"Is she going to be okay?" Madeline touched the dog's back.

Doc handed Jackson the slip of paper. "A broken leg, but she'll heal quickly enough. You paying?"

"I can…" Madeline reached for the bill.

Jackson shook his head. "No, I'll pay for this."

Madeline took the puppy and held her close. The same puppy she hadn't been too fond of yesterday. Jackson wrote out a check for the vet bill and walked her out the door.

"What's the deal between you and Doc?" she asked as Jackson opened the truck door for her.

"He caught me parking with his daughter about sixteen years ago and he has a long memory." Jackson waited for her to get in the truck and then he leaned in close. "And back then he had a pretty good aim with his shotgun."

"He shot you?"

"Nope, he shot the tires off my truck. I had a hard time explaining that one to my dad."

He closed the door and walked around to the driver's side. The story had grown over time and with numerous tellings, but his version was still the truth. And maybe knowing it would show Madeline why he was the last person she needed her name connected with.

But maybe it was a little too late to be thinking about that.

Chapter Eleven

Dawson Community Church cancelled Wednesday-night services. With just three weeks until Christmas and less than two weeks before the living nativity was scheduled to begin, it was decided they needed more practice, so everyone involved would meet at Dawson Community Center. Madeline had planned on picking Jade up after school but Jackson told her he'd bring her with him.

Madeline pulled into the community center parking lot shortly before six. People were already there. Lights had been plugged in outside, huge shop lights with bright halogen bulbs. She walked up to the building, searching the crowds for that familiar face.

Searching for Jackson. She shook her head and told herself to stop. Before long Jade would be going back to her mother. Jackson would go back to his life and she'd go back to living in her empty house, uncluttered, unencumbered, empty. And she would be happy for that day to come.

Really she would.

"Madeline."

She turned quickly, spotted Jade and smiled. "You have ketchup on your chin."

Jade scrubbed at her face with her hand. "Better?"

"Yeah, sure." Madeline rubbed away the last smudge of ketchup. "What did you have for dinner?"

"Jackson made corn dogs."

"Nice." She turned, saw Jackson walk through the door and averted her gaze, returning her attention to the girl in front of her. "Did you have a good day?"

"Yeah, but he's a grouch."

Madeline nodded and decided to let it go. "Come downstairs with me. I have to get dressed and you can hang with me. If you want?"

"Yeah, I want. How's the puppy?"

"Same as this morning, pitiful. I think she isn't as bad as she wants us to think."

Jade laughed at that. "I think she loves the attention." And then the girl's smile faded. "I'm going to miss her."

Because this weekend they were going to Oklahoma City to try and find her mother. "I know, but you'll get to see her again."

"When?" Jade walked next to her, small and slim, a kid who worked hard at being strong.

"Soon. I promise."

"Right."

Madeline turned to the girl. "Jade, I keep my promises."

"Yeah, probably."

"Hey, where are you two going?" Jackson appeared next to Madeline.

"Downstairs to get dressed. Don't you have something to build?" Madeline had realized something lately. She didn't know how to have an easygoing conversation with a man. She tried but it came out more like an order, less like banter.

"I do have work to do. I'll catch up with you later."

Madeline nodded and then he left. She ignored Jade's knowing glances and headed downstairs. Next to her Jade giggled.

"What's so funny?"

"The two of you, acting like you don't like each other or like you haven't been spending a lot of time together."

"We haven't been spending time…" Okay, they had, but not because they wanted to. He had made her a cup of tea Monday after they got home from the vet. He'd listened as she told him little details about her childhood. He'd given advice about finding Sara.

"Yeah, you like him," Jade teased.

"No, I don't. I mean, I do, but not…" She groaned at the direction the conversation had taken. "Jade, I'm not discussing this with you."

"Fine, that's okay. But can you do me a favor?"

They were in the kitchen of the community center, surrounded by people, and Madeline didn't know if she wanted to continue the conversation around so many pairs of ears. But Jade's hazel eyes locked with hers, begging.

"What is it?"

"Tell him to keep me. I'm his daughter and I can't go back."

"Jade, I can't make this decision for him."

"Then you keep me. Call family services and tell

them that my mom isn't fit. You're a teacher, they'll believe you."

"I can't do that."

"Of course not. If I hadn't messed up and gotten the address wrong, you'd still be doing your own thing and you wouldn't be bothered with us."

Madeline hugged the girl. "Yes, I would still have my uncomplicated, uncluttered life. I would be sitting alone in the evening in a quiet house with no one to talk to."

Although a little silence would be nice. With Jade in her home, in her life, silence seemed to be a thing of the past. When Jade left, would Jackson also be a thing of the past?

"I need to get in costume." She brushed off the thoughts that didn't make sense.

"What do I do?" Jade followed her into the dressing room.

"You can come with me and watch."

Jade sat down on a stool and watched as Madeline got ready.

"A woman called my da…" Jade looked down and shrugged. "Called Jackson today."

"Jade, that's personal." Madeline tied the fabric belt around the waist of the costume.

"Yeah, I guess. I heard him tell her he couldn't see her right now. And I think she must have asked when he could see her and he said he didn't think he'd be seeing her anytime soon."

Madeline pretended she wasn't listening because hadn't she just said that this information was personal?

She didn't need to know what Jackson told women that called his home. Honestly, she didn't care.

Much.

Jackson slid the paper with the DNA results back into his pocket along with the other medical information. He had work to do. There were people everywhere. He sighed and walked through the crowd to the back of the manger. He'd been helping with the star, getting it in place so that it would shine over Bethlehem and the baby Jesus.

Beautiful Star of Bethlehem. He could almost hear his great grandmother singing the song. The memory brought a smile and he hadn't had much to smile about today. He had a lot to think about.

When he turned from the tower holding the star he saw Madeline and Jade walking together, heads bent toward one another, whispering and smiling. He smiled, seeing the two of them together. Yeah, he had a lot to think about.

Later he'd talk to Madeline. He stopped working for a minute to think about that decision. He'd been thinking about her all day, thinking about talking to her, about telling her his news, how his day had gone.

And then he'd anticipated her reaction to the medical tests and the secret he didn't want to share. He watched her walk into place, surrounded by sheep. Jade watched from a short distance away.

Someone walked up behind him. He turned, nodded and tipped his hat to Wyatt Johnson. Wyatt grinned big and turned his attention from Jackson to Madeline, back to Jackson.

"Watch out, that one will get under your skin." Wyatt Johnson smirked a little. Payback for what Jackson had told him last year.

"I don't think so, Wyatt."

Wyatt laughed, loud. People turned to stare and Wyatt thumped him on the back, jolting him and making him flinch a little.

"Watch the ribs, if you don't mind." Jackson rolled his shoulders to unkink the muscles.

"That's right, you got tossed last week. You aren't the first guy around here with some broken ribs."

"I'm not as young as I used to be." He grimaced, knowing he sounded way too much like a country song.

"Right, you're not. So what's wrong with taking time to get to know one of the nicest single females in this town?" Wyatt watched his own wife head their way. Something stabbed at Jackson's heart. Jealousy? Nah, couldn't be.

"Nothing wrong with it, Wyatt. But I think she's a little out of my league."

"She probably is." Wyatt raised his hand to thump Jackson on the back a second time and Jackson moved to the side.

"Could you not?"

"Oh, sorry, didn't know you were so weak."

"Right, weak."

"You're not your normal humorous self." Wyatt turned to watch the beginning of the living nativity as it got underway. His voice lowered. "Seriously, is there anything I can do to help?"

"No, not right now." Jackson shoved his hands in

his pocket, feeling the paper that he'd gotten that day. "I'm good."

"Well, it was good to see you in church on Sunday. You plan on coming back this Sunday?"

"No." He had to explain, not leave Wyatt hanging. Although that would have been fun. He watched the progression of Mary on the donkey, Joseph at her side.

He finally turned and smiled at Wyatt who had the good sense not to push, but he looked pretty tense with all of those unasked questions rolling around inside him.

"Wyatt, I'll be back. I'm taking Jade to Oklahoma City this weekend." He watched Mary and Joseph exit the inn, looking young and perplexed. "But I'm coming back. I guess I got tired of going and having to face questions, a few accusing looks, my own guilt."

"So what's changed?"

Jackson didn't mean to but he looked in the direction of Jade. And Madeline. He tried to brush it off, to pretend it had nothing to do with either of them. It really did have more to do with him.

"I guess a guy has to face his life. Time to make some changes."

"She's a cute kid."

Jackson nodded but didn't say more. Yeah, Jade was cute. She looked like him. She had his eyes. Sometimes it looked as if she had his smile.

"She's great," Jackson agreed. She had somehow survived a childhood that hadn't been much of a childhood and a mother who hadn't been a mother.

He refocused on Madeline as a shepherdess. As he watched the angels appeared. Madeline went down on her knees, covering her head with her arm. Jackson walked away from Wyatt. He walked closer to the scene of the shepherds leaving the field and walking toward the manger. He stood close as Mary revealed her newborn son and angels began to sing. The shepherds bowed at her feet.

Jackson stood there waiting for normal to return. But it wouldn't and he knew that. He'd changed. Maybe this was the new normal? Maybe this was his new life? Something had to be wrong with him. He'd turned down a date today with a woman he'd gone out with off and on for the last two years. She was a lawyer's daughter and owned a clothing boutique in Tulsa. She was uncomplicated.

He'd turned her down because of the shepherdess kneeling not ten feet from him. The same shepherdess who looked up at that moment and caught him staring. Yeah, he was definitely losing control of his life.

Jade saw him standing there, watching. She smiled big and bounced away from the group she'd been crowded in with A kid who thought she was his. He thought about her future and it left a pretty big space in his heart because she deserved a home, a life with people who cared about her.

Tomorrow he would try again to contact her mother. And if he couldn't, then what? He had a load of bulls to take to Oklahoma City. He could try to find her. But he couldn't keep Jade indefinitely. He couldn't expect Madeline to raise her. He'd considered talking to his parents.

But this one was in his court.

The program ended. Jade stood at his side, a skinny

kid in a big, puffy coat. Her cheeks were pink from the cold and her nose was red. She smiled up at him.

"This is great." Her tone was all happiness and sunshine.

"Yeah, it is." He pulled her close to his side for an instant and thought about moments in the future and how it would change everything for her.

"Is it time to go now?"

He nodded and watched as Madeline spoke to a few people and then slipped away from the crowd. He watched her. He couldn't stop watching her. He smiled as she walked toward him, toward Jade.

"That was great." He thought about the three of them, arm in arm, leaving together.

"Thank you. It feels as if it is all coming together."

"Yeah, it does." He felt Jade move away from him, but he couldn't stop staring at the woman in a shepherd's costume. He couldn't stop thinking about holding her close, making her feel safe.

"I'm going inside." Jade punched his arm. "They're serving hot chocolate and cookies."

"Go for it. We'll leave soon," he called out after her. She raised a hand to let him know she'd heard. It made him feel like a dad. Strange, really strange that it could happen so easily, this change in his life.

"Are you okay?" Madeline stood in front of him still. She had zeroed in on his mood. She knew how to do that and it unnerved him a little.

"I'm good." He didn't reach into his pocket for the piece of paper. "I'm going to try again to contact her mother. If I can't, I have to drive down there and look for her."

Madeline's gaze drifted to the church, to the door Jade had just skipped through. "I know. It's a shame though. I mean, I know I can't keep her, but I wish she could stay."

He reached for Madeline's hand. "Let's walk."

"Oh, okay." She hesitated, glancing toward the church. Small crowds gathered in front of the building, talking. A few people looked their way.

Yeah, rumors, gossip. He knew the drill.

"We can talk later," he said, because he didn't want to give people a reason to talk.

"Is this about Jade?"

He nodded once and released her hand. When he did she touched his arm. It would have been easy to hold on to her, to make this about him, not about Jade. But it was about Jade. In the short span of a week his life had become all about a kid.

And a woman.

"I should go." What he meant was he should escape.

"No, you should come inside."

Madeline hooked her arm through his. He knew that took a lot for her. He knew that easy gestures weren't always easy, sometimes they took real courage. He pulled her close to his side and leaned to drop a kiss on the top of her head.

"Inside, huh? Right into the midst of gossip and speculation?"

She laughed a little. "Are you afraid?"

"Shaking in my boots."

"I'll be with you." She said it in a breathless way and he looked down to see if her expression matched. She looked up at him, surprise flickering in her eyes.

He had to dig up a little of the old Jackson to get hold of this situation. "Promises, promises, Maddie."

She didn't pull away. Instead she turned, still holding his arm and they headed toward the church. She didn't let go. He didn't want her to.

Chapter Twelve

The phone rang and rang as Madeline unlocked her front door. She tried to hurry but her fingers were numb from cold. Jade stood next to her, hopping up and down a little. The wind whipped against them, a cold, north wind.

Finally she pushed the door open and they rushed into the warmth of the living room, greeted by wood smoke and Angel barking from the laundry room. Jade ran past her, heading for the dog, of course. She could hear the girl calling to the animal as she hurried through the house.

"Don't throw clothes everywhere," Madeline warned and then in a quieter voice because it didn't matter added, "I have a hall tree."

She hung her coat and kicked out of her boots before picking up the phone and checking the caller ID. The number didn't look familiar. It didn't have a local area code. She pushed the number for voicemail and listened. Her heart raced as the message played and then she slammed the phone down.

Not at Christmas. She didn't want to do this at Christmas. Forgiveness needed to happen, she got that. She even thought she had forgiven. But she didn't want her mother forcing her way into this life, a safe life with safe people.

Her world had already been upended by a young girl and a confirmed bachelor who wanted safe help. She was safe. Her life was safe. She plopped down in the big easy chair she'd bought when she first moved in.

The perfect chair for quiet evenings alone, reading a book, drinking tea. Safe.

Loud laughter reminded her she didn't have a quiet evening ahead of her. Then footsteps. Jade ran into the room carrying the puppy that licked and licked her face.

"She's glad to see you." Madeline smiled in spite of herself. Being alone was overrated. Jade made noise and clutter worth it.

This weekend the girl would be gone. Madeline's heart broke a little for her, because she knew how it hurt to be jerked around at that age. Maybe she'd keep Jade. Maybe she'd file for custody if Jackson didn't plan on doing something.

Why wouldn't he? He was her dad. He had to do something.

"Can I go to work with you tomorrow?" Jade plopped down on the sofa with the dog.

"I can't take you to work with me." She would have loved to. Jade needed to be in school. "Jackson is going to spend the day with you. He has a lot of work to do, he said, and you can help."

"Oh, that's cool." Jade leaned in for the puppy to lick her face again. "I love this dog. I've never had one."

Madeline smiled as she watched dog and child. "Me, neither. I think you love her more than I do."

"Do you love my da…" Madeline's heart broke a little more for Jade, even if this did sound like a tricky question coming at her. "Jackson?"

"We should go to bed." Cop-out.

Jade hugged the puppy and giggled. "She needs to go outside. And you do love him."

"I don't. Jade, love is more complicated and takes more than two people being thrown together. It is more than just simple emotions. It's about two people being connected, really caring about each other. It's about wanting to share lives and everything, good or bad, that goes with life. It takes time to find and build a love like that."

"I think you could love each other, get married and we'd be a family." Jade's tone was wistful and sad. "Don't you think?"

Madeline sighed because she didn't know what to say. She let her heart trip over the idea of being in love with Jackson Cooper. Complicated. He made her life way too complicated, and she avoided complicated as often as possible.

"I think it really is bedtime. You're so tired you're delirious." Madeline pushed herself out of her favorite chair and reached for Jade's hand. "It's cold but the puppy has to go outside."

Jade giggled. "Too late. You should see your laundry room."

"I'm seriously going to make Jackson Cooper come over here and clean up the mess. By the time this is over he's going to owe me a new floor."

"Yep, you love him."

She swatted Jade, a playful swat. "Give me the dog and you go brush your teeth."

All of the right mom words were coming out. It took her by surprise that she knew those things to say, because she'd never had a mother who said them. And now her mother wanted to be in her life.

No. Madeline couldn't go there. She could forgive, but letting the woman in her life, that she couldn't do. Jade headed into the hall but she stopped and glanced back.

"Are you okay?" The girl bit down on her bottom lip and her eyes, so much like Jackson's, studied Madeline's face with intensity that unnerved.

"I'm good, just tired."

"Okay, I'll brush my teeth." Jade smiled a sweet smile. "I think he could love you back."

"Jade, go." Madeline cringed on the inside. That definitely sounded like a mom voice.

The phone rang again. Madeline held the puppy in her arms and stared at the caller ID. The same number. She closed her eyes and waited for it to stop ringing. Slowly her hand descended, picking it up. Because she wouldn't run anymore. She couldn't. She had to face the past to move on with her life.

"Hello?"

"Madeline? It's me. It's your mother."

Madeline's world went dark for a moment. It spun. It faded and then righted itself. The puppy licked her face. She set her down on the floor and held the phone against her ear.

"Madeline?"

"I'm here." *Breathe. Breathe.* She leaned against the wall, trying to block images of her mother's face, smiling, telling her it would be okay. But it wasn't okay. Her mother led her to the man who abused her. Tore her life apart. Her mother waited for her. Held her. Told her she was sorry.

Sorry?

"I know you don't want to talk to me."

"Really, so why are you calling?" Madeline sank to the floor. The puppy crawled into her lap. Jackson had been right about having a dog.

"I'm calling because I have to. I need to." Her mother sobbed from hundreds of miles away. "I'm in Tulsa."

"No." Not hundreds of miles. Tulsa. A little more than an hour's drive. "No."

She waited but the world kept spinning. Faster and faster.

"I want to see you."

"No." She couldn't get another word out. She couldn't form another response. She couldn't even tell the woman on the other end to go away.

Because a part of her still wanted a mother? Because she knew she needed to forgive?

But not this woman. Not now.

"Madeline, I was young. I made mistakes."

"Mistakes?" Madeline shuddered as she released a breath. "Mistakes are something a person makes in their checkbook. Mistakes are when you say the wrong thing or buy the wrong car. Those are mistakes. You didn't make a mistake. You allowed your only daughter to be abused."

"I know." A long silence, sobbing on the other end

that Madeline couldn't be sorry for. But she was. "I hurt you. I wanted you to know that I was afraid, too."

"Oh, okay, well, thank you for sharing that. I'm sorry you were afraid."

"This isn't going well."

Madeline closed her eyes and tears slid down her cheeks.

"No, it isn't. I can't talk to you right now."

"Maybe soon? I have a job and an apartment in Tulsa. I wanted to be close to you so I moved here."

"I have to go." Madeline hung up.

A few minutes later Jade kneeled in front of her. She didn't take the dog. Instead she curled close and hugged Madeline. "Are you okay?"

Madeline nodded. She tried to smile and reassure Jade, but she couldn't. Her heart ached. Her throat tightened with the tears, the emotion. She wanted to crawl inside herself, the way she'd done as a teenager. She wanted to hide from the pain and close herself off from feeling.

But she couldn't go back. God had done too much in her life. She couldn't go back to being the person who hid from life.

Jade hugged her hard and let go. "I'll be back."

Madeline nodded. She knew Jade walked away. The puppy, limping and hopping, followed. Madeline hugged her knees close to her chest and took a deep breath. She had to get it together.

She needed to take care of Jade, not let the girl take care of her. She leaned her head on her knees and prayed for strength to get through whatever her mother would throw at her in the coming weeks. She prayed for strength to truly forgive.

And then the front door opened. Madeline looked up. Jade stood nearby. She pointed at Madeline and Jackson nodded. In the blink of an eye Jade disappeared and Jackson was at her side. He leaned and lifted her into his arms.

"Why are you here?" Madeline leaned into his shoulder, finding it hard to believe that he had showed up when he did. Jade had called him, of course she had. And he was here. Her heart wanted to open up like a flower in early spring reaching for the sun.

He carried her to the couch and sat down with her held against him, his arms strong and holding her close to his side. She closed her eyes. This is what safe feels like, she told herself. To be held.

She thought of all the times God had held her. Through the toughest times of her life. Held and kept her anchored in faith.

"Jade called. She was worried."

"I'm fine." And then she cried. She flooded his shirt with her tears and he stroked her hair and told her everything would be okay.

She believed him.

"What happened?" He reached for the tissue box on her table and handed it to her, but he didn't stop holding her, making her feel safe.

"Do I have to talk about this?"

"Not if you don't want to." He wrapped her in protective arms and held her tight. She leaned into his strength and she couldn't force herself to move.

"My mother has not only found me, she called and

she's living in Tulsa. She'll be there when I decide I want her in my life."

Jackson sighed. She felt the rise and fall of his chest. His hand slid down her back. "I know this isn't easy, but I know that you're strong. And you know I'll be here."

"I know." Did she? Why would he be here for her? She couldn't ask those questions. For the moment she had someone in her life who promised to be there for her.

Jade had asked her if she loved him. No, of course not. She was a grown woman. She knew better than to think she'd fallen in love with him. They'd been thrown together for a short time because of a teenager and a dog. They'd somehow forged a friendship.

"Maddie, I mean it." His voice, soft and husky, warm near her ear. She wasn't in love with Jackson. Attracted to him, definitely. But love?

She looked up, intending to tell him something brave and witty, if only she could think of something. When her lips parted he leaned and met her with a kiss that made her forget doubts, fears, pain. He brushed her lips with his, feather-soft, once, twice. She clung to him, exploring this moment, no fear, no desire to run, only a need to stay in his arms. His lips touched hers again, lingering this time.

The dog barked; Jackson pulled away. His eyes widened a little and he smiled. "Maddie, Maddie, you do push a man to forget his convictions."

"Right, Jackson, that's me, the temptress."

They both laughed and he pulled her close. "More than you know."

The dog hopped into the room. A moment later Jade

followed, a knowing little grin on her face. "I'm going to bed."

Jackson stood and pulled the girl into an easy hug. He kissed the top of her head and ruffled her hair. "Thanks for calling me."

"Anytime." Jade's gaze dropped to Madeline. "I took the dog out."

The evidence was in her face. The pink cheeks. The red nose. Her eyes glistened a little.

"Jade, are you okay?"

Jade nodded. "I'm good."

Madeline patted the couch next to her and Jade plopped down. Madeline hugged her tight. "It really is going to be okay."

"I know it is. Right?" Jade looked up at Jackson.

Madeline followed the look and what she saw frightened her. Jackson put on a good front. He smiled and Jade probably believed him, that everything would be okay. The look in his eyes, a look he sent Madeline, told her otherwise.

Jade seemed convinced. "Good night."

The girl hurried down the hall, the dog trying to follow.

"What's going on?" Madeline asked as Jackson paced her floor.

Jackson pulled a piece of paper from his pocket and tossed it her way. He put a finger to his lips and she got it. Everything wasn't okay. He sat down next to her again.

What she read slammed her heart. She knew he must have felt this way or worse when he read the results. The

DNA test showed that Jade Baker could not be Jackson Cooper's biological daughter.

She didn't know what to say.

Madeline handed him back the paper and she couldn't look at him, couldn't see the sadness in his eyes. Or would it be relief?

When she did look at him, she saw concern and worry, not relief. It made her heart soar a little.

"Now what?"

"I'm not sure what to do." He rubbed the back of his neck and then leaned back on the sofa, closing his eyes.

Madeline didn't know what to say. She reached for his hand and waited, because he needed time and she knew he needed a friend. A friend. He had those. He had family. And he was sitting next to her, on her couch, lost.

"Jackson, we have to find her mother." She held his hand tight, wishing she could do more.

His thumb brushed her fingers. "Yeah, I know. Thank you for being a part of this. 'We' sounds much better than me, alone."

She wondered about that. He seemed good at being alone.

"Of course I'll do what I can. I love her, too."

"I know." He let out a long sigh. "I have to tell her she isn't mine. And I have to take her back to Oklahoma City to her mother."

"I'll go with you." The words rushed out. Jackson's hand tightened on hers. He lifted it and held her palm to his lips.

He moved to the edge of the couch, leaning for a moment over clasped hands. Madeline's hand rested on his back and he turned, smiling.

"And I have to go now. Because you're amazing and I…should really go."

She followed him to the door, trying to figure out the sudden change.

"Maddie…" He leaned and kissed her goodbye, soft and slow, ending with a sigh as he walked away.

Madeline wanted to run after him. She wanted to call him a coward for running. She was the one who ran but she hadn't. This time she hadn't run. She hadn't hidden inside herself.

She watched him drive away, headlights in the dark night. Somewhere a coyote howled. She could hear trucks on the distant highway. Lost, she stood there in the cold of the open door because Jade might have a point. A teenager understood Madeline's feelings better than she understood them herself.

Jackson fired up the tractor the next morning and hooked a round bale to take out to the cattle in the back pasture. Madeline hadn't gotten there yet with Jade but Travis had shown up and he'd be in the barn when they arrived.

He drove along the fenceline, stopping to open a gate when he got to the field where they were grazing the beef cattle. He hopped back in the tractor and eased it through, then got out to close the gate again. He latched it tight because he had no intention of chasing down a hundred plus head of cattle today. Sleet had started to fall an hour earlier. Nothing major but enough to make the cold pretty miserable.

As he climbed back in the tractor he heard a pitiful sound. He stood on the step and looked around but didn't see anything out of the ordinary. The cattle were a good hundred yards out. They were grouped together, fighting the wind and sleet. As he headed their way they started to move. He'd brought a bale out yesterday but he planned on moving several bales today. He also needed to corral the young bulls he would be selling this weekend to a breeder just outside of Oklahoma City.

The City, as it was more popularly referred to. When someone was going to the City, everyone knew what they meant—Oklahoma City.

A dark form in the grass caught his attention. He lowered the bale of hay and backed off from it. The cattle were already moving in, even though they still had hay. He'd need to check the automatic waterer, to make sure it wasn't frozen.

He hated the cold. Even in the enclosed tractor, complete with heat, he felt it down to his bones. The wind whistled. Maybe the sound of the wind made it seem even colder. Whatever, he was ready for spring already and winter hadn't really hit yet.

The dark shape moved and he saw that it was a calf. The form next to it didn't move. He headed the tractor in that direction. Not a good morning for a downed cow. As he got closer the cow still didn't move. She didn't even raise her head.

Even worse. He jumped down from the idling tractor and eased toward the bawling calf. Cold air gusted, blowing against him. The calf appeared to be a few hours old, and half frozen. The sleet coated its dark fur, still wet, but icy.

"Not a good way to start your life, little guy." He

scooped up the bawling calf, took a last look at the momma cow to make sure his assumption was correct.

She was gone. He walked away, holding the calf. Part of farm life. Yeah, he knew that. He'd learned the lesson early in life. Sometimes animals died. People died. He guessed for some people it got easier.

He reached to open the tractor door and pushed the calf inside the cab, following it. "Now what in the world are we going to do with you?"

A few minutes later the tractor rolled toward the barn and he knew what he'd do with this calf. Madeline's car parked in front of the barn gave him the answer he needed. He drove past the barn to the equipment barn. Tractors, an old farm truck and a couple of stock trailers were parked under the roof of the three-sided, open-front building.

Jade ran toward him as he got out of the tractor and headed for the barn. She didn't seem to notice the cold and he remembered how his grandfather had always said that cold got colder as a man got older. He grinned, remembering.

"A calf!" Jade's eyes lit up. "Where's its mom?"

"Gone." He didn't want to say more. He didn't want to see her eyes full of tears. But he knew it had to happen. Just like eventually he'd have to tell her that she wasn't his.

"What happened?" Madeline had walked up behind Jade. She looked so good this morning, he wanted to grab her up in his arms and thank her for being in his life.

He didn't know who would be more shocked if he did that. Probably better if he let it go. The tender vulnerability in her eyes last night warned him to go easy, move slowly.

Jade was petting the sticky, wet calf.

"I found him with his mother. It happens." He hated that it did. "We need to get him a bottle and get him warmed up."

"He won't die, will he?" Jade's eyes widened as she looked from him to the calf.

"Of course he won't." Jackson led them all into the barn. Travis had left. "Where'd Trav go?"

"He had to get home and start packing for Tulsa." Madeline's voice trailed off when she said the name of the nearest city. "School got cancelled due to the weather."

"Yeah, I can imagine that. Let's get this little guy settled and a few chores done and I'll take you girls to the Mad Cow."

For lunch. And he didn't care what people said or how they talked.

"What can we do?" Madeline followed him into the feed room.

"I'll hold him if you can grab that bottle and mix the calf starter. In that rubber tub, a scoop of the starter and then fill the bottle with water from the sink in the bathroom through that door." He pointed to the door across from them. "Jade, grab a towel out of that cabinet and let's get him dried off."

"Got it." Madeline already had the lid off the tub. Jade pulled a towel from the cabinet and rubbed it over the calf.

"A little harder than that, kiddo. We need to get him dry and warmed up."

"Poor calf," she crooned as she rubbed the calf he'd set on the floor of the feed room. "Everyone should have a mom."

And that sent an arrow to his heart. Every kid should have a family, too. His mom had tried to give a home to as many as possible. He'd learned at an early age that family didn't necessarily have to be about blood connections and DNA.

"Here it is." Madeline returned, a city girl in jeans and a heavy coat, lace-up suede boots to keep her feet warm. She knew how to blend.

She handed him the bottle, her hands covered in crocheted gloves that were probably pretty worthless in the cold, especially if they got wet.

"You need better gloves." He shoved the bottle into the fighting calf's mouth. The calf turned his head one way and then the other. "Hold his head."

"Okay. Why doesn't he want it?"

"It isn't his momma. Give him a minute to realize it's food and he'll take to it."

Madeline held the calf's head and Jackson opened his mouth. The calf let out a little moo and then clamped down on the giant-size baby bottle.

"There he goes."

Jade moved close. "Aww, just like a baby."

Jackson laughed. "Yeah, a baby who will someday weigh close to a ton, have horns and be able to run you into the ground. Don't let him fool you. He isn't a pet."

"But he's cute," Madeline insisted. He'd put the calf on the wood floor and it wagged its tail and pushed against the bottle he had handed over to Jade. Slobber flew, dripped down the calf's chin. Jade laughed and held tight to the bottle.

"He's strong."

"He is strong," Jackson agreed. "And cute. But still, he's going to grow up to be…"

"A big, mean bull." Madeline repeated his warning with a little laugh.

He shot her a smile and watched her cheeks turn pink. Yeah, he hadn't lost it completely.

"Right."

Madeline kneeled next to the calf. "You aren't planning on sending this thing home with me, are you?"

Jackson widened his eyes and pointed to his chest. "Me, do that to you?"

"Yeah, you're going to do that to me." She pulled off her city-girl gloves and stroked the calf's back. "Where would I put a calf?"

"You have an empty barn and a corral."

The sucking air sound meant an empty bottle. Jade pulled the bottle from the calf's mouth and it chased after her, butting against her, wanting more. She laughed and stuck out her fingers. The calf brought his long tongue around her hand.

"What do we do now?" Jade kneeled in front of the little bull calf.

"For now we'll put him in a stall with plenty of straw to sleep on and feed him again later."

"He'll be all alone." Madeline stroked the calf and looked at him with kind of pleading, kind of accusing eyes. Great, an orphaned calf and two big-hearted females.

"Yes, he will. But that's about the only option. He

wouldn't survive on his own in the pasture." He picked up the calf and headed toward an empty stall, trying to figure out a way to undo the sad look in Madeline's eyes. It hadn't been but a couple of weeks ago that he'd just do what he had to do and that would have been the end of it.

A female around the place changed everything. They brought emotion into farming. He sighed and shook his head because now he couldn't walk away without it bugging him, too.

He put the calf in the stall and turned, smiling because he was going to be the hero. "I'll get a goat to keep him company."

"A goat?"

"Yeah, Ryder Johnson has a few goats that he sometimes pairs up with foals. We'll stop by there on our way back from the Mad Cow."

Jade leaned in, looking at the bawling, unhappy calf. "Can't we get him a friend now?"

He shook his head and pulled out his phone. "Let me call Ryder."

He made the call and fifteen minutes later Ryder pulled up to the barn and led a big, fat goat into Jackson's barn. Ryder grinned, tipped his hat and handed the lead rope of the goat to Jade.

"Told you to buy a goat." He shot the comment at Jackson.

"Right, I should have listened to you." Jackson opened the stall door and the goat walked right in, eyed her new companion in unblinking silence and grabbed a mouthful of straw.

The calf stopped crying as the goat moved closer.

"Perfect." Madeline smiled and watched as the calf

followed the goat around the stall. Jackson shook his head. It was that easy to make her smile.

And he'd never cared more about making a woman happy. That thought made him want to jump in his truck and drive far and fast from this situation and this moment. Realizations like that one didn't come around very often.

It had never happened to him before.

"Now, can we go to lunch?" He slipped a convincing arm around her waist and moved her toward the door. Ryder walked on out but turned as they followed.

"Let me know if you need anything else." Ryder grinned. "Like advice."

"I doubt I need advice from you." Jackson glared and Ryder didn't seem to notice.

"Of course not. I mean, why would you need advice? You've been ranching all your life."

"Exactly. I'm very good at ranching."

And they both knew they weren't talking about ranching. Madeline walked away, fortunately not getting it. She followed Jade to the fence and one of the horses walked up to let them rub her neck.

"Nothing changes a man like a good woman and a kid."

Ryder pushed his hat down on his head a little tighter.

"I haven't changed." Jackson didn't have a woman or a kid, not really. He watched them walk down the fence line and he knew it bugged him, that Jade wasn't his. That Madeline wasn't his.

"Gotta go. Andie and the twins are ransacking the house. She's decorating. They're chewing and dragging stuff everywhere."

"It'll be a great Christmas for you all."

"Yeah, it will. See you later, Jackson. I think your Christmas is going to be different than you expected, too."

Jackson would have agreed, but he knew that the DNA test undid any ideas he'd had about Jade having a Cooper Creek Christmas. He wondered if she'd have any Christmas at all with her mother.

For a brief second he tried to tell himself it wasn't his problem, but it was and it cut deep, thinking about her alone at Christmas.

He whistled, loud and shrill. Madeline and Jade turned and headed his direction. "Let's get some lunch."

They all climbed into the truck together. Madeline in the middle next to him. Jade did that on purpose every time.

Chapter Thirteen

The Mad Cow Diner looked like Christmas come early. Madeline walked in next to Jackson and Jade. She tried to pretend she went to lunch with someone like Jackson every day. But the stares from the locals reminded her that she couldn't fool them or herself. She'd been here a year and she'd never dated. When well-meaning friends tried to match her up with a nice guy, she always said a polite "No, thank you."

She stared at the Christmas tree and decorations, trying to ignore the heat creeping up her neck. Jade grabbed her hand and pulled her toward a nativity, hand-carved by a local artist. The tree sparkled with clear lights and Christmas music played softly on hidden speakers.

Last year she'd been in town just a few months and she'd joined Vera for Christmas at the Mad Cow. Vera always had a big meal for folks in town without family. Madeline had received the same invitation for this year.

Vera walked out of the kitchen, wiping her hands on her apron. She grinned big when she saw them. "Well, Merry Christmas."

Madeline smiled back. Vera had switched from her normal blue dress to a red dress, white apron and a Santa hat.

"Merry Christmas, Vera." Madeline accepted the other woman's warm hug and skittered a look sideways to find Jackson heading their way.

"Isn't that nativity beautiful?" Vera put an arm around Jade. "A man in our church carved that for me. I love the look of love on Mary's face. She'd just had the most perfect baby in the world, and she had to wonder why God had brought this moment to her. I always wonder how she felt, being so young and being put in that situation. I think she must have felt as awed as the shepherds."

"I think the cows were awed, too." Jade grinned as she looked at the scene. "We have a calf."

"Do we?" Vera's brows arched and she turned to look at Jackson.

He shrugged and let it go. But Vera didn't. Her gaze shot up and she smiled. "Why, Jackson Cooper, look at that, Madeline is under the mistletoe."

"Vera." Madeline tried to step away.

Jackson caught her hand, a wicked grin on his face. He smiled at Vera and then at her again. His hand on hers was rough and warm. "We can't ignore mistletoe. Vera would be crushed."

"I would indeed." Vera smiled big. "I move it every morning because I want to keep things interesting."

"But—" Madeline looked around the restaurant, half-full and everyone staring at them. A table of women giggled and pointed.

Jackson grinned and her heart stopped protesting.

She stopped wanting to escape. How did he do that? When he stepped close she wobbled a little and he slid a hand to her back, steadying her. "One little kiss won't hurt."

She nodded but wanted to disagree. It could hurt, very much. He leaned and dropped the sweetest of kisses on her mouth. When he pulled back, his smile had faded.

"Maddie, I'm all out of self-control. Good Jackson has left the building."

Vera laughed. "From the look on her face, I think Good Maddie has left the building, too."

Madeline shook her head. "I'm very much still here."

Vera clucked a little and moved them in the direction of a corner booth, out of view. She said, "I think what the two of you need is a nice bowl of chicken and dumplings. Weather like we're having calls for comfort food. The weatherman said today that we've had two weeks of below normal temperatures."

"Chicken and dumplings do sound good, Vera." Jackson's hand remained on Madeline's back and he reached for Jade who had stopped to look at Christmas cards taped to the wall. "This way, kiddo."

As they walked people were talking behind their hands and nodding in their direction. Madeline pulled her jacket a little tighter around herself and blinked fast to clear her vision. Why did moments like this make her want to hide again?

Being stared at, whispered about. It had all been too much a part of her life all those years ago. Being interviewed by police, going before judges and lawyers, facing her mother that last time. Her heart squeezed tight.

A hand touched her arm, guiding her to the booth

and into a seat. She scooted across the bench and took the spot closest to the window, sighing with relief when Jade sat next to her.

"What are we going to do for the rest of the afternoon?"

Madeline looked up from her menu when Jackson asked the question. Jade, seated next to her, grinned. "I'd like to ride a horse."

"We could do that, in the arena. This weather isn't great for riding." Jackson's gaze settled on Madeline and she didn't have an answer. He didn't look away for a long minute and she focused on the menu, unable to meet the questions in his eyes.

"What about Christmas shopping?" He smiled up at the waitress approaching with an order pad.

They stopped to order and then Jackson returned to the previous conversation, pulling them back to the subject with him.

"So, Christmas shopping?" He picked up the wrapper from his straw and turned it into a paper wad that he flicked, hitting Jade in the nose. "I'm kind of an expert on shopping with women. It comes from having a half dozen sisters."

"Christmas shopping sounds fun." Madeline stirred sugar into the super-strong coffee that Vera was famous for.

"We can drive into Grove." Jackson reached for the sugar bowl that Jade had nearly emptied into her iced tea. "I think that's enough."

Jade didn't smile. She didn't laugh. "I have to go home tomorrow. I won't be here for Christmas."

Madeline ducked her head and waited for Jackson's

answer. But her heart broke for Jade who just wanted a family for Christmas.

"Jade, I'm not going to leave you on your own. I promise."

Jade shrugged her slim shoulders like it didn't matter. But it did matter. It mattered more than any of them could say. To a girl who had nothing, not even family, it mattered.

"You don't even think you're my dad."

Jackson leaned forward, resting his arms on the table. "What do you mean by that?"

"Why else would you need a DNA test?" Jade fiddled with her napkin, tearing it into little pieces. "You're looking for a way to skip out on me."

"I'm not." He tossed his hat on the bench and brushed a hand through his hair. "Jade, I'm a bachelor. I've been single and on my own for a long time. I'm not going to know how to make 'dad' decisions right off the bat."

"Right, yeah, whatever." Jade hunkered, her shoulders curved forward and her head down. "I'll be okay."

"Jade, you'll be more than okay. I promise."

The waitress appeared with their chicken and dumplings, as well as a big basket of rolls and salads for the three of them.

"Let's eat and have a good day. Tomorrow we'll figure something out."

Jade nodded but she wouldn't look up, wouldn't make eye contact with either of them. She blew on a steaming bite of chicken and dumplings but didn't take the bite. Instead she looked down at the bowl, tears dripping down her cheeks. Madeline touched her hand and smiled when Jade looked up at her.

"It'll be okay. I know people have told you that before, but Jackson isn't going to let anything happen to you. He's going to be there for you."

And then Madeline looked at Jackson, pleading without words for him to keep the promise she'd just made for him. He had to be the person this little girl needed. Someone had to be there for Jade.

Two hours later Jackson still couldn't shake the way Madeline's words back at the Mad Cow had shaken him. Jackson in Charge wasn't the name of this little family drama. The only person Jackson really knew how to take care of was Jackson.

Somehow, though, a kid and a woman had become a big part of his life. He walked behind them as they browsed the second flea market of the day. They were looking at fancy little tea cups that wouldn't hold more than a thimble of liquid. While they looked at tea cups he tried to remember who he had been a week ago.

"This one is pretty." Jade picked up a cup and handed it to Madeline who held it up to the light and examined it.

The guy gene didn't allow him to see a thing different about that cup. It looked like every other cup they'd looked at.

"It's beautiful." Madeline turned to him, big smile, eyes dark and pulling him in. He was about to tell her he agreed.

He couldn't stop himself.

"It is pretty." He blinked because he didn't drink tea. He didn't shop in flea markets for old tea cups that other people had been drinking out of for years.

She laughed and he knew he'd blown it. "You're not good at this."

"Sorry, I'm not a tea person. Or a cup person."

"Or a flea market person." Madeline put the cup back on the shelf. "We should go to a store with guy stuff. Fishing poles and guns."

"Madeline, do you want that cup?"

She shook her head. "Even I wouldn't spend that much for a cup. Let's go, before you break out in hives."

How far gone was a guy when he picked up the flowery tea cup and carried it to the counter? As he paid he told himself this was going to pass. But watching the delight on Madeline's face when he handed her that bag holding the perfect tea cup, he wasn't quite sure. He wondered if he needed to go back and buy another dozen of those cups, because if each one put a smile on her face, it was worth it.

She led him out of the store by the hand, Jade skipping ahead of them.

"What am I going to do?" He watched the girl walk ahead of them, window shopping.

"Tell her the truth." Matter of fact Madeline.

"Yeah, sounds easy, doesn't it?"

"It won't be. She wants to be a Cooper. And who could blame her. She wants you for a dad. Any little girl would."

That did more than surprise him. He stopped walking, but kept his eye on the teenager a short distance ahead of them. Okay, he couldn't let it go. He turned to look at Madeline.

"Why in the world would a kid want me for a dad?"

"Really?" Madeline watched Jade, too. "You don't

get that? You have everything to offer. You're a good man with a wonderful home and a family. You can take care of her, make her feel safe."

"Keep talking, you're starting to convince me." He grinned down at Madeline and she turned away, cheeks a little pink. "I never thought you'd think so highly of me, Maddie Patton."

"I'm not talking for me. I'm talking for a young girl who has grown up in a pretty unstable home."

"But I'm not that man, Maddie. I'm not dad material. I'm a bachelor who does a barely decent job at taking care of himself. And the most important fact is the one we both know. I'm not her dad."

"No, but you're the closest thing she has to one."

"What am I supposed to do about that?" He was the closest thing Jade Baker had to a dad. That didn't say much, but he knew it was true. He wasn't anyone's dad. But this girl needed someone to be there for her.

This relationship couldn't be walked away from. This wasn't a Friday night in Tulsa with a waitress who only expected one night, a decent dinner and empty words. This was a kid who expected someone to be there for her forever.

It was Madeline, standing next to him, believing he'd do the right thing. He whistled softly and shook his head. She was looking for the same thing, someone to be there for her, forever.

"Hey, what's going on back there?" Jade turned from a window and hurried back to them, sliding a little on a slick spot in the sidewalk.

When would he tell her? The thought came to him,

that he didn't have to tell her. He could let her believe the DNA test came back positive.

But he wouldn't lie to her.

"We're coming." He smiled and headed up the sidewalk with Madeline at his side. "See anything you couldn't live without?"

She shrugged slim shoulders. "I thought we could go in that jewelry store. They have homemade jewelry."

"Let's go." He opened the door for the two women to walk in ahead of him.

It looked like trouble to Jackson. A jewelry store plus two females equaled serious trouble any way he looked at it. Not that he hadn't given women jewelry before. For Christmas. To say goodbye. Once, a long time ago he'd bought a promise ring for a girl in school. After another month of dating he realized forever felt like, well, forever. He'd taken the ring back and her brother had knocked him almost into eternity.

His phone rang, saving him from the ohhing and ahhing as Jade and Madeline went from display cabinet to display cabinet. Saved by the bell, he walked outside to take the call.

"Jackson Cooper, bring my daughter back." The voice on the other end didn't sound at all familiar. The words slurred and mumbled, forcing him to plug his opposite ear.

"I can't hear you."

"This is Gloria. Bring my daughter back. She's not your kid."

"So you did get the messages I left." He walked a short distance away from the front of the jewelry store. "Listen, Gloria, I can't really talk right now. I'm bringing her back tomorrow. But we're going to discuss this situation."

"We aren't going to discuss anything. She's my kid and I could have you arrested."

Anger shot through him, white hot and making his heart beat hard in his neck. He swallowed a lot of things he knew he shouldn't say in favor of carefully chosen words.

"Don't worry, the police know that I have her. My question to you is, why didn't you call sooner? Why didn't you file a missing persons report?"

"That's none of your business. Jade knows how to take care of herself."

The anger took a pivotal turn for the worse and he had to stand there for a long minute, finding a way to respond without making the situation worse. "Gloria, she's thirteen."

Gloria laughed, loud and harsh. "Right, and you care?"

"Yeah, I care."

"Just bring her home."

The phone went dead. Jackson stood with the cell phone in his hand watching the steady stream of traffic down the street. A hand touched his arm. He turned and Madeline gave him a cautious look.

"Problem?"

He shook his head and pocketed his phone. "Nothing I can't handle. Let's go back inside and see if Jade found something wonderful she can't live without."

"She found several items that fit that description."

"What about you?"

"No, I'm not a jewelry person. And as interesting as

their jewelry is, I'm more of an antiques girl. There's something about owning something that someone treasured for years, or generations."

"Gotcha." He touched her back with one hand and reached to push the door open with the other. Antiques. He filed that away for future reference.

The whirlwind of a teenager grabbed him and for the next fifteen minutes pointed out every awesome thing she could find. And then she told him she didn't want anything. She was happy just to look. Jackson hugged her tight. If he'd had a kid, he'd want her to be just like this one. He'd want her to be wild about living life, meeting people and experiencing new things.

He bought her a matching set of jewelry and she threw her arms around his neck and whispered, "I love you, Dad."

Over her shoulder he caught Madeline's soft-hearted expression, eyes filling with unshed tears. "You're welcome, kiddo."

She deserved a dad. Tomorrow he would have to tell her the truth. He knew, from talking to Gloria, that if he didn't, Gloria would. It would hurt less coming from him. Nothing in the world would keep it from hurting, though.

"We should probably head home." He paid for the jewelry and handed the bag, all decorated in bows and swirls, to Jade.

Madeline stood next to the door waiting for them. "Good idea. I have to be at practice in two hours and I bet that puppy is going crazy wanting outside. And that's your fault, Jackson Cooper."

"My fault?" He opened the door for them. "What, exactly, is my fault?"

"The puppy at my house making who knows what kind of mess."

"Oh yeah, the puppy. Okay, that probably is a little bit my fault."

"So you'll come over and clean up her puppy messes?"

"Nope, but I'll buy you dinner tomorrow evening." Jackson gave her his best smile because he couldn't take a chance that she'd say no.

"Tomorrow? But you'll be in Oklahoma City." Her eyes widened and her chin came up a slight notch as she got what he meant.

"You said you would go with us."

Madeline remained quiet as Jade moved ahead of them, drifting to the front of a store that held a display of tie-dyed shirts.

"She has to go home, doesn't she?" Madeline slowed her steps, and Jackson matched his to hers.

"I wish she didn't, but Gloria is pretty determined. She wants her daughter home and she pointed out that Jade isn't mine."

"She put your name on the birth certificate."

"I know. But the DNA proves otherwise."

"So this is the end."

Jackson nodded and he couldn't look Madeline in the eyes. Yeah, this was the end. Jade had to go home. Madeline would be out of his life. Everything would go back to normal. He'd go back to his life. They'd each go back to their respective lives. Whatever lesson he'd been expected to learn would be over.

It sounded easy but it hurt like crazy to think about it. Tomorrow his life would be his own again. No, he wouldn't be throwing a party anytime soon.

Chapter Fourteen

A quiet house. Madeline walked through her front door after work on Friday and thought about how this quiet used to be normal. No Jade. No Angel the puppy. Heather Cooper was babysitting the dog for her until they got back from taking Jade to Oklahoma City. No noise and no clutter.

After today her life was her own again. No more Jackson Cooper messing around in her business, or her emotions. She should sigh a sigh of relief over that one. Good riddance!

She dropped her bag by the hall tree and kicked off her boots. But she didn't have a lot of time. Jackson wanted to leave for Oklahoma City in an hour. That meant packing an overnight bag, changing clothes and tidying up a little before he got there to pick her up.

The plan included them staying one night in Oklahoma City. She would stay in a separate hotel room with Jade, to keep the girl safe and watch her. Tomorrow morning they would take Jade to her mother. And then they'd head home. Alone.

End of story. End of this little chapter in her life. This very complicated, cluttered chapter. As she walked through the hall the phone rang. She ignored it. It quit ringing but immediately started again. Madeline reached for it as she headed to her room to grab extra clothes.

"Hello."

"Madeline, it's me. It's your mother."

Madeline cringed and then she groaned. "Stop calling me."

"It's almost Christmas. I just wondered if maybe you would reconsider seeing me. Please. If you would just see me, just once?"

"Do you know what happened to Sara?" Madeline grabbed jeans out of her closet and two sweaters. She shoved pajamas into her bag and extra warm socks.

A long pause and then her mother spoke again. "Honey, I'm sorry."

"Sorry? I think we've established that. You're sorry and you want to be forgiven." Madeline leaned against the wall and closed her eyes. And as much as she fought the urge to stay angry, to stay bitter, she wanted to forgive. The little girl in her cried out for her mother.

Over the years, every now and then, she'd thought about what it would be like if her mother came back. If her mother could be the person she wanted her to be, needed her to be. That dream had seemed far better than the thought of always being alone with no family to turn to.

"Madeline, Sara…" Across the line Madeline heard a sniffle and then a sob. "Honey, she killed herself the night that she took you to town. She wanted you safe, I think. She did what I should have done."

Madeline walked to the window and looked out at the barren December landscape painted in shades of brown and gray. Bleak. Winter was always so bleak.

This moment felt like winter. It ached deep down inside, frozen and cold.

"I have to get off the phone now." Madeline held the phone to her ear as she slipped into jeans.

"Maybe before Christmas we can talk again?"

Madeline nodded even though the woman on the other end couldn't see. "I'll pray about it."

"Thank you. Oh, Madeline, thank you."

The call ended. Madeline sat on the edge of the bed and thought about the girl who hadn't really been her sister. Sara hadn't saved herself. She had given up. And no one had ever told Madeline. They'd allowed her to search, to ask questions, and they'd hidden the truth from her.

Maybe she could have found the truth if she'd tried a little harder? The one thing she couldn't have done was save Sara.

A car honked. She shoved her makeup bag and extra clothes into an overnight bag, slid her feet into boots and jerked her coat off the hall tree on her way out the door.

Jade jumped out of the truck and motioned for Madeline to climb in. Always pushing her into the middle. Madeline shook her head and climbed in. Jackson smiled big as she slid across the leather seat. He tipped his hat a little and winked. As she slid close she realized how good he smelled. And how good it felt to sit next to him.

The door slammed and Jade reached for her seatbelt. She didn't smile, though. Instead she watched out the window, shoulders slumped. Madeline touched her arm and Jade turned, smiling just a little.

"It'll be okay."

Jade shrugged. "Yeah, sure it will."

"We're not walking out of your life, Jade." Jackson shifted gears, his hand brushing Madeline's knee. She scooted a little closer to Jade.

"Right, I know." Jade looked out the window again, ignoring them.

Were they so different, she and Jade? Madeline thought not. Both had mothers they wanted to escape from. Madeline had escaped once and then she'd had to escape again. And again. She wasn't going to run anymore. This time she would face her mother. She'd been learning that facing fears sometimes meant overcoming them, seeing them for the tiny ant hills they were rather than the mountains they appeared to be.

Maybe her mother would be another mountain conquered.

Maybe someday Jade would conquer her mountains, her giants. It took faith, learning to rely on faith.

A hand touched Madeline's. She turned her attention from Jade to the man sitting next to her. Jackson Cooper. Her fears had changed from how he could hurt her, to how he could break her heart.

She hadn't expected that.

"How was your day?" He slid a quick look her way before turning his attention back to the road.

"Good day at school. My mother called again." She meant to be strong but her voice broke a little. Jackson shot her another quick look.

"You okay?"

"Good. I'm good." An easy smile to prove the point.

"Are we going to stop and eat?" Jade turned from the window to ask the question. "Are you taking me home as soon as we get to Oklahoma City?"

"We will eat. I do need to check in with your mom as soon as we get to town, but I thought you could stay with us tonight. I reserved two rooms, one for the two of you and one for me."

"Cool, a hotel. The only hotel I've ever stayed in was the shelter when Mom…" Jade's words faded off and she turned her attention back to the window. "How come you had to bring bulls?"

Madeline glanced back at the trailer hooked to the truck.

"I'm selling them." Jackson looked in the rearview mirror. "We'll stop at a ranch outside of the city, unload the cattle and drop the trailer. I'll pick the trailer up on our way back home."

"*Your* way back home," Jade corrected with a big frown.

"Jade, this isn't goodbye."

"Yeah, I know." She reached to turn up the radio. "Silent Night" filled the cab of the truck.

Madeline started singing. Jackson glanced at her, a quick look at her profile. Jade kept staring out the window for a minute but then she couldn't help herself. He figured that's what Madeline intended. Pretty soon Jade and Madeline were both singing. An elbow jabbed his gut.

"Broken ribs, remember?" He grunted and grimaced a little.

"Sing." Madeline smiled up at him, innocent and sweet.

He hadn't sung "Silent Night" in years but he joined them for the chorus. The chorus went high. They laughed at him.

"Hey, you said to sing."

"We changed our minds." Jade looked pained and stuck her fingers in her ears. "Please don't sing again."

"Give me another chance." He cranked the volume to George Strait singing a Christmas song. "This is more like it."

Madeline openly laughed. "You're not even going to tell us that you compare to George Strait."

He winked and grinned at her. "I'm a cowboy. I have jeans and a...cute grin."

"You're full of yourself." She shook her head and started singing.

For the next two hours they sang to the radio. Jade finally fell asleep. He didn't know if Madeline had intended for it to be such a great distraction, but it had worked. He owed her.

Jackson slowed the truck for the turn that would take them to the small town where he had a buyer for the bull calves in the trailer.

"Are we almost there?" Jade blinked a few times and then rubbed the sleep from her eyes.

"Almost." Jackson took the next right. The trailer lurched and the truck pulled a little. "We'll eat after we drop these calves."

"I'm starving." Jade again. She stretched and then leaned her head on Madeline.

He pulled up the driveway, dialed his phone and listened to the man on the other end give directions on which gate to back up to with the trailer.

"Give me fifteen minutes. The two of you can stay in here where it's warm."

Madeline nodded and watched him get out of the truck. He looked back in at her. Lately he'd wondered a lot what she thought about him. If he had any sense at all he wouldn't want an answer to that question.

Thirty minutes later Jackson was back in the truck and they were on the road. He cranked the heat and tossed his gloves on the floor of the truck. "Man, it's freezing out there."

"Is that sleet?" Madeline nodded, indicating moisture hitting the windshield.

"Yeah, I think it is. And maybe freezing rain. We need to get to Oklahoma City." He glanced at his watch. "I wonder if it's doing this in Tulsa."

His parents and brother were in Tulsa heading up a charity bull riding event for Travis's favorite charity, a group home for children taken from their parents. Kids like Jade. Hopefully the weather didn't mean the event got cancelled.

The frozen stuff hit the windshield. He flipped on his wipers and turned the heat to defrost. They were driving through Oklahoma City and already cars were sliding off into the ditch. Good thing he'd left that stock trailer behind. He'd pick it up on his way home.

"Can we eat now?"

Jackson shook his head. "No, we're going to see your mom first. And then we'll head for our hotel and order from room service."

Out of the corner of his eye he saw Jade wringing her hands and biting her lip.

"Jade…" He stopped because he wouldn't tell her again that it would be okay. She'd heard it enough. He didn't know what would happen, so how could he make promises?

The GPS gave directions to the address Jade's mom had given him. It was dark and the houses were dark. People stood on porches, walked out to cars. Houses were boarded up and looked empty. The house they stopped in front of didn't look much better than the abandoned houses.

"Home sweet home." Jade opened her door and got out.

The freezing rain had stopped but it was still cold. Jackson slid a little as he got out. He reached back in for Madeline. Jade had already headed up the sidewalk.

Gloria, not the Gloria he remembered from years ago, but a thinner version with stringy hair and a gaunt face, stepped outside. She shivered in her thin T-shirt and skin-tight jeans.

"Did you tell her you're not her dad?"

Jackson shot Jade a look, saw her face pale, her eyes widen.

"Not like this, Gloria."

"Well, she's got to stop living in a fantasy world, thinking she's some princess who got lost. This is it, sweetheart, home sweet home."

"Gloria, stop." Jackson rushed up the steps, reaching for Jade as the girl bolted.

"You should have told me." Jade slipped from his

grasp and ran down the steps, down the sidewalk. At the street she turned. "I thought I could trust you."

"Jade, you can." But how could she trust anyone? "Come back and talk."

When he realized she didn't plan on talking, he went after her. But she was gone. She disappeared into the dark night. Madeline ran to his side, yelling for Jade to come back. They walked down the street together, past houses with loud music cranked. People shouted and cars honked.

"Where'd she go?" Madeline shivered next to him.

"It's hard to tell. Maybe she has a friend around here somewhere. Maybe Gloria knows."

They walked back to the house. Gloria had gone inside.

"How does this happen?" Madeline asked as they walked to the front door. "How does a life get this out of control?"

"Wrong choices build up." Jackson shrugged and slid an arm around the shivering woman who didn't have to be here with him. "So, your mom called again?"

"She wants to see me. I'm thinking I might. I don't know. She told me that Sara killed herself."

Jackson pulled her close to his side. "I'm sorry."

She nodded and reached to knock on the door. "The important thing now is finding Jade."

Gloria opened the door. In the light from the living room her skin looked yellow and dry. She scowled at them as if she couldn't remember who they were or why they were there.

"What?"

"We didn't find Jade." Jackson pushed the door open. "Mind if we come in?"

"I'd rather you not."

"Right, but we are." He led Madeline into the smoke-filled living room. It stank of old food, cigarettes and unchanged cat litter. "Where do you think she went?"

"What do you care? You're not her dad." Gloria plopped down on the sofa and lit another cigarette.

"My name is on her birth certificate. You did that."

She shrugged. "Yeah, well, I couldn't think of anyone else to put on there. I wanted her to have a dad. You seemed decent."

"Did you think I was her dad, Gloria?"

"No, not really. I just thought if something ever happened to me, you'd be contacted and the kind of family you came from, you wouldn't leave a kid on her own."

He tensed and shoved his hands into his pockets. He'd never wanted to hurt a woman, not once in his life. This one pushed him pretty close to that point. "Where is she?"

"Probably at that preacher's house. Maybe at a friend's house. She'll be home tomorrow. Once she calms down and realizes her little vacation is over."

"Don't you care about her at all?" Madeline's voice shook and Jackson reached for her hand. "She's a child. She needs you."

Gloria stood, got in Madeline's face, the whites of her eyes as yellow as her skin. "Don't come in here and tell me how to raise my daughter, Princess. Yeah, you're one of those do-gooders who ain't never had to suffer."

"You have no idea what you're talking about." Madeline stood tall. "But I do know that Jade deserves for you to be her mother."

"You take her then." Gloria dropped back to her seat on the couch and waved them away. "You take her."

"Take her?" Jackson stepped closer. He kneeled to put himself at eye level. "Gloria, are you okay?"

She turned away but not before he saw tears streaking down her cheeks. "Hepatitis. But it doesn't matter. I'm done with that kid running away every time something happens that she doesn't like. You're not her dad, but your name is on the birth certificate. Take her with you. Give her to your family or something."

She coughed into her hand and then lit another cigarette.

"You all need to go. I have somewhere I need to be." She slid her feet into shoes and grabbed a jacket off the chair next to her. "I don't know where she is. Come back tomorrow and maybe she'll be here."

As she got up and started to walk away Jackson grabbed her thin arm, ignoring the marks on her arms. He tried to remember the person he'd met fourteen years ago. A young woman and her sister traveling and having adventures.

"What about Jade?"

Gloria laughed, a croaking sound that ended in a cough. "Take her, Jackson. I don't want her. Give her to your girlfriend. Take her to your family. Or call the police and have them pick her up. I've had a good time not worrying about her."

"Really?" Madeline stepped between Gloria and the door. "Is that really how you feel about your daughter?"

Gloria stopped to grab a beat-up, dirty purse. "Get out of my house."

"No, I want to know if that's how you really feel about your child." Madeline shook so hard Jackson didn't know if she'd stay on her feet or fall over. But she didn't appear to be about to back down. She had the look of a mother tiger about to do battle for her cub and he wanted to hug her.

"Look around you." Gloria swung a thin arm around the dirty living room. "This is it. This is all I have. One more mouth to feed. That's what Jade is. She needs stuff. She's always wanting new clothes. She wants to go places."

"You'll sign over custody?" Jackson stepped close to Madeline. "I'll get a lawyer tomorrow and have something temporary drawn up."

"Yeah, sure." Gloria's eyes glistened. "I'll sign."

Jackson pulled out his wallet. "Take this."

"You buying my kid, Jackson?"

"No, Gloria, I'm helping out someone who used to be a friend."

Gloria motioned them out of her house without saying anything and then she walked down the sidewalk. Jackson stood on the front porch, unsure of how this whole situation had happened.

"What do I do now?" He glanced down at Madeline.

"Find your daughter?"

Yeah, and he had no idea where to start. Somewhere on this street of mostly dark houses, a few with a sprinkling of Christmas lights or a tree showing through a window, Jade had taken refuge. She was hiding from them, thinking he had let her down.

Madeline reached for his hand. "We'll find her."

We.

Chapter Fifteen

They didn't find her. Madeline woke up the next morning with the sun peeking through the heavy curtains of the hotel and an empty feeling in the region of her heart. They'd driven for hours. They'd stopped and asked people on the street if they'd seen a young girl. They'd called the local police for help.

Jade had disappeared. Madeline looked at the other bed, still made. Jade should have been in that bed. She should have been safe, knowing that Jackson loved her the way a father loved a daughter.

That thought did fill Madeline's heart. It filled up empty spaces, that Jackson could love Jade that way, in a way that would make a girl like Jade feel safe, secure, not afraid. If only Jade knew.

Madeline forced herself to get up and get ready for another day. She prayed, the way they'd stopped and prayed last night, she and Jackson, that they'd find Jade safe. She closed her eyes thinking of that moment that Jackson had reached for her hand and said they'd forgotten something.

How could they have forgotten to pray?

She opened her eyes and looked in the mirror. She prayed again, but this time for herself, not for Jade. Her heart had moved into foreign and very dangerous territory. Her heart, crazy, inexperienced organ that it was, wanted to run away with emotions that were new.

Someone pounded on her door. She peeked through the peephole and saw Jackson standing in the hall. He had his hat in his hands and he was looking up, waiting. She pulled the door open.

"Any news?"

He shook his head. "None. Let's grab some breakfast and we'll see if we can find her."

Madeline looked back into her room. "Should I pack my stuff?"

"No, I already reserved the rooms for a second night. If we find Jade, we can go home, but if we don't, we have a place to come back to."

"We'll find her." She grabbed her purse and coat and pulled the door closed behind her. "She's hurt and she's running but she'll be back."

Hurt and running were two things Madeline knew from experience.

Outside the hotel it was difficult to tell that there were any problems in the world. They'd stayed in a quaint section of Oklahoma City called Bricktown. Arriving late last night Madeline had seen the twinkling of Christmas lights and heard music, but neither of them had been in the mood to enjoy the city.

They'd gotten a cup of coffee and headed to their individual rooms. Now, Bricktown surrounded them. Bricktown, once a warehouse district, a place where industry thrived, had been reinvented, and turned into an entertainment district with restaurants and other attractions.

They walked along the canal, watching steam rise from the water. Neither talked for a long time.

"We should eat something." Jackson led her toward a restaurant that appeared to be open. "I could use coffee."

"That sounds good." Madeline walked through the door he opened for her.

Weeks ago she would have looked down, avoided touching him as she walked through the door of the Mad Cow. Today she looked up, smiled and hoped he'd return the gesture. She wanted to comfort him, to reassure him.

The door eased closed. Jackson leaned, touching his forehead to hers. "Thank you."

She nodded, still close to him, unable to move away. "You're welcome."

"What am I going to do with a kid?" He laughed a little and then pulled back from her. "What was I thinking?"

"You were thinking that Jade needs a family and you can give her a wonderful family."

The hostess led them to a table. When they were seated Jackson reached for her hands. "I'm not a family. I'm me. I'm a single, almost thirty-four-year-old man who has never had a relationship that lasted longer than two months. To be honest, Madeline, you're about the best relationship I've ever had."

"That's not promising, is it?" She pulled her hands from his and reached for the menu, a laminated card stuck between the sugar bowl and the napkin holder.

"I think it is." He nodded at the waitress when she brought a pot of coffee to their table.

Madeline smiled up at the waitress. "I'll take biscuits and gravy."

Jackson ordered the same. "I called a lawyer this morning. He's a friend of my brother Blake's and he lives here in Oklahoma City. He's writing something up for us and he's going to meet us at Gloria's."

"That's good. I only wish we could find Jade and tell her."

"We're going to find her. I'm not leaving here without her."

After they'd finished eating, they walked the block to the parking garage. Jackson spent part of the time talking on the phone, first to his parents, then the police and then the lawyer. Finally he slid the phone into his pocket and Madeline asked the question that had been on her mind since the previous day.

"Jackson, from the very beginning, you seemed to know that Jade wasn't yours."

He pulled out his truck key and kept walking. Madeline had to pick up her pace to keep up. He had her door open and she stopped, waiting for him to answer. He helped her in the truck and then he stood in the open door.

"I knew she wasn't mine because I can't have kids." He closed the door and walked away.

Madeline leaned back in the seat, closing her eyes against the pain she'd seen in his eyes. When he got in next to her she opened her eyes and looked at him. He started the truck and shifted into Reverse without speaking.

"I'm sorry. It's none of my business."

"No, it isn't. But now you know. She isn't mine. It was never possible. I had a bad case of the mumps as a kid…" His voice trailed off and he focused on driving.

"But you didn't tell her. You allowed her to stay."

Jackson sighed and yanked off his hat. He tossed it on the seat between them and he didn't look at her. Madeline reached, touching her fingers to his. He moved his hand so that their fingers laced together.

"Madeline, I let her stay because I thought 'what if?' And I let her stay because she was a kid who wanted a family bad enough she was willing to hitch a ride and forge a note to find one. I also didn't want her taken into custody, not at Christmas."

"So am I the only one who knows your secret?"

"That I can't have kids? My family knows."

She shook her head. "No, I mean the other secret. The part about you being one of the most decent men in Dawson."

"You've forgotten that I'm the Jackson that dates a different woman every week. I'm the guy who keeps my mother and grandmother on their knees praying I'll come back to church."

"Right, you're that Jackson." But he wasn't that Jackson at all. Not anymore.

He glanced at her and laughed. "Don't get that look in your eyes like you've discovered something wonderful and noble about me, or some secret that explains my wicked ways. I am who I am, Madeline."

They finished the drive to Gloria's in silence. Madeline didn't need to ask for further explanations. Jackson was who he was. Note to self: don't get attached to a cowboy who breaks hearts for a hobby. Even when that cowboy is noble to the core.

Jade was sitting on the front porch of her mother's house. Jackson pulled up and a big, dark blue sedan pulled up right behind him. That would be the lawyer and his wife, the notary. As Jackson got out of the truck, Jade walked into the house, ignoring him.

Madeline was ignoring him, too. That was for the best. She was tea. He was coffee. She would someday want to get married and have babies. He could picture her in a little house, a baby in her arms, some nice guy coming home from his office job.

He wanted to hurt that nice guy with the office job. But right now wasn't the time to be plotting against fictional people in Madeline's life. Now he had to deal with Jade. That had to be his focus.

"George, do you have the paper?" Jackson held his hand out, shook the hand of the lawyer and then took the paper he handed over.

"Right here. Are you sure about this?"

"Yeah, I'm sure. I've never been more sure about anything." Almost anything. Madeline stood a short distance away. When he smiled at her she looked away.

Gloria opened the front door of her house and dragged her daughter out. Jade jerked away from her mother. She stood on the porch, still wearing the clothes she'd worn the day before. Today, though, her look of defiance had multiplied. She seemed to be daring all of them to speak to her.

Madeline didn't seem to care what Jade's look said. She walked right up the steps and gathered the girl into her arms. She whispered and Jade shot him a look. Her eyes got big, watered, and her nose turned pink.

What in the world was he thinking?

"Jade, do you want to go home with me?" He handed the paper to Gloria. "Sign this."

She jerked it from his hand and looked it over. "Fine, give me a pen and get her out of here."

Her words were cold, callous. Jackson didn't know if Jade noticed, but her mother's eyes didn't reflect that tone. Her eyes watered and she had to look away, to brush the tears from her cheeks.

Gloria signed the paper. Jackson signed it. The lawyer signed it. Jackson turned to Jade. "Hug your mother."

"She isn't my mother."

Madeline gasped and Jackson shot her a look. He didn't need another emotional female in this mix. He turned to Jade, now officially in his custody. "Hug your mother."

Jade had walked off the porch but she stomped back up the steps and she hugged Gloria. Gloria held her tight for a minute and then let her go quick. She stepped back and looked away. "You go with Jackson and try to behave. I want you to visit."

"She'll visit." Jackson didn't know what to do now. This time he let Madeline handle it. She hugged Gloria and gave her a phone number. In case she needed anything.

They were walking down the sidewalk when Gloria ran down and grabbed Jade again. She held her daughter tight and then whispered, "I did my best. I'm sorry."

Jade stared at her mother, unsure. "I know. Thank you for letting me go with Jackson."

"Yeah, okay." And then Gloria ran back up the steps and into the house.

"Let's go home." Jackson opened the door. Madeline climbed in last this time. She put Jade between them and he figured that said it all.

On the drive home he had plenty of time to think about the situation he'd put himself in. Jade slept next to him, her head resting on Madeline's shoulder. Madeline had fallen asleep as well.

He turned the radio on low but he didn't hear the music. He had too much to think about. Like what in the world would he do with a teenager? He didn't want to dump Jade on his parents. He'd take her to his sister Heather and then figure out a plan. He guessed he'd need a live-in housekeeper. He'd also have to put her in school as soon as possible.

When he stopped to pick up the trailer, Madeline woke up.

"I guess we're not home?"

He shook his head. "Just an hour out of the city."

By the time he got back in the truck she had fallen back to sleep. He looked at her, sleeping like that, and he wondered what it would be like, to have a life with a woman like Madeline. A man would be blessed to have her as a wife.

He wanted to be that man.

In thirty-three years he'd never had that thought. Not this way, in a way that settled in his gut, twisted him up inside. Yeah, there had been women, most of them not exactly the kind he'd take home to his mother, that he'd dreamed about marrying.

This woman, though, she'd gotten under his skin. He

could see her raising a bunch of kids, growing old with a guy, having grandchildren.

Children and grandchildren. He knew someday she'd have those things. She'd have everything she deserved. But not with him.

She'd get married. He'd stay in his old farmhouse, raising Jade, sometimes dating. Maybe he wouldn't date. That game was getting old, as old as he was.

He drove through Dawson, one main street, convenience store, feed store, Vera's. He waved as a neighboring farmer walked out of the feed store. At the edge of town he turned on the paved county road that led to Cooper property, and Madeline's little house in the middle of the vast acreage that belonged to his family.

"Madeline, we're almost there."

She woke up, blinked a few times and rubbed sleep from her eyes. "Wow, I slept the entire way?"

"We had a rough day yesterday. You needed the sleep."

When he pulled in her driveway, she gathered up her purse and overnight bag. "I would walk you to the door, but I'd better get her home."

"That's okay, I'm a big girl." She smiled at him, a sweet as honey smile. "Goodbye, Jackson."

He tipped his hat and smiled. "Goodbye, Madeline."

She had already jumped out of the truck and was going up the sidewalk to her front door. She stopped on the porch and waved.

Goodbye, Madeline. As she drove to the community center for practice, Madeline tried to forget that empty goodbye a few days ago. She'd known when she stepped into Jackson's life that he was a player. She'd known that the only reason he'd dragged her into his life was to help him with Jade.

She parked her car and walked up to the church. Beth Hightree met her at the steps.

"You look down tonight."

"I'm not down. I mean, not really. I'm just tired."

Beth nodded and Madeline thought she'd let it go. It would be good if she let it go. "I heard that Jackson brought Jade back home with him."

"He did."

"And she isn't his?" Beth walked with her through the old church sanctuary.

"Nope. But his name is on her birth certificate."

"Amazing. He's always had a big heart."

A big heart. Madeline nodded but she didn't want to talk about this anymore. She wanted to forget that Jackson had a big heart, that he cared about people. She wanted to remember him the way she used to think of him, as the man who knew how to charm, to smile and flirt but not remember a woman's name.

Beth continued to stare at her, obviously wanting an answer.

"He has a big heart." There, she'd agreed. Now let it go. Move on.

Beth laughed a little and reached to hug Madeline. "Oh, honey, you've fallen in love with that awful rogue."

"No, I haven't." Madeline reached for her shepherd's robe. "I helped him out when he needed help. End of story. Which is why I haven't talked to him since Saturday." She hadn't meant to add that.

"And you're going to let it go, just like that? Maybe he's been busy with Jade and hasn't had a spare minute to get in touch with you." Beth helped her pull down the rough, cotton gown. She handed Madeline the belt.

"Or maybe he's moved on. He's Jackson Cooper. Isn't that what he does?"

Beth took the belt from her hands and looped it twice around her waist, tying it at the side.

"In the past that's what he did. But I think he probably misses you as much as you miss him."

"This isn't me missing him. This is me being tired and ready for Christmas to be over."

"Right, you want Christmas to be over. You love Christmas."

"I do love Christmas." She loved the music, the decorations and most of all what the story meant to her life and to her faith. "I love it without the drama. And I don't mean the living nativity. I mean Jackson drama, Jade, and now my mother."

"She's contacted you again?"

Madeline pulled the shawl over her head to cover her hair.

"She wants to see me."

"You can't."

Madeline met her friend's concerned gaze. "I think I have to. I've thought about not seeing her. But I think I need closure. I need to face her. I have to do this or it will always control me."

"If you want, I'll go with you."

They hugged and Madeline nodded. "I'd love for you to go with me. I'm not running anymore, Beth. I'm not going to flee in fear that she'll find me. If I face her, I won't have to run again. I can stay here and let this be my home."

"I'm glad because I wouldn't want you to leave." Beth smiled a teasing smile. "And I think Jackson would miss you, too."

"I think what we need to do is get up there for this last practice."

Because she could only deal with one thing at a time. She would deal with her mother, with forgiving. Jackson was something she didn't want to think about. She didn't want to think about how he made her feel, or how much it hurt to think of that very quiet goodbye.

Jackson had needed a friend. Madeline smiled as they walked out of the dressing room. "You know, I'm just the person a guy calls when he needs a really big favor."

"I think the Jackson I know, that I grew up with, doesn't call a woman to rescue him."

No, he didn't call at all. He said goodbye without even adding the cliché, "I'll call you." Goodbye means goodbye.

Chapter Sixteen

A few days before Christmas, Jackson walked through his house and it hit him that everything felt empty. Jade was staying with his grandmother for a few days. Madeline hadn't spoken to him since the day he dropped her off at her house.

The Christmas tree lights were unplugged. There were no gifts under his tree. It felt as much like Christmas as a hot day in July. Jackson Cooper, this is your life. This was reality.

He'd always liked it this way, empty, clean, quiet. Until it got filled up with Jade and Madeline, this life had been fine with him. They'd given him a brief glimpse into another world.

The doorbell chimed and the dog ran through the living room barking. Jackson yelled that he'd be there in a minute. When he opened the door his grandmother marched in, looking like a woman on a mission. With his grandmother, it was all about appearances. She had on her favorite hat, gloves and a dress coat over a pantsuit. And everyone knew that Myrna Cooper loved her blue jeans. Suits were only for business and church. He grinned as she swooped in and he knew that he was her business.

"Where's Jade?" He looked behind her, looked at her car parked sideways in the drive.

"She's with Heather. They went Christmas shopping. Dear goodness, turn on some lights, this place looks and feels like a morgue. It's Christmas. Are you Scrooge?"

She walked ahead of him, flipping on lights, opening curtains. She plugged in the tree. "Nice tree. Buy some decorations next year."

"I like the homemade ones." Made by Madeline and Jade.

"Well, I never thought of you as the pitiful grandson."

"What does that mean?" He followed her into the kitchen where she turned on the coffeemaker. "I hear Travis brought a woman home with him. Harden's daughter?"

"Yeah, she's a looker."

Jackson laughed. "Gram, you're one of a kind."

She shrugged bony shoulders and turned to point a finger at him. Rings sparkled and bracelets clinked on her arms. "You're a mess."

"Could you explain what this visit is all about?"

"I'm here to save you."

"I think I've been saved. I'm even back in church. What more could you want?"

"I'm here to save you from your pitiful self. It was sweet of you to bring Jade back and give her a home, but you can't expect the rest of the family to raise her."

"I'm going to raise her."

"I know you are. You're going to find yourself a wife

and you're going to raise that child the way she deserves, with you as a dad and with a decent woman as a mom."

"Gram, I'm not getting married."

"Oh, posh, stop that nonsense." She pulled a ring off her finger and handed it to him. "This ring was my grandmother's. I guess it's older than dirt, but it means something to me. It's about family, about history. You take this ring and you ask Madeline Patton to marry you."

He choked a little and put the ring back in her hand. "I don't know what you're up to, Gram, but I'm not asking Madeline to marry me."

"You hard-headed fool. That girl loves you and I'm pretty sure you love her, too."

He poured two cups of coffee. "I'm not in love. She helped me out. We're friends."

She frowned at him. "You're going to make me lose my witness if you don't stop acting so noble. Fine, you aren't sure. Date her for a while and then ask her to marry you."

"I'm not going to marry Madeline Patton."

Gram patted his cheek with a cool hand. He braced himself for it. Three little pats and then a good whack. He blinked and shook his head.

"Jackson, stop feeling sorry for yourself. Marry the girl."

She pushed the ring back into his hand. "And I don't want your coffee. It's always too strong and it gives me heartburn. I want you to invite Madeline to Christmas with the Coopers. She shouldn't be alone and you shouldn't want her to be alone."

"I'll think about it."

That pointy finger poked him in the gut. "You'd better do more than think about it. Now, I'm going home and I want you to get out of this house and go Christmas shopping. This place is a disgrace."

"Thanks, Gram, glad you approve."

She laughed as she walked through the house, grabbing her coat on her way out the door. "I love you, Jackson. You're my favorite."

"Gram, you say that to all of us."

She turned, smiling big. "I mean it, too."

That evening Jackson took Jade to see the living nativity. They took the tour of Bethlehem, met the innkeeper who turned Mary and Joseph away and then were led to the manger where the baby Jesus had been born. Through the crowds of people Jackson watched for the shepherdess who had touched his heart in a way he'd never expected.

Six months ago his brother Lucky had told him that someday he'd pay. He guessed this was what Lucky had meant. A woman had finally changed everything for him. She made him think about someone sitting next to him in those rocking chairs on his front porch.

He watched as she kneeled before Mary, Joseph and the baby Jesus. From Heather he'd learned that two days ago she had gone to Tulsa to see her mother. Beth had gone with her. He should have been the one to go with her.

Angels sang. The people in the crowd sang. The story of the birth of Jesus. The lighted star cast a bright light over the area, illuminating everything. Including the tears streaking down Madeline's cheeks.

"Are we going to talk to Madeline?" Jade had hold of

his hand. Today he'd gone shopping and when Heather brought Jade to his house, the girl had screamed and raced around the house because of the gifts under the tree. His grandmother had been right. He'd played the part of Scrooge a little too well.

"Yes, we'll talk to her."

Jade led him through the crowd. Madeline had walked away from the other shepherds. She saw them heading her way and she froze.

"Madeline." Jackson didn't know what to say. He tried to remember a time in his life when a woman had left him speechless.

This had to be a first.

"Jackson." She smiled at Jade. "Hey, Jade, how are you?"

"I'm great. I have a ton of presents under the tree. And there are some for you, too."

"What?" Her gaze shot to Jackson's, asking questions.

The ball was in his court.

"We were wondering if you'd come to Christmas with us."

She looked at Jade and then at him. "Christmas?"

"With us," he repeated.

"Please." Jade grabbed her hand. "It won't be Christmas if you aren't with us."

Jackson reached for Jade. "She might have other plans. Do you have other plans?"

"No, I don't have other plans."

"Then you'll come." Jade didn't let her answer, but grabbed her in an exuberant hug. "Yeah!"

"Jade, she didn't say she would." Jackson shook his head. "I'm sorry."

"I'll go with you. What time?"

"We'll pick you up Christmas morning. Early. Maybe seven."

"I'll be ready."

Jackson took a step back because it would have been easy to reach out, to hold her. When it came to Madeline he was still fighting for self-control.

Christmas with the Coopers. Madeline spent the next two days worrying, telling herself not to worry, being excited and then telling herself to stop. She had to get control of her emotions, shove them back in a box where they were safe.

Jackson had invited her for Jade's sake. Or maybe because the Coopers knew she'd be alone and they were just being polite. She didn't have to be alone on Christmas. Just over an hour away she had a mother living in Tulsa. Not that she was ready for serious family bonding with Marjorie. Not yet. They had talked. Marjorie had explained about growing up being shipped from relative to relative, getting pregnant and being on the streets until she'd formed a friendship with a group of people she thought would take care of her.

Madeline felt sorry for her mother. But the scars of the past were deep and healing would take time.

Beth Hightree had offered to let Madeline spend Christmas with her family, the Bradshaws. She didn't want to intrude on their family gathering, either. Yet she'd said yes to Jackson and Jade.

She'd even bought them gifts. Books for Jade because

she loved to read. For Jackson, a coffee mug and gourmet coffee. She'd made candy to take for the rest of the Coopers. And there were a lot of them. Although a few would be missing. Reese had recently been sent to Afghanistan. Dylan had taken a load of bulls to California and on his way home he'd hit bad weather. He wouldn't be home for a day or two. That meant he'd miss Christmas with his family.

On Christmas morning she paced the living room, waiting for Jackson to show up. Hadn't he said he'd pick her up? What if he'd meant for her to drive herself? She paced back to the kitchen because she didn't want to look overly eager should he show up. If he hadn't changed his mind.

Her heart kept telling her to trust him, to give him a chance. If she didn't want to be judged for her past, Jackson shouldn't be judged for his. Not that he'd been the victim. She groaned at the wild storm of thoughts sweeping through her mind.

Deep breath, calm down. He hadn't invited her for any reason other than that Jade probably wanted her there. Another deep breath. That made perfect sense. Jade had missed her.

The doorbell rang and the puppy, cast-free now, ran in circles, barking and jumping. Madeline slowed her pace and walked calmly to the door. She opened it and a bouquet of flowers and balloons attacked.

"Oops, sorry." Jackson moved the bouquet and smiled.

Her heart did a triple back flip. He grinned and pushed his hat back a little.

"What's this?"

He handed her the vase. "Merry Christmas."

"Thank you." She tried to smell the white roses and red carnations but balloon strings were everywhere. "These probably don't mess on the floor or chew up slippers."

"Not that I've heard of, but if they do, let me know." He followed her inside and she carried the vase of flowers to the kitchen table.

When Madeline turned, he was standing right behind her. She stepped back and looked up, afraid, excited, a million different things at once. Afraid of him, afraid of what he'd say or wouldn't say.

"We should go." She reached for her purse.

"Where's your coat?"

"Hanging on the hall tree."

Jackson nodded and instead of walking away, he reached for her hand to stop her. "You forgot to read the note on the flowers."

"I didn't see it."

Jackson reached for the note and opened it. He cleared his throat. "Allow me."

"Okay." Her voice trembled. Her hands trembled. Her heart did something that felt like trembling. Or longing?

"Dear Madeline, will you go steady with a cowboy who might be, very possibly is, in love with you?"

"Are you in love with me?"

"Honey, I'm so in love with you I can't see straight."

He touched her cheek. Then he leaned, still holding her close, and kissed her sweetly, stealing her heart, taking her places she'd never imagined. In his arms she was cherished. She was loved.

When he backed away, she rested her head on his shoulder. "I love you, too. I was just so afraid."

"Afraid?"

She nodded and then looked up. "Afraid that you wouldn't love me. Everything in my past, I just thought…"

He kissed her again. "You're strong, brave and beautiful. Yeah, sometimes that is too much. It floors me that you're even standing here with a renegade like me."

"I don't know what to say." She didn't know what she could say, not without losing it right there, standing in front of him.

"Madeline, you have to go into this knowing that I can't have children. I'll adopt as many as you want to fill that old farmhouse with. But that's something I've been running from for a long time."

"We have Jade."

"We." He hugged her tight. "I love it when we're a 'we.'"

Jackson reached into his pocket, laughing a little at the surprised look on Madeline's face. "I know we just started going steady—" he glanced at his watch "—two minutes ago, so this probably seems like the shortest courtship in the world, but I have another question I'd like to ask, and if I don't do this right, my grandmother is going to flog me good."

"Okay."

"Now bear with me, I'm not as young as I used to be and you might have to help me get up."

She laughed. He shot her a look, trying to appear offended that she'd laugh at him.

"Jackson, please don't."

"Are you really going to laugh at a man who is trying to propose the way his Gram expects him to propose, the way a gentleman proposes?"

She laughed until tears sprang from her eyes. Jackson reached for a napkin on the kitchen table and handed it to her.

"Now let's start over. And please, no laughing. I got a two-hour lesson on courting and proposals last night." He winked and Madeline turned pink. "I think Gram might have mentioned that the courting part of the process should last at least six months and then the proposal. But I've always been a renegade when it comes to love. I'm afraid if I don't get this ring on your finger, you'll chicken out or realize I'm not much of a catch."

"Jackson, I love you. But really, I do think we should, um, date? For a few months at least."

"Stop talking, you're throwing me off my groove. You know, I used to have a groove until you came along and completely threw me for a loop." He took off his hat and tossed it on the table. With her hand in his he dropped to one knee and fished the ring out of his pocket again.

"Please, stop." Tears poured down her cheeks. Jackson stopped.

"Are you going to say no?" He didn't know how long he could stay on one knee. He wasn't many weeks this side of being tossed into a wall.

She shook her head. "I'm not going to say no, but it's so much and it's Christmas and…"

He grinned big and she smiled. "And you love me because I'm crazy and nothing like any other man you've ever met. Madeline, you need a man like me, someone strong and stubborn. I'm not going to let you go. I'm not going to hurt you."

The ring in his hand, more than a hundred years old, sparkled and the metal heated in his hand. He slid it on her finger. "My great-grandfather gave this ring to his wife. When my grandmother got married, they gave it to her to wear. She wanted you to have it because she wanted you to know that when you marry me, you're a Cooper. We marry for life and we hold on to each other through life's storms."

"Did your grandmother tell you to say all of that?"

He grinned and shook his head, but then he nodded. "Some of it."

Madeline fell to her knees in front of him. He forgot about his aching knees when she cupped his cheeks in her sweet hands and moved close, touching her lips to his.

He forgot about everything but Madeline and how it felt to hold her in his arms. He'd spent a lifetime thinking he'd never get caught, only to find out that it wasn't about getting caught, it was about falling. And falling.

With Madeline, he thought he'd be falling in love with her for the rest of their lives. He told her that and she wrapped her arms around his neck and buried her face in his shoulder.

"Madeline, will you marry me?"

She nodded. "I will."

"Then you'd better help me up and we'd better get to the house before they send out a search party."

She stood, reaching for his hands and pulling him to his feet.

"Where's Jade?" Madeline's eyes watered and her nose was pink.

"I'm right here."

They turned and Jade was standing in the door of the kitchen with Angel the puppy. "I think that was about the sappiest proposal ever."

Madeline reached for his hand and held it tight. "I think it was the sweetest proposal ever."

Jade ran forward and hugged them both. "The best part is that I'm going to have a family. Merry Christmas!"

"Merry Christmas, Jade." Jackson hugged the girl who was his. It didn't matter what the DNA test said—in his heart, she was his daughter. They were a family, and he'd never had a better Christmas or been more blessed in his life.

Epilogue

June

Jade looked out the window of the Sunday school classroom they were using to dress for the wedding and she whistled softly. "Maddie, you have to see this."

Beth ran to the window and shook her head. "No, Jade, she doesn't. It's a surprise."

Madeline tried to slide past Beth but several pairs of hands caught her and kept her from getting a look outside.

"No, ma'am, don't even think about it." Angie Cooper held her veil. "Jackson went to a lot of trouble and you're not going to ruin it for him."

Madeline closed her eyes but she giggled. "You remember his proposal, right?"

Angie laughed. "He couldn't walk right for a week. And he was supposed to keep the ring until after you'd dated a few months."

"Exactly. So I really need to see what's out there. Someone, please?" Madeline looked around the room, hoping for someone willing to spill the secret. Her bridesmaids, Jenna, Beth, Heather and Jade, all shook their heads.

The only other person in the room shook her head, too. Madeline's mother, Marjorie, was a thin, tiny woman. She no longer looked beaten down by life. Her eyes had a spark that hadn't been there months ago when they'd met in Tulsa. They were getting to know each other again.

Madeline had a family. She smiled at Jade, remembering a teenager who had defied everyone to get that exact same thing for herself.

Jade twirled in her pale yellow dress. "I love this dress."

"Don't get it dirty," Madeline warned. "Or trip over the hem."

"I won't." Jade weaved, dizzy from turning in circles. "I wish I could go to Hawaii with you."

"Sorry, this is a honeymoon for two. When we get home we'll take you to Florida, remember?"

"I remember." Jade's smile brightened. "And I get to stay with Grandma Angie while you're gone."

"Yes, you do." Madeline looked in the mirror at her simple, white dress. Straight lines, no beading or lace. She'd never thought about weddings or what she would wear. She'd never dreamed of honeymoons or even the man who would change her life.

And yet he had existed anyway. All of those years of closing herself off, afraid to feel, afraid of being hurt again, and God already had the perfect man for her.

Jackson Cooper. She smiled at her reflection in the mirror. In a million years she wouldn't have thought he would be the one. It wasn't that long ago that she'd avoided looking him in the eye when he helped pick up her spilled groceries.

Today he would stand before God, in the presence of these people, and he would become her husband.

She would become Madeline Cooper. Maddie Cooper. She closed her eyes as love and contentment overflowed. When she opened them, Beth stood behind her, smiling.

"Look what God did, Madeline. He took all of your fears, your past, your insecurity upon Himself and gave you this new life, this new hope."

The door opened. Jackson's sister Sophia, self-appointed wedding coordinator, smiled and motioned them all out the door.

"Time to get this show on the road."

"Very romantic, Sophie." Heather patted her sister on the cheek as they filed out of the room.

"I don't have time for romance."

"Of course you do." Angie Cooper shook her head and then kissed her older daughter's cheek. "Romance will find you."

Tim Cooper, Jackson's dad, stood at the entrance to the church sanctuary, ready to walk Madeline down the aisle. He looked so handsome in his Western-cut tuxedo. But Madeline's gaze slid past him to the front of the church. Tim placed her hand on his arm and they started down the aisle, the bridesmaids walking in front of them.

Madeline had eyes only for the man at the front of the church. Jackson Cooper, the man she would spend her life with. Fifteen minutes later he slipped a wedding band on her finger, sliding it against the ring his grandmother had provided. They said "I do" and he pulled her to him, kissing her as if he would never let her go. And then he led her down the aisle and out the doors of the church.

To her surprise a white open carriage was parked in front of the church. Adorned with white roses, it was pulled by four white horses. A man in white livery stood next to the door of the carriage, holding it open for them.

"Surprise." Jackson leaned and kissed her cheek.

"It's a wonderful surprise."

"Throw the bouquet," someone shouted.

Madeline turned her back to the crowd and tossed the yellow daisies and white roses. The bouquet landed right in Sophia Cooper's hands.

* * * * *

AN ASPEN CREEK CHRISTMAS

Roxanne Rustand

To Danielle, Ben, Lilly, Violet and Finn,
with all my love.

Acknowledgments

Many thanks to Dr. Erin L. Garman, DVM, for her wonderful assistance with the veterinary details in this story. Any errors are mine alone!

And also, many thanks to Lisa Mondello for her research assistance on foster care and adoption.

And we know that in all things
God works for the good of those who love him,
who have been called according to his purpose.
—*Romans* 8:28

Chapter One

Hannah Dorchester studied her travel-weary, disheveled niece and nephew sitting across from her in the McDonald's booth.

Neither had spoken since she'd picked them up at the Minneapolis–St. Paul airport a half hour ago, except to refuse every restaurant she could think of that might be open on Thanksgiving evening—hence, the fast food.

Though even in this child-friendly atmosphere they hadn't touched a bite of their meals. And no wonder. Today they'd faced yet another huge change in their young lives.

After they were orphaned seven months ago in Texas when their parents died in a head-on collision with a semi, their elderly great-aunt Cynthia in Dallas had been adamant about gaining custody.

But two weeks ago she'd tripped over a toy truck and broke her hip badly. She'd then informed Hannah she simply couldn't handle the children any longer—not while facing a long and painful recuperation.

Hannah had immediately begun the process of gaining out-of-state custody of the children. With a family law attorney at her side, she'd then gone to court to gain temporary guardianship.

Given that there were no other options besides Hannah or long-term foster care, social services and the court—bless them all—had expedited the process.

Scowling, Molly poked at the paper wrapping of her cheeseburger, then shoved it aside. "I don't even know why we had to come way up here. I don't *like* Wisconsin."

"You've never been here, honey." Hannah chose her words carefully. "It takes a long time to recover from a broken hip, and now Aunt Cynthia realizes she can't keep you and your brother any longer, because she… um…just isn't young enough to raise two children. But I know you're going to make some great friends here. And if you start missing her, maybe we can all go down for a visit—"

"She didn't even like us," Molly scoffed. "She was *mean*."

Hannah blinked. Cynthia was an elegant, austere woman who had never been particularly friendly during the few times Hannah had seen her. But *mean*? "Maybe she just isn't used to being around kids."

"She kept saying our uncle Ethan would be coming to take us, and he'd make us behave or else. 'Cause he's some kind of soldier."

Ethan?

Hannah swallowed hard, willing away the painful memories of the man she hadn't seen for thirteen years. A man she never, ever, wanted to see again. "I'm sure she didn't really mean—"

"Why would he want us? We never even met him." Molly angled an accusing glare at Hannah, then dropped her gaze to her lap. Her voice dropped to a whisper. "And even you didn't want us till now."

"I did, honey. Believe me. But Texas prefers to keep children in their home state, if possible, so they'll face less disruption. The judge decided Cynthia could provide a good home and keep you in your same schools."

Left unsaid was the fact that Cynthia, a wealthy widow who owned a major western wear company, kept a team of lawyers on retainer who had made very sure that her wishes were met. Hannah hadn't stood a chance in family court back then.

But now Cynthia's determination made more sense. Ethan was Cynthia's nephew. She'd apparently wanted to keep the children in Dallas, so the transition to his guardianship would be easier.

He'd probably even insisted on it.

Yet, seven months after the car wreck, he'd never showed up—no surprise there—and Cynthia was no longer capable, so now Hannah finally had a chance to give these kids the stable, loving home they deserved.

"We've got an hour drive ahead of us. Would you like to bring your food along?" she asked gently, wishing she could reach through the wall of grief surrounding them both.

Cole, only six years old, lifted his teary gaze briefly, shook his head and then slumped lower in his seat. "My m-mommy always h-had turkey an' everything on Thanksgiving."

His voice was so soft, so broken, that Hannah's heart clenched. "I know, sweetheart. But since you traveled today, I thought maybe we could have our big dinner tomorrow. Is that all right?"

The bleak expression in his eyes reaffirmed what she already knew.

This wasn't about the pumpkin pie or the holiday feast. It was about memories of happier times...and about loss. He just wanted his parents back.

And that could never be.

The next morning Hannah awoke early and made herself a cup of coffee, eager for the kids to wake up.

How life had changed in the blink of an eye—and how grateful she was for this wonderful blessing—a chance to finally surround her sister's children with love and healing.

Until two weeks ago she'd devoted herself to her career as a physician's assistant at the Aspen Creek Clinic and the ongoing renovation of this pretty little cottage on a hill north of Aspen Creek. Her only roomies had been the assorted rescue animals she took in, rehabbed and re-homed.

She'd had so much to arrange in a hurry after Cynthia's injury—both here and down in Texas—that there'd been no time to create a welcoming home for Molly and Cole. So they'd stayed a couple extra nights with one of Cynthia's friends while Hannah flew home to get the house ready.

Exhausted after their day of air travel and the sixty-mile drive from the airport, both children had been dazed and silent when she'd driven into her driveway at ten o'clock last night. They'd barely looked at their rooms before tumbling into bed without a whimper.

She'd checked on them several times during the night, but sometime during the early morning hours Cole had quietly dragged his quilt into Molly's room and went back to sleep wrapped up like a mummy on the floor at the side of her bed.

Hannah's stomach tightened. The poor little guy. Had he been scared? How had she failed to hear him?

Please, Lord, let this be an easy transition for them. They've been through so, so much.

A white-faced golden retriever limped to her side and bumped her hand, eliciting an ear rub. "So what do you think?" she whispered. "Will they be happy here?"

The dog, one of her rescues who had yet to find the perfect forever home, waved her flag of a tail and stared up at Hannah with pure adoration in her cloudy eyes. "I'd like to think you're telling me yes, Maisie."

The old dog crept silently into Molly's room and sniffed at Cole's makeshift sleeping bag, then gently curled up next to him.

The little boy stirred, mumbling something in his sleep. Cuddling closer to her warmth, he flung an arm over her soft neck.

Hannah felt her eyes burn at the dog's instinctive compassion. She'd started to tiptoe away when the puffy pink-and-purple comforter stirred on the bed.

Molly sat up and frowned as she surveyed the bedroom, her long, curly brown hair framing her face.

"Good morning, sweetie," Hannah whispered, stepping just inside the door. "What do you think of your new room?"

The walls were now a pale rose, the woodwork a crisp white. The bookshelves and a bedroom set were ivory with gold trim. Keeley, who owned an antique shop in town, had brought lovely lace curtains as well as a stained-glass lamp in pink, green and blue for the bedside table.

It was a fairy tale of a room that Hannah would have loved for herself as a child, but Molly just shrugged.

"Are you hungry for breakfast?"

Molly shook her head and flopped back down on her pillow, pulling the quilt up to her nose.

"Remember when I came to see you in Texas last time and made chocolate chip pancakes? I can make them this morning, or I have that chocolate cereal that you like."

"No." Molly yanked at the quilt to cover her head and turned toward the wall, clearly ending any further conversation.

Hannah tiptoed down the short hall to the kitchen, where a trio of cats sat staring at the refrigerator door, apparently willing it to provide an extra meal.

She stepped over a basset hound snoring in the middle of the floor, nudged the cats aside to grab a gallon of milk and then made her homemade version of a café-au-lait in her favorite mug.

Settling down at the breakfast bar overlooking the living room, she contemplated the stack of twelve, extra-large, newly delivered FedEx boxes sitting just inside the front door.

Each had felt like it had to weigh over fifty pounds when she'd dragged them in from the porch. Each had given her a pang of sorrow.

They represented the remnants of her sister's life, after Cynthia had summarily sent all the adult clothing to Goodwill and hired an auction house to dispose of the apartment furnishings.

It was heartbreaking to think that everything left of the children's lives had been distilled into just twelve cartons.

The question now was how she should most tactfully deal with all of this without upsetting them. Would they cry at the finality of seeing those labels and the contents? Things they'd seen in their old home, before a drunken truck driver had plowed into their parents' car and everything went so terribly wrong?

Hannah pushed away from the breakfast counter and moved over to the boxes to read the labels written in Cynthia's elegant hand.

Hannah quickly stowed Dee and Rob's boxes out of sight in her own bedroom closet to consider later. Then she lugged one of the Home Office boxes across the living room and began searching for school and health records, categorizing the contents into neat piles on the sofa.

At a knock on the door she looked up, startled at the silhouette of a tall, broad-shouldered man standing outside the front door. The basset hound gave a single, bored woof and went back to sleep.

She was usually working at the clinic during the day, so none of her friends would think to visit her at this time of the morning. It was probably just another shipment of boxes from Cynthia—who must have paid a fortune for such quick delivery.

She pulled back the lace curtain to look outside before unlocking the dead bolt.

She froze. It was Ethan Williams.

And he'd *seen* her. There was no way she could step away from the door and pretend she wasn't home.

From all the way down in Texas—or wherever it was that he'd been—Ethan had somehow found her, deep in this pine forest, five miles out of Aspen Creek on a winding gravel road.

He was the last person she'd ever wanted to see again. The cruelest man she'd ever met. And she knew his arrival spelled just one thing.

Trouble.

One glance at Hannah's horrified expression through the multipaned window in the door and Ethan knew his chances of being allowed inside were slim to none.

He deserved that and worse. But he'd traveled a long way. This visit wasn't about the troubled history between them. It was about the kids and their welfare, and he knew he had to handle this carefully or there'd be a battle every step of the way. It wasn't one he planned to lose.

After a long moment of hesitation, Hannah closed her eyes briefly, as if saying a silent prayer, then cracked the door open without releasing the safety chain. She focused her gaze somewhere above his left shoulder. "Yes?"

He drew in a jagged breath.

She was even more beautiful than when he'd seen her last—thirteen years ago. Slim, shapely, with honey-gold hair that fell to her shoulders in waves and startling, light blue eyes.

They'd first met at his brother Rob's wedding rehearsal, and their mutual attraction had been immediate. He hadn't taken his eyes off her for a second during the rehearsal and wedding, and despite all the years since then, he now felt that same rush of emotion all over again.

From a lifelong habit he nearly offered his right hand—or what was left of it—but caught himself just in time. "It's been a long time, Hannah. But you haven't changed a bit."

"If that's a compliment, don't think it will get you anywhere, Ethan. I've grown up since you last saw me and I'm not the fool I was when we first met. Understand?"

He nodded, edging the toe of his boot forward and bracing his left hand high on the door frame in case she tried to shut the door in his face. "Totally. Two adults. All business. That's fair enough."

"I can't imagine what business we would have after all these years." She bit her lower lip then reluctantly unhooked the safety chain. "Come in, but try to be quiet. The kids are still sleeping." She waved him past two tall stacks of boxes and toward a sofa and upholstered chairs arranged in front of a fieldstone fireplace.

The sofa was covered with stacks of papers, apparently taken from a shipping carton sitting on an ottoman, so he eased into one of the chairs, setting his jaw against the familiar stab of pain in his right knee.

Open suitcases stood just inside the door with children's clothing cascading out onto the floor, while a heap of winter jackets lay tossed over a chair.

Three cats, positioned like sphinx guardians in front of the refrigerator, glared at him from across the room.

"Nice place you have here," he said as he surveyed

the warm amber walls and abundance of multipaned windows looking out into the timber.

"It's a mess right now. We got back from the airport pretty late last night."

"Beautiful country."

"I've got ten fenced acres, with state forest surrounding the house on three sides." She perched stiffly on the arm of the upholstered chair opposite his, still avoiding his eyes. "This is a perfect place to raise the kids. There's lots of room to play."

He ignored her pointed tone. "After coming up your road, I'm glad I chose an SUV instead of a sedan at the airport. You must not get much traffic up here."

She didn't return his smile. "There are only a few homes on Spruce Road. I'm at the end of the line, actually. Public access to the government preserve is south of here. But I'm sure you didn't come all this way to discuss real estate."

"No." He'd rehearsed his speech during the flight north. Weighed different approaches. Honed his logic, to best make his points clear and get this done as efficiently as possible.

If only he'd returned to Dallas a few weeks sooner, before Cynthia's injury, the children's transition into his care would have gone smoothly. But from the steely glint in Hannah's eyes, he already knew *that* wasn't going to happen.

His conversations with Cynthia and social services in Dallas had made it clear that the situation was now far more complicated.

Maybe the children hadn't had time to settle in and bond with her, but Hannah had been granted temporary custody and had already brought the children north. He couldn't legally swoop in and whisk them back to Texas now—even though it was the right thing to do.

Unless he could convince her that it would be best for everyone involved. And why wouldn't she be relieved? The Hannah he remembered had been flighty, irresponsible. Surely she would understand that if he took the kids, her life would be a lot easier.

She crossed her legs and folded her arms over her chest. "Well?"

"I'm here to see Molly and Cole."

"Because…?"

"They're my niece and nephew," he said easily, "just as they are yours."

"You've missed them a lot, I'm sure." Her eyes narrowed. "Since you've seen them so often."

The ever-present phantom pain in his right arm began to pulse in deep, stabbing waves in response to his rising tension. "I've been overseas in the military. As you probably know."

"But you never went home to see your family? Not even," she added in a measured tone, her gaze fixed on his, "when the kids were born? Or your own brother's funeral? At least, I didn't see you there."

"I wasn't."

He hadn't been able to arrange for leave in time to fly back from the Middle East for the christenings. And as for the double funeral this spring…

He flinched as a cascade of images slammed through his brain. Gunfire. Explosions. Screams and blood and wrenching pain. And, finally, blessed darkness. That first long, hard and drug-fogged month at Walter Reed had left him incapable of anything more than simply existing.

"The kids say they've never met you."

"I saw Molly when she was toddler, and I made it back when Cole was starting to walk, but they were probably too young to remember. I plan to make that up to them, though."

"By finally finding time to visit them way up here?" The veiled note of sarcasm in Hannah's voice was unmistakable.

"Actually, now that I'm stateside, I want to take them back to Texas, where they belong."

"No." Her eyes flashed fire and she shook her head decisively. "I don't think so."

She'd definitely changed.

When he'd spent those three weeks with Hannah years ago, she'd been a fun, lighthearted nineteen-year-old with a sense of adventure and daring that matched his own.

Impulsive and giddy, she'd dared him to go cliff diving at the reservoir and had matched him shot for shot at a gun range. She'd invited him on five-mile runs in the moonlight, after the oppressive heat of those Texas summer days had faded.

She'd also been impetuous and immature, he'd realized in retrospect, though at the time he'd been sure she was his soul mate—if there was such a thing. He hadn't wanted to miss a minute of her company during the brief time he'd been stateside.

But now, instead of a sparkling sense of fun in her eyes, he saw only keen intelligence, absolute determination and a heartfelt wish that he would simply disappear.

After what he'd done to her, he expected nothing more.

But that didn't mean he was going to give in. No matter how difficult it was going to be, he owed it to Rob to make sure his kids were raised right, and were raised where they belonged.

"You do know that your custody is just temporary."

"That doesn't mean it will end. I spent considerable time with the children's caseworker, my Texas lawyer and in court. Even in a situation like this, involving out-of-state custody, the children's welfare and happiness are still paramount. So we'll have home visits and interviews by a caseworker after thirty days to evaluate how the kids are doing. Then again at three and six months—at which time I will petition for permanent custody and ultimately adopt them, if Molly and Cole agree."

He ground his teeth. Perhaps the nineteen-year-old he'd dated had grown up—but she was *not* the right person to take on this responsibility. "Clearly, there are lots of uncertainties. Is it fair to get them settled clear up here, when they'll need to move again?"

"That won't be the case."

He cleared his throat. "We need to straighten out this situation, the sooner the better. I honestly think they'd be better off coming back to Texas with me. You'd be free of responsibility, and they could be back in a familiar school, with their friends. Close to relatives and—"

Her smile vanished. "Close to what other relatives? Cynthia? Who didn't want to deal with them? And their uncle Ethan? Who travels the world? Who else is there to give them consistent day-to-day time and attention?

Your dad is in a residential facility. Your mom and grandfather are gone. Would you need to hire a nanny for the months you're away?"

"What can you offer them?"

"A stable home. A *loving* home in the country with lots of animals and a huge fenced yard. I have lots of close friends with children they can play with. A warm church family. This is a friendly small town, where people know each other well and watch out for each other. Good schools. And," she added, meeting his eyes squarely, "I work at the Aspen Creek Clinic, so they'll have the best of medical care. I can guarantee it."

"It seems you've given this some thought."

"Since the day of the accident—not just when you showed up at my door. The kids don't even know you, Ethan. I heard Cole asking who you were and wondering why you'd never visited—at least that he could remember. Anyway, I'm their godmother—which ought to tell you something about their parents' wishes."

He snorted at that. "And I'm their godfather, so I guess we're even."

Her mouth dropped open. "I don't believe it. No one ever mentioned a thing about that. You certainly weren't at the christenings."

"I was stationed out of the country and couldn't make it back in time. I guess I was never able to make it back for anything important," he admitted with a twinge of regret. "But that doesn't mean I can't make up for lost time. And I plan to, even if it means that we need to take this back to court."

Hannah flung a hand in the air to silence him and glanced over her shoulder.

A little boy in Batman pajamas suddenly appeared in the arched doorway that probably led to the bedrooms, his hand on a white-faced golden retriever. He blinked at the sunlight streaming in through the wall of windows facing the driveway and forest beyond.

Hannah immediately went to him, kneeled and gave him a hug. "Good morning, sweetie. Did you have a good night's sleep?"

He rubbed his eyes and gave Ethan a brief, blank look, then regarded her with an achingly solemn expression. "Do we have to go back on the plane now?"

"No, of course not." She rested a gentle hand on his cheek. "Do you remember what your great-aunt Cynthia said before you left Texas?"

"She said we had to come here." His lower lip trembled and his eyes welled with tears. "But Mommy and Daddy are there, and our toys, and everything. And I *gotta* go back."

Chapter Two

Her heart breaking at Cole's grief and confusion, Hannah briefly closed her eyes. *Lord, please help me say the right things and help him understand. He's so very young for all of this to happen.*

"Your mommy and daddy will love you forever and ever, and would want to be with you more than anything," she said softly. "But they're in heaven now, sweetheart. When you grow very old and go to heaven, you'll be with them again, I promise."

She rested her hands gently on his shoulders and nodded toward Ethan. "But you have relatives on earth who love you very much, like your uncle Ethan and me. We want to make sure you are safe, and happy. And that you'll get to do all the fun things boys like to do."

She bit her lower lip, wanting to tell him that she would be the one to keep him safe and happy forever. But with Ethan lurking in a chair across the room, she couldn't risk adding more hurt to the little boy's life.

Would she even stand a chance against Ethan and

his aunt if they challenged her custody in court? Could she afford enough legal representation to stop them?

"Your toys are in those boxes by the front door, and I see you made friends with Maisie," she continued with a smile. "Did I tell you that there are lots of other friends here for you to meet?"

He met her eyes then dropped his gaze to the floor.

"Bootsie, the basset hound, is sleeping over there on the kitchen floor and the kitties by the fridge are Eenie, Meanie—the most playful one—and Moe. And outside I have some really fun surprises to show you once you get dressed and have some breakfast." She tipped her head toward the suitcases. "Do you want to pick out some clothes for today or should I?"

He lifted a shoulder in a faint shrug, so she dug through his suitcase and found jeans and a bright red sweatshirt. "Can you get dressed all by yourself?"

At that, his lower lip stuck out. "I'm six. Anybody in first grade can do that."

She chuckled. "Of course they can. So here you go, buddy. You can change in your room, okay? And I'll go check on your sister. Maybe she's ready to wake up, too."

After he dressed and she'd settled him at the counter with a bowl of cereal and a glass of juice, Hannah knocked lightly on Molly's door and stepped just inside when she heard no answer.

The eleven-year-old was dressed—in her clothes from yesterday—and huddled in the corner by the bed, her arms wrapped around her knees.

Hannah dropped to the floor next to her. "Tough

morning, with all of these changes," she said softly. "I'm so sorry."

"I want to go *home*." Molly bit her lower lip. "But I don't know where that is anymore."

"You must feel like a leaf blowing in the wind. From Texas to Oklahoma for a year, then back to Texas last April. Right?"

"'Cause Dad kept losing his jobs," Molly said bitterly. "But he said things would be better if we went back to Texas. He *promised*."

Glancing through the open bedroom door, Hannah saw Ethan shift in his chair and frown at Molly's words. Had he known that little detail about his shiftless brother? About all the promises, all of the failures?

Probably not. At Cole's christening, her sister Dee had mentioned that Ethan rarely came back to Texas when on leave, and Rob had been adept at covering his failures with bluster and bravado.

With so little contact with his family, Ethan somehow imagined he should be the one to raise these kids? If he was like his brother, it would mean just one more chapter marked with disappointment in Molly's and Cole's lives.

"If you ever miss being with your great-aunt Cynthia, you can call her anytime. Or even visit her when she feels better."

"I don't miss her. Just home." Molly swallowed hard. "But now everything there is gone and there's no way we can go back. It would never be the same." Molly glared at Hannah. "You won't ever be our mom. I'll *never* call you that."

"Of course not. When you were little, you called me

Auntie Hannah." Hannah rested a comforting hand on Molly's, but the child jerked her hand away. "You can call me Aunt Hannah or just Hannah. Does that sound okay?"

Molly gave a faint, dismissive shrug.

"Sweetheart, I loved my sister very much, and I don't want to take her place. I just want you to be happy again someday."

"Then I need to be with my old friends at school. Not here." Molly dropped her forehead to her upraised knees.

With all the times her family had moved in the past three years, Hannah knew the poor girl had barely had the time to make new friends before changing schools and starting over. Though she wasn't ready to hear it, Aspen Creek would be her first chance to actually put down roots.

"Speaking of friends, I have some for you to meet—right here."

Molly shuddered. "I'm not staying and I don't *want* to meet anyone."

Hannah rose. "I think you'll feel differently in a moment. After breakfast, we'll have some introductions. Okay?"

"I don't *like* breakfast."

Hannah had known there'd be plenty of problems ahead, and that choosing her battles would be the key to making this work. Today's breakfast just wasn't one of them.

Cole finished his cereal, then swiveled in circles on his bar stool several times before pulling to a stop and pinning his gaze on Ethan. "You're my uncle?"

Ethan nodded.

Cole's eyes narrowed. "I never met you."

"That's because I'm usually very far away." Ethan cleared his throat. Did he explain that he was Rob's brother or would mentioning the kid's dad make him cry?

He'd always been uneasy around children, never having a clue what to say. If he upset the boy, would it make everything even more difficult in the future?

He definitely didn't want to mess this up on the first day.

He summoned a smile. "You did meet me, Cole... but you were just a little guy then."

From Cole's stubborn expression, he wasn't buying it. "If you're my uncle, how come you didn't come see us all the time like Hannah? She came lots of times on a plane, and even brought us presents. Every time."

"Well, I couldn't come to see you often because I'm a soldier. So I've been gone a lot, way on the other side of the world."

"Shooting guns and stuff like on TV?" The boy's eyes widened with worry and a touch of fear. "Do you kill people for *real*?"

"Uh..." He searched for the right thing to say to the boy, who slid off his stool and backed up beside Hannah, and figured a vague answer was best. "Soldiers do a lot of things—not just fight."

Cole considered that for a moment, his expression still wary. "So I could take you to show-and-tell, with your guns and everything?"

Ethan shuddered at that. "That would not be a good idea, buddy. Guns aren't safe—especially at school."

He looked up and found Hannah glaring at him, her arms folded over her chest and her eyes as cold as steel.

"You can thank your aunt Cynthia for how he feels about you. Apparently she told Molly and Cole that you were a tough guy. One who would really straighten them out. If you ever showed up, anyway."

"Why on earth would she—" He heaved a sigh, suddenly knowing all too well.

Even when he and Rob were kids, she'd been a stickler about her designer clothes, her elegant lifestyle. She'd always watched them like a hawk during their rare visits to her pristine home. Having Rob's two kids underfoot all those months had probably been unbelievably stressful for a woman who had always prized perfection over warm family emotions.

Ethan cleared his throat, searching for a different topic. "So, do you, um, like to ride bikes?"

"Don't got one." The child's face fell, his eyes filled with stark grief. "Mom said she'd get me a bike after we moved. But she died."

"I—I'm…" The boy's words felt like a fist to Ethan's gut and he floundered to a halt. "I'm so sorry about that."

Knowing Rob, there probably hadn't been any extra money for a new bike anyway, even though Ethan had loaned him a lot of money over the years.

His brother had always had just one more emergency, one more bout of overdue bills, and promises that it wouldn't happen again. And, always, a case of amnesia when it came to paying any of it back.

"I'm not batting a thousand here, am I?" Ethan muttered, looking up at Hannah.

"Nope." Her eyes narrowed on him. "And just in case you haven't noticed, never think this situation is easy."

Cole looked between them, clearly confused by their exchange.

"Time for a new topic," Hannah muttered as she put Cole's bowl and cup in the sink. She smiled down at him. "We have our first snowstorm of the year predicted on Sunday, so right now I think we should be shopping for sleds. But come spring I'll make sure you and your sister have new bikes. Now—are you ready for a surprise?"

His eyes round and serious, Cole nodded.

Molly appeared in the kitchen, her expression dour, and Ethan felt his heart clench at seeing her long, curly brown hair and big green eyes. Cole was fair and blond like his mom, but Molly was nearly identical to her dad at that same age—even down to her stubborn chin, the sprinkle of freckles over her nose and slender frame.

"Stay where you are, so you don't get trampled. I'll be right back." Hannah went through a door leading into the attached garage, leaving it open behind her.

A moment later a river of puppies exploded into the kitchen. Black ones. White ones. Gold. Spotted and speckled. They tumbled across the floor with squeals of excitement and chased each other throughout the kitchen and living room. The basset snored on.

Giggling, Cole dropped to the floor, quickly overcome with puppies trying to crawl over his legs. But though a glimmer of a smile briefly touched her lips, Molly held on to her aloof expression and backed away.

Ethan winced as a white pup with a black spot over

one eye careened against his bad right ankle then landed in a heap on his other foot.

Forgetting his usual caution, he reached down and scooped it up, cradling its fat bottom in his good hand to look into its pudgy face. "Who are you, little guy?"

"I haven't named any of them yet," Hannah said. "That might be a good job for Molly and Cole."

She glanced at Ethan's weak ankle, where his brace probably showed beneath the hem of his jeans, and cocked her head, obviously curious but too polite to ask. But when she lifted her gaze, her attention caught on his prosthetic hand and her mouth dropped open. She quickly looked away. "I… I didn't realize. I'm so sorry, Ethan. Are, um, you all right now?"

Unwanted attention.

Shallow sympathy.

Platitudes.

He gritted his teeth. After leaving the hospital he'd encountered those reactions at every turn and he wanted none of it.

He knew he was fortunate to still have both legs. Fortunate to finally be walking unaided and to have a state-of-the-art prosthesis that once again made him a functional human being.

But he still struggled with a surge of instant resentment whenever he saw pity in someone's eyes. So many soldiers had to deal with far worse and deserved sympathy far more than he did. And all too many—some of the best friends he'd ever had—never had a chance to come home.

He shrugged off her sentiment and surveyed the

puppy pandemonium. "This is like trying to count minnows in a bucket. How many of them are there?"

"An even dozen." She hitched her chin toward the garage. "The mom was a stray and she was brought here just before she whelped."

"Quite a bonanza."

Hannah picked up two of the black-and-white-spotted pups and snuggled them against her neck. "Not a record litter, but more than enough. She'll be spayed before I try to find her a good home."

Molly looked up at Hannah. "They all live here?"

"Not in the house. The mom and pups have a fenced cage, heat lamp and warm bed in the garage, with a doggie door out to the fenced backyard. I bring the little guys inside for socialization several times a day and give their poor mom a break." Hannah grinned at her. "Now that you're here, you can help me play with them. I have more friends to show you, but that can wait until I do chores."

Now Molly had a half dozen of them crawling over her feet and when she crouched, they tried to lick her face. "You have even more puppies?"

"No…not right now. But there are some other rescues in the barn."

The joy of the romping puppies was too infectious not to elicit a smile and Ethan found himself chuckling at their antics. "Isn't there a humane shelter in town?"

"On the other side of the county, but not anywhere close to Aspen Creek. So there are several of us who try to help. We have fund-raisers every year to help with food, spaying, neutering and vaccinations."

Two of the pups started chasing each other around

the living room, skidding on the hardwood floors and braided rugs. One of them scrambled onto the sofa and scattered the stacks of paper like falling leaves in a stiff wind.

Molly's smile faded as she focused on the big cardboard box by the sofa. "'Rob and Dee's home office and health records,'" she read aloud. She turned to give Hannah an accusing look. "You're snooping through my mom and dad's stuff?"

Hannah paled at her harsh tone. "I wasn't snooping, honey. Cynthia collected all of their important papers and sent them to me. They came this morning. We'll need your health records and other documents for when we get you set up with a doctor, dentist and the school."

Molly's mouth hardened. "Well, if you think you're gonna find money or something, good luck with that, because we didn't have any. Sometimes Mom didn't have enough money for the grocery store. Not even at Christmas, and that made her cry."

Ethan tensed, remembering all the times his brother had asked him for loans. Had things been even worse for them than Rob could admit? "I'm so sorry. If I'd known..."

Hannah glanced up at him with a frown, then gave the children a faint smile. "You know what? I think these pups would love to run and play with you two in the backyard. Want to grab your jackets? Then after you're done playing, I want you to meet Penelope."

She had the kids bundled up and the whole lot of them—exuberant puppies and kids—outside in minutes. He'd watched every move and still didn't know quite how she'd done it with puppies running everywhere and Cole too excited to stand still.

Cole ran around the yard with the pups, though Molly perched on a picnic table and chewed her fingernails, doing her best to look bored.

Despite the awkward history between them and his determination to take the kids back to Texas, Ethan couldn't help feeling a newfound appreciation for Hannah as they stood on the back deck to watch the melee. "You're good with them."

"Never had any of my own, of course, but one learns." She shrugged. "Corralling kids when armed with vaccination syringes does take some practice."

"You mentioned the clinic earlier. Are you a nurse?"

"I'm a PA—physician's assistant."

He blinked, surprised. "Where did you go to school?"

"I've got a Masters from UW-Lacrosse. My clinical phase was at Mayo."

He whistled softly. "When we first met, you had a part-time job at a burger place and didn't have a clue about your future."

"I always planned on college," she said simply, keeping a close eye on Cole. "I just needed to save money first."

"You never married?" The question escaped before he thought it through and he'd have done anything to snatch it back.

A long, awkward silence stretched between them.

"No," she said finally, angling a glance at him that could have sliced through steel. "Though I understand you did—your brother was more than happy to let me know that you'd gone on to far better things. Rapidly, in fact."

He felt heat crawl up his neck. After the hard life he'd led and the things he'd done for his country, he wouldn't have imagined that he was capable of such a reaction, yet here it was—heart-stopping regret, awash with embarrassment over what a fool he'd been. But he'd paid for it, in spades.

Janet had been one of the biggest mistakes of his life.

"I regret a lot of things in my life. That's one of them."

"I never asked Dee or Rob about you over the years. The subject was strictly off limits, and they knew it," she said. "But since no one is here with you, I assume the marriage didn't last."

"Never guess that every twenty-one-year-old guy is actually mature." He gave a humorless laugh. "I was lonely and impetuous. Janet worked on the base and was on the rebound. Let's just say it was not a match made in heaven. The ink was barely dry on the certificate when Janet's ex turned up and she left me."

Her gaze fixed on forest beyond the backyard, Hannah didn't answer for a long moment. "And that's what I was, too. Just a brief fling."

"No." His heart wrenched at what she believed and what had been the truth. He'd dreamed of her for years afterward, regretting what he'd done. "You were the one who stole my heart and never gave it back."

She raised an incredulous eyebrow and snorted. "That's not how I remember things, but it's all in the past and I'm pretty sure we both dodged the proverbial bullet. All for the best."

Hannah descended the deck stairs. "Hey, kids, can you help round up these guys? C'mon, puppies—dinnertime!"

Some of the little critters followed, others went the opposite way. One black-and-white pup industriously tugged at Cole's shoelace, trying to wrestle it free. But in a few minutes they all disappeared into the garage with Cole and Hannah, where metal food dishes rattled and Cole's laughter rose above the din.

After Hannah retrieved the mixed-breed mom from a separate outside enclosure and took her to her brood, she stepped outside and started for a weathered-wood shed at the far end of the yard.

It looked like a classic, hip-roofed barn the size of a double garage, with a walk door on the side and two big, sliding barn doors at one end. A wood-fenced corral enclosed a small pasture behind it and to one side there was some sort of pen surrounded with a high chain-link fence.

"I don't suppose anyone wants to see what I've got in here?" she called over her shoulder.

Cole followed at her heels as Hannah disappeared into the shed, while Molly just hunched over her folded arms on the picnic table and made no move to follow.

Ethan strolled over to her and sat at the opposite end of the table. "So…what do you think about all of this?" he ventured after a few minutes of silence.

She lifted her gaze to the surrounding forest and scowled. "It's not Texas. And it's *cold*."

"True."

A thin whinny echoed from inside the barn. One of the sliding doors opened and Hannah emerged leading a woolly Shetland pony with Cole on top. She led the little buckskin in a slow circle then toward the picnic table.

Cole beamed. "This is Penelope. She's really old."

"She's a rescue, as well. It's probably time to hop off, but she should gain some weight in a few months and feel stronger, and after that maybe you can ride her a bit longer." Hannah reached up and helped Cole dismount before pulling a small brush from her jacket pocket. "In the meantime, you can lead her if you want and bring her carrots. She also needs to be brushed every day. Anyone here interested in doing that?"

Cole nodded, accepting the brush. He began brushing Penelope's neck. "She's pretty."

"I heard you talking to Cole in the house," Molly said to Ethan after watching her brother for a while. "And I don't get it, either."

"What's that?"

"How you could be our uncle—our *only* uncle, but we never met you. Not ever." Her mouth flattened. "Maybe we shouldn't believe you."

He considered that. "But it's true. Your dad and I were brothers. He was three years older than me. Let's see… He had a great sense of humor, he could charm his way out of trouble and he was great at every sport he tried. He had a long scar on his left inner arm from when we were playing in your great-grandfather's workshop. Did he ever tell you how it happened?"

Her lower lip trembled. "He said his brother snapped a piece of wire at him."

Typical Rob. "No. He stretched out a coiled length of wire, planning to snap it at me. But he lost his grip on one end and it zinged back. He actually had to have eight stitches."

Her brows drew together. "He had a collie. What was its name?"

"Radar." Ethan smiled. "I'm glad to see you're such a smart girl. It's good to be cautious with someone you don't know."

She turned to give him a long look. "You don't look like my dad. And—" The moment her gaze dropped to his right hand, her eyes filled with horror and she recoiled. "What is *that*?"

Cole stopped brushing the pony and craned his neck for a better view. His mouth dropped open. "Wow."

Ethan had just gotten out of Ward 57—Amputee Alley—at Walter Reed a week ago, a place where the loss of his hand and damaged leg were minor compared to so many who had lost a great deal more. Compared to the three men in his platoon who had paid the ultimate price the day of the explosion.

But seeing the kids gawk at his missing hand reminded him that he would always be different in this civilian world. And to them, he might even seem scary.

"I was in Iraq. An insurgent lobbed a grenade into the back of our transport vehicle. I lost my hand." He flexed the fingers, demonstrating the dexterity of his prosthesis. "This gives me back some of that function."

Cole's eyes rounded. "So now you're like a bionic robot guy—with superpowers?"

"Somebody has seen way too many movies," he said with what he hoped was an easy smile. "But it would be tough having just one hand and my prosthesis does help a lot."

"It…it looks like real *skin* on it," Molly whispered.

Ethan nodded. "Supposed to. But that's just a skin-colored cosmetic cover, so it doesn't draw attention. I don't always wear it."

Molly surveyed him from head to toe, her eyes filled with blatant curiosity.

"No other mechanical parts," he said, guessing at her unspoken question. "Though several bones in my right leg were shattered. I still wear a brace."

"Forever?"

He shrugged. "I hope not."

"I'm so sorry about all you've been through, Ethan," Hannah murmured. "When did it happen?"

He glanced at Molly and Cole, once again unsure of what to say in front of them. "Last spring. A couple weeks…before."

Hannah winced and closed her eyes briefly. "And that's why you couldn't come back for the funeral. I'm sorry about what I said to you earlier. I had no idea that you were injured. Cynthia should have said something to me at the funeral…or later."

"She didn't know yet. She and I were rarely in touch over the years."

Cole turned back to brushing the pony.

Molly seemed to have lost interest in the conversation, as well. She wandered along the fenced perimeter of the backyard and peered into a chain link at one end of the barn, jumping back when an explosion of black-and-white feathers flew into the air.

"That's Mabel," Hannah called out. "She's gets herself in a kerfuffle at the least thing, but Ruth and Louise are a little less silly. They're probably taking a nice sensible nap inside the barn, where it's warm."

Molly looked over her shoulder. "You rescue *chickens*?"

"A lady near town had them. When she passed away, her family brought them here. They actually do lay eggs once in a while, but not so much now that it's winter."

"Chickens. Back in Texas, I expect they would have been dinner by now," Ethan mused.

A glint of humor sparked in her eyes. "Maybe so, but I could never eat something that has a name—or such individual personalities as those hens do."

Her gaze dropped to his jeans and he realized he'd been idly massaging the deep hollow along his outer right thigh, where the explosion had ripped away most of the muscle. "Does your leg still ache a lot?"

He shrugged. "Not really."

"Right. And poor old Mabel has an IQ of two hundred."

He snorted.

"Still, I haven't noticed you limp at all."

"Only if I'm tired, or walk too far. Or," he added with a short, humorless laugh, "if I step on it wrong. Which means a return to active duty isn't yet on the horizon."

She lowered her voice. "I can only imagine how many surgeries you've been through and the months of rehab."

"I have no memory of the explosion, and very little of the month afterward. And later—with the ongoing surgeries and the intensive rehab—I wasn't able to focus on much else. I didn't look at email or snail mail for months."

She rested a gentle hand on his arm. "And no wonder. I'm so—"

"I don't want sympathy," he retorted, his voice too harsh. "I never should have—"

He stopped himself in time and looked away. Until this moment, he'd never talked about the explosion or its aftermath. Not even through his wasted months in support groups or the attempts of a private counselor. Regrets were a waste of time, because he deserved what had happened to him.

Nothing would ever change the truth of what occurred that day. And nothing could ever erase his guilt.

Chapter Three

At the sound of a car pulling to a stop outside, Hannah glanced at her watch and gave the table a final, critical glance.

Four settings of her grandmother's china were placed on the cranberry tablecloth, flanked with her own silverware, folded linen napkins and her mother's sparkly water goblets.

Warm, flaky biscuits were already nestled in a napkin-lined basket and, from the sound of approaching footsteps outside, the rest of the dinner had arrived.

She hurried to the front door and ushered in Keeley and Sophie, some of her best friends in town. The aroma of roasted turkey, buttery sage dressing and sweet potatoes flooded her senses.

She closed her eyes and inhaled. "This is incredible. I can't believe you did all of this for us!"

Keeley and Sophie set the food on the counter. "We have at least one more trip in," Sophie said with a cheerful smile as she turned for the front door. "Then we'll leave you in peace."

Ethan, seated in one of the upholstered chairs by the fireplace, stood and turned to face them with an easy grin.

Keeley blinked and darted a quick, questioning glance at Hannah, her eyebrows raised. Sophie stumbled to a halt and simply stared.

Disconcerted, Hannah cleared her throat. "Uh, Ethan Williams, I'd like you to meet my dear friends, Keeley North and Sophie McLaren. They knew things were going to be a little crazy here and volunteered to bring Thanksgiving dinner. And, um, Keeley and Sophie, Ethan is—or was—my sister's brother-in-law. He came to see his niece and nephew."

Sophie looked as if she were on the verge of melting into a puddle of awe and admiration over the unexpected visitor.

Keeley recovered more quickly. "Nice to meet you, Ethan."

When he made no move to step closer and offer a handshake, she slid another glance at Hannah then gave him a welcoming smile. "Did you travel far?"

"I flew in from Dallas—this morning."

"Well, I'm sure the children were happy to see you," Keeley murmured. "As you'll see, we brought way, way too much food, and I hope you'll all enjoy it."

Sophie finally found her voice. "I've been dying to meet the kids. Where are they?"

Hannah tipped her head toward the bedrooms. "Just hold on a minute."

"We'll go ahead and finish bringing in the food."

Ethan followed the two women outside to help, and

soon containers of mashed potatoes and gravy, green bean casserole and three pies filled the counter.

Molly edged to the threshold of her room and glanced at the newcomers, then bowed her head, but Hannah had to go into Cole's bedroom to convince him to come out.

Keeley beamed at them both. "I am so happy to meet you two. Molly and Cole, right? I hope we'll get to see a lot of you around town."

"I hope so, too," Sophie echoed. "My son Eli is in fourth grade, and I know he'll be very excited about meeting you both."

"Tell Hannah to bring you by my shop anytime," Keeley added. "I always have fresh homemade cookies for special visitors."

Hannah glanced between them. "Can you join us for dinner? It would only take a moment to add some place settings."

"Wish I could," Sophie said with a wistful smile. "We have a lot of catching up to do. But Josh is on call at the ER today, so I need to be home with Eli."

"And I need to get back to my store. The day after Thanksgiving is usually really busy. But I hope you'll all enjoy the meal."

Hannah walked them out to Keeley's SUV. "This was so kind of you—going to all this work. I can't thank you enough. I know the kids missed having their Thanksgiving dinner yesterday."

"Poor kids," Sophie said in a somber tone. "I can't imagine how tough this year has been for them. And what's with the uncle? The kids were down in Texas and got on their plane just yesterday, yet he's already made a trip from Dallas up here? What's really going on?"

Hannah darted a look back at the house. "It's...a long story, but basically he says he wants custody."

Keeley gasped. "Isn't it a little late?"

"And what about the kids—uprooted then being hauled right back?" Sophie chimed in. "That's just not right."

"I agree. Totally. And I plan to fight him every step of the way, if it comes to that. But he is their uncle, so I can hardly shove him out the door...at least not yet."

Sophie's eyes widened. "You're going to let him stay here?"

"We haven't discussed how long he'll be in Wisconsin or where he'll stay. I hope he'll be leaving in a day or so. But, no, I don't think it's appropriate for him to stay here. I don't have an empty guest room now, anyway."

Keeley gently gripped Hannah's forearm. "You'd better get back inside before the food goes cold. But call me—day or night—if you need help or just need to talk. Okay?"

"And me, too," Sophie whispered. "This place is so isolated, now I'll wonder if you're even safe here."

Hannah smiled at them both. "I taught personal safety classes at the community college for four years, remember? And I have 9-1-1 on speed dial. We'll be fine."

But as she watched them drive away, Ethan's words slipped into her thoughts.

He'd mentioned an explosion.

She shivered, imagining all he'd gone through. The pain. The loss of a limb and thus the loss of his life as he'd known it. The surgeries and long, painful therapy. Probably even PTSD.

Given his proximity to that explosion and the extent of his physical damage, had he also suffered a TBI—traumatic brain injury? Unfortunately it was all too likely.

A soldier could fully recover from a TBI...or face disabling symptoms for a lifetime.

During the clinical phase of her physician's assistant program she'd seen one such problem firsthand when a vet with severe mood swings sent an orderly to the floor at her feet, out cold.

Ethan had the right to his privacy, but she needed to keep two young children safe. So she would keep on her guard. Watch him carefully. And she would talk to him privately when the moment seemed right.

But in the meantime, she would also keep her cell close at hand.

Ethan watched the kids as they sat at the table pushing bits of turkey around their plates, their eyes downcast. Neither had eaten enough to keep a sparrow alive.

Were they remembering Thanksgiving dinners from years past, when their family was still complete? How could that grief and loss ever be repaired?

"This is the best meal I've had in a dozen years," he said reverently into the strained silence as he forked up another bite of mashed potatoes and rich gravy. "Everything is delicious."

Molly looked up from sculpting a mountain range with her potatoes and frowned at him. "A dozen years. Really?"

He nodded. "I've been stationed in various places overseas all that time and almost never made it back for a Thanksgiving dinner in the States. Your aunt Hannah has some mighty nice friends to go to all this effort for you."

Tears started down Cole's face. Hannah moved to his side and wrapped him in a gentle embrace. "I know coming here is a big change, after all those months at Aunt Cynthia's. And I know how tough it is, honey."

Had Ethan's words about home-cooked meals reminded him of his mom? Cole's thin shoulders shook and his tears flowed faster. "I... I just want my m-mom back," he whispered brokenly. "A-and my dad."

"I know you do, sweetheart. I miss your mom a lot, too. And I know that right now you both feel hopeless and overwhelmed." Hannah gently rubbed his back. "You'll never forget your parents and you'll never stop loving them. But in time, I promise it will become easier."

Molly fixed her gaze on her brother, her lower lip trembling. She abruptly pushed away from the table and fled to her room, slamming the door behind her.

Ethan had led men into battle. He'd faced off against the enemy too many times to count. But now he stared after the girl with a searing sense of helplessness. "Should I go after her?" he asked finally.

"Not just yet. Give her some time."

Cole pulled away from Hannah's embrace and slouched lower in his chair, draping an arm over Maisie. The old dog hadn't moved from his side since they'd all sat for dinner and now she sidled even closer to rest her head on his lap. "Can I go to my room?"

"Would you like some pie first?" Hannah ruffled his hair. "Sophie brought pumpkin, cherry and a French silk—that's like a creamy chocolate pudding. Or, I have chocolate chip ice cream."

"No thanks."

Ethan watched the boy trudge away, the retriever at his side, then stood to help Hannah clear the plates and serving dishes. "I wish there was something I could do, right now, to make them happy."

"What it will take is prayer and love, and lots of time. But time is elusive, because it's all so relative. Now they're going through this year of firsts—the grief of birthdays and holidays without their mom and dad." Hannah began emptying the leftovers into plastic containers and loading the serving dishes and glassware into the dishwasher. "They will adjust, but every big life event will bring it all back. Confirmation. Graduation. Weddings. It just goes on, because they'll wish they still had their parents to share those times. But you know all that—Rob said you two lost your mom early, right?"

"She walked out on us when we were in grade school and we only saw her once after that. She moved to Maine, remarried, then died at thirty-five. Jay-walking, of all things."

"But your grandpa raised you, correct? Rob used to say he was quite a pistol—and the grumpiest person he'd ever met." She looked over her shoulder while stowing the leftovers in the refrigerator. "It must not have been easy for you boys."

"One way to put it, I guess."

After living with a single father who'd had a short temper, little interest in parenthood and a career involving a lot of travel, the parade of live-in babysitters had finally ended when Dad ditched Rob and Ethan at their grandfather's house. Ethan could still hear Dad yelling that he couldn't cope with them any longer and he wasn't going to try.

"I'm so sorry," Hannah murmured as she began filling the sink with hot, sudsy water.

He shrugged. "My parents never should have married each other, and having two kids couldn't cement bonds that didn't exist. But I guess these things happen." He eyed the flatware and the stack of plates. "Can those go in the dishwasher?"

"Not the good china or silverware."

"Do you want me to wash or dry?"

She glanced at the oversize clock above the sink. "Thanks, but it'll take just a minute to wash these few things and I'll let it all air-dry. Anyway, it's already getting dark. Are you heading into town for the night? Or the airport?"

"Town."

She washed and rinsed a plate and gently rested it in the drying rack, then took a deep breath and turned to face him. "And then what? Do you have any plans?"

When he'd talked to one of his aunt's attorneys in Dallas and insisted that he wanted to pursue custody, she'd confirmed what Hannah had told him earlier today. There would be monthly visits by a caseworker to see how well the children were adapting to Hannah and their new home before permanent custody would be granted—probably after ninety days if all the reports were good.

She'd also warned him that he could petition for custody, but if the children were well settled and content in their new home, it was unlikely that the court would agree to any further disruption of their lives.

But it was the attorney's additional words that kept playing through Ethan's thoughts.

The situation would be evaluated—especially regarding how well the children were bonding—and with whom. Which led him to believe that he still had a chance.

He was a stranger to them, so that was now a moot point. But the attorney had suggested he spend as much time as possible with the children—without upsetting them or challenging Hannah in any way—prior to the first thirty-day custody evaluation.

If he wanted any chance at all, the children needed to be comfortable with him, and want to join him in Texas.

Hannah looked at him expectantly, clearly waiting for an answer.

"I'm staying in town, at least until Christmas."

Her jaw dropped. "In Aspen Creek? Don't you have a home in Dallas…or somewhere?"

"Just a condo—but it's always been more of a storage unit than a place to live." He shrugged. "Right now I'm on medical leave, so there's no place I need to be. A month or so here would be as good as any place else."

"To do what? Have…a…a vacation?"

"Of sorts."

Her face pale, she fidgeted with the dishcloth, wiping at the already spotless kitchen counter. "You have a place to stay?"

"Reservations at a B and B on this side of town that also has some year-round cabins. I haven't checked in yet, but the off-season rate was better than any of the other places I found online."

"Y-you arranged all of this before even flying north?" She worried her bottom lip with her teeth. "What else have you planned?"

"I want to spend time with my niece and nephew."

"Now—when they've barely arrived here? Is that fair to them?"

"It's time I got to know them—something I failed to do before. As their uncle, I understand I have that right, but I won't interfere."

"But they'll be in school starting this Monday, up through December twenty-third." Her voice took on a desperate note. "They'll be in school all day. They'll have homework and will be spending time with kids they're going to meet at church and school…"

"Understood, but surely I can see them now and then. Isn't it good for them to know more about what little family they have left? I promise I won't be in the way."

"Not much," she muttered under her breath. "Why not come later, when they've had a chance to get settled? Maybe Easter."

"Rob and I had a childhood filled with acrimony and irresponsible adults who didn't much care about us. That isn't going to happen to Molly and Cole."

"There will be no such acrimony and lack of responsibility here, I assure you. I love these kids."

Love? Maybe. But he knew all too well how flighty and irresponsible she could be, and he wasn't going to take any chances. "I need to make sure my brother's children have a much better life than he and I did. I owe him this much."

She sagged against the counter and he could see the realization dawning in her eyes. "Which means you *are* serious about wanting custody. This trip is all about you trying to win them over before permanent custody is finalized."

"I want what's best for them, Hannah. A loving, stable home, in a familiar place. Except for their dad's misguided move to Oklahoma last year for another job that didn't pan out, they have always lived in Texas."

"A nice sentiment. But will you really follow through—or will you lose interest and foist them off on some nanny when you go overseas again? You did say that your return to active duty isn't yet on the horizon, so you obviously hope to leave again." She blew out a slow breath. "I don't mean to keep bringing up the past, but I seem to recall that your good intentions don't always amount to much. You once made some very serious promises to me."

"A whirlwind romance when we were too young to know better."

"You were already in the service, which implies responsibility and honor to me. You made promises and then you not only reneged on them but you disappeared without a word. Without an apology. Without explanation. Not even a goodbye. I was packed, ready and excited, Ethan. And you left me standing on the courthouse steps. *Alone*."

"There's nothing I can do to change that now. I only wish it was possible to make up for what I did."

She gave a short laugh. "Not necessary. Eventually I realized two things—that I was lucky to have escaped marriage to a man I couldn't trust. And, I escaped repeating history."

"History?"

"My dad was military, as you might remember," she said bitterly. "He ran our home like a barracks, and woe to anyone who challenged his authority or failed to measure up. But he'd always promised to come home—no matter where he was sent or what he did." She turned away.

"But he couldn't keep that promise?" Ethan asked gently.

"A new recruit went crazy on the base one nice, sunny day. Shot Dad six times in the chest while shouting nonsense about war and the evil army officer who was sending him home. I was just twelve, visiting Dad's office on Career Day. I saw him die. I thought I would be next. But then his killer turned the gun on himself. The whole floor was awash in blood and I was too scared and shocked to even move."

"I'm so sorry, Hannah."

"I swore then that I wanted nothing more to do with military life when I grew up. Living with Dad had been tough, but seeing him die because he wore a uniform was a thousand times worse. Military families are amazing, strong people, and we all owe them so much for what they sacrifice every day. But I'm just not that strong—and I could never handle that life again."

He'd seen the horrors of war for over a decade. Dealt with his nightmares as best he could. But he could not imagine what that terrible day had done to an innocent child.

"So you see," she added softly, "you jilted me. You

made me a laughingstock in town. But you also saved me from a life of living with my worst fears. I won't ever trust you again on any count, but I guess I also owe you my thanks."

Chapter Four

"So this is downtown Aspen Creek, guys. All of the shop owners have been decorating for this weekend, and the Christmas Committee has been putting up decorations in the town square." Hannah parked at the north end of Main Street in front of the shoe store and looked over her shoulder. "Next, I want to buy winter boots for you both, then we'll walk down to the square so you can see the crew decorating the pine trees. If you aren't too tired after supper, we can come back for the lighting ceremony and a sleigh ride."

Cole perked up at that. "With horses?"

"Yes, indeed." She grinned at Cole and his sister, happy that her plans for the day seemed to be working out. An introduction to the festive downtown area, a yummy lunch somewhere and then maybe a movie might be a good start at helping the two kids feel at home. She hoped. And surely they'd enjoy the Christmas lights and carolers tonight—Aspen Creek's kick-off weekend for the holidays.

"A stable near town always brings a pair of dappled gray Percherons and a beautiful sleigh for evening sleigh rides," she continued. "They're here Saturdays and Sundays during the Christmas season. I love hearing those heavy brass jingle bells coming down the street."

Cole unbuckled his seat belt and leaned forward. "Can we go more than once?"

"Of course we can."

Molly directed a disinterested glance out the window, then picked at the snowflake design on her new wool mittens. "Can't have a sleigh. No snow."

Hannah laughed. "You're right about that. When there isn't any snow, they bring a pretty carriage with a fringed roof and big wooden wheels with red and white spokes. If the weather forecast holds, we might have enough for a real sleigh for tomorrow."

Her cell phone chirped and she grabbed it out of her purse. Her happy mood vanished. *Ethan*. She hesitated then took the call with a resigned sigh. "Yes?"

"You mentioned going into town today. Can I treat you all to lunch somewhere?"

She glanced at her watch. She'd gone through the children's clothing boxes this morning to check on what they needed for the colder climate and then she'd taken the kids shopping. After an hour at the Children's Shoppe, both of them now had extra sweatshirts and warm pullover sweaters, goose-down jackets and snow pants in their favorite colors, with mittens to match.

But she still needed to buy them snow boots and sleds, and take them down to the town square. If there was enough time, they could also drop in on Keeley's antiques store for cookies.

And admittedly—stop somewhere for lunch. "I…
guess so. In an hour?"

"Perfect. Do you have a favorite place?"

Despite her resolutions regarding Ethan, the deep
timbre of his voice still sent an unwanted tingle of
awareness shivering over her skin.

"I think the kids would like the Creek Malt Shop. It's
fairly new, but has 1950s décor, and they make malts
with scoops of real ice cream. Their burgers are the best
in town and they have old-fashioned pinball machines
in the back—no charge." She glanced at the kids. "What
do you two think—sound good?"

When they nodded, she returned to the call. "The
Malt Shop faces the town square. We were heading
down there to see the holiday decorations after we finish shopping, anyway. We'll be there in an hour."

She ended the call and sighed. They would show up
to meet him, but she doubted she could eat a single bite.
Her stomach was already tying itself into a tight knot.

She'd stayed awake until two in the morning, worrying about what the future would bring with Ethan in
the mix. Praying that he might see the flaws in his plan
and just give up and go back to Dallas.

But, nope—he was still here. And he was already
finding ways to keep in touch.

Which proved that she'd better plan to keep on her
toes.

Ethan idly ran a fingertip through the condensation
on his malt glass and settled back in the booth. He
glanced at his watch once more.

The hesitance in Hannah's voice had been unmistakable over the phone. Would she even show up?

His booth was right in front of a plateglass window looking out over the street and, beyond that, the town square where clusters of folks were busy winding strands of Christmas lights on the dozen pine trees scattered throughout the little park.

A larger team was tackling the towering blue spruce in the center, utilizing a cherry picker to reach the very top.

Though it was only the Saturday after Thanksgiving Day, Christmas music already blared from loudspeakers in the square, and even through the window, he could hear the banter and laughter from the crowd as they worked.

Christmas seemed to be everywhere.

Even in this hamburger joint, there had to be a dozen tabletop-sizes Christmas trees with twinkly lights perched on shelves, counters and in the corners. Wreaths and Christmas stockings hung on the walls. Over each booth and table a sprig of mistletoe hung from the ceiling on a bright red ribbon.

It was as if Christmas had exploded in here, and it made him edgy. *Bah humbug.*

He caught sight of Hannah—her shimmering, pale blond hair unmistakable, even from a distance—weaving through the crowd across the street, where she was making slow progress by chatting to every person she met. Cole walked at her side, wearing a puffy, bright red jacket. Molly, in a similar hot-pink jacket, followed a few yards behind with a sullen expression.

They finally made their way across the street and

he saw Hannah square her shoulders and take a deep breath before ushering the kids inside the Malt Shop. From her grim expression she didn't seem at all happy to be there.

In a moment they arrived at his booth. Molly and Hannah slid in opposite him and Cole scrambled next to Ethan. The faint, familiar scent of Hannah's perfume wafted in the air, reminding him of the past they'd shared. One he needed to forget.

"Sorry if we're a bit late," Hannah murmured as she grabbed menus from the rack behind the napkin dispenser and dealt them out.

"I got a new coat and mittens and boots," Cole announced. "And other stuff, 'cause it's cold here."

Molly rolled her eyes and dropped her gaze to her menu.

"Looks like you got a new coat, as well," Ethan said to her. "Have you found your sleds yet?"

She shook her head.

"We never had sleds before," Cole announced. "'Cause we didn't get enough snow. But Aunt Hannah says we'll get *lots* tonight. Five whole inches!"

"The most I ever saw in Dallas was a few flurries." Ethan shifted his gaze to Hannah. "So I've never gone shopping for sleds, either. Can I come along?"

She gave him a stiff smile. "Of course. The hardware store is a couple of blocks over and it usually has a good supply."

Cole's eyes lit up. "Maybe you can both get a sled, too, and then we can all go. Aunt Hannah says she'll bring hot cocoa and marshmallows and cookies. So we have *lots* of energy."

Ethan chuckled. "Somehow I don't think you'll run out of that anytime soon."

"But you'll come sledding, right? And for the carriage ride tonight?"

"Well…" He angled another glance up at Hannah. "Is that all right with you?"

The corner of her eye twitched but she nodded. "Aspen Creek Park is just a mile north of town and there are good sliding hills near the campground. The snowplows don't usually clear the country roads before the afternoon on Sundays, though. So…" She considered for a moment. "Maybe two o'clock tomorrow?"

"Deal."

"And the carriage ride, too?" Cole insisted.

A waitress in a red-striped uniform appeared at the table with a tray of water glasses and a smile. "As you can see, we're kinda busy, so just wave to me when you're ready to order."

"I want a cheeseburger and a chocolate malt, with French fries," Cole announced instantly.

"Same," Molly muttered.

"That didn't take long. Hot-fudge shake and a grilled chicken sandwich for me," Hannah said without looking at her menu. "Ethan?"

"Cheeseburger and fries. I've already got my malt."

Molly eyed the colorful flashing lights on the pinball machines at the back and gave the waitress a pleading look. "Can we play?"

"Sure. Nice change from all those computer games, if you ask me. Unless someone else comes in and wants a turn, you can play as long as you like." The waitress grinned. "At least, until your food comes. I'm sure your parents can keep an eye on you from right here."

Hannah's gaze flew to Molly—expecting a meltdown over the waitress's assumption. But the kids launched out of the booth and made a beeline for the bank of pinball machines without a backward glance.

"Whew," she whispered, her hands clenched on the tabletop. "That was close. I'm finding casual conversations can be quite a minefield with people who aren't yet aware of our circumstances. I'm sure the word is spreading, but still..."

It would probably be the same in Texas, Ethan realized, though he couldn't help but think it would be easier if the kids were at least on their home turf. And come to think of it, there would be a few people who could make assumptions. He didn't know people there anymore except Cynthia and his dad. He'd been gone all of his adult life.

"I know this will be a hard Christmas for the kids, with their parents gone. It's going to bring back so many memories of the happier times." Hannah twisted in her seat for a better view of the pinball machines. "But Christmas is my favorite time of year, and I'm excited about sharing the whole Aspen Creek holiday experience with them. I hope they'll have some good times, anyway. Maybe make some new memories. This town is amazing from now until the last day of December."

"What makes it so special?"

"A quaint little tourist town like Aspen Creek really celebrates. Lighted wreaths on all of the old-fashioned lampposts, twinkling lights everywhere, and the festivities go on and on. Carolers. Games. A skating rink in the town square. A lighting ceremony there this evening. We draw large crowds of weekend shoppers from the Twin Cities and Chicago because of it. I love the horse-drawn sleigh rides in town on weekend evenings, and our Christmas Eve candlelight service at the Aspen Creek Community Church is always beyond beautiful. I just hope the kids will enjoy it all."

She'd come into the café looking tense, but now her eyes sparkled and she gave him her first real smile. The sheer strength of it sent a jolt straight to his chest. "I suppose they will."

"Sorry." She gave a quick, self-conscious laugh. "You look a little stunned, but when I get started on Christmas in Aspen Creek, I start to babble. My friends tease me about being one of Santa's elves."

Hearing her love of Christmas touched a hollow place in his heart. Made him wish he could attend every event and try to absorb some of the joy she radiated, and awaken in himself some measure of Christmas spirit.

But Christmas stirred no happy memories. It was fraught with a lifetime of disappointment—failed wishes and lost dreams. It was something to get past, to forget. There'd been no Norman Rockwell holidays in his childhood and none later, either.

And, right now, all of these local festivities carried a great deal of risk to his plans. Would the kids become so enthralled by Hannah's joy and this fairy tale of a town that they wouldn't want to move back to Dallas with him?

He listened to the bells and chimes of the antique pinball machines at the back of the café and watched the kids' rapt attention as the pretty lights flashed.

And once again he kicked himself for not getting back to Dallas sooner. No matter what his doctors and therapists had said, he should've toughed it out on his own without those last months of therapy.

Then he would have been home before Cynthia's injury and could've picked up Molly and Cole before Hannah whisked them off to Wisconsin.

Where there were puppies and ponies and dazzling Christmas events that might make them want to stay with her for good.

Chapter Five

Hannah looped an arm around Molly's and Cole's shoulders and gathered them close for a hug as more people arrived in the town square for the lighting ceremony.

Darkness had fallen while she was doing the animal chores back home and now light snow was drifting downward in gentle swirls to frost the pine trees and sparkle on the children's stocking caps and jackets.

With no wind and the temp hovering just below freezing, it would be relatively comfortable out here for the hour-long program, but maybe her little Texans weren't accustomed enough to the cold. "Be sure to tell me if you're getting chilly, okay? We can go home whenever you want."

"I want a sleigh ride for *sure*." Cole tipped his head back to catch snowflakes on his tongue, and even Molly joined in.

"The church is selling hot chocolate and Christmas cookies, so if you—"

"Yes!" Cole exclaimed, tugging on the hem of her yellow ski jacket. "Please?"

Nodding to people she knew from church or the clinic, Hannah led the kids to the food stand at the other side of the square. Painted white with green vertical stripes, its red canvas roof was strung with icicle lights.

Inside, Beth Stone and Olivia Lawson, two of Hannah's friends from the local book club, were dressed in Mrs. Santa caps and white wigs. Over their winter coats they wore aprons adorned with jingle bells and giant neck-to-knee Christmas trees bedecked with flashing lights.

Both of them beamed when Hannah finally reached the head of the line. Cole looked up at their outfits in confusion. "There are two Mrs. Santas?"

"We're just her helpers for today," Olivia assured him with a kindly smile. "She's very busy this time of year."

"Keeley told us about you two," Beth said with a warm smile as she handed Molly and Cole gingerbread men and hot chocolate topped with pastel marshmallows. "We're both so happy to meet you!"

"Thanks," Molly mumbled. Cole shyly nodded.

"Love those aprons," Hannah teased as she handed over a ten dollar bill. "They're just so understated."

Beth laughed. "We're good until the AA batteries wear down. If you really like them, I stocked some extras in the gift area of my bookstore."

Olivia, an elegant and slender woman of seventy, craned her neck to search the nearby crowd. "So where's this Texas cowboy of yours? Keeley tells me he's quite a hunk."

"A what?" The term was so unexpected from a sophisticated, reserved woman like Olivia that Hannah sputtered on her first sip of cocoa, laughing.

And just then she felt the back of her neck start to burn and knew that, without a doubt, the hunk had to be standing right behind her. Embarrassment flooded her cheeks with heat.

"Hey, kids. Hannah." His voice rumbled against her ear.

Mortified, she froze for a moment. Had it sounded like she was laughing at him?

Cole turned around and, bless his heart, broke the awkward silence. "We dint know you're a cowboy, Uncle Ethan," he breathed in awe. "That's even better than a soldier 'cause you get to have horses *and* a gun."

"He's not a cowboy, stupid," Molly said, elbowing him and sending his cup of hot cocoa sloshing dangerously. But then she looked up at Ethan and frowned. "Are you?"

"Nope. Your aunt Hannah is closer to that than I am. She's got the horse."

Surprised at his gracious reply, Hannah felt even more awkward about her inadvertent insult.

Molly rolled her eyes. "Penelope isn't any bigger than I am."

He lifted a shoulder and smiled at her. "Maybe the next one will be taller. But if you want to see something big, wait until you see the team headed this way."

"Where? Can we go now?" Cole spun around, trying to peer through the crowd milling in the square. This time his hot chocolate spilled over his mitten and onto his new snow boots.

Panic flooded into his face and he jerked back, his lower lip trembling. "Sorry. I'm really sorry, Hannah."

The ramifications of his fearful reaction sent a chill through Hannah. She met Ethan's gaze and frowned, then bent to Cole's level. "It's only a cup of cocoa, sweetie. No big deal. I'll get you a refill."

He stared helplessly at her, like a rabbit caught in a trap, his eyes sheened with unshed tears.

"Really, it's not a problem, kiddo," she said with a smile. She gave him a hug. "And we will go see the horses when they start giving rides after the program. Promise."

Keeley silently telegraphed unspoken concern as she leaned over the counter to hand Hannah a new cup of cocoa. Hannah shook her head slowly in return before shepherding the children toward the benches set up in the middle of the square.

The thought of a sweet little six-year-old boy fearing punishment made her heart clench.

Someone had been severe with the poor little guy. His father? A former babysitter? *Cynthia?* None of them would be in his life again, but this was yet one more subject to bring up gently with him when the time was right.

She sat on a bench toward the back of the crowd with Molly and Cole on either side of her. Ethan sat next to Cole and draped an arm over his thin shoulders.

"Hey, buddy, I hear there's going to be lots of snow for sledding tomorrow. Are you excited about using your new sled?"

Cole nodded, his head bowed.

"I wonder which one will be the fastest," Ethan

mused. "I've never had a sled before, so this will be really fun."

Cole gave him a sideways glance. "Never?"

"Nope. And I've never ice-skated, either. I noticed an ice rink on the other side of the square, so maybe that's something we could all do, too."

"Molly and me don't have skates."

"I'll bet we can work something out. When we were at the hardware store for the sleds, I noticed that they have a used skate exchange. Good idea for kids who are always growing, right?" He leaned forward to catch Molly's eye. "What about you? I can see you now— spinning on your skates like a ballerina. Would you like that?"

Molly shrugged and plopped back in her seat, though maybe there'd been the faintest glimmer of interest in her eyes.

The mayor stood at the podium, tapped the microphone and wished everyone a happy Christmas season, then stepped aside. A dozen carolers wearing Santa hats took his place and began singing Christmas carols and hymns, encouraging everyone to sing along.

The beauty of this night, with snowflakes falling and her sister's two children at her side, filled Hannah with love and gratitude. When Cole reached over to hold her hand, she felt overwhelmed by her many blessings.

She lifted her eyes skyward. *Dee, I promise that your children will be safe and loved, and I'll do everything in my power to raise them as you wanted to.*

As the sweet strains of "Silent Night" drifted off into the night, the mayor stepped back up to the podium and shouted, "Merry Christmas!"

With a flip of a switch, all of the trees on the square blazed with light. The tallest, a massive old blue spruce towering thirty feet into the sky, sparkled with thousands of tiny white lights.

"Wow," Molly breathed. "It's so pretty here! Like a fairy land."

Hannah gave her a one-armed hug. "I know. I come every year and I never get tired of it. These gorgeous lights will be on until New Year's Day."

Cole tugged on her jacket. "Can we go see the horses now? What if there's a big line and we can't have a ride?"

"Problem solved. People used to get cold waiting in line, so the town council decided to sell advance tickets for various time slots. I bought ours this morning on-line." Hannah reached into her jacket pocket and pulled out an envelope. "People can still line up for any empty seats, but this way we don't have to wait. All four of us—you, too, Ethan—need to be on the other side of the square in ten minutes."

Cole and Molly darted ahead. Ethan fell into step with Hannah, both keeping an eye on the kids.

A dusting of snow sparkled in Ethan's raven hair and on the shoulders of his navy jacket. She suppressed the impulse to brush away the snow and jammed her hands into her pockets. "So, what did you think?"

He angled a glance at her as they strode after the kids. "Nice evening."

"Just nice? I thought it was beautiful. All of the carolers, the moment the town square was lit up and—look down the street—all of the wreaths on the streetlamps are now lit up, as well. And check out the lovely shop windows. The town has a contest every year for those displays. I just can't get enough of it all."

He chuckled at that. "I can tell."

She frowned, thinking over the day. "You didn't need to buy four sleds, you know. I hope you didn't feel obligated when Cole went crazy over all those choices. I can certainly pay you back."

He looked affronted. "No. Actually, while I'm here, I'd like to help with their expenses. It seems only fair. You must have spent a lot on the winter clothes you bought them today."

Hannah felt her hackles rise. "Not necessary. It was fun getting them outfitted with some of the things they'll need here."

Just ahead, Molly and Cole stopped along the sidewalk where two massive grays, in gleaming black leather and silver harnesses, stood patiently. One shook its head, sending the bells on its harness jingling.

Cole danced excitedly. "Just look at the horses, Aunt Hannah. They're pretty! And look at the carriage—it has ribbons and bells and Christmas lights!"

Hannah approached the driver, who was dressed in a Santa suit and already calling for those with tickets for the first trip, and then motioned to Ethan and the children. "This is it—our scheduled ride. Climb aboard!"

There were two rows of bench seats behind the raised front seat for the driver. Cole and Molly sat in middle with two other children who were already on board. Ethan and Hannah ended up in the back, wedged together by another seated couple.

Hannah tried to scoot over to avoid being pressed

so tightly against Ethan, but to no avail. "I'm sorry," she whispered.

"No problem." He lifted an arm and curved it around her shoulders, which gave them both a bit more room. "Seems like old times—in my old Chevy truck."

He remembered that?

From the moment he'd appeared at her door she'd been wary of him, suspicious of his motives and worried about the possibility of a looming legal battle over the children's future. She'd carefully ignored his physical appeal—he was simply a tall, incredibly good-looking guy, nothing more. But that hadn't been difficult. She'd only had to recall her hurt and anger at the callous way she'd been jilted—and his brother's cruel words afterward—to put that foolishness to rest.

But now, sitting so close to him, feeling the warmth of his leg against her jeans and his hard-muscled body pressed against hers, she could sense his strength even through the layers of their jackets. He made her feel safe. Protected.

Which made no sense since she knew she couldn't trust him one bit. Not when something really counted.

The carriage dipped to one side as the driver lumbered up onto his seat and then twisted around to doff his cap in greeting. "Well, folks, happy holidays to you all! I'm Pete. Frank and Earl here have been pulling this carriage for five years, so we should have a good, steady ride for the next half hour. Grab the folded lap robes stored under your seats if you get cold. Any questions before we start?"

Molly raised a timid hand. "Can you ride these horses?"

Pete chuckled. "Sure. Some folks ride draft horses, but I've gotten old and prefer driving. Creaky bones, I guess."

He shook out some slack in the reins and clucked at the team. They dutifully plodded forward, the bells on their harnesses rhythmically jingling, the leather creaking.

The carriage swayed as the horses clopped down Main Street beneath the swags of Christmas lights suspended across the street between lampposts.

"This is just lovely," Hannah murmured, glancing up at Ethan.

The rhythmic hoof beats, the warm scent of the horses and the aroma of the surrounding pine forest were almost mesmerizing.

The strong line of his jaw and his five-o'clock shadow were more than a little mesmerizing, too.

She pulled her gaze away and leaned forward. "Look to the left, kids. See that antiques and gift shop with the icicle lights hanging in the windows? It belongs to Keeley, who helped bring us Thanksgiving dinner yesterday. We ran out of time today, but we'll stop by another day. She wants you to try her yummy cookies."

Cole turned around. "She's nice."

Guessing at his thoughts, she smiled. "You'll both have lots of friends here, soon. I promise. You'll get to meet lots of kids at church tomorrow, and on Monday you'll see them in school, too."

"I don't want to go to school. Or church, either," Molly muttered without turning around. "I won't know *anybody*."

The girl next to her had been staring at the Christmas

lights and bickering with her brother. But now she angled a curious look at Molly. "What grade are you in?"

"Sixth."

"I'm in eighth. But my cousin Joanie is in sixth." The girl shuddered. "I hope you don't get Mrs. Stone for math. I heard she's tough."

Molly shot a desperate glance at Hannah. "Did I? I *hate* math."

"You're all set to start, but I don't remember everything on the class schedule they sent me. Except that you got Mrs. Fisher for English. She goes to my church and is really nice, I promise. We can check the schedule when we get home."

Molly bowed her head. "It's dumb to change schools now, after everybody has already made friends. I'll never catch up, anyway. Everything will be different and I'll look stupid."

"Well, I'm Faith, and you know me. And I'll tell Joanie you're really cool, so then you'll know her. She's cool, too." The other girl gave her a gentle, teasing shoulder bump. "And you aren't the only new one at school. We got two new kids in my classes just last week. Anyway, Christmas vacation comes up soon and after that it's like we're all starting new."

Molly shot her a grateful look then settled back in her seat.

"Thank goodness for small favors," Hannah said under her breath. "Monday might not be so hard, after all."

Chapter Six

The next morning Cole and Molly stood at the living room windows in their new flannel pajamas and stared out at the winter wonderland of white in awe.

"This is more than five inches," Molly whispered. "It has to be."

Hannah laughed. "A good foot so far. The new forecast predicts about fifteen inches with a possibility of forty-mile-an-hour wind gusts. So what do you think of all this?"

"Does this mean school will be canceled tomorrow?" The desperate note of hope in Molly's voice was unmistakable. "We never got anything like this in Dallas."

"I can't say what will happen with school. We'll listen to the radio or check the internet for closing announcements. But don't forget Faith and her cousin Joanie. You'll have two friends right at the start."

Molly shot a glum look at her. "I don't even know what Joanie looks like."

"After the carriage ride yesterday I started thinking, and I believe that family may have just started attending my church. So if the plow comes in time—which I doubt—we could go into town for the service and you'd probably get to meet Joanie and some of the other kids, too. Wouldn't that be great?"

Molly plopped into one of the upholstered chairs, her legs dangling over the armrest. "I guess."

"That was one of my goals for today, anyhow. Another was to make sure we had fun sledding." She shook her head. "But Old Man Winter sure isn't cooperating. And though I know you don't want to hear it, I want to make sure you both are all set for school tomorrow."

"What about my class schedule?"

"I've got it right there on the counter, next to the phone."

Molly hurried to get it. Squeezed her eyes tight. Then slowly unfolded the letter. "Mrs. Fisher… Miss Hayward… Mr. Coe… Mrs. Belkin…" She fell silent for a long moment then slapped the schedule onto the counter. "And Mrs. Stone. Math. I knew I wouldn't be lucky, I just *knew* it," she wailed. "I'm bad at math, so of *course* I got the mean one. I'm going to fail."

"You heard the opinion of just one student," Hannah said mildly. "And Faith didn't even have that teacher. Secondhand information isn't always right. Maybe Faith's friend was a slacker who didn't do his or her homework."

"Or maybe she tried super hard and the teacher failed her just out of spite," Molly retorted.

"I don't imagine that will happen. Anyway, math isn't subjective. Your answers are either right or wrong. But I can promise you that whatever happens, I will help. Okay?"

"Can we go sledding right now?" Cole looked up from pressing his fingertips against the frosted edges of the windowpanes, his eyes bright with excitement and anticipation. "You got us boots and snow pants."

"You're definitely all set, but there aren't good sliding hills nearby—the forest is too dense. We'll need to drive down to Aspen Creek Park for that—but not in this weather."

Cole's face fell. "Can't we try?"

"We have to wait for the snowplow. I can't promise when he'll come—especially if the wind picks up. Blowing and drifting can be a real problem out here, so sometimes the county pulls the plows off the road. Then we just have to wait."

"But you have a big car. I bet it could go."

"Even if my SUV could make it, it's not worth taking any chances. We might get there but not make it back today, and who would feed all the animals?"

"Does that mean Uncle Ethan can't get here, either?"

The ceiling lights in the kitchen flickered ominously and Molly's eyes rounded. "What was that?"

"No worries. Sometimes the power goes out during storms if a line goes down somewhere. We usually get it back within a few hours."

"So in the meantime we could freeze to death, right? And not be found till spring?"

Hannah smothered a smile at Molly's dramatics. "Not a chance. We have the wood-burning fireplace, plus I have lots of candles, flashlights and several kerosene lamps, so we won't be sitting in the dark. I also have a generator to keep just the essentials going." Hannah moved to the fireplace and opened the glass doors.

"In fact, I think a little fire would be cheery right now, don't you?"

Cole followed her. "Can I help?"

Hannah sat on the raised hearth and pointed to the alcove next to the fireplace. "Can you hand me some good pieces of firewood? Four or five should be plenty right now."

Reaching inside the firebox, she opened the damper then helped him arrange the wood and tinder. She struck the match and in a few minutes the sweet scent of burning pine wafted into the air.

As warmth began to radiate into the room, Maisie, Bootsie and all three cats claimed spots right in front of the fire.

She dusted off her hands. "Great job. Thanks, Cole. Now, who wants to help make chocolate chip cookies?"

"Me," Cole said softly. "I used to make cookies with my mom. I know how."

"Super. And you know what? She might have used the same family favorite recipe that she and I got from our mom. How about you, Molly? Want to help?"

"Not me." Molly headed for her room. "I'm going to read and pray that we get enough snow that school closes for the rest of the year."

Ethan turned up the heat of the windshield defroster and peered at the wall of white ahead of him. Following a snowplow had kept his speed at twenty-five, but the snow was too deep to try passing and he doubted he could make it through the drifts ahead of the plow anyhow. With such limited visibility he'd probably end up stuck in a ditch.

He'd passed the turnoff for Aspen Creek Park a few miles back, so the main highway would soon veer to the east, while Spruce Road continued north through the deepening forest for another mile to Hannah's place.

With only a couple homes on Spruce, it probably wasn't a high priority, and if the plow didn't head up that way, the rest of this trip was going to be a true test of what his rental SUV could do.

He'd probably end up finishing the trip on foot, or choosing the wiser course of giving up and turning back for town. How far would he get, trudging through this snow with a brace and a bum leg?

But if the forecasters were right and this storm worsened, how safe were Hannah and the kids up here in such an isolated area if the power went out, the furnace quit or her phone went dead?

If he didn't reach them now, he wouldn't rest easy back in town until he did.

Another blast of wind buffeted the side of his SUV and turned the visibility to zero. When the snow cleared he could see the plow rumbling away on the sharp curve to the east. Spruce Road opened up ahead of him like a white tunnel beneath an arched dome of the winter-bare branches of the trees lining either side.

He debated for a second then headed up the lane.

His prayers had never amounted to much—he doubted they'd even been heard much less answered. If God had listened, his best friends would still be alive.

But now he said one under his breath as he leaned forward to peer into the blinding world of white, his hands gripping the steering wheel.

The SUV steadily plowed through the snow, bucking

through drifts, shimmying over ice patches. He passed a mailbox, then one more. The driveways leading back into the woods were obscured by drifts.

Finally he caught a faint view of a dead end sign through the falling snow and then Hannah's mailbox.

For the second time in years he said a prayer. And this time it was heartfelt thanks.

Gathering the grocery bags on the seat next to him, Ethan stepped out into a knee-deep drift and his bad leg buckled. Only his grip on the SUV's door kept him upright.

He limped to the front entry, cringing at each step, and knocked. From inside came a cacophony of barking and the sounds of dogs clawing at the door. A moment later Hannah peeked through the small window.

She unlocked the door and stared at him in surprise. "What are you doing out in this weather? Have the plows come through already?"

"Just on the highway."

"And you still managed to make it up Spruce Road? That couldn't have been easy." With a twinkle in her eyes, she stepped aside to usher him in. "Especially for a Southern driver."

"It isn't that we can't drive in snow, we're just smart enough to live where it isn't an issue."

He set the groceries on the floor, shucked off his boots and hung his jacket on the coatrack by the door. He savored the aroma of warm chocolate chip cookies. "Who's baking?"

"Me and Aunt Hannah. Molly didn't want to help, so she went outside to see the chickens and the pony." Cole stared at Ethan from the kitchen then rushed to grab his own coat. "You got here! That means we can go sledding!"

"Not so fast, buddy." Ethan ruffled his blond hair. "I was really fortunate to get here. But the roads aren't good at all."

The boy's shoulders slumped. "We gotta have snow to go sledding. But then we *get* snow and we can't go anywhere. It isn't fair."

"There will be lots of other times. So many that you might even get tired of it, kiddo." Hannah nodded toward the window. "And, remember, your job is to watch out for the snowplow. Unless it comes too close to dark, we'll still try to go today."

Ethan hoped not. The thought of repeatedly trudging up a long hill only for a quick trip down made his knee throb as he carried the two grocery sacks to the kitchen counter. Though he forced himself to walk with a steady gait, he looked up and found Hannah's gaze riveted on his right leg. *Busted.*

"What happened to you? You weren't limping like that before."

"Took a wrong step when I got out of the SUV. It's nothing."

"Right. If you take a seat and prop up that leg on an ottoman, I'll give you a cold pack."

"It's fine."

"No, it's not. Sit." She fluffed up a couple of sofa pillows. "Chair or sofa?"

From her steely look of determination, he knew he might as well give in. "Chair, I guess. But no ice pack."

She put one pillow against the backrest, waited for

him to get settled and then put the other pillow on the ottoman to elevate his leg.

She glanced at him. "Do you mind?"

He started to wave her away but she'd already crouched next to the ottoman. She studied his leg for a moment then ran deft hands down his jeans from mid-thigh to ankle, gently probing here and there.

Warmth radiated through him at her light, professional touch, and he found himself drawn to the way the flickering fire turned her hair to molten gold.

Then her light fingertips brushed over the mid-calf area of his right leg. He drew in a sharp breath and forced himself to not flinch.

Her gaze flew up to meet his. "Does it hurt here? Or…here?"

Always, but he wasn't about to admit it.

"So…what happened?"

He shrugged. "Shattered tibia and fibula. Took three surgeries to rebuild them."

"Would it be more comfortable if you took your brace off while you're resting?"

"No."

She gave a searching look. "So tell me about your pain meds."

"Huh?"

"Tell me about your pain meds," she repeated. "Do they give you adequate relief? Or have you been trying to taper?"

He set his jaw. "I quit the prescriptions right after I was discharged. I manage without anything, except for maybe an ibuprofen now and then."

"Toughing out pain isn't macho, Ethan. Not when

something mild can help keep you moving so you can maintain your muscle mass, strength and mobility."

"Which I am doing."

She rose. "If you say so. But if you have problems, come to the Aspen Creek Clinic. Dr. Talbot is there Monday, Wednesday and Friday, and she's excellent. I'm usually there Monday through Friday."

Though he had no intention of going, he nodded. "I'll keep that in mind."

"And, of course, there's a VA hospital in the Twin Cities, plus some VA clinics that are a bit closer."

"Right."

She blew out a slow breath. "Why do I think it's a waste of time talking about this?"

"I've had good medical care, but I'm done. I figure that now it's up to me."

She frowned at him. "Let's move on to something easier then. Your jeans are damp from the snow—knees on down—so you must be chilled. Can I throw them in the dryer for you?"

"Uh...no. But thanks."

"I probably have a large enough robe around here someplace. Or maybe some sweatpants would be better." Her eyes twinkled and a flicker of a grin touched her lips. "I have hot pink or lime."

He snorted at that. "The jeans will dry."

"Not very fast, but suit yourself." She snagged a brightly colored lap quilt from the back of the sofa and draped it over his legs, threw another log on the fire and went into the kitchen. He could see her piling chocolate chip cookies on a plate.

"Coffee or cocoa?"

He shifted his attention to the crackling fire, thankful for the warmth radiating into the living room. "I'm good."

"No—make a choice. I've got cookies here, too."

"Coffee, I guess. Thanks. While you're over there, you might want to check those grocery sacks and put things away."

She lifted the edge of one of the sacks and peered inside. "Two dozen eggs, butter, a loaf of bread…"

"I wasn't sure if you were low on any of the basics, so I grabbed a few things in town in case you wouldn't be able to get out for a while."

"Thank you. This was so thoughtful." She cocked her head, listening to the wind howling outside, then prepared a hot cup of coffee for him with the Keurig machine on the counter. "And it was probably a really good idea. The wind wasn't supposed to pick up until later on, but it sounds like it's already here. I'm not sure if you'll even be able to make it back down the road to the highway, if you wait much longer. You should probably go right away."

"Not until I'm sure that you're all set for this weather. Do you have plenty of firewood?"

"There's a big stack in that alcove by the fireplace, and I've got two cords under a tarp next to the back porch." She gave him a plate with the mug of coffee and the cookies. "So we're good."

"What about all the animals? I can help you with chores before I go."

She smiled at that. "Thanks for the offer, but I think you'll want to keep off that leg for a while. There's not much to do—the chickens always roost inside the barn when it's this cold, so I just need to close the little door to their outside run. They already have free-choice feed and an electric waterer that doesn't freeze."

"What about the pony?"

"It's too early now, but before dark I'll close Penelope in for the night, bed her down and feed her. She can go in or out at will during the day, but the silly thing wants to stay outside no matter what—rain, sleet or snow. I just hate to think of her outside all night in the wind and cold."

Cole, still standing at the front windows, looked over his shoulder. "The plow still hasn't come. Why not?"

"They're probably taking care of all the main roads first, honey. Why don't you find a board game in your room or bring out your Legos? That would be a lot more fun than watching for the snowplow, wouldn't it?"

Cole's shoulders slumped as he disappeared into his room.

Ethan lifted his coffee in salute. "Perfect coffee. Cookies, too."

"Glad you like them." She glanced toward Cole's open bedroom door and then moved to the sofa next to Ethan's chair and leaned forward, her elbows braced on her thighs. She lowered her voice. "I was hoping I'd have a chance to talk to you privately. It's about Cole."

Ethan set his coffee cup on the small end table next to his chair. He already had a good idea about what she wanted to discuss, but he didn't have the answer. Not for sure. "The incident with the spilled cocoa last night?"

"Exactly. It broke my heart to see his reaction. He was so frightened—like he was expecting to be se-

verely scolded. And it makes me worry about who—
and when—someone treated him that way."

"I can't see my brother ever treating Cole like that.
Distant? Yeah. Not giving the kid enough attention?
Probably. Rob was usually caught up in his own big
dreams and financial dramas."

"And Dee was a good mom, I'm sure of it. I visited
whenever I could, and I never heard my sister raise her
voice unless one of the kids was really out of line and
refused to listen. They loved her to pieces. Cole followed her around like a little duckling."

"I saw that, too—what little time I was around."

Glancing at Cole's bedroom door again, where the
sound of a battery-operated toy car now buzzed around
the room, Hannah took a deep breath. "And that leaves
your aunt Cynthia. And some babysitters, I suppose. But
Dee didn't work outside the home, so there wouldn't
have been many of those."

Ethan stared at the flames dancing in the fireplace,
remembering Cynthia's anger when he and Rob had
accidentally broken a vase while playing in her living
room. He'd been in kindergarten, and facing her cold
fury had made him feel like his world was about to end.
"Cynthia means well. I can't imagine her laying a hand
on anyone. But she's not Mary Poppins."

Hannah nodded. "I saw her at Rob and Dee's funeral, of course, and after that I went down several
times over the summer to see Molly and Cole. As you
can imagine, they were just devastated. But they were
also shell-shocked and terribly withdrawn. I would have
gone down to see them more often, but Cynthia privately told me—coldly *discouraged* me—from even

that much contact. She said it only confused the children during such a fragile time. She said they were much worse after my visits."

"But she's not in the picture any longer. So what are you trying to say?"

"Just that Cole's fear over spilling the cup of cocoa worries me. A lot. And now you're here, talking about wanting to take the kids back to Texas. Where there are no grandparents to help you out. No other aunts or cousins or lifelong friends around, either."

"I can't instantly manufacture a support system, if that's what you're getting at."

"So where does that leave them, if you go back on active duty, or find a job, or simply want a date night with someone? I didn't ever see Cynthia screaming at the kids, but from the way she's treated me, I think it's a very distinct possibility that she might. If—by chance—you gain even partial custody, I want you to promise that woman will not have any lengthy contact with Molly and Cole."

"Agreed."

"And I…" Hannah faltered. "You do?"

She looked so surprised at his immediate acquiescence that he felt a sudden heaviness in his heart. Did she really think him so uncaring, so totally unsuitable to raise Molly and Cole?

"Whatever you think of me, I only want the best for them. And whatever her faults, I'm sure Cynthia wanted that, too. But she hasn't mellowed into a sweet, patient old lady, and I don't imagine she'd even want to have any part of caring for them in the future. So that case is closed. I promise."

"Still—" The sound of the little race car stopped and Hannah paused, listening.

"Hannah," Cole called out. "I need your help with Candy Land. It's up too high."

"Excuse me." Hannah rose and headed for Cole's room.

Curious about what she'd done for the boy's room with such short notice, Ethan swept aside the lap quilt and hobbled after her. He leaned a shoulder against the door frame and watched her reach for the game on a shelf, then he surveyed the room.

He felt his heart swell until it barely fit in his chest. It was everything he and Rob had never had as boys. Perfect for making Cole feel at home.

The walls were light blue, with a dinosaur wallpaper border along the top and dinosaur curtains on the double window facing the backyard.

The boyish furniture was rustic oak that could take a lot of abuse—a big dresser topped with a dinosaur-themed lamp and the kind of bunk bed with a place for a desk in its lower level. But instead of desk, a fort had been constructed in that space, complete with a window and camo-print canvas hanging across a little doorway.

Filling another wall, floor-to-ceiling shelves were already filled with toys and books. It looked as if Cole had lived there all his life.

Hannah handed the board game to Cole. "Do you want to play in here or out by the fireplace?"

He promptly headed toward the living room. Hannah glanced at Ethan then studied the room. "Well, what do you think?"

"How did you ever get this ready so fast?"

"Craigslist and a lot of friends. This used to be my office, so it was loaded with my stuff, and the walls were pale peach with lacy curtains. As you can imagine, we worked like mad to make it into a boy's room."

The back door squealed open and slammed shut. Boots thumped onto the floor and then Molly came around the corner in stockinged feet, her cheeks rosy.

"You were out there a long time," Hannah said. "You must be really cold. Do you want some cocoa?"

"No thanks," Molly mumbled. She went into her room and shut the door behind her.

"Sorry about that. I would show you her room, but I guess we're still in an adjustment phase, so I'm going to just let her be for a while. With school on Monday on top of everything else, I think she needs some space."

In the living room Cole was setting up the game. He looked up at Hannah and Ethan with such hopefulness in his eyes that Ethan just couldn't say no.

Ethan smiled. "Can I play a round with you before I go?"

From outside at the front of the house came a loud *zzzzzt* and a bang. Instantly all of the lights went out and the refrigerator stopped humming. The lights flared on for a second then went dead.

Ethan jerked and spun around, adrenaline surging through him at the sound of enemy fire. The choking smell of smoke and blood, hot metal and burning rubber.

He was in the back of that doomed transport vehicle, trapped by the explosion and shrapnel—

"Are you okay?" Hannah murmured. Her hand hovered over his arm then she cautiously drew it back. "You know where you are, right?"

He blinked, confusion spinning through his brain. He forced himself to focus on her face and the turbulent emotions began to calm, leaving raw embarrassment in their wake.

The cats curled up in front of the fireplace had darted for hiding places. The two old dogs had barely stirred. And Cole was looking up at him as if he'd seen a ghost. "What was that sound outside?" he cried. "You were scared!"

"He was just surprised, Cole. That loud noise was probably because a tree limb fell over the power line close by." Hannah gave him a reassuring hug. "Or maybe it was a careless squirrel."

Cole's eyes widened. "A huge, monster squirrel? Like Godzilla?"

"Nope. Now and then a regular ole squirrel fries itself at the top of the tall power pole out in front—by touching the pole and the power line at the same time. It's happened three times in the past six months, so now maybe the power company will finally install the squirrel guard they've been promising."

She reached for her cell phone, scanned the directory and called the power company. After a five-minute wait she spoke to someone.

"Well, guys. They say there are lines down all over the county due to this storm, and thousands of people are without power. They won't get to us until sometime tomorrow, and that's if the road is plowed by then. Apparently the main roads in and out of town are drifted shut and the plows have stopped until the wind dies down."

Ethan stood at the front window and forced himself to concentrate on slow, steady breathing as he stared out at the heavy snowfall driven horizontal by the strong winds.

The curtain of snow obscured both his SUV and the county road that hit a dead end just past Hannah's house. And at just three o'clock, the daylight was already fading. "It's now or never, if I'm going to get back to town, but from the sound of things, it isn't worth trying."

Hannah joined him at the window. "Not if it's so bad the plows quit."

He frowned. "I'm glad to be here, though. I hate to think of you and the kids alone out here if anything goes wrong."

"We'll be fine—I've lived here for five years, and this storm isn't anything new, believe me. But I appreciate the concern." She went to the fireplace and added another log. "I'm going to let the pups run outside for a few minutes, then bring them in here to romp. Then I'll check the generator and get it ready, bring in more firewood and get the kerosene lamps set up. After that I'll go take care of the outside chores. I think you should either play Candy Land with Cole or go back to the chair and rest that leg."

"Candy Land it is." He laughed aloud. "But what a list you have. Reminds me of a country oldie I've heard on the radio about a guy giving his wife a long list of chores starting with 'Put another log on the fire…'"

She chuckled. "If memory serves, she's leaving him

by the end of that one. But my chores won't take too long."

She headed for the door leading to the garage and jerked to a halt. Then spun toward the window over the sink.

"Fire! Oh, no—*fire!*" Hannah jerked on her boots, hopping on one foot and then the other as she hurried to the back door. Shoving her arms into the sleeves of her jacket, she jerked up the zipper and wrenched open the door. "Call 9-1-1 and tell them the barn is on fire. Hurry. The fire number for this place is 478."

Ethan hurried after her, punching in 9-1-1 and making the call as he hobbled to his jacket and boots and pulled them on.

She was going into that blaze to save those stupid chickens and pony. She was as impetuous and foolhardy as she'd been thirteen years ago.

Only this time, it could kill her.

Chapter Seven

Hannah plowed through the wide, deep snowdrift in the backyard. It reached her upper thighs and each step was a struggle—as if she were trying to swim through a vat of thick, cold molasses. High winds threatened to knock her off her feet.

Ahead, the blaze licked at the walls of the barn on the two sides she could see. Something exploded inside—maybe an aerosol can, fueling the flames even higher.

Her heart clenched. She wasn't going to reach the animals in time. *Please, Lord, make Penelope go outside. And please help me save those poor chickens.*

She spared a quick glance over her shoulder. Ethan was closing the distance between them, his face grim. Back at the house, Molly and Cole stood in the open doorway to the deck, their faces pale with fear.

"If the dispatcher calls back with any questions, tell them the barn is on fire at Hannah Dorchester's place, Spruce Road," Ethan shouted back at them. "Got it? Dorchester. Fire number 478. Write it down—478. And shut that door!"

The wind slammed snow into Hannah's face and down her neck as she pivoted and again struggled toward the barn through the snow. Her lungs burning and throat raw with exertion in the cold, she'd begun to feel the searing heat of the blaze when Ethan closed a strong hand on her shoulder and pulled her to a halt.

"No," he shouted above the keening wind. "Don't!"

"I'm not stupid—I'm not going inside. If the hens are in their run, I've got to try to grab them and get them away from the heat. And I'm praying Penelope hasn't panicked and gone back into the barn. Do you see her?"

He scanned the area near the barn, squinting against the driving snow. "No—wait. Is that her back in the trees?"

Thickly covered in snow from ears to tail, Penelope looked more like the mound of a ski run mogul than a pony, but she'd stayed at the far end of her corral instead of running into the familiar safety of the barn. If it were true that some horses did that, at least Penelope had more common sense.

Hannah reached under her jacket and unbuckled her leather belt. "Can you reach her and put this around her neck? I'll come back for her in a minute. She's going to the garage."

"Wait!"

She ignored him and darted to the chicken run at the other end of the little barn, knowing there was little hope. The roosting chickens had probably already died from the smoke.

But now she heard angry squawking and the beating of wings against the chain-link fencing that formed a roof over the pen, meant to protect them from hawks and owls.

Wind-driven flames were already starting to reach this end of the barn and from somewhere inside she heard the screech of weakened timber giving way.

There's so little time. She slipped inside the outside pen through its narrow walk door. Grabbing two of the hens, she slowly made her way to a large, empty kennel inside the garage, fighting the deep snow and the wind that threatened to send her back two steps for each one forward. She locked them in a Great Dane–sized kennel and then hurried back for the final bird.

Ethan—now limping painfully as he made his way through the heavy snow—and Penelope arrived minutes later. Inside the garage Hannah sagged against the bumper of her SUV with exhaustion and relief.

"Penelope can wander around in here for the night, I guess. I've got a couple bales of cedar shavings I can put down in the corner on the far side for her, and some in the cage for the chickens. Not perfect, but it will do."

"Better here than out in a blizzard." Ethan scraped the thick blanket of snow off the pony's back and neck with the side of his hand. "That barn will be a total loss."

"I know." She looked into the high-walled pen where the pups were sleeping in a warm pile while their mother, Lucy, kept a watchful eye on Ethan and the pony. "At least everyone is safe. I'd better get inside and check on the kids. Molly ought to be old enough to keep an eye on Cole for a little while, but you never know."

The two were standing just inside the door when

Hannah and Ethan walked in, their faces tense with worry.

"We were afraid you'd get burned up. The fireman called and said he couldn't come." Cole looked back and forth between Ethan and Hannah. "Is the pony okay? And the chickens, too?"

Hannah ruffled his blond hair. "They're fine. Now they're up here in the garage where they can stay warm and dry tonight."

Cole's anxiety seemed to ease, but she wasn't sure about Molly.

Hannah gave her a closer look. It wasn't tension or fear on her face. It was misery. Sheer misery, coupled with overwhelming guilt. "Molly?"

"I didn't mean to do it. *Honest.*" The girl's lower lip trembled and tears filled her eyes.

"You mean the fire?" Hannah exchanged glances with Ethan, then led Molly to a chair at the kitchen table and sat next to her while Cole and Ethan headed for the living room. "It could have started for a lot of different reasons. What could you have done to cause a fire?"

Molly's tears spilled down her face. "I thought the hens were too cold. Ruth kept fluffing up her feathers like she needed to be warmer and that funny-looking heater wasn't even very hot…but I couldn't find a way to turn it up. So I moved it closer to where they roost. What if it made their feathers catch fire?"

"I didn't see a single singed feather. They even had enough sense to flee to their outside pen."

"But—"

"A heat lamp with a bare bulb and no wire guard would be a big risk for sure. But the people who brought those hens here also brought the flat-panel heater from their coop, which is much safer. It's just mild, radiant heat that brings up the temp a few degrees."

"I... I thought..."

"Anything electrical could probably short out somehow, but if that happened to the heater, it wouldn't be your fault. Maybe there was some mouse damage to the wiring somewhere in the barn." Hannah rested a gentle hand on Molly's cheek. "I'll call the insurance company and fire department Monday morning. I'm sure they'll want to figure it out for the insurance claim. No worries, okay?"

"Where will the animals stay now? Will they be all right?"

"They'll be fine. After I get the snow cleared off the driveway tomorrow, I'll start parking outside, until I can figure out a replacement for the barn. That probably can't happen until spring, but we'll get by."

Molly nodded somberly.

"With all this excitement I haven't noticed the time. What would you like me to start for supper?"

"I'm not really hungry. But thanks, anyway."

Hannah sighed as she watched Molly go back to her room, then she rose and went to check on Cole. He and Ethan were on the floor, bathed in the warm light of the fireplace and well into a round of Candy Land. As always, Maisie was pressed close to Cole's side as if she knew how much hurt he still held inside.

The picture of Ethan and Cole, with their heads nearly together as they concentrated on the board game, made Hannah's heart squeeze.

She'd thought of Ethan as her nemesis for thirteen

long years. Remembered every last detail of the weekend of his betrayal and his callous departure for active duty without a farewell, much less an apology.

He'd torn her heart in two.

Ever since she'd thought of him as heartless. Cruel. Someone she never wanted to see again. Someone she could never forgive.

Eventually she had, after a lot of prayer. But it had been a grudging forgiveness. An obligation, once she'd really thought about the words of the Lord's Prayer she said every night.

And then Ethan showed up on her doorstep two days ago and turned her safe world upside down.

Her heart had warned her to stay clear of him from that very first moment. Yet…he was a warrior, one who had sacrificed for his country. One who—like all soldiers—deserved the heartfelt thanks of every American, including her. Even if she wished he'd leave Aspen Creek and never come back.

But now she'd seen another side of him and wondered if she'd been wrong about him all along.

A cruel man didn't play Candy Land with a little boy and clearly try to lose.

A heartless man didn't trudge through deep snow, feeling pain with every step, to rescue an elderly pony, or try to break through a young girl's shell of grief and loss with gentle words.

Her cell phone chimed, pulling her out of her troubled thoughts.

"Bill Jacobs here. Fire department." She'd known the fire chief and his wife Marnie since her EMT days, before she'd gone on to her hectic clinical phase of study at Mayo.

She smiled into the phone. "I'll bet you're having a busy day."

"Too much. Family of five—their dog woke them up late this morning before they all died of carbon monoxide poisoning. I'm still thanking God for that dog. Three little kids, right before Christmas..." He swallowed hard. "Then there was a fire at the apartments west of town and we had to call for trucks from two other towns for that one. And then Keeley North's dad wandered off this afternoon. In the middle of a blizzard, no less."

Hannah drew in a sharp breath. "Please tell me he's all right."

"Dr. Talbot was covering the ER when we finally found him and brought him in. Frostbite, hypothermia, but he'll be okay. She said he's too cantankerous to die."

"Poor Keeley. She must have been beside herself."

"While I was still there, she was talking to the doc about finding a memory care unit for him." Bill sneezed. "Anyway, I'm real sorry we couldn't make it out on your call—we were already spread too thin and the snow is so bad I don't think we could've even made it up your road. If it had been a house fire, we would have tried hard to get there. But I understand it was that old shed out back?"

"Small barn. We didn't lose any animals, but I'm sure it's a total loss. I'll call the insurance company tomorrow."

"Is it still actively burning anywhere?"

"Once the roof and framework were gone, I could

see the hay smoldering. After all the wet snow falling on the hay, I imagine it will continue for some time. There's nothing else close to the barn at risk, though."

"I'll try to get out there tomorrow, too, in case there's any question about how it started. Will you be at the clinic or at home?"

"Clinic. But I'm just working nine to three Monday through Friday until New Year's because my niece and nephew are here. Permanently, I hope."

"The wife and I were real sorry to hear the news about your sister." He hesitated, cleared his throat. "Just a warning—you know that Gladys Rexworth will surely hear about your fire from some gossip or another. She'll think it's a good excuse to stir up the city council again about shutting down your rescue operation."

"She's already tried, but I'm licensed and have passed every inspection, and so have the other two women who take in strays. She and the rest of the city council should just be thankful they don't have to add a shelter to their annual budget. Though, if the town grows any more, they'll need to."

"And cut back on their beautification projects? They'd consider that a bitter pill." He snorted. "But I've got to say one thing—Gladys seems to have a very personal vendetta against you, and I'd hate to be in your shoes. Any idea what got her started?"

"Um…can't say," she told him.

Which was completely true, and long after the call ended, Hannah stared out the window at the deepening dusk.

She knew full well why Gladys had held on to her grudge. Why she had tried to ruin Hannah's career at the clinic with her gossip, and would now try again to end the animal rescue out of sheer spite.

But because of strict medical privacy laws, there wasn't a thing Hannah could do to stop her.

Ethan helped Hannah set up the generator outside, in the lee of the garage, to maintain the electricity for the appliances, water heater and well pump, since the power was still out.

The fireplace, Hannah said, was usually adequate for enough warmth so the water pipes didn't freeze, though everyone would be wearing warm sweaters and extra socks.

While she let the dogs and puppies outside for a brief run and filled their food and water dishes, he brought several armloads of firewood inside and filled the two kerosene lanterns.

Now the pups were running helter-skelter through the house, sliding on the hardwood floors and yipping at each other as they wrestled. Cole was in the midst of the melee, nearly bowled over by their sloppy puppy kisses and trying to hold a pudgy little brown-and-white one that was wriggling in his arms.

The cats had immediately disappeared in the face of the onslaught pouring in the door. The basset hound hadn't stirred from his warm spot by the fireplace.

Old Maisie had retreated to the fireplace as well, clearly overwhelmed by all the exuberance.

"I'm going to start supper," Hannah announced, peering into the refrigerator. "We've still got lots of leftovers to use up from dinner on Friday, if that's all right with everyone. After that, we've got several pans of lasagna and some casseroles that friends dropped by for the freezer. Let's eat in about an hour, okay?"

"All sounds good to me." Ethan surveyed the flashlights and candles sitting on the kitchen counter, then shouldered on his coat. "It looks like you're all set in here, but I'd like to check out your garage and see if something better could be done for the pony. I noticed the plywood walls of the puppy pen. Is there any extra plywood out there? Or extra 2x4s?"

"Stacked against the south wall and also up in the eaves. I can come out to help as soon as I get this all started."

"Can I help?"

Cole looked up him with such longing that Ethan felt his heart catch. Was the boy missing the days of projects with his dad, or was it that he longed for the male companionship that Rob had rarely shared? "Of course, buddy. I need a helper and you'll be perfect. Put your jacket and boots on, though."

Out in the garage Ethan discovered Penelope in the narrow space between Hannah's SUV and the house, with her head deep into one of the garbage cans, its aluminum lid on the floor and much of the contents scattered at her feet.

"Looks like you're having a good time," he muttered, tossing the trash back into the can and settling the lid on tight. "If this means you'll be having a bellyache, I don't think your vet will be making house calls tonight."

Across the garage he discovered the stack of 2x4s and a couple sheets of plywood. Eyeballing the back corner of the garage, he cut some of the wood with a handsaw then began building an L-shaped framework that could support sections of plywood four feet tall and eight feet long.

Cole appeared at his elbow. "Can I hammer something?"

"You bet. Watch out for your fingers, though." Ethan steadied the boards while Cole gave a nail a tentative tap then missed the nail entirely. "Good job. This is really hard with such a heavy hammer and that little nail. Try again."

Cole sent a worried look at Ethan and then whacked at the nail again, sending it sideways.

"I guess I don't know how."

"Everyone starts out like this—and with practice, learns to do better. Your dad and I didn't do half as good as you when we were your age."

"Really?"

"Really. It just takes time. And maybe a smaller hammer." Ethan searched the small workbench near the puppy pen and found a lighter tack hammer. "Try this one."

Cole two-handed it and missed the nail then hit it on the second try with a resounding thwack.

"That, my man, was excellent."

Beaming, Cole tried it several more times before putting down the hammer. "My arms are tired," he confessed. "Sorry."

"I could still use your help, though. The nails are in that red bucket by your feet. Can you hand them to me, one by one? This will go a lot faster and then Penelope can have her own stall tonight."

Cole nodded, his face filled with pride.

The pony wandered over and stood behind Ethan to

oversee the project, her warm breath and muzzle whiskers tickling the back of his neck. In an hour the simple framework was assembled, the plywood panels hammered onto the frame.

The door into the house opened and Hannah stepped out into the garage. "Wow. That is amazing, you two. It's perfect!"

Cole looked up at her with shy pride. "I'm just the helper."

"And he's really good at it, too. Without Cole I couldn't have done half as much." He gestured to a three-foot opening on one side. "This is for a gate, but I couldn't find any spare hinges on the workbench."

"I don't think there are any. Did you look in the buckets of odds and ends under the workbench?"

"No luck. I figured I could temporarily suspend the door—" he held up a section of plywood "—and fasten it on both sides with hook-and-eye closures, like the ones for old-fashioned screen doors. I found a few of those. The next time you go to town, you could pick up a couple of proper hinges."

"Thank you, thank you," she said fervently. "I really didn't like the thought of the pony roaming the garage all night. The cement floor is just too hard for her old bones and she could get into all sorts of trouble."

Hannah picked a heavy, plastic-wrapped bale of compressed pine-shaving bedding from a stack at the front of her SUV, slit it open in the new stall, then got two more bags while Ethan finished the temporary gate.

After fluffing the bedding with a pitchfork, the hard bale of shavings expanded into a deep, soft bed so the pony could comfortably lay down. Hannah put her hands on her hips and surveyed the results. "This is fantastic, Ethan and Cole. I'm so grateful to you both. Especially as it could be months before it's warm enough to start building a new shed."

Cole grinned from ear to ear at her praise. "Can she have some of the hay by the puppy pen?"

"Since all the rest of the hay in the barn is probably smoldering, yes, indeed. I'm so glad I brought up so many bales to insulate the outside walls of that pen."

Ethan glanced around for a bucket. "Can I use that for the pony's water?"

Hannah nodded. "I'll get it—I'll need to fill it from the bathtub faucet, and it will be heavy."

He raised an eyebrow.

"Look, you might be a tough guy, but I see you limping worse than ever. As much as I appreciate your help, going out to the barn through those drifts didn't do that leg any favors."

She grabbed the bucket before he could get to it and grinned. "It's time to come in for supper, anyway, and probably time for that ice pack you didn't want."

Chapter Eight

"I don't know how many times Molly asked about school tomorrow," Hannah murmured as she snuggled deeper under her afghan on the sofa and sipped a cup of hot cocoa. "I wonder if she'll even sleep tonight."

"At least there should be a two-hour delay or a cancellation," Ethan said.

"Just more hours for her to worry about her entrance into enemy territory." Remembering the words of the older girl on the carriage ride, Hannah had offered to call some church friends and track down Joanie, who was apparently Molly's age. Would Molly want to think up some random questions about school to ask her, as a way to make contact?

Mortified, Molly had violently shook her head at that, saying Joanie would think her a total loser if she needed her aunt to find her a friend. Then she'd announced she was going to bed.

"I've already been told that I can drop her off in front of the school, but I was *not* to go in and embarrass her." Hannah sighed. "The elementary school actually wants parents to bring children inside and make sure their names are checked off, and the same routine after school. But Molly wants me to be invisible. Was I ever like that when I was her age? I hope not."

"Ask your mom." A corner of Ethan's mouth lifted in a quick grin. "You might be surprised."

"Actually, I wouldn't be, now that I think about it. Dad tolerated no back talk, no straying from proper behavior and absolutely no shirking of duties. I was more like a cadet than a daughter whenever he was around."

"How did your mom feel about that?"

"I'm sure my parents loved each other in their own way, but Mom is like a different person now that he's gone."

"Losing him must have been tough on her."

"Yeah, of course. But now it's like she's blossomed. She earned a Master's degree in nursing and moved to Minneapolis. Every time I talk to her on the phone she's happily volunteering for something, or going off to some social event. I guess she must have felt like she was under Dad's thumb, too."

Ethan looked at her and their eyes met, held. "So you were being honest when you said the reprieve from eloping with me really was all for the good. Right?"

Her pulse stumbled. "Honestly? It broke my heart. Maybe things would have been different for us. Better. I was sure of it at the time. But afterward I focused on my regimented childhood and figured I'd just been blessed with a fortunate escape."

His mouth quirked. "Ouch."

The wind continued to howl outside, buffeting the house with snow. The intimacy of this night, with the house darkened except for the soft glow of the kerosene lantern on the kitchen counter and the flickering fireplace, made it easier to talk about wounds that had never quite healed.

"Why did you do it? I used to wonder, a lot. Was I such a terrible mistake? Had you already started seeing the woman you married?"

"I was stupid. Too young. You were everything I'd ever wanted—more than I ever could have hoped for. But I knew nothing about marriage. Nothing about lifetime commitment. I sure didn't have an example of that at home, and I was terrified of being a failure." He stared into the fire. "Of failing you."

"So you ran."

"That afternoon I heard I had to report for duty by five—a week sooner than expected. So, yes, I ran. Didn't know how to explain or apologize. I knew I could face an enemy in combat but had no idea how to face you."

"So I was that fierce," she teased gently.

"You were that sweet and beautiful. And trusting. I threw away something I knew I'd never find again."

Her chest tightened and her throat felt too thick with emotion to speak.

He shook his head slowly. "So now—"

From Cole's bedroom came a terrified scream. And then another, even louder. Maisie hurried out of his room to Hannah's side and pawed at her, clearly indicating her worry.

Ethan blanched, his gaze darting around the room.

Hannah raced from the couch into Cole's room with Ethan and the dog at her heels.

His wide eyes glazed and unseeing, Cole was sitting up in his bunk bed with the blankets twisted around him. Flailing his arms, he seemed to be trying to fend off a legion of unseen monsters, his screams going on and on in the darkness.

Hannah moved next to him. "Everything is all right," she murmured in a low voice. "You're at your aunt Hannah's house, in a nice, warm bed. Your uncle Ethan is here, too, so you are very safe."

But the inconsolable screaming didn't stop. If anything, his screams escalated.

"He probably doesn't really hear me, but I just want to offer comfort," Hannah said as she glanced at Ethan over her shoulder.

"Poor kid. Is he sick? In pain? Do we need to get him to the ER?"

"Night terrors," she said quietly, though Ethan could probably barely hear her. "First time since he got here, but don't worry—they aren't uncommon."

Ethan moved to her side. "Like a nightmare?"

"Not really. He's not awake, and he won't remember this in the morning." She gently circled one of his trembling wrists with her hand. "Poor guy. His pulse is racing."

"Shouldn't you wake him up?"

"I know it's hard to listen to him screaming, but he'll settle down eventually and still be asleep. If I try to force him awake, he might be confused and scared, and unable to get back to sleep for a long while. So if this ever happens when I'm not around, don't talk loudly or try to shake him awake. And if he gets out of bed, just quietly guide him back."

Ethan's eyes filled with helplessness and worry. "How do you…?"

"I've had a number of parents come into the clinic with kids who do this. It's sometimes just random. Sometimes it's from stress or fear, or sleeping in a strange place. Or big life changes."

"And Cole has faced all of that, and more," Ethan said somberly.

"For all I know, he might have had night terrors many other times, even before his parents passed away, though my sister never mentioned it." She looked at Cole, whose screams were quieting. "I think this bunk bed was a mistake if he is going to be experiencing these now and then. Some kids and adults will fall out of bed or even sleepwalk. He's too high up for that."

Cole still stared sightlessly ahead, but then he hiccupped and finally lay back down.

"This is going to be tricky, Ethan. But let's let him be quiet and settle down for a few minutes, then I wonder if you can reach up there and quietly pick him up while I pull his mattress down to the floor. Tomorrow I'll turn that lower bunk level into a regular bed."

"I wish he wouldn't scream like that," Molly mumbled from the doorway. "He wakes me up and then gives *me* nightmares just listening to him."

Hannah gently rubbed Cole's back. "I'm sorry, honey, but I think it's all over now. Go back to bed, okay?"

She yawned and gave Cole a bleary look. "Cynthia took him to the doctor right away when he did this. But there wasn't anything wrong."

"Did he ever have these problems before your parents' accident?"

"I dunno. I never heard him." Molly shrugged and shuffled back to her room.

It was nearly midnight by the time Cole was settled in his bed on the floor, with an arm flung over Maisie, who had curled up next to him. Her lips whiffled softly with doggy snores.

"That was quite an experience," Ethan said on a long sigh as they left Cole's room.

"And after quite a day. Are you sure you'll be okay on the sofa? There's a little room upstairs with a single bed if you'd rather, but that room is mostly storage. It'll be really cold."

He laughed at that. "Believe me, the sofa and that big stack of blankets on it or that upstairs room would be ten times better than any place I had to sleep in Iraq."

"Can I get you any acetaminophen or ibuprofen?"

"I'm good."

She lingered just inside the living room. "Um, if you get hungry, help yourself to anything in the cupboards or fridge. Especially the turkey. I don't think we'll ever be able to finish all of it."

Cole's night terror episode had been a perfect lead-in to the questions she wanted to ask, but now it was late and she could only imagine how uncomfortable it was for Ethan to be still standing on that bad leg, no matter what he claimed.

"Good night, Ethan. If you need more blankets or different pillows, you'll find them in the hall closet."

He crossed his arms and gave her an assessing look. "Well, what is it?"

"What?"

"You look like you've wanted to say something for

the past half hour. You might as well get it over with."
He lifted an eyebrow. "If you'd rather I didn't stay, I
can start up your snowblower and work on the drive,
and then see what that SUV can do about getting me
back to town."

"No way. The last time I looked, some of the drifts
were well over three feet, and it must be worse close to
town. The fire chief told me hours ago that the main
highway to town was already impassable. Anyway, the
kids are happy that you're staying for the night."

"Then, what is it?"

She edged into the living room, sat on the arm of
one of the chairs and squared her shoulders. "I know
it isn't my place to pry. But I couldn't help but notice
your reactions the moment the power went out with a
bang. Or when Cole started screaming."

He took the other chair, his eyes never leaving her
face. "And?"

"Both times, it seemed like you'd been transported
back to a different place. Like you weren't even here."

"Is that a problem for you?" he asked.

She raised a hand in frustration. "You're being ob-
tuse. You have to know what I'm getting at."

He didn't answer.

"You were in a dangerous part of the world. You were
badly injured," she continued doggedly. "You must have
seen and done things the rest of us can't even imagine.
So I'd guess PTSD is a part of your life now. And after
an explosion close enough to take your hand, a traumatic brain injury—concussion—would not be unexpected. So is a TBI in your picture, too?"

"You were right in the first place. It isn't really your place to pry."

She huffed out an impatient breath. "Well, then. Let me try again. You were at Walter Reed for how many months? Before Rob and Dee's car accident, and you said you were released sometime this month. So...seven months, maybe eight?"

He looked away.

"I don't think anyone could have gone through all you did without some PTSD and a concussion—possibly severe—from such a close-proximity blast. They must have assessed you carefully and provided treatment. Did they say anything about long-term effects? Did they send you to support groups? A counselor?"

When he didn't reply, she had her answer. "Of course they did, but you either didn't attend or didn't participate when you did go."

A muscle ticked along the side of his jaw.

"I'm not trying to badger you or sound like an interfering mother, honest." She gave a self-deprecating laugh. "I just want to know where you're at with this, because you want time with the kids. You even say you want full custody, though I plan to oppose that every step of the way because I feel they'll be happier here in the country. Near a close-knit, friendly little town instead of some big-city condo. But during whatever amount of time they spend with you, are you truly capable of keeping them safe?"

"Of course I am," he said, his voice level.

"I know you mean that, and you want it to be true. But I also know that blast injuries can cause a big list of long-term repercussions with TBI, and that PTSD can last for decades, especially if not addressed. Depression, episodes of irritability, anger issues and memory loss are just a few…and they can make family life difficult. So again, I'm asking. How are you, really? I want to know if you really are capable of dealing with these kids, or if your goal of custody is based on a sense of duty and responsibility to your brother."

He scrubbed a palm down his face then leaned forward and propped his elbows on his thighs. "Yes, I had a concussion—they tell me I was knocked out for about an hour. But after that I was in a hospital for a long time—plenty of time for that to heal. All of my symptoms—the headaches, dizziness, vertigo, confusion—were gone in a couple weeks."

"Thank goodness," Hannah breathed. "I'm glad to hear it."

"As for the PTSD, how common is that these days? I'm working past it month by month. It doesn't affect me every day. And I'm not the only soldier who hasn't wanted the support groups—I've heard only fifty percent of us actually seek help."

"The effect can last for decades, Ethan. Some people never realize how much better they could feel if they only sought help."

He shrugged. "Maybe I am startled by loud noises. It's self-preservation for anyone after being in the Middle East so long. And who wouldn't have nightmares after some of the things you see over there? But I've been dealing with it on my own and doing fine. End of story."

"I see."

"So you don't need to worry about it. I promise you I have no issues that affect my ability to take care of the kids. None." He glanced at his wristwatch. "And with that, I'd like to turn in. It's been a long day."

"Good night." She hesitated, wanting this conversation to end on a more casual note, but then headed for her room. She shut the door quietly and leaned on it, thinking over all he'd done and said since first arriving at her door.

Funny, how people changed. He'd been a handsome daredevil when they'd first met—the kind of bad boy who could light up a movie screen or make a girl fall in love and want to take off on wild and crazy adventures with him, whatever the danger.

But he was different now. A man seasoned by years in the military, a man driven by responsibility and honor to right the wrongs of his irresponsible brother.

And he was a man with a good heart, who could be kind and gentle with kids and animals, yet still possessed the kind of indefinable charisma that drew her as much now as it had thirteen years ago. Even more so, as a man instead of the reckless boy he'd once been.

But between the two of them, he was *not* the one who should have custody of the children.

So whatever her personal attraction to him, she couldn't lose sight of her most important goal: helping Molly and Cole adapt to their new life in Aspen Creek. And making sure they felt loved and secure, before a caseworker arrived to judge whether or not this move had been the right one.

And she had just thirty days to do it.

* * *

Ethan stared at the flickering light of the fireplace long after Hannah said good-night, an ugly torrent of dark memories and troubled emotions making it impossible to sleep. He'd managed to bury all of it in some deep recess of his mind, where it could no longer take over his every waking thought and visit him in nightmares.

But now Hannah's persistent questions had set it all free.

Or maybe it had happened because he'd seen the terror on Cole's face and had heard him screaming inconsolably on and on and on, until he'd finally fallen back onto his pillow, exhausted. What kind of childish horrors had spun through his brain to incite such fear?

Ethan knew all too well about nightmares and the true horrors of this world.

Wounded and dying women and children, the heartbreaking collateral damage of war. Body parts and rivers of blood, and young men barely old enough to vote screaming in pain, begging for help as they lay dying. Begging for the chance to go home again.

His two best buddies—who had died because of him.

He'd seen the insurgent lob a grenade into the back of the transport vehicle. He'd lunged for it. But the others crammed inside had been dozing and he hadn't been able to crawl over them in time to throw it out.

The explosion had turned that vehicle into a scene of carnage.

If he'd only moved faster, he could have prevented it. If he could have fought off his loss of consciousness, he could have stemmed arterial wounds and saved the lives of his two closest buddies.

But he'd failed, and the crushing guilt would be like an anvil in his chest forever.

Chapter Nine

At seven the next morning Hannah started a pot of coffee and checked the local weather—clear and cold—and the closing announcements on the laptop she kept on the kitchen counter.

With the schools still planning a two-hour delay, she could let the kids sleep in a while longer, though if the county plow didn't come by they wouldn't need to worry about going anywhere at all.

Ethan was already outside using the snowblower, though from the looks of things it was barely making a dent in the deep snowdrift that had crossed the front yard and banked halfway up the windows along the side of his SUV.

After calling the clinic to let the receptionist know she wouldn't be in until ten at the earliest, she began her morning routine of letting the dogs and puppies outside, cleaning cages and litter boxes, and filling the food and water dishes.

Penelope nickered when Hannah appeared in the garage, anticipating her special, geriatric horse pellets, which were now likely a pile of ash. Hannah brought her more hay, water and a handful of baby carrots as a treat.

"Sorry," she murmured as she rubbed just the right spot behind the pony's furry ears. "No pellets today."

The pony suddenly swiveled her ears and snorted, her head high. And soon Hannah could hear it, too—the distant, familiar rumble of a snowplow making its way up Spruce Road.

"Well, old girl—looks like you're in luck. We'll be able to get into town and get you more feed, after all."

At ten fifteen Hannah stamped the snow from her boots in the entryway of the Aspen Creek Clinic and then stopped at the front desk for a printout of her patient schedule.

The waiting room walls were now strung with clear Christmas lights and jewel-toned metallic ornaments hung from the ceiling over the reception counter and the office area behind it.

Hannah admired the sparkly lights. "Wow—great job of decorating, Connie."

"I'm only halfway done. Wait till you see this place tomorrow."

"I can't wait. Sorry about the delay getting here. Did you have to reschedule many of my patients?"

"Most of them were country people who were snowed in and couldn't make it into town, either." The fiftysomething receptionist glanced at her computer screen. "And those who live in town sounded just as happy not to brave the roads. I cleared the schedule until eleven just in case you were delayed even further, so now you've got some time to catch your breath. How did it go with the kiddos this morning?"

"You raised three kids. How in the world did you manage?" Hannah rolled her eyes. "I felt like a field commander. Getting them fed, dressed and loaded into the car was quite a feat, because neither of them wanted to go to school."

"Your niece is in sixth grade, right? Tough age for a new school— especially midyear."

"I know. She was so nervous about walking into school—but adamant about me not going in with her. I'm praying that she'll find some friendly faces in her classes."

Connie offered a sympathetic smile. "Middle school years are the worst. And Cole?"

"First grade. Parents and guardians need to walk in with the younger kids, so I'm glad about that. I got to introduce him to his new teacher, and I saw a few boys I know from church, so I introduced him to them, too."

Connie tapped the tip of a pencil against her lips. "You know, I think my neighbor has a first-grader. Maybe we can get them together for a playdate sometime."

"That would be wonderful." Hannah glanced at her watch. "I need to make a few phone calls, so I'll be in my office."

"Oh…and, Hannah?" Connie's voice wafted down the hall. "So sorry to hear about your fire. I heard about it on the scanner."

Hannah walked past the first four exam rooms to her office and stepped inside, feeling, as always, a little rush of pleasure at having this private space to call her own. At her first job, in the next town over, she'd shared a cramped office with the director of nursing. No windows, no extra space, and the dreary mustard walls had made each day depressing. But here she'd been allowed to decorate just as she wished.

The walls were now a bright ivory that made the most of the sunshine streaming through the two large windows facing the west. She'd found the L-shaped oak desk and matching wall of bookshelves at an estate sale.

She sank into the leather swivel chair behind her desk and flipped through the pile of message slips, copies of new doctor's orders, today's hospital admission list and assorted mail left in a pile on her desk, then listened to her phone messages.

It looked like a busy day, so far.

Eight scheduled clinic appointments, afternoon rounds in the small, ten-bed hospital wing, with four patients to see there, and two quarterly assessments for residents in the twenty-bed, long-term-care unit.

At the sound of footsteps coming down the hall, she looked up and smiled. "Connie, could you check with—"

But it wasn't Connie who stood glowering at her from the open doorway.

"Gladys." Hannah cleared her throat. "Is there something I can do for you?"

"Certainly not." The woman breezed into the office and planted her hands on the back of one of the barrel chairs, her long, red-lacquered nail digging deep into the upholstery. "I'm no longer a patient at this clinic, to my relief."

In her seventies, with the austere, patrician elegance

of someone wealthy and powerful, Gladys never hesitated to make a scene, and never seemed to care who saw it.

At least there weren't any patients waiting in the nearby exam rooms.

Hannah waited as the woman glanced around the office and sniffed her displeasure.

"I just wanted you to know that I've heard about your little debacle yesterday, and how you've risked the lives of those poor animals in your care."

"Debacle?" Hannah blinked. "A shed on my property caught fire. No animals were even in it. Not one animal was harmed."

As usual, the woman ignored her. "I'm appalled at your so-called rescue operation. Amateurs have no business placing homeless animals at risk. I've called the state inspectors—again—and expect they will be visiting you very soon. You will see, missy, that you aren't so powerful as you think."

She was back to harping on their unfortunate, shared past history. *Again.*

Dr. Martin, long since retired, had apparently caved to her every whim regarding her prescriptions—probably to ensure her hefty donations to the hospital continued. The hospital had profited well—case in point, the new hospital wing named in her family's honor.

But Dr. Martin hadn't done her any favors.

Powerful sleeping pills, antianxiety meds, pain meds—she'd been insistent on them all, and livid when Hannah had refused to provide refill prescriptions. That Hannah had alerted Dr. Martin's replacements about the situation had been the last straw as far as Gladys was concerned.

When Gladys could no longer use her wealth to get whatever she wanted, she'd started going somewhere else for her health care. Hannah prayed it was someplace good.

"If you did call the state, that's fine." Hannah sighed. "As you know already, I have my nonprofit animal shelter license, as do the other two women in town who volunteer to help with rescues. We've each been properly inspected and approved, after meeting the required standards of care. We pay our annual fees."

Gladys drew herself up, reminding Hannah of a huffy bantam hen. "We shall see about that. I know that—"

Connie appeared in the doorway, tentatively waving a slip of paper. "Excuse me—so sorry to interrupt. I have an emergency message from the doctor. Can you pick up line three? It's urgent. And private."

Gladys glowered at Hannah, then pivoted and strode out of the office, her high heels clicking down the hallway.

"Is that really a message?" Hannah asked dryly.

Connie swept imaginary perspiration from her forehead. "No. But I could hear that woman clear down at the reception desk and figured you'd want her gone before patients started arriving. What's with her, anyway? Just because she's on the city council doesn't mean she can run roughshod over people."

"She's unhappy about a lot of things, I guess—but not about anything I can change. I just keep praying that she will mellow…or finally see the errors of her ways. But I'm beginning to doubt it will ever happen."

By three o'clock Hannah was finished for the day and more than eager to pick up Cole and Molly at school.

She'd worried about them all day, hoping they liked their teachers and had found it easy to find some new friends and gain acceptance, so important at their ages.

She'd just said farewell to Connie and started out the door when she heard the phone ring behind her and the loudspeakers crackle.

"Code Orange—ER. Code Blue—ER. Code Orange—ER."

A mass casualty, with at least one critical patient heading for the ER.

She turned around to find Connie gripping the phone receiver, her face white as chalk. "A van with a family of six kids. T-boned by a dually pickup at an icy inter-section. One ambulance and three EMT units on the way. ETA fifteen minutes."

Hannah hesitated.

Ethan was the only other adult the kids had met in this town, besides their teachers or, briefly, Keeley and Sophie, who would still be at work.

He was only one they would recognize and trust to pick them up at school.

But the risk was clear.

Would he recall this day, and use it to prove to the caseworkers that Hannah's job made it too difficult for her to provide care for them in an emergency? Would he twist this to his benefit?

But there was no one else she could ask, and she'd have to deal with that later.

She whipped out her cell phone, checked the directory and scrawled a cell number for Connie. "Ethan Williams is the children's uncle from Dallas, and he's in town. Please call him. Ask him to pick up the kids at school, and give him the directions. Tell him I don't know when I'll be done here, but I'll try to text."

"But the schools—will they let a stranger do that?"

"Please call the school to explain. They'll see the hospital number on their caller ID. But text me if I need to call them personally."

And then Hannah began to run.

His mission had been a success, despite wary assessments by the principals at both schools and their demand that he show his driver's license.

Ethan looked at the two kids in his rearview mirror. "How was your first day at school?"

Total silence.

"Okay, what was the best part? There must have been something good."

Not one peep.

"Something bad?" It was probably wrong to ask, but now he was curious.

"I hated it," Molly ground out.

"Why?"

"It was just like when we moved back to Dallas last spring. Everyone looks at you like you're weird or have a disease. They whisper to each other about it and stare at you. And I just want to die." She shrugged. "You asked."

"That bad, huh."

She folded her arms over her chest. "I'm not going back there again. If you make me, I'm gonna run away, and then everyone will be sorry."

"I see." He kept a solemn face as he mulled over her words, sorry about her unhappiness but also amused at her childish logic. "So where would you go? It's mighty cold and snowy outside."

She glared at him.

"Well, then, how about you, Cole? What was the best part of today at school?"

"Chicken nuggets."

"Anything else?"

"We couldn't have recess outside, but we played dodgeball in the gym."

"Sounds like a good first day to me." He turned to look over his shoulder at the two of them. "Okay, then, now that you're buckled in, where would you like to go? Are you hungry?"

Molly dropped her chin down to the backpack she held on her lap, face glum. Cole darted a glance at him then looked away.

"The thing is, I don't have a key to Hannah's house, though she might have one hidden somewhere outside. But she isn't answering her phone so I can't take you out there just yet."

The backseat remained silent.

"So what do you think of this? Hannah said the pony's feed was lost in the fire, and I don't think she's had time to buy more. So, we could go to the feed store outside of town and buy some sacks of whatever it is that

Penelope eats. Then we could go to the malt shop and get whatever you want."

"Could we play a game there?" Cole's voice was barely audible, but the hope in his eyes touched Ethan's heart.

"Of course. And after that we could go back to that hardware store and see if we can find us all some ice skates. I saw the rink in the town square on my way to pick you two up, and it looked pretty nice. What do you say?"

Molly fidgeted. "I don't know how to skate."

"I don't, either," Cole piped up.

"Neither do I, but I'll bet we can learn."

"What if kids from school are skating?" Molly pleaded, clearly thinking it would be a social disaster. "They'll think I look really dumb."

After he finally coaxed an agreement from both of them, he drove to the feed store, where the clerk knew Hannah well and looked up her account to figure out which feed Ethan needed to buy.

At the malt shop, the kids each ordered hot-fudge sundaes with extra whipped cream, then only ate half before going back to play the pinball machines.

From the sounds of the chimes, they weren't scoring, but at least they seemed enthralled by the colorful lights.

Keeping one eye on the kids, Ethan opened the new paperback he'd bought today, but his thoughts kept straying to the call from the hospital receptionist.

A horrific accident.

Victims being stabilized, four leaving the local hospital by helicopter. Several surgeries being dealt with here…and Hannah was in the thick of it.

He hadn't realized what a range of services PAs could provide, much less that she was qualified to assist the doctor performing the emergency surgeries. But the receptionist had certainly filled him in, leaving him with the uncomfortable feeling that he'd been underestimating Hannah from the first time they'd met. Irresponsible? Flighty and immature?

Maybe back then, but she'd also been bright. She'd charted her course, buckled down and now carried a lot of responsibility on her delicate shoulders.

He could no longer discount her out of hand as someone who couldn't handle the responsibility of taking on Molly and Cole.

Not that he planned to give up.

A group of kids came into the malt shop, laughing and jostling each other as they headed for the pinball machines. Molly and Cole promptly returned to Ethan's side.

"You don't want to play anymore? I could go over there with you, if you want."

"No." Molly shook her head. "Can we leave? *Please?*"

"Okay. Next up, skates at the hardware store."

Which turned out to be more complicated than he'd thought, and a lot more expensive.

Still, the young clerk seemed knowledgeable and took his time fitting Molly and Cole with lightly used skates offering good ankle support, and found a well-used and abused pair of adult hockey skates for Ethan, as well.

A mother and her son were shopping at the same time. "If you're going to skate at the town square, you should know that helmets are mandatory," she said with a kindly smile. She showed him the red, white and blue helmet in her shopping basket.

He returned her smile. "Thanks."

"I'm Margaret. And this is my son Trevor. I'd guess he's about the same age as your daughter—sixth grade?"

The kid looked like one of the overly cute boy-band singers Ethan had once glimpsed on television. Apparently even Molly thought he was cute because she blushed a furious shade of red and looked away, clearly mortified.

"She's my niece. And, yes, she's in sixth," Ethan confirmed. "Molly and her brother are from Dallas and just started school today."

From the anguished sound Molly made, it seemed as if she wished Ethan would drop dead and the boy would disappear before she imploded from embarrassment.

"Well, that's real nice," the woman said, apparently oblivious to Molly's groan. "I love your familiar accents. We moved up from Oklahoma two years ago, so your kids and mine have your Southern roots in common. Maybe y'all will have some classes together."

The boy tipped his head and looked Molly over. "I saw you in Stone's math class, and maybe English. I can't believe I got Stone—I was really hoping I would."

Molly lifted her chin a few millimeters, but didn't quite meet his gaze. "I heard she's really awful."

He grinned. "Only if you don't try. She's actually way cool. She skydives and stuff like that. Sometimes she tells us about it in class."

His mom touched his shoulder and tipped her head

toward the cash register. "Trevor's dad is waiting in the car, so we need to get going. Nice to meet you."

Molly surreptitiously watched them leave, her eyes filled with awe. She let out a deep breath.

"So, looks like you made a friend," Ethan murmured. "Maybe you'll see him again at the ice rink or in school."

"Uncle Ethan!" But her mortified tone certainly didn't jibe with the glow in her starstruck eyes.

Chapter Ten

Hannah texted Ethan at five o'clock. When he didn't answer, she tried again at five thirty and at a quarter of six.

Then she began to worry.

The past three hours had been hectic and tense. Frantic family members poured into the hospital and milled around the waiting room and hallway, desperately waiting for news about the three accident victims still in the Aspen Creek ER and those who had been airlifted.

Now that it was all over, Hannah zipped her coat and hurried to her SUV. After turning the key she waited a few minutes for it to warm up.

It had been almost three hours since the kids had gotten out of school, but there'd been no word from Ethan beyond a brief text telling her he'd successfully picked them up. Had he taken them to her house?

The other possibility made her stomach clench.

What if he'd taken off with them for Texas, and planned to petition the court with his urgent need to take over their custody?

She could call the sheriff, report them missing, but were they, really? With the SUV's ubiquitous Minnesota plates and not knowing the license plate number, finding that vehicle in the Wisconsin-Minnesota area would be like finding the proverbial needle in a haystack.

Her pulse pounding, she pressed her gloved fingertips against her temples, willing away the beginnings of a headache. *Please, Lord, let them all be here in town. Please.*

She shifted into Drive and headed slowly toward Main Street, searching the parked cars on either side of the street near the cafés and restaurants. Nothing. Not even near the malt shop, or the busy town square, where she could see a colorful crowd gliding on the ice rink or...

She blinked. Circled the square again. Then began checking the dimly lit side-street parking surrounding the square while trying to call Ethan's phone.

Her breath caught. There it was. A silver SUV, Minnesota plates. She veered to the side of the street, double parked and hurried to the vehicle. Sure enough, Molly and Cole's backpacks were inside.

Relief made her knees weaken, followed by a surge of anger at Ethan's thoughtlessness. He should have responded to her texts. She was the children's guardian and he had no right to...

Be thankful, a still, small voice whispered. *They're here, and they are safe.*

She took a steadying breath. Parked her SUV in the first empty spot she found and then strode toward the ice rink.

Safe or not, Ethan had definitely illustrated that he

was still careless and irresponsible, no better than he'd been thirteen years ago. And once again she would learn her lesson well.

"Uh, oh." Wobbling on his skates, Cole tugged on Ethan's sleeve. "Are we in trouble? Hannah's coming and she looks *mad*."

Ethan held Cole's other hand and steadied him. It took just a second to find Hannah in the crowd. Her long blond hair swung with each purposeful stride as she approached the four-foot-high wooden wall surrounding the ice rink. And yes, indeed—she definitely didn't look happy.

"We'd better go see what she wants, buddy. Ready?" Ethan glided slowly across the rink with Cole in tow.

Molly was still clinging to the fence off to one side, awkward as a scarecrow on her skates. But a girl in a purple coat was talking to her now and gesturing toward the center of the rink.

Molly let go of the fence and reached for the girl's arm but flailed wildly, her feet going in opposite directions. She lurched forward to grab the fence, missed and landed on her rear.

But instead of scowling, she was grinning at the other girl. *Grinning*. Ethan did a double take. That glimpse of her smile made every bump and bruise and penny of this adventure worthwhile, along with the aching muscles and tendons he'd have tomorrow.

Except now Hannah had reached the rink fence, her mouth flattened in a grim line and her eyes flashing fire.

Ethan continued toward her slowly, thankful Cole

was with him. She seemed to be upset, but surely she wouldn't make a big scene in front of Cole and so many townspeople whom she probably knew.

"Why didn't you answer my texts?" she demanded in a low voice. "I've been frantic."

Surprised, he raised an eyebrow. "You asked me to pick up the kids and I did."

"But now it's after six o'clock. And I had no idea where you were." Her eyes narrowed. "It didn't cross your mind to let me know?"

Yep, she was angry, all right, but he could also see the worry in her eyes. Had anyone ever been that concerned about Rob and him?

All around him, he could see parents hovering over their kids, watchful of every step. Consoling the little ones who fell, cheering on every tiny success.

It was like watching the old sitcom reruns where the loving mom always wore pearls, heels and a ruffled apron, and the dad dispensed calm, sage advice from a favorite chair. He'd watched those shows as a kid with longing, mystified by a world so different from his own.

He could remember Dad as irritable and impatient over his unexpected role as a single dad after mom left. Gramps wasn't much better. Rob and he had mostly experienced an unstable childhood of changes beyond their control.

He jerked his thoughts back to the present. "I did text, and told you I'd picked them up. I don't have a key to your house, so I called the ER to leave a message for you, wondering if you usually leave a key hidden somewhere. The guy who answered sounded pretty stressed out. He said you were assisting in surgery and couldn't be interrupted. He said he'd give you the message."

"I never got it. But I've been trying to text you and you never answered. Not once."

"My phone is in the SUV, hooked up to the charger. But it only charges if the vehicle is running, so it's still basically dead."

Her agitation seemed to fade. "Where have you been?"

"After I got the kids, we went to get pony food, then to the malt shop. After that, we bought skates, where I think Molly fell for a cute guy from her math class, then we came here. Where, if you take a look to the right, you'll see that Molly is making a new friend. I think. Unless she crashes and nails the poor girl again with her skate blades."

Hannah's steely expression softened. "She needs a friend so much. I'm sorry, Ethan. I was terrified that something had happened."

He eased closer to the fence. "You mean you were terrified that I might have taken the kids. A rather surprising lack of trust, if you ask me."

She looked away, a delicate rose tint blooming on her cheekbones. "It's been a stressful day, in a lot of ways. I apologize for thinking the worst, when you were doing such a good job with them. I was just so worried."

"On that note, I didn't have a key, so your dogs have been in the house since ten this morning. I can finish up here and drop the kids off, if you want to get home to take care of things there."

"I hate to have you make the trip, but that would be super—oh, look!"

He followed her gaze to the far side of the rink where Molly was clinging to her new friend's arm as they slowly, painfully, made their way along the ice. Molly's knees buckled and she went down, but the girl patiently offered her hand and Molly quickly scrambled back to her feet.

"Believe it or not," Ethan drawled, "it's going a lot better."

"Me, too," Cole chirped, his cheeks ruddy from the cold. "I'm better. Let go, Uncle Ethan."

Cole edged onto the ice with a wide-legged stance, moving his skates with tiny forward-and-back scissor motions that gained him little progress. "See?" He looked over his shoulder. "I can stand up!"

Hannah cheered. "Wonderful! I'm so proud of you."

"I haven't been the best teacher, but I saw a sign offering lessons. That might help." Ethan grinned.

Looking up at him, she rested a hand on his. "Great idea. I'll definitely check it out. Thanks again, Ethan, for everything. I'm going to make a quick stop at the grocery store and then be on my way home."

"We'll be there as soon as I can round them up, though it might take a while." But Molly's new friend was nowhere to be seen and Cole was trying to pick himself off the ice.

So maybe it wouldn't take as long as he thought.

Hannah parked in front of her garage just as Ethan's headlights swung into the driveway. When none of his car doors opened, she went to the front driver's-side door and rapped lightly on the window.

He rolled the window partway down. "We'll be in—just give us a minute."

"Something wrong?" She peered in the backseat window, where Cole appeared to be pouting and Molly wore a scowl. She stepped back to Ethan's window. "Oh, dear."

He nodded. "We've been talking about people who are friends and those who aren't. And how you can't really make others play nice."

"So...something happened at the ice rink?"

Ethan nodded. "The girl who befriended Molly pretty much stabbed her in the back as soon as some other girls came out on the ice." He looked at the rearview mirror. "Right, Molly? She wasn't kind at all. But I promise you, you'll meet nice people before long."

"I hate it here," Molly burst out. "Those girls were *laughing* at me. And the kids at school are all *mean*. They hate me, and say I talk like a stupid cowboy. I'm not going back there. Not ever."

"I love your Texas accent, sweetie," Hannah said. "And others will, too. I think it makes you very cool."

Molly didn't budge.

"I don't blame you for feeling upset, but let's go into the house, okay? It's cold out here and we can talk later." Hannah opened Cole's door and helped him out, then grabbed the ice skates that were on the floor.

Ethan went to the back of his SUV and carried a fifty-pound sack of horse feed into the garage, then retrieved her groceries from the backseat of the Subaru and carried them into the house, with Cole on his heels.

Molly still sat in the backseat, her face filled with misery.

"Honey, I know you're upset. But please come inside, okay? You're going to get really cold out here."

At the sound of a faint, pitiful whimper, Hannah straightened and looked around the yard. "Do you hear something?"

Molly's scowl deepened and she sunk lower in her seat. But then she must have heard it, too, because she straightened and looked out her window.

The overcast sky cast only a faint glow over the heavy drifts of snow in the yard and the high banks the snowplow had left along each side of the road.

"That sound didn't come from the house or garage," Hannah said quietly. "It sounds to me like something is hurt."

Molly got out of the car and joined her as she scanned the yard. "There—" She pointed to the base of the metal flagpole by the garage. "What is it?"

She hurried toward the small, quivering shape.

"No, Molly. Stay back," Hannah called out sharply as she went after the girl.

Now she could make out the shape—a skeletal dog of some kind that had been chained to the flagpole while they were away. Chained outside in the snow. With no shelter, in rapidly dropped temperatures.

"Don't get too close. She's terrified and she might bite."

But Molly ignored her and crouched, murmuring gentle words. Still, the dog cowered as far away from her as the chain allowed, its tail tucked between its legs.

Molly lifted tear-filled eyes to Hannah. "Just *look* at her. She's all bones, and there's something weird about her neck—it looks crusty. What if we hadn't come back tonight? She would have frozen to death out here. Who would do such a terrible thing?"

Far too many horrible people, Hannah thought. Molly's tender heart hadn't yet encountered the wretched people who locked dogs away in dirty kennels and never let them out, or kept them on chains in miserable conditions.

Which was exactly why Hannah had begun her private, no-kill rescue. "The one good thing is that someone cared enough to bring her here, where she'll now have a chance."

"W-will she be okay?"

"I'm going to get some treats for her and hope to make friends before we try to move her inside."

But Molly was already edging closer to the stray, oblivious to the risk of approaching a dog this scared. Her sympathy would doubtless overcome all caution if she was left for even a minute without adult supervision.

"On second thought—can *you* go get a little stainless-steel food pan, put some kibble in it and bring it to me? And switch on the outside floodlights when you come back out."

Molly raced into the garage and returned in a flash with an overflowing food pan. "What do I do—should I put it down in front of her?"

"No. Come over here behind me and let's see if this works."

Hannah crouched and tossed a piece of kibble a couple feet in front of the dog. The animal yelped and fought the chain, but she was already at its end and had no escape. When she settled, her bony sides were heaving and she was wobbling on her feet.

"That's a good pup," Hannah murmured in a gentle, soothing voice. "You'll be glad to come inside. Yes, you will. A nice warm bed, doggie friends, good food."

She tossed more kibble, and this time the poor thing just quivered. Then she edged forward with her head down and ears flattened. She gave Hannah a long, wary look, then suspiciously sniffed at the kibble before wolfing it down.

"Can she sleep in my room tonight?" Molly whispered. "Please?"

"Not yet. I think she's been injured. She's scared. Just coming into the garage would be a big transition right now. She might not be accustomed to any sort of indoor shelter."

"But she's so cold," Molly pleaded. "Look at her shaking."

"The garage is heated. I just keep the temp low so the transition of the animals going outside isn't so abrupt." Hannah tossed more kibble, a few inches closer to her own feet. The dog took a half step closer and eyed the food. Then she backed up.

"She's probably shaking from fear as well as hypothermia. The poor girl doesn't have any body fat at all and I hate to think what I'll find under that wet, matted coat."

"Can you take care of...of whatever is wrong?"

"I'm going to talk to the vet in the morning and see if I can take her in for an exam before I go to work."

"It's so cool that you do this." Molly looked at Hannah with newfound respect. "But how will you get her there? She looks so scared."

"If she's too frightened to be lured into my car, I'll

see if the vet can stop by. I don't want to waste any time if she needs antibiotics or other treatment, and I very much doubt she's had any vaccinations. I also need her checked for an identification chip."

Molly rocked back on her heels, aghast. "Why?"

"She could have been stolen from a good home and then mistreated, or maybe she ran away from nice owners and got lost, then fell into the wrong hands. There might be children who miss her terribly. Or, sadly, maybe it was her real owner who is responsible for this."

Molly's eyes widened with horror and started to fill with tears.

"You should probably go inside," Hannah said quickly. "Take your bath and get your pajamas on. You must be cold out here."

Molly shook her head. "No. I'm staying."

"Just a few more minutes then." Hannah tossed another piece of kibble and this time the dog crept cautiously forward on its belly to within a few feet of them. She nabbed the morsel and didn't retreat.

"What a good girl you are," Hannah crooned in a soft, low voice. "You'll be so pretty when you put on a few pounds and have a nice bath. Where have you been to end up looking like this?"

"What should we call her, Aunt Hannah? She can't just be 'the dog.'"

Hannah glanced at her and smiled. "Since you were the one who found her, I think you should decide."

"Belle."

"From the cartoon?"

Molly shook her head firmly. "Because she is going to be beautiful. I just know it."

"Perfect. Then Belle it is."

After another ten minutes of patience, the dog finally edged forward enough to sniff Hannah's hand. Another fifteen and she finally accepted gentle strokes against the side of her head, though her tail was still clamped between her back legs and the hair along her spine raised.

"Molly, can you do me a favor? I've got her distracted right now. Can you give us a wide berth and slowly, quietly, unfasten the chain from the flagpole? Then bring that end to me. Try to not let it jingle too much."

After taking care of the chain, Molly watched with rapt attention as Hannah slowly eased the frightened dog into the garage and offered her a pan of water.

The chickens were already roosting for the night and didn't stir, but Lucy barked once, then looked over the fence surrounding her pen at the newcomer with frank curiosity. Once the garage door was shut, Hannah breathed a sigh of relief.

Whatever happened now, at least the poor thing couldn't panic and escape into the cold winter night.

"Now I need to fix a big pen for her, with lots of blankets, and she'll be comfy for the night. And I also need to put the other dogs out one last time. So, young lady," Hannah said firmly, though she couldn't quite contain a smile. "You've been a great help, but now it's almost nine o'clock and this time I mean it. Go get ready for bed. I'll be in shortly, so we can talk about your tough day at school."

Chapter Eleven

When Hannah finally finished her chores outside, she walked into the house and found Ethan on the living room floor, where he and Cole were playing yet another game of Candy Land.

"I figured you and Molly were busy outside, so I thought I'd better stay with Cole until you came in," Ethan said as he stood. "I wasn't sure what to do about bath time, though, so I just let him get into his pajamas. He's also had a bedtime snack, and just a couple minutes ago he brushed his teeth. Molly is taking a shower."

"Wow. Thank so much, Ethan. I appreciate it." She smiled down at Cole. "So, let's go read some stories, all right? Just a few, though. I should have been in an hour ago to get you to bed. Sorry."

"I had fun with Uncle Ethan. You can go back outside if you want, 'cause we're playing a game."

"You'll have to finish another time. Can you say good-night to your uncle?"

Cole hesitated, then stood and plowed into Ethan and

wrapped his arms around Ethan's good leg. "Thanks! Come again, okay? *Someday* you're gonna win."

"I doubt that. You are way too good." Ethan ruffled the boy's hair and let his hand linger, as if he were savoring a moment he didn't want to end. "Sleep tight, okay?"

Hannah walked into Cole's room and flipped on the light. She gasped. "Ethan—did you do this?"

He sauntered into the room. "I hope it's all right. I didn't want to think about Cole using a mattress on the floor again, so he and I studied the situation while you were outside. Is it all right?"

"All right? It's perfect. Thank you so much."

He shrugged. "It was pretty easy. We switched some of the pieces so he has a regular twin bed now, and the spare pieces are in the upstairs storeroom in case you want to switch things back again."

Overcome with the sudden temptation to give him a kiss of thanks on the cheek, she took a quick step back, knowing it might unleash a flood of emotions she could not afford. The children were all that mattered right now. "It's wonderful. Absolutely wonderful."

"I like it, too," Cole said, climbing under the covers. "I'm not so high up, in case I have to go to the bathroom. And Maisie can even be on my bed, see?" The dog, curled up at the foot of the bed, thumped her tail once at the sound of her name.

"This is perfect in every way," Hannah said, her heart overflowing with love for this sweet little boy. And with sadness, too. Dee had missed so much of her children's lives already. "Let's say our prayers now, okay? And then we'd better let you get a good night's sleep."

Cole dutifully recited his prayers. She kissed him good-night, turned on his night-light and went out to the living room, where Ethan was pensively staring into the fire he'd started earlier, his thumbs hooked in his back jeans' pockets.

"Molly is done in the shower and back in her room," he said in a low voice. "She looks pretty tired."

"I'm not surprised. Now, for the tricky part," Hannah said quietly. "Convincing her to go back to school tomorrow. And waiting for more night terrors—or not. I'll be praying that Cole will be all right."

"I was just heading out, but do you want me to stay a while longer?" he asked with a self-deprecating smile. "Not that I have any experience with either problem, but I could offer moral support."

"We'll manage. Could I offer you a cup of decaf or cocoa for the road?" she asked lightly. "Or leftover turkey? I'd be very happy to send some with you if you have a fridge."

"I've got just a tiny fridge, so I think I'll pass. Thanks, though." He reached for an envelope on the mantel and handed it to her. "This was taped to your front door when we all got home. Addressed to you, of course."

She slid a finger under the flap and withdrew a single sheet of paper. "Apparently the fire chief—who is also the local fire inspector—came out today. This is the report I can give to the insurance company."

"What did he decide?"

"Molly will be so glad to hear this. She was worried

that the fire was her fault, because she had moved the chicken's panel heater. But Bill figures it was an electrical short at the other end of the barn. Frayed wires, probably thanks to mice."

"So you shouldn't have any issues with the insurance coverage."

"I don't think so. It should just be a matter of getting the check and waiting for warm enough weather to start building another small barn." She paced the length of the living room then turned back. "I've had to make do with that old building, but this time, I want to work on plans and make it right. Clean, spacious, bright, with better exercise runs, for starters."

"A facility like that would cost many times what you'll get from your insurance claim."

"But it would be a start, anyway." She thought for a moment. "I'll have to talk to the other women who run home-based rescues like mine. Maybe we can try once again to stir up interest for a permanent shelter in town. Get the city council involved. Fund-raise and all that."

He smiled. "I believe you have more energy than anyone I ever met."

She laughed at that. "Energy, but not a whole lot of money. And I'm afraid I have an enemy on the city council. But it doesn't hurt to dream, right?"

Something sad flashed in his eyes. "No, I guess not."

She walked him to the front door. "Thanks again for taking the kids this afternoon. I have friends I could've called, but I didn't know if Molly and Cole would be comfortable with anyone except you. Not yet."

He lifted a shoulder dismissively. "No problem.

They're why I'm in Wisconsin, and I'm glad to be with them any time I can. Never hesitate to ask."

"About that…" She bit her lower lip. "I wonder if I could ask you for another favor?"

"What do you need?"

"That new dog needs a ride to the vet clinic tomorrow morning. I called Darcy—the vet—tonight on her cell, and she said she could fit us in at nine, but I have appointments starting at nine. I hate to wait till the weekend."

"No problem. Anything else?"

"Maybe. I don't know when it might happen, but there might be an inspection of my rescue facilities sometime soon. The inspector probably won't give me any advance warning, but when he arrives he'll need access to my garage. So at some point, if I can't get away from the clinic, I might need to ask you to go unlock it for him."

"No problem with that, either."

"Super. I'll show you where the spare key is. And, Ethan… I'm sorry I was so testy about where you were with the kids. I never should have assumed…"

"It's been a long time since we were together, Hannah, and we no longer know each other that well. People change. And it's no secret that our goals are polar opposites when it comes to the kids."

"Still…"

"No, your first priority is them, and that's how it should be," he said gravely. "So I'd say you were simply acting on instinct to keep them safe."

"But I didn't mean to—"

He cut her off. "Don't overthink this, Hannah. Just forget it."

Their eyes met. Locked. And then he gave her a faint, sad smile. "I've made mistakes in my life. A lot of them. But the more I'm here, the more I realize that my worst one was when I let you go."

He'd imagined himself doing any number of things on Tuesday while the kids were in school and Hannah was working at the health clinic.

Holding the leash of an emaciated, cowering dog and feeling the glares of the other three clients in a vet's waiting room was not one of them.

They had a right to look outraged at Belle's condition. He felt exactly the same way. But if they only knew how long it had taken him to beg and cajole this dog from her pen to his car, they'd be awarding him a medal.

As it was, he was pretty sure the lady in the corner chair, with a Westie as white and pristine as fresh snow, was surreptitiously calling the cops to have him arrested for animal abuse.

"Come here, sweet girl," he murmured. Belle was at the end of her leash, under the chair, as if she expected him to attack at any moment. She clearly wasn't planning to budge.

The judgmental stares aside, he'd felt his heart clench painfully at his first good view of her this morning. Her bony frame and the open sores on every bony prominence made him long to make her last owner regret he'd ever been born. What kind of person could do something like this to a helpless dog?

"Mr. Williams?" A young woman in a pink uniform

with KayCee on her name badge appeared in the doorway leading to the exam rooms. Her jaw dropped. "Oh, my goodness. Hannah called and told us about this one. But I never..." She took a deep breath. "Will she lead?"

"Not really. I can only get her to move along with bits of turkey." He gave the girl a wry smile. "Hannah just happened to have some leftovers, and I figured it was important to get her here one way or another."

"Let me try." She took the leash from him and crooned to Belle. She reached under the chair to pet her head, but the dog jerked back in abject fear.

Ethan offered her the Ziploc bag of tiny bits of turkey. "This works better. I promise."

"I read that turkey is toxic to dogs," the woman with the Westie announced, her eyes narrowed.

KayCee tipped her head toward an array of handouts on one of the end tables. "Turkey skin and fat can cause pancreatitis in dogs, and they can choke on the bones. But our vet says a little bit of the white meat is okay."

Ethan felt the glares of the other clients boring into his back as he, Belle and the vet tech slowly made their way down the hall, though by now Belle had planted her butt on the floor and was leaning back with all her might as she was being towed toward an alcove with a scale.

She feebly resisted before stepping onto the platform. The digital screen read 24.4 pounds.

"That can't be good," Ethan muttered.

The girl jotted the results on her clipboard. She ushered them into the next exam room. "Dr. Leighton will be in shortly. Just have a seat."

Here, amid the scent of sanitizer and the barking

of dogs from somewhere in the back of the building, Belle seemed to decide Ethan was her only ally in this frightening place.

She pressed her bony side tightly against his leg, her breathing fast and shallow and her head bowed in abject defeat. He ran his hand lightly along her back in long, slow strokes, then began rubbing gently behind her ears.

"What a good girl you are," he soothed. "In no time at all, you'll be romping with those other dogs at Hannah's place and sleeping on someone's bed."

Molly's, he guessed. When Hannah had called him this morning about the vet appointment, she'd said that she'd found Molly out in the garage this morning, curled up by the dog's pen.

A thirtysomething woman in a lab coat, with shiny brown hair twisted into a knot on the top of her head, stepped into the room.

"Goodness," she exclaimed as she surveyed the quivering dog. "Where have you been, poor thing?"

"Did Hannah explain when she called?"

"Yes, she did." The woman extended her hand. "Dr. Leighton. You must be Ethan?"

He nodded.

"And this must be Belle." She crouched and offered the back of her hand for Belle to consider, then ran gentle hands over the dog's emaciated frame. Whining, Belle cringed under her touch.

"She looks like she might be a springer spaniel cross, maybe with some shepherd in the mix. Without doing a DNA test, we can't really be sure, but that doesn't matter. She's a good twenty pounds under weight and if she'd gone much longer she would've gone into irreversible organ failure."

"Can you write down what she should be eating?"

The vet nodded. "Hannah has been through this before, but yes—I'll send home instructions."

"And those awful sores on her neck and hips?"

"Looks like her choke chain collar was too tight and became imbedded in her neck, and those are pressure sores over her hip bones. She must have been chained someplace where she had little or no bedding and hardly any space to move. Terrible."

Ethan winced. "Also, Hannah wants you to check for an identification chip."

"The tech can do that in a bit. In fact, we need to keep Belle for a few days. That collar has to be surgically removed. Believe it or not, she's a young dog. I'd guess around two." Dr. Leighton shook her head firmly. "Everything you see can be fixed. She deserves a far better life, and Hannah and I are going to make sure she gets it."

As if Belle understood the vet's tone and body language, if not the words, her tail began to slowly wag.

Ethan watched as the vet continued her exam, and realized he was learning about more than just Leighton's caring attitude.

His stay in Wisconsin was also revealing just how much he had misjudged Hannah all those years ago.

From choosing a challenging career where she could help people every single day, to her dedication to saving abused and abandoned animals, the depths of Hannah's own compassionate heart were far greater than he ever would have guessed.

Coupled with her love and protectiveness toward the children, he now knew she'd be a formidable opponent indeed, if their custody battle ended up in a court of law.

Chapter Twelve

Molly trudged out to Hannah's Subaru, her trademark sulk firmly in place. She joined Cole in the backseat without a word.

"So, how was your second day at school?"

"I hate this place and I want to go home. To *Texas*."

Was that what she truly wanted? Would she really be happier living with Ethan, after all—or was she simply longing for the days before her parents died?

The children's happiness was paramount, but there were so many uncertainties in that equation that Hannah didn't even want to think about it. Not yet.

Molly had fallen asleep last night before Hannah had made it to her bedroom, so there had been no chance for a much-needed discussion. And with the return of Cole's night terrors, Molly had awakened in the middle of the night, and then tossed and turned.

Lack of sleep hadn't made the child's day any better.

Molly picked at a loose thread on her backpack strap. "How is Belle?"

"She's at the vet clinic right now."

Molly jerked upright, her eyes wide with alarm. "They wouldn't— They couldn't—"

"They're taking good care of her, I promise. They're giving her IV fluids and antibiotics, and they've started treating the ulcers."

"I don't believe you. Maybe they'll decide to put her to sleep." Molly's lower lip trembled. "I want to see her. Can we go there? Right now?"

"That happened with our kitty," Cole mumbled. "She went to the vet and never came back."

Oh, dear. Hannah turned her SUV toward the vet clinic. "I'm so sorry to hear that, Cole. Was she very old and sick?"

Cole shook his head. "She couldn't come to our new 'partment so Dad sent her to heaven."

Instead of a shelter? Hannah had a feeling there was more to the story, but maybe Dee just hadn't explained it very well.

"There might have been a very good reason, sweetie. Sometime animals are suffering too much, and it's more kind to let them go."

"No," Cole insisted with a stubborn shake of his head. "She couldn't come to the 'partment when we moved. It wasn't fair."

If he was right, Hannah totally agreed. "Well, just to show you that Belle is receiving good care, we're going to the clinic. Okay? It's just a few blocks away."

Molly and Cole sat silently in the backseat until Hannah pulled into the parking lot, but they both beat her into the clinic.

Hannah followed them inside. "I have a couple of

kids here who are worried about Belle—the dog I sent in this morning. Can we see her?"

Marilyn, the sixtysomething receptionist, shook her head. "I'm sorry—"

"No!" Molly screamed. "You *killed* her?"

"Of course not," Marilyn said gently. "The vet is doing some surgery on her right now, but she should be fine."

Molly looked up at Hannah with a stricken expression. "I want to see her," she begged. "*Please*. What if she dies? I didn't even get to say goodbye."

This wasn't just about the dog, Molly realized with a pang of sorrow. It was about life and loss and grief that had to weigh on these kids every single day.

The parents they loved had left one day and never returned. How did a child ever recover from that?

"About how long until Belle is finished?"

"Maybe a half hour, but I'm not sure." Marilyn lowered her voice. "Darcy made sure it was the last appointment of the day, just in case it took longer. Imbedded choke chain. Deep."

Hannah swallowed hard then summoned a cheery smile. "Okay, kids, it's going to be a long while, and even then Belle will need to recover from anesthesia. Let's walk down Main Street."

"I want to stay." Molly plopped down on the nearest chair.

"Molly, there's nothing to do here, and it will be a long wait. Why don't we check out Keeley's cookies at her antiques store, then we can stop at the Christmas Shoppe. I'd like you both to pick out some new decorations for our Christmas tree so we can go out and cut our tree tomorrow. By then it will be time to come back and see Belle."

Feeling as if she were being followed by two reluctant ducklings, Hannah headed down Main Street. The sky was overcast with the feeling of snow in the air and dusk was falling earlier every passing day. All of the storefronts were decorated and brightly lit. Overhead, Christmas lights were twinkling on every lamppost.

At Keeley's store, the stained-glass lamps and sparkling antique chandeliers inside cast a welcoming glow onto the sidewalk. Hannah ushered the kids into the store. "This is where your pretty stained-glass bedside lamp came from, Molly. Keeley gave it to you as a gift."

Molly nodded.

From behind the cash register Keeley waved and pointed to the table with a coffeemaker, a pitcher of ice water and an array of decorated Christmas cookies on a crystal platter covered with a glass dome, then continued to wait on a customer.

"I don't suppose this would be your favorite kind of store, Cole. But would you like to look around or would you rather sit at the ice-cream table by the window and have your cookies?"

Cole zoomed to the window and settled on a wrought-iron chair. He looked up in awe at a vintage lamp with cartoon figures chasing each other around the rim of the shade.

After wandering aimlessly through the store, Molly joined her brother, her gaze fixed on a two-foot Christmas tree adorned with antique decorations in the corner. The sadness in her eyes was palpable.

"I love Christmas," Hannah said as she brought over the platter and two paper plates.

Cole tentatively picked a Santa cookie and looked up at her.

"Aren't these pretty? I'm sure it's okay if you want two."

Molly halfheartedly picked the cookie closest to her on the platter. Her gaze veered back to the tree. "It's not like Christmas this year," she said softly. "Not the same at all."

Hannah set the platter back on the serving table and brought over two waters and a black coffee. "I don't suppose it will be. But we will always have Christmas. Every year, we celebrate the birth of the Christ child, just as you did before, and that will never, ever, change. I promise. And every year, we'll have presents under a tree and Christmas stockings. And I hope we can talk about your Christmas memories—and try to make new ones, too."

"We had a tree in a box," Cole announced.

"An artificial tree then. I'll bet it was nice."

He nodded. "And we had favorite decorations—ones we made at school. One had my picture on it from pre-school."

Hannah's eyes started to burn. The shipping boxes from Texas weren't all emptied yet—just the ones with the children's clothes, toys and books. The others were stored away in the bedroom upstairs. But she'd looked inside each one and knew for a fact that none of them had contained Christmas ornaments.

Cynthia had probably seen it all as rubbish and discarded it. And in the process, she'd destroyed one more connection the kids could have had with their past.

"After your cookies, we're going to buy some Christmas ornaments, and those will be yours forever. But do you know what? I'd love it if we could make some, too. Those would be so special—and we could do it every year."

"Hey, guys." Keeley sauntered over and pulled up a fourth chair to join them. "I'm so glad you stopped in. How's everything going?"

Cole shyly ducked his head. Molly traced her finger across her cookie and didn't look up.

"I am so thrilled to have these two with me," Hannah said. "I hope I can find lots of fun things for them to do. Any ideas?"

"Let me think. You've been on a sleigh ride?"

"But it had wheels," Cole said, taking another bite of his cookie.

"Then that's what you should do, now that we have snow. It's only a few days until the weekend and the sleigh rides start again." Keeley worried at her lower lip with her teeth, thinking. "The kids at church will be caroling that night, too, as they walk down Main Street. Have you two met any of the kids at church yet?"

Hannah shook her head. "They haven't. We were snowed in Sunday morning, unfortunately. Mingling with those kids would've made this first week at school easier, I think. But maybe we'll run into some of them at the Advent service on Wednesday."

Molly eyes widened in alarm. "You aren't going to, like, make me *talk* to them. Right?"

"That would be awful, no doubt." Hannah hid a

smile. "But if you see someone from school who looks kinda nice, you might ask a question about school, or about the youth group at church or about what they like to do around here for fun."

"Sounds like a good plan," Keeley agreed. "Even adults find it hard to meet people in a new town, and if you don't try, it can be very lonely."

"Lots of people have moved here during the last few years," Hannah added. "Did you know Keeley's fiancé is from Texas like you are?" At Cole's sudden attention, she nodded. "And Connor is a real cowboy. Now he trains and shows horses here in Wisconsin, but he grew up on a ranch out West. When the weather is nicer, maybe we can go out to the horse ranch where he works, so you can ride."

Even Molly perked up at that. *"Really?"*

"Absolutely. But right now we'd better scoot over to the Christmas Shoppe, so we can get back to the vet clinic before it closes. Thank Keeley for the lovely cookies and we can be on our way."

Cole and Molly bundled up into their coats and mittens, dutifully murmured their thanks and went out to the sidewalk.

Hannah hesitated at the door and looked back. "Thanks, Keel."

Keeley joined her at the entryway and they both looked out the front window at the children running their hands over the snow-frosted bench just outside. "So how are things going—really?"

"They're still grieving, of course. And I knew moving here wouldn't be easy. But sometimes…" Hannah felt tears start burning in her eyes, but she willed them away. "Sometimes they say or do something that rips my heart in pieces. We were just at the vet clinic, and Molly…"

Hannah swallowed hard, unable to go on for a moment. "Can you imagine the pain of losing your parents and having no chance to say goodbye? How can they ever recover from that?"

Keeley gave Hannah a brief, comforting hug. "You will just keep loving them, Hannah. Make them feel loved, and safe, and honor their memories. Do you remember the funeral for the Jones' boy a few years ago?"

"I'll never forget it."

"I remember his distraught mom asking us how she could ever get through her grief and you said…"

Hannah managed a wobbly smile. "By holding on to the faith that he was already with the Lord in heaven, beyond all suffering, and that she would be with him again."

"You'll all get through this in time. I promise. There isn't another person who could handle the challenges better than you will."

Impatient now, the kids were both looking through the front window at her, their hands framing their faces as they peered through the breath-frosted glass.

Hannah felt her heart warm and give an extra little thump. "I'll be praying every single day that you're right, Keel. Because nothing matters to me more."

Hannah had envisioned a long and careful search through the Christmas Shoppe while Molly and Cole searched for their perfect ornaments for the tree.

But it took all of five minutes with Molly finding a

springer spaniel ornament that looked vaguely like Belle on a display tree right inside the door, and Cole finding a golden retriever one that looked a lot like Maisie on the same tree.

Evening shoppers were beginning to fill the sidewalks as they stepped out of the store, and holiday music filtered into the chilly, early evening air through loudspeakers on the lampposts.

A light dusting of snow had landed over the town, making Hannah feel as if she were walking in an old-fashioned snow globe.

In just a few minutes they were back at the clinic.

Marilyn greeted them with a smile. "I'm glad you made it back. We'll be closing in fifteen minutes."

Molly fidgeted from one foot to the other. "Can we see Belle?"

"Of course you can. Dr. Leighton is gone, but I can take you back there. But you have to promise that you won't touch anything or get too close to the cages. And, especially, do not poke your fingers into the cages trying to pet the animals. We have four post-ops back there, and dogs that are sweet at home can be quite nervous in a vet clinic."

When both kids nodded, she led the way to the back of the clinic. A night-light warmed the darkness with a soft glow.

Three dogs were immediately awake and barking when Marilyn turned on the fluorescent lights. "Your Belle is over here, to the left. The last time I looked in on her she was quite subdued, but she's in poor condition and doesn't have a lot of energy yet. She also took a little longer than usual to wake up after the anesthesia."

Belle was crouched at the back of her cage, her ears flattened and tail tucked when Molly approached.

"She looks so *miserable*," Molly whispered. "I don't think she even remembers me."

"I'm sure she's scared. Here she is, in another new place with strangers, and on some pain meds that might make her a little woozy. I'm sure she's never had an IV drip before, or NG tube feedings. But Dr. Leighton thinks she'll be a lot perkier tomorrow."

"And then we can take her home?"

Marilyn pursed her lips. "That, I couldn't say. I'm sure we'll have a better idea in a day or two. You wouldn't want her home too soon, only to get weak and sick, would you?"

Molly shook her head vigorously. "I want her to be well."

Cole pointed to three dogs in the cages along the back wall. "Why are they here? Are they all sick, too?"

"Let's see. One neuter, one spay. Those two will go home tomorrow. One got away from his owner and was hit by a car, so he had his femur repaired this afternoon."

"I'd like to be a vet someday," Molly murmured, looking around the room with awe.

"Good for you. There's a high percentage of female vets these days." Marilyn ushered them out of the recovery room and switched off the overhead lights. "Study hard, get good grades and take all the math and science classes you can in high school. It will help a lot when you take the pre-vet classes in college."

Molly looked up at Marilyn with shining eyes. "I will. There's nothing in the world I want more."

* * *

Hannah checked the new text message on her phone and sighed. Until she'd brought the children north, she'd never hesitated to put in extra hours at work. Every day brought new challenges and she loved both the patients and the staff she worked with.

But now, she just wanted to be home when the kids weren't in school. To that end she'd shortened her clinic hours and asked to be taken off the on-call schedule until after Christmas. But apparently the other PA in town was out sick.

She tapped her phone for Ethan's number. The call went straight to voice mail, so she waited a minute, tried again and left a brief message. Where was he?

She glanced in the rearview mirror as she shifted her vehicle into Drive. Cole slumped in his seat, his face pale and drawn. "Are you all right?"

He nodded, not meeting her gaze in the rearview mirror.

"I guess this was a pretty big day for you two." She turned onto Main Street. "Did you have a good time?"

No one answered.

"I hope you don't mind, but I need to stop by Ethan's cabin to see if he's available tomorrow, just in case I get called back to work. Is that okay with you?"

When neither of them answered, she directed another glance up at the mirror.

Molly glowered back at her. "We don't need a babysitter."

"Maybe not, but I don't feel comfortable with you two alone out in the country."

"Mom let us stay home when she went to the store. Nothing happened then."

"Maybe not, but it will make me feel a lot better if there's an adult around." At the other end of town she braked at the four-way stop sign in front of the coffee shop. "Okay?"

"Isn't that his car?" Cole piped up. "Right over there."

Sure enough, it was the SUV with Minnesota plates.

Hannah parked in the next open space, and led the way into the coffee shop. Busy as usual, most of the tables were filled and a number of people were eating at the long lunch counter.

"There he is," Cole chirped, pointing toward the back. "Talking to that pretty lady standing by his booth."

Hannah's heart stumbled.

Dressed in a lipstick-red wool jacket and short skirt, the woman's clothing molded every perfect curve. Glittering diamonds flashed at her ears and wrists. With the four-inch heels of her tall black leather boots and the thick, wavy blonde hair spilling down her back, she looked like she'd just stepped off the cover of *Vogue*.

She was obviously a wealthy young woman, and from the silvery trill of her laughter, she and Ethan were enjoying a delightful conversation. No wonder he hadn't answered Hannah's calls. He had much better things to do.

Forcing back a flare of unexpected jealousy, Hannah glanced down at her own puffy black jacket—the one that probably added twenty pounds to her silhouette, and the khaki slacks badly stained with formula a baby had spit up on her at the clinic.

But jealousy was a ridiculous response.

Ethan and she had no personal relationship. None— beyond the politely adversarial situation they'd been locked in since he'd appeared at her door. He was free to flirt with anyone he chose, and it didn't matter to her at all. And if his taste now ran toward women like this one, he probably thought Hannah was pathetic.

"Uh… Ethan looks like he's busy. Let's go," she murmured.

But Cole was already racing to the booth, with Molly on his heels, so there was no turning back.

The blonde looked down at them with horror, then raised her gaze and gave Hannah a sweeping, dismissive glance. "You have a *family*?" she snapped, turning back to Ethan. Then she spun on her heel and walked out of the coffee shop.

"Boy, she was *mad*, Uncle Ethan," Cole exclaimed as he watched her disappear through the front door. "Was she a movie star or something?"

"She just stopped to visit, I guess."

"Sorry we interrupted," Hannah said dryly. "I can run after her and tell her that you are totally available, if you'd like."

"Please don't."

"Hannah's better, anyway," Molly muttered. "At least she's nice."

Faint praise, but even that much was a surprise and Hannah gave her shoulders a quick, one-armed hug. "We saw your car and stopped, because I tried to call a little while ago."

Ethan gestured at his coffee cup. "Join me?"

"No, I've got to get the kids home, but thanks, anyway. I just learned that I need to be on call tomorrow evening. If I do get called in, can you spend some time with the kids?" She flicked a glance at the front door of the coffee shop. "Unless you'll be seeing your…friend, that is."

He grinned at Molly and Cole. "Nope. Hands down, I'd rather spend time with you two, any day."

"Thanks, Ethan." Hannah waggled an eyebrow up and down. "And just to make sure no one is bored, I have a cool project for the three of you. Just wait and see."

Chapter Thirteen

Ethan had already noticed that Hannah's ten acres held a lot of trees.

What he hadn't noticed was that there was an immeasurable number of pine trees out there, but apparently *none* of them were perfect enough for a Christmas tree.

Cole ran from one tree to the next, studying each one from every angle and then moving on. His standard of perfection was the artificial tree his parents had put up every year, and none of these live ones fit the bill.

No wonder. What self-respecting tree would want to look like a scraggly replica with plastic needles?

Trailing well behind, Molly wanted something "super tall and wide at the bottom" like the one she'd seen on a book cover in the school library.

But it was already five and soon it would be getting dark.

Carrying the saw, Ethan trudged doggedly after them through the deep, pristine snow, his bad leg aching a little more with every step.

He had a feeling Hannah could have found a way to

expedite this process, but she'd been called back to the hospital and probably wouldn't be home until seven.

Hannah's "cool project" was proving to be cool in every sense of the word.

She'd asked him to find a Christmas tree with the kids, but every time he tried to take a stand about going no farther into the forest, he was met with wails about this being their very first tree to cut down and it had to be *perfect*.

Good luck with that.

Yet this was the first time he'd seen the kids show any real enthusiasm about their first Christmas without their mom and dad. So how could he deny them anything within his power?

Ethan's knee buckled, sending him face-first into a mound of snow and the boulder hidden beneath that deceptive mantle of white.

Stars exploded in his brain.

He wobbled, dizzy and disoriented as he tried to push off the rock and regain his feet. Now the entire forest seemed be spinning in disjointed loops that dipped and swayed, and sent him careening against the trunk of a tree.

Closing his eyes, he held on to the tree trunk and took slow, deep breaths. Waited to regain his balance.

A flash of motion flickered at the corner of his eye and he pivoted toward it in time to see a magnificent buck with a massive rack not twenty yards away. Regal, the deer took several slow steps with its head held high, then bounded away into the forest.

"Kids," Ethan whispered, "did you see that?"

He pivoted slowly toward where he'd last seen Molly, then to where Cole had been just a moment ago.

Both of them were gone.

"Molly! Cole!"

The forest remained dead silent. Even the breeze had gone still.

He resolutely changed course toward the last place he'd seen Cole, slipping on unseen, downed tree trunks hidden under mounds of snow, stumbling over rocks.

At the top of a small rise he finally connected with Cole's boot prints, which headed off to the west and a rugged hill covered with thickets of low, thorny branches.

Now his heart was beating double-time, as much from worry as the exertion of plowing through deep snow. Where on earth had the boy gone?

"Cole! Molly!" He waited. Listened. Then continued onward. In less than an hour it would be too dark to see the tracks.

He briefly closed his eyes, remembering all of the times he'd been desperate—trying to reach a wounded buddy under fire. Searching through a bombed-out city of rubble and despair, determined to take out any snipers before they got to him and his men first.

God hadn't ever answered his prayers then and after a while he'd given up.

But now, with two kids missing and a below-freezing night ahead, he dredged up those rusty words and began to pray. *Please, God, I know I'm not worthy. But please, please help me find those two innocent kids—they don't deserve to die out here.*

Then he struck out again, scanning the terrain for any sign of the kids as he went.

The tracks were veering south, thank goodness, in the general direction of Hannah's house. And there were Molly's tracks, too.

But why would they have turned back without a word?

Or had they? When he looked down again, the tracks had vanished. Had that buck been a figment of his imagination, too?

Scrubbing a hand over his face, he stared in wonder at the blood on his glove and tried to sort through his thoughts. Figure out where he'd gone wrong.

But he couldn't remember a thing.

Hannah searched the house then looked out into the backyard.

Ethan's SUV was in the driveway, the house unlocked. But none of the lights had been turned on against the approaching darkness, so maybe they were still outside, dragging a pine tree behind them like a caveman's trophy kill.

She smiled to herself, wondering how long that decision had taken. She'd told Ethan to stay within the fenced border of her property just for that very reason.

It was all too easy to be lured farther and farther into the forest by the prospect of a perfect tree waiting just out of reach, and then become confused and lost—especially at dusk. But if he'd followed directions, he and the kids would always run into her fence line sooner or later and be able to find their way home.

Shoving her feet into her snow boots, she shrugged

into her heavy down jacket, pulled on a hat and mittens and headed outside beyond the charred remains of the barn.

"Ethan?" She cupped her hands to her face. "Molly! Cole!"

She listened and then crossed the old pony corral and let herself out into the ten acres of timber, watching for any sign of movement.

Worry began to grip her heart in a tight vise. Ethan had been a soldier for thirteen years. How could he get lost in a ten-acre wooded pasture? How could they all be missing?

She called out to them again. This time she heard Molly's faint response and she hurried in that direction, thankful she'd thought to stuff her cell phone in a jacket pocket in case she had to call for help.

Over the next rise she gasped in relief. Molly and Cole were trudging toward her, struggling to make it through the deep snow. They both looked exhausted.

She enveloped both of them in a group hug. "I was so worried about you two. Where have you been—and where is Ethan?"

Molly's lower lip trembled. "We don't *know*. We were hunting for a tree and suddenly he was gone. We called and called and tried to find him, but then it was getting dark and we had to try to get h-home. What if something got him—like a bear?" She cast a fearful look over her shoulder. "What if it's still out there and it's coming af-after us?"

Hannah brushed a kiss against her forehead. "There definitely are bears in Wisconsin, but I haven't ever seen one on my property, and there haven't been any reported in this area for years."

She called Ethan's name several times. "You know what? I'm going to get you two up to the house and then I'll come back out and try to find him. Okay?"

Panicked, Cole gripped her arm. "No—I don't want you to. Please don't leave us there!"

"Don't worry, sweetie. It'll be fine." She gave him another hug then moved a few steps away and yelled Ethan's name again.

A shadow stumbled through the trees, too indistinct to make out for sure, but she held her breath, praying it was him. If it wasn't, how could she ever find him in the dark?

He drew closer and she blew out a breath in relief. "Thank goodness, Ethan. We were so worried! Where have you been?"

"I...don't know." His words were strangely slow and measured, as if he had to think about each one. He was limping badly.

In the dim light his face was oddly dark on one side. But it wasn't until she'd hurried to his side that she realized what it was. Blood, still dripping from a gash hidden somewhere in his hair.

"Come on, kids, we're going for a ride." She hooked her arm under his and walked him slowly into the house to grab her purse, then pulled her car keys from her pocket and loaded everyone into her car. "ER, here we come."

Ethan leaned against the headrest, his eyes closed. He'd heard Hannah call the ER on the drive into

town. He'd started to protest and then had lost his train
of thought.

But now they were suddenly at the hospital and she'd
pulled up under the overhang at the ER entrance. A
nurse pushing a wheelchair barreled out of the automatic glass doors and she was bearing down on his
side of the car.

His fuzzy thoughts began to clear as his alarm grew.

"Wait—I don't need to be here," he protested as the
nurse wrenched open his door and reached for his seat
belt buckle.

Hannah rounded the front of her vehicle and took his
arm. "Maybe not, but do me a favor and let Ann take
you inside. Let's get you cleaned up a bit—you might
need a couple of sutures."

Sutures. He could handle that. He awkwardly transferred into the wheelchair, wincing at the stab of pain
in his knee as he pivoted.

Hannah bent into his field of vision and took his
good hand in hers. "Ethan, I need to take the kids over
to Keeley's house, but I'll be right back. Ann is a great
nurse and Sophie's husband, Dr. McLaren, is here, so
they'll start checking you out, okay?"

She straightened, turned away from him and lowered
her voice. "He was disoriented when I found him, and
seemed unusually drowsy on the way here. He's a soldier on medical leave…with a history of TBI. Recently
discharged from Walter Reed."

Ethan looked back at the Subaru, where Molly's pale,
frightened face was pressed against the back window.
His thoughts snapped into crystal-clear focus.

He started to get out of the wheelchair. "I just need to get back to my cabin. A little sleep and I'll be fine."

"Not the best idea, sir. Not with a head injury." The nurse pressed him gently back down and wheeled him through the glass doors into the blinding light of the ER, and on to an exam room where a man was already waiting.

"I'm Dr. McLaren," he said crisply. "I hear you've had an adventure tonight."

"I took my niece and nephew out into Hannah's timber to look for a Christmas tree. I slipped in the snow and fell. Nothing more than that."

"Did you ever agree on one?" The doc's mouth quirked into a brief smile. "My family never does. I finally learned it involves a lot less mileage to check out the Christmas tree lots instead of tramping through Hannah's woods with a saw."

Ethan laughed at that, which made his head start to pound. "I'm sure coming here was just a waste of your time."

"We still want to have a look. Ann is going to take your history and get that laceration cleaned up so we can take a better look. In the meantime, I need to check on another patient here in the ER, but I'll be back shortly."

The nurse returned with a laptop computer on a rolling stand, helped him up on a gurney and cleaned up his face with deft, gentle fingers. She applied a dressing and then began peppering him with questions about his medical history and medications, her fingers flying over the keys with every answer.

Next she began a lengthy assessment of his orientation, motor response and balance, an all-too familiar litany of procedures that he'd been through more times than he could count.

"Well, sir," she concluded with a warm smile, "the doctor is busy with something right now, but he should be with you shortly. Hannah's friend lives close by, so I'm sure she will be back soon."

After pointing out the call light and handing him a TV remote—not a good sign regarding how long he might have to wait—she disappeared.

Hannah appeared at the side of his gurney. "You've been asleep," she murmured. "How are you feeling? A little dizzy?"

Asleep? He glanced up at the large clock on the wall, though now he wasn't sure about the time he'd arrived. With Hannah hovering over him like a worried hen, he wasn't going to ask.

Footsteps entered the room and now Dr. McLaren was on the other side of the gurney flipping through several pages on a clipboard. "So, tell me your name."

He rolled his eyes, though he knew it would be faster to just go along. "Ethan Williams. It's December second, and I'm here because of a minor thump on the head. And... I'm fine."

"I see that you're on no meds. No chronic diseases. Blood pressure, temp and pulse are fine. You've been through quite a bit, though." McLaren studied Ethan's prosthetic hand. "Amazing what they can do these days. How are you doing with this?"

"Well enough. Though my niece Molly might beg to differ. She asked me to re-braid her hair after I brought her and Cole to Hannah's after school. I couldn't do it without the tactile sense for managing something so fine and slippery."

"You could in time—it's just another new skill to work on." He looked down at the clipboard. "So…about your head. You said you didn't lose consciousness after your fall—at least that you were aware of. Right?"

Ethan nodded.

"Good. Your Glasgow score was 15 when you first arrived, and also ten minutes ago. Since 15 is normal and 3 is dead, you're at the best end of the spectrum there." McLaren studied him over the top rim of his glasses. "While you've been waiting here, have you had any bouts of confusion? Disorientation? Nausea?"

Ethan shook his head.

"You were a little foggy when you arrived—you didn't respond to several questions and appeared to be hypersensitive to the lights. That's not surprising with a mild concussion. But as far as tests go, an X-ray wouldn't be of benefit with minor head trauma."

"So I'm done here?"

"At this point, your assessment results don't indicate a need for a CT scan, either. But given your history of a blast-related TBI, I want to keep you overnight for observation. I also need to do a little suturing, and then we can move you into one of the hospital rooms just down the hall."

After the doctor left the room, Hannah stepped back to his side. "I'm so sorry. I feel responsible for this. If I hadn't mentioned finding a Christmas tree, this wouldn't have happened."

"If I'd been more careful, it wouldn't have happened," he retorted. "I'm just sorry the kids didn't find their tree."

"No matter. What really matters is that you're all right." She smiled down at him but her eyes were filled with concern. "I need to pick up Molly and Cole, then I want to slip into the back of the church for the last part of the Advent service if we can. Afterward I'll need to get them home for bed, but the staff here knows they can call me at any time."

She put his cell phone on his bedside table. "And here is your cell, if you need to reach me."

Staring at the stark, white walls of the exam room, he realized that as soon as she left, he was going to miss her. A lot.

"I'll be back in the morning as soon as I drop the kids off at school," she continued. "Don't give the staff any trouble, okay? If the docs decide you do need a CT or something, don't give them any grief. Both Dr. McLaren and Dr. Talbot are excellent physicians and they know what they're doing."

"Fine," he grumbled.

Her eyes sparkled with sudden humor. "I'm sure you will be. I'll hear about it if you're any trouble."

She leaned over and kissed his cheek. Hesitated, then gave him another kiss that brushed his mouth and lingered, sending a dizzying rush of warmth straight to his heart.

Then she was gone.

Chapter Fourteen

What in the world had she been thinking? Hannah tightened her grip on the steering wheel, thankful for the darkness that hid the deep blush burning its way up her cheeks from the kids sitting in the backseat.

She'd kissed him. Despite knowing full well that he was a heartbreaker. The kind of guy who didn't stay around. And it hadn't been just the light, good-luck kiss of an acquaintance, either.

She'd done it at the hospital, where any passer-by might have seen her, taken note, and then happily shared the observation at the coffee shop tomorrow morning, which would then set the rumor mill on fire.

That, she could handle with an offhand dismissal and a shrug. Eventually.

But far worse, she'd crossed an invisible boundary between Ethan and herself. One that had placed any romantic feelings between them squarely in the past.

And in doing so she'd stirred up the old emotions that she'd been denying since the day he arrived.

He wasn't just a threat to the secure, permanent home

she longed to provide for the children. He was also a threat to her heart.

But he was here because of the children. Not her. And in a few weeks he would be gone. She'd best not forget that.

Hannah drove up the snowy side streets toward the Aspen Creek Community Church perched on a hill overlooking the town. High snowbanks left by the snowplows at the street intersections made each one an adventure, when she could only ease forward and hope no one else was coming.

"I never seen snow like this at home," Cole said from the backseat. "When can we go sledding?"

"Tomorrow," Hannah promised as she pulled into a parking spot at the far end of the church parking lot. "But only if we have time after choosing our Christmas tree."

"We'll be fast. I *promise*. Maybe we can go find one tonight and then go sliding right after school?"

Hannah chuckled. "It's already dark out. Too late. But we'll make sure you have plenty of time tomorrow."

She led the kids across the parking lot to the steps leading up to the church, struck as always by the simple beauty of its tall, old-fashioned white spire reaching toward the sky.

The welcoming light from within shone through the stained glass of the dozen tall, arched windows that marched down each side of the building. "Isn't it beautiful?" she asked. "I always feel as if I've just come home."

Even with the strains of "Joy to the World" floating from within, Molly lagged behind, the grim set of her mouth more suited to the gallows than a lovely old church.

Inside, Hannah collected a bulletin from an usher and led the way to a back pew. They'd arrived too late for the brief Advent sermon and most of the service, except for a soloist and one more hymn, but the dimmed lights and the candles glowing at the front of the church still filled her with a familiar sense of peace.

She glanced at Molly's stony expression and closed her eyes. *Please, Lord, help me reach this child. Her burdens are so heavy right now. I can't even imagine her sense of grief and loss, and I only want to do what's right for her and her brother. Please.*

Pastor Mark stepped out in front of the altar. "Welcome to our visitors and members. We hope you'll join us downstairs after every service for refreshments and the chance to get to know each other better. Blessings and peace to you all, now and always."

He moved back to his seat behind the pulpit and a haunting a cappella, crystalline voice rose from the choir balcony. "Mary, did you know, that your baby boy…"

A complete hush fell over the congregation. Not so much as a paper bulletin rustled.

Except for the smallest, muffled sob next to Hannah. Molly, her face crumpled with raw grief, tears streaming down her face.

Tears filled Hannah's eyes as she pulled the child into her arms and held her close, rocking her as she would a baby as Molly's tears fell and her shoulders shook with her silent sobs.

Cole edged closer, his heartbroken gaze pinned on

his sister. Hannah shifted and slid an arm around his narrow shoulders, too.

"This was Momma's favorite song," he whispered sadly. "She always sang it to us at Christmas. Then she kissed us and said we were *her* babies, and she loved us more than the whole world. Only she can't do it anymore."

His words felt like a blow to Hannah's heart. "A mother loves her babies forever and ever, honey," she whispered, kissing the top of his head. "When you hear that song, think of her singing to you from heaven."

The soloist finished and the pastor led the congregation in prayer. Then the organist started a prelude to "O Holy Night" and everyone stood for the final hymn.

Molly's tears faded to hiccups and she started to pull away, but Hannah gave her an extra squeeze before letting her go. "Are you all right, sweetheart?"

Molly rubbed at her face with her hands and looked away.

"I know this has been hard—terribly hard," Hannah whispered. "But I promise you that things will get better. It just takes a lot of time."

Molly didn't answer.

"We can just go home or we could slip into the bathroom downstairs right now and let you wash your face. Then we could stay a little while," Hannah coaxed, hoping her plan wasn't a big mistake. "There'll be all sorts of Christmas cookies and treats down there, with cocoa and punch. Would you mind—for just a few minutes? It might be fun."

Somber now, Cole nodded.

Molly heaved a deep, resigned sigh.

With another verse of the hymn left, Hannah slipped out of the pew, led them downstairs and waited while Molly went into the bathroom to wash away her tears.

The congregation was pouring down the stairs when Molly came out and moved to Hannah's side. "Let's get in line, so you can pick out some cookies, okay?"

Molly shook her head. "I just want to go home."

At Cole's pleading look, Hannah tipped her head toward one of the tables. "Cole wants something. If you want to wait right there, we'll join you in a minute."

A vaguely familiar girl looked at Molly from across the room then turned to grab the arm of a younger girl standing next to her and they both came over. "I'm Faith. Remember, from the carriage ride? This is my cousin Joanie."

The younger girl's cheeks reddened.

"She's kinda shy," Faith added diffidently. "She's in sixth grade, like you, but she's been home sick from school this week so you haven't seen her yet."

"I'm better now," Joanie said with a tentative smile. "Faith says we might be in the same classes."

Another cluster of people came down the stairs and got in line for refreshments, including a tall, remarkably good-looking boy standing with his parents. Lawyers in town, Molly remembered after a moment's thought.

The boy surveyed the room with a bored expression until his gaze landed on Molly. He brightened and strolled across the floor to her side.

Faith and Joanie stared in awe, their eyes shifting between Molly and the newcomer.

"Hey, Molly," he said. "I didn't know you belong to our church."

"Hey, Trevor." Molly shuffled her feet, a faint pink blush blooming in her cheeks. "My aunt does. So I guess my brother and I will, too."

"Cool. So, are you joining the youth group?"

"I...um... I don't know." Molly gave Hannah a swift, questioning look.

"You can if you want to." Hannah smiled. "I keep reading in the church bulletin about all the things they do, so I'm sure it would be a lot of fun."

"We do good stuff, too. Like helping at the nursing home or reading to little kids."

Barely able to contain a smile, Hannah silently withdrew and headed for some friends in line for coffee.

This evening wouldn't change everything for Molly, but it was definitely a start.

Thank you, Lord, for leading me to come here tonight, even though we were late. And thank you, thank you, for bringing Molly a chance to finally make some friends.

Ethan had been watching the clock in his hospital room since four in the morning, trying to forget Hannah's sweet, unexpected kiss whenever he wasn't counting the minutes until the doc made his rounds and released him.

At least the discharge papers were on his bedside table, but he still needed Hannah to spring him from jail.

Which led him right back to thinking about Hannah's kiss.

He was sure she'd meant it as a friendly good-night and nothing more.

But trying to forget the warmth of her lips on his was like trying to ignore fireworks on the Fourth of July, because now his thoughts were spinning with a kaleidoscope of memories of those weeks they'd shared years ago.

Since his arrival in Wisconsin he'd carefully focused on the children. Tried to avoid the inadvertent meeting of accidental glances. Dodged the unintentional brush of a hand that might reawaken the fierce chemistry that had once been between them.

He snorted under his breath. It hadn't taken a touch or a glance or a casual kiss. Just arriving that first day and seeing Hannah at her front door had brought it all rushing back, and more. She, on the other hand, had seemed unaffected—beyond her deep concern about the children.

After seven months in Ward 57 in Walter Reed, every whiff of disinfectant, every squeal of med cart wheels on the polished floors, every glimpse of a uniform set his teeth on edge and made his stomach twist.

If not for the fact that he had no car here at the hospital and no keys for his cabin, he would've left the hospital hours ago, as soon as the hall lights dimmed and the third shift came on duty.

At nine o'clock sharp his cell phone rang. Expecting Hannah, he did a double take at the Dallas phone number on the screen. David Benson, a high school acquaintance who had joined the marines the same time Ethan had chosen the army.

"Hey, buddy, I heard you had some tough luck."

Ethan leaned back against the pillows and closed his eyes, wishing he hadn't taken the call. "I'm good."

"Not what I heard from Tommy Joe. He says you were in quite a blast last spring. Lost some of your moving parts."

Ethan let his thumb hover over the off button on his phone, then reconsidered with a sigh. "I'm a bionic man, my nephew says. Just a hand."

David whistled. "Tough luck."

"That would be the guys who didn't get to come home. I'm all right."

"I s'pose it's too early to say if you want to get back to active duty."

"Some do, with prosthetics," Ethan shot back. The defensive note in his voice made him cringe. "I'm not yet sure about what I'll do."

"True enough, but I wanted to run something past you, buddy." David cleared his throat. "I didn't re-up this last time around. I wanted to be closer to my kids. See them grow up. Another marine and I have a business here in Dallas, and we need a couple more guys with the right military background—ASAP. I thought of you first."

"Doing what?"

"Personal protection. Bodyguards. High-security courier services, and so forth."

Intrigued, Ethan leaned forward. "You've actually got this business running?"

"Six months. We can't keep up, to tell the truth. Both of us are working fifty-sixty-hour weeks and have turned away business, so it's time to expand. Interested?"

A few weeks ago Ethan would have said no. Getting back into active duty was the only thing he knew.

The only thing he was good at. But now, with Molly and Cole and the custody issue, he was no longer sure.

And then there was Hannah.

Where their relationship was heading was still a guess—he doubted she would give him her trust easily after he'd so cruelly jilted her years ago, and every time he saw her, he regretted his stupidity even more. How could he have thrown away something that precious?

But he still needed to think about career options. And, if he found there was no chance at all with her, he wouldn't care what he did or where he had to live. Nothing else would matter.

"So this job would be in Dallas?" he asked cautiously.

"For now, but we're thinking about expanding into other big-city markets."

"Minneapolis–St. Paul?"

"Very likely."

"Wisconsin?"

"Uh, maybe. The bigger cities might be possible, if that's something you'd want to develop sometime in the future."

Ethan grabbed a piece of paper and a pen from the bedside table and began taking notes as David launched into an extensive description of the business, its clientele and future plans.

"So," David said after pulling in a slow breath. "Sound interesting to you?"

"I guess so."

"I'm going out of town next week, but my schedule is open on the fifteenth and I could meet with you that afternoon if you can get down here."

"I'll give it some serious thought."

At a light rap on the door Ethan ended the call and straightened, expecting Hannah.

A middle-aged woman in a dark skirt and cranberry sweater walked in instead. She approached his bedside and briskly shook his hand. "Georgie Anderson, Social Worker."

He sank back against the raised head of his bed, wishing he'd feigned sleep, but he didn't have the heart to order her out of his room. She looked like the quintessential cookie-baking grandma.

"I understand you had a bit of a fall yesterday, but you're going home today. Wonderful news," she said. "You're feeling back to normal?"

Like he would admit to anything that might keep him here longer? "Yes. All good."

"To get right down to it, Dr. McLaren asked me to come by before you leave. He wanted me to drop off some brochures about the local veteran's support groups, as well as the VA clinic in Maplewood."

Now that he looked a little closer, she was more like a ruler-toting schoolmarm than someone's sweet old grandma. He sighed, gestured toward his bedside table. "I'll look at it later."

"Somehow, I doubt that. Dr. McLaren is concerned about you. Not just your concussion yesterday, but about what you've been through in the service. When you two talked last night, you were open about the problems you face with PTSD and said that you've rejected help in the past."

He'd said that? He blinked. The woman's voice faded into the background as he mentally reviewed the hours since he'd been brought into the ER. Sure, he'd been a little foggy—not uncommon after even a mild concussion. But when had he ever talked about his PTSD— much less to a veritable stranger?

She rested a hand on his forearm and drew him back to attention. "You aren't the only one facing this. One of our groups has a member who suffered for twenty years on his own. Refused to acknowledge that burden. Refused help. He says he never realized what was wrong in his life—he just figured he was a failure at jobs, at relationships. He never knew he could feel so much better, until he finally ditched his stubborn pride and began dealing with his problems. He's now the leader of the Saturday morning group here at the hospital, in case you're interested."

Her offer was calm and professional, but the glint in her eyes held a different message.

So was he finally ready to try?

Chapter Fifteen

Hannah checked the slow cooker, with chili simmering away in the kitchen, turned on the oven light to check on the corn bread, then returned to the living room and studied the freshly cut Christmas tree.

She'd been right.

With the lure of finally going to the sledding hill at Aspen Creek Park, Molly and Cole had converged on a nicely shaped blue spruce within fifteen minutes, had taken turns sawing at its base and had both helped drag it to the house.

The sledding hadn't lasted long given the minus-five-degree windchill. But they'd both stuck it out for five runs down the longest hill before happily heading back to the SUV to defrost with a thermos of hot cocoa on the way home.

At a knock on the door Cole ran to the front and peered out the sidelight window. "It's Uncle Ethan!"

Cole unlocked the door and opened it wide. "We went sledding! And we got a tree!"

Ethan laughed as he shucked off his boots and coat

and brought a square bakery box into the kitchen and handed it to Hannah. "Dessert—since you invited me for supper. I hope someone here likes chocolate."

"No doubt about it." She eyed him closely. He'd looked pale and drawn when she'd picked him up at the hospital and had taken him back to his cabin this morning, but at least now his color was better. "How's that head of yours?"

"Fine."

"No headache?"

"I'm good."

Which was a non-answer if she'd ever heard one, but it was his business, not hers. "Glad to hear it, but I hope you've been taking things easy."

He winked at her. "Followed doctor's orders, as always."

His dimples deepened whenever he smiled, and that twinkle in his eyes made her heart take an extra beat. It was getting harder to remember that he might be polite and friendly, but he was staying in town "at least until Christmas," because he wanted to connect with Molly and Cole and then try to gain full custody. It wasn't because he was her friend…or anything more.

So why on earth had she kissed him last evening at the hospital? She still couldn't get that out of her thoughts.

It didn't take much analysis, she realized. She was drawn to him more now than she'd ever been. An indefinable magnetism hummed between them like an invisible force.

But it was more than that. With every passing day that he was here, she found more things about him that drew her. His kindness. His warm affection for the kids. The way he was so willing to help out with anything— even to the point of taking a terrified stray to the vet clinic.

He was so different from the guy he'd been at twenty-one. His years in the military had matured him into a solid, dependable man who seemed trustworthy. Safe. Could things between them actually work out this time?

He turned back to living room and studied the tree. "Where was that one hiding yesterday? It's perfect."

Molly, sprawled on the floor in front of the fireplace, looked up from her homework. "Aunt Hannah said we had to wait to decorate until you came."

"Yeah. 'Cause you're taller and can reach the high branches." Cole went to a stack of red boxes with green lids. "Can we start now?"

"Supper first." Hannah set four salads and the corn bread on the round oak table in the kitchen. "Have a chair, then we'll say grace before I bring the chili over. Would anyone like to lead the prayer?"

After a moment of silence, she reached for Molly's hand on her left and Ethan's hand on her right. When everyone was connected, she bowed her head. "Thank you, Lord, for this wonderful day. For Ethan's good health and release from the hospital. For the friends Molly has made, and the ones whom Cole will meet soon. For this meal, and for the coming celebration of your birth. In Jesus's name we pray, amen."

Just as she finished serving the chili, someone rapped on the front door. "Excuse me, I'll be right back."

Ethan followed, hovering protectively at her shoulder, a soldier ready to take out an enemy. "I can answer the door, if you'd like."

Through the window she saw a portly man with a briefcase and a clipboard in the crook of his arm. "It's all right. I know why he's here." She hesitated then opened the door. "Can I help you?"

"Fred Larsen. I'm here to follow up on a complaint regarding your rescue facilities." His wary gaze lifted to survey Ethan. "Uh, if it's not…um, inconvenient."

"I've been expecting you." Hannah dredged up a smile. "I know you can't say, but I've no doubt it was called in by Gladys Rexworth. She has never actually set foot on this property, but she heard about the fire here and probably made assumptions. She told me that she would be calling your office."

Apparently satisfied that the chubby man was harmless, Ethan left to rejoin the kids at the kitchen table. The inspector watched him go, then seemed to recover his composure. "Can I see your animal facilities, please?"

"No problem at all. If you haven't had supper, you're welcome to join us."

"Thank you, but I'd better proceed." He referred to his clipboard. "I'll need to see your records regarding vet care, intakes and adoptions. But first—how many animals are here right now?"

"Three cats and two dogs living in the house. There was a fire in the small barn out back last Sunday, attributed to an electrical short. The inspector thought it was probably due to mice chewing on a wire."

"Any animal deaths?"

"It was basically a pony shed and hay storage, and a

place to keep three chickens that were left here. They're all fine—just temporarily in the garage. We're also starting to think about fund-raising for a centralized shelter in town."

The man's eyebrows rose. "Wait—you have chickens and a pony in the garage?"

"Plus twelve puppies and their mother, who was dropped off here a few days before she whelped. Obviously, I'm not parking my vehicle in the garage anymore. Someone dropped off another dog on Monday, but she's at the vet right now, in terrible shape."

"She'll be euthanized?"

"Absolutely not. She's emaciated, and she was clearly abused, but she'll be fine with good care. If you want to check in on her, she's at Dr. Leighton's clinic in town."

"I see."

Hannah led the way into the garage. He walked from one pen to the next, noting food and water dishes and studying the dimensions of the pens. "This all is fine, but the regulations for dogs also require daily exercise and contact with people. How are you handling that?"

"The backyard is fully fenced, so I turn the adult dogs out four times a day, and the pony has a small pasture. The pups have been going out with just their mom, unless the weather is bad. Socialization is inside the house with me, and now, also with my niece and nephew." She smiled. "When we go back into the house, I'll let Lucy go outside and show you what we do with the pups. Are you done out here?"

He wrote a few more notes on his paper then nodded. "My big-ring notebooks for shelter activities are on the kitchen counter by the phone. Feel free to look through them all. I'll be inside in just a second."

A few minutes later she peeked through the kitchen door. "Here they come—everyone ready?"

Cole and Molly had finished their supper and were back in the living room with Ethan. Giggling, they both sat on the area rug as the flood of puppies poured through the door.

Startled, the inspector took a step back, then he started to laugh. "What a family!"

"I think they're thrilled to have the kids living here now, and it should help them be better family dogs when they are available for adoption. They'll already be used to cats and kids."

"So when will you add them to your website?"

"Usually at eight weeks, but that falls during the week before Christmas and I don't want to risk them ending up as impulse buys for presents. Too many of those poor dogs end up back in shelters."

He finished paging through the notebooks then shook her hand. "I think you're doing a great job, here. The animals are all at excellent weight. The pens are clean and comfortable. Congratulations on a job well done."

After he left, Molly gently swept aside the puppies wrestling on her lap and went to the kitchen, where Hannah was eating her chili at the counter. "What did he mean about your website?"

"Well, we need to spread the word about adoptable animals, so three of us in town maintain a website showing all of the available animals. People can call or email if they are interested in one in particular, then make an appointment to see it."

"Just like that? They pick one and take it home?"

Hannah smiled at her concern. "It's definitely not just like that, I promise. They have to fill out a long form and prove they either have a fenced yard or use a buried fence and radio collars to keep dogs at home. We never want to send a dog to a place where it will spend its life chained outside. That's horrible. Dogs are pack animals and crave being with people or each other."

"Wow. Can I see that website?"

Hannah put her chili bowl in the sink. "Sure."

With a few clicks she reached the Aspen Creek Rescue site. "Here…do you want to look through it?"

Molly settled on a tall stool at the breakfast bar and wandered through the site, then clicked on Available Animals. She looked up at Hannah in horror. "Penelope is here. You *can't* send her away!"

"That's what we do, sweetie. Keep strays or discarded animals safe, and rehabilitate the ones that need a new start. Then we try to find them a forever home. It's really hard sometimes. But it's good to know when an animal will finally be with someone who loves them."

Frowning, Molly scrolled down farther. "And Lucy? Her *puppies*? You can't!"

"If you check closer, you'll see they are listed as unavailable until after January first, not now. Just think about it, Molly. Eventually that would be a total of thirteen big dogs. How could I ever keep them all? It would be a big pack eating me out of house and home. And none would have the same love and attention as if they had their very own family."

Molly shot a look at Cole, who was lying on the

floor drawing pictures with Maisie sleeping at his side, then she directed a fierce, accusing glare at Hannah. "Even Maisie is in here," she demanded in outrage. "How could you do that? My brother *loves* her. Doesn't that matter? I suppose you're going to put poor Belle on the list next."

"You are absolutely right about Maisie. He not only loves her, I know he needs her. Especially right now. It's been so busy around here this past week that I wasn't even thinking about the website." Hannah pulled the computer over and deleted Maisie's listing. "There. Done. Now—let's go decorate the tree before it gets too late."

An instrumental Christmas CD provided soft background music as Ethan wound the final string of white lights around the tree, plugged it into the surge protector with the others and flipped the switch. The tree came alive with a bright glow—as if covered in stars.

Cole stared at it in awe. "It's the prettiest *ever*. And it smells so good!"

"Now we need to open those other boxes and hang the decorations," Hannah said. "But, first, here are the ones you kids picked out at the Christmas Shoppe. Maybe they should go on first so you can find the very best spots."

She handed them over and watched the children ponder their great decision. Then each hung their decoration at eye level. "Absolutely perfect."

Ethan watched as three big totes were opened and the ornaments added to the tree one by one, the kids entranced by the sparkling, shiny baubles. Many of the decorations were whimsical animal figures, Santas and angels, some were miniature nativity sets—an array of unmatched memories from Christmases over the years—so unlike Cynthia's annual white tree with silver ornaments and metallic silver bows.

After he helped hang the highest decorations on the tree, he joined the kids in stepping away to take in the full effect. "I agree with Cole. This is indeed the most beautiful tree I've ever seen. You all did a super job."

"And now I have something else to hang up," Hannah announced, pulling a large paper sack from behind a chair. "Hmm. I wonder what these could be? I'll hand them out, then we can open them all at once. Okay?"

She looked into the sack and made a production of lifting out something wrapped in green tissue and tied with a red ribbon. "I think this is for Molly!"

She handed it over and then pulled out a similar package in red tissue and tied with a green ribbon. "This is for Cole!"

She frowned, tilted her head, and reached into the sack again. "I think there's something else in here, but I'm not sure. Yes! It's for Ethan!"

He hesitated, so she leaned over and thrust it in his hand. The brush of her slender fingertips against his hand sent a sizzle of warmth up his arm.

He looked at her in surprise, painfully aware that he hadn't brought gifts for anyone else. A little shocked by his physical reaction to her touch. "I... I didn't realize that I should have brought something. I'm sorry."

"No, don't be. This is just something everyone needs before Christmas. Okay—ready, set, open!"

He held his own package and watched the kids tear

into theirs, trying to remember if he'd ever experienced a real family Christmas—with a fragrant, fresh tree or such beautiful music. Certainly not after his mother had walked out…and before that there'd been the endless tension between his parents.

"Wow!" Cole exclaimed, unfurling a big red-felt Christmas stocking covered with dogs and cats and Christmas elves, and dusted with sparkling sequins. "Now Santa can come!"

Molly's was the same, only in green with a big silver bow at the top. Her eyes sparkled when she looked up. "It's so *pretty*, Aunt Hannah. I love it! But what about you—don't you have one?"

"I've had mine since I was a little girl, and it's somewhere in the Christmas decoration boxes. I'll get it out tomorrow."

Hugging his stocking to his chest, Cole eyed the package in Ethan's hands. "Open yours, Uncle Ethan. Maybe you got dogs, too!"

The fire crackling in the fireplace and the Christmas tree lights were now the only illumination in the room, creating a cozy, festive air. It was like being in the midst of a Norman Rockwell painting, surrounded by a deep sense of family, celebration and love. Something so foreign to his life that he could barely name the emotions welling up inside.

If he lived to be a hundred, he would never forget this moment. And he would wish for it again, every single year.

He opened the package slowly, expecting that maybe Hannah had found a stocking in camo print. But when he unfurled it, his breath caught on the lump in his throat. It was black felt, with shiny silver, gold, red and green ribbons sewn in a crisscross pattern on its front surface. "Uncle Ethan" was written across the black cuff at the top in elegant silver script.

"It's beautiful, Hannah. Just…beautiful. Thanks."

How did he begin to thank her for this evening? For what she was awakening in his solitary, guarded heart?

Chapter Sixteen

The following week passed in a blur of running errands, sledding, skating and a Christmas party at the church for the kids.

Ethan was with them more often than not, which delighted the kids and—Hannah had to admit—warmed her heart, too.

Watching him out on the ice with Cole and Molly under the lights on Friday evening, she could well imagine him as a watchful, loving father someday.

"So how's it going?" Keeley strolled up to Hannah and gave her a friendly, teasing shoulder bump. "And why aren't you out on the ice, too?"

"I've never been good on skates. Weak ankles," Hannah admitted. "I'm less danger to others if I'm right here along the fence. How about you?"

"I'm beat. I spent an hour after closing restocking the store shelves and now I just want to go home."

Keeley followed Ethan and Cole's progress as they slowly made their way around the edge of the rink, Ethan holding Cole's hand. "He's sure good with the kids," she observed quietly. "How are you two getting along?"

Hannah shrugged. "Fine, I guess. The kids seem to really like him."

Keeley gave her a sideways smirk. "And how about you?"

"It's…complicated."

"How so?"

"He understandably wants to spend time with the kids, and how can I say no to that? They deserve to know their only uncle now that their dad is gone. And being difficult about it could have a negative impact when custody is reviewed."

"No…how about *you*?" Keeley repeated.

Hannah swallowed.

"If you were ready to elope with him, you must have been head over heels for him back then. Who wouldn't, with those heartthrob looks?"

"And don't forget the charisma," Hannah added with a resigned sigh. "He drew me like a magnet and I never thought twice."

"And no one else ever compared?"

Hannah gave a helpless shrug. "No one else even came close. But it isn't just that superficial appeal. Maybe I only sensed it before, but now I see it. His gentleness with the children, the rescue animals. His quiet sense of humor. Lots of things. Important things. But none of that changes anything."

"Maybe if you tried…"

"I'm doing my best to keep my feelings out of this. Soon he'll be gone. End of story."

"Maybe not." Keeley pursed her lips. "Did Beth tell you that her husband wants to talk to Ethan?"

"Whatever for?" Turning to face her, Hannah rested an elbow on the top of the ice-rink fence.

"A business opportunity of some kind. Something about selling and installing home security systems. Alarms, I think." Keeley lifted an eyebrow. "If it interests him, maybe he'll want to stay."

Molly thudded into the solid-wood fencing next to them and flung her arms over the top rail. Her pink hat was askew, her cheeks rosy with the cold.

"I'm ready to go," she said breathlessly. "Joanie went home and my feet are cold."

Keeley grinned at her. "You're doing great on those skates. Next year maybe you'll want to start figure-skating lessons."

Molly rolled her eyes. "I'm only eleven and I think it's already too late. Have you seen those little kids twirling and going backward? Some even do jumps."

"Never too late to start, kiddo. Well, guys, I think I'm heading home." Keeley slanted a grin at Hannah. "That goes for you, too, girlfriend. If you really want something, it's never too late."

Hannah's heart stumbled whenever she slowed down enough to glance at the calendar. Each day meant precious time with Molly and Cole, and she wanted to savor every moment. So how had the week flown by so fast?

Christmas Eve was now just thirteen days away.

No matter how much she tried to make this a happy holiday season, no matter how much she planned and prayed and shopped and baked, she didn't know how the children were going to feel during this first Christmas Eve without their parents.

It might be okay, or they could feel an overwhelming sense of loss, experience a huge meltdown and be swamped with grief. All of the long talks and compassionate hugs in the world could not replace what they'd lost.

Worse, the children's caseworker was technically supposed to come at thirty days, which fell on the day after Christmas. But the woman had just called to say she would be traveling over the holidays and would come to Hannah's sometimes before Christmas Eve.

What if she came on a bad day—when the kids were distraught and inconsolable, and could only talk about going back to Texas?

The thought of losing them tore at Hannah's heart and made it impossible to sleep. On those nights, she just hit the carpet on her knees and begged for the wisdom to make the best choices for the children and the strength to face whatever was ahead.

Hannah shook off her thoughts, finished her coffee and squared her shoulders. "We'd better get going. Is everyone ready? It's time to go get Belle."

Molly shot out of her bedroom like a rocket, with Cole close at her heels. "I can't believe she can actually come home!"

"Remember, guys. She's had to fight a very serious infection where the vet had to cut away that metal choke collar. She's been very ill, and she's still weak. She might just want to be left alone. So you can't rush her. Promise?"

Her coat half on, Molly gave Hannah a stricken look.

"But today is the Advent Blessing of the Animals at the town square. She *needs* that, Aunt Hannah. Trevor and Joanie are bringing their dogs, but Belle is the one who truly needs it. *Please?*"

"And I want to bring Maisie, 'cause she's old. Can I *please*? She needs it, too."

Belle was such a wild card that Hannah didn't know what to say. She was thrilled the kids had made friends at church and that their childlike faith was so firm and trusting.

But Belle had been as fearful as a feral animal when first dumped in the front yard. After twelve days of being cared for by the veterinary staff, she might now be an entirely different dog. Then again, a crowd of strangers might be the worst possible situation for her.

"I can't risk anyone being bitten. Not you two, not anyone at the ceremony. So, first, we need to talk to Dr. Leighton about what she thinks. Unless she feels Belle would be totally safe, I just don't think it's a good idea. And it isn't fair to the dog to bring her into a situation she isn't ready for. Deal?"

Molly thought for a moment. "Maybe we could park close and leave Belle in a kennel in the car. I could stay with her, while you and Cole are at the service. I'll bet God will know that we tried, so he'll bless her, too."

"What a wonderful idea." Hannah gave her a quick hug. "I'm proud of you for thinking of it."

"Is Uncle Ethan coming?"

"He said he would try, but I'm not sure. Do you remember my friend Beth who owns the bookstore? Her husband Devlin was in the army, like Ethan was, and

Beth thought the two of them should meet for coffee. I imagine they'll have a lot to talk about."

At the vet clinic, Dr. Leighton confirmed what Hannah had already guessed. While all of the daily handling had calmed the dog down, her quieter behavior had been within this close environment. Out amid the bustle of crowds and the pets brought for the service, Belle's behavior might be unpredictable.

The vet tech brought Belle out on a leash. Tentative, watchful, the dog tensed when she saw Hannah and the kids and tried to turn back to the kennel room.

"My goodness—she must have gained five or six pounds already!" Hannah exclaimed.

"Not quite, but she's doing better. She's just receiving smaller feedings four times a day, dry kibble without any canned food mixed in. I'll send home some cream for her hips."

"How is her neck?"

"Still healing, so I need to see her again in a week. This dog harness doesn't hit those raw areas so it works better than a standard collar."

Molly edged closer and the dog froze, but soon her tail began waving slowly. "I think she remembers us. Can I lead her to the car?"

"Not quite yet." Dr. Leighton smiled. "Belle had no idea how to respond on a leash when we started. She's finally getting the hang of it, but if she got away she'd be very hard to catch."

Hannah loaded Belle into the wire kennel in the rear compartment of the Subaru and then she helped Cole get into the backseat with Maisie and Molly.

"Okay, kids. We're off to the town square. I think

Belle will be just fine in the back while we're all gone to the service. Okay? I just can't leave Molly alone in the car and, of course, I need to be with Cole. Can't be in two places at once."

Molly nodded. "But will she be warm enough?"

"There's a doubled folded blanket in the cage to lay on, and we won't be gone long." A parking space opened up as Hannah began searching for a spot close to the service. "This is perfect. Now zip up your coats and let's hurry."

The pastor was just starting when they reached the small crowd gathered in front of the old-fashioned band shell. "Some churches take a day for the blessing of animals in October, some choose other days. We thought it would be wonderful to honor our beloved pets during Advent, before Christmas, in remembrance of the animals in the stable where baby Jesus was born, and the camels that brought the wise men. We'll have a prayer for kindness and compassion toward all animals, and a reading, and then you can line up with your pets for their individual blessing. With a forecast of heavy snow heading this way, we won't be here long."

The pastor finished his prayer and gave a quick reading, then motioned for people to come forward and get in line with their pets.

A brisk wind now funneled through the trees, sending snow swirling around their feet. Molly snuggled closer to Hannah's side and threaded her arm through the crook of Hannah's elbow. On her other side, Cole nestled closer, too, with Maisie pressed at his other side. "I'm c-cold," he whispered.

"Do you want to leave?"

"No. I gotta stay. For Maisie."

"Well, keep a close eye on her. If she starts to shiver, we'll have to leave." She urged him toward the line of owners and pets. "I'll be right here, watching you."

At the other side of the crowd Hannah spied Trevor with his parents and a black Lab. "Look, honey—it's your friend."

Molly rolled her eyes but a minute later she edged through the people standing at the back and soon the two of them were laughing over something. Hannah smiled. Molly had joined the church youth group this past week, and it promised to be a big part of her growing comfort in Aspen Creek—exactly what she'd needed after so much upheaval in her life this past year.

Hannah sensed someone approaching on the sidewalk behind her and she felt a light frisson of awareness dance across her skin. She didn't need to hear his voice to know it was Ethan. When he draped an arm around her shoulders, she felt a rush of warmth rocket through her and had to resist the urge to melt into that casual embrace.

"Hey, stranger," he said in a low voice. "Having fun?"

"We're here for a short service," she whispered. "I think the kids expected to see more of their friends with their pets, but the forecast must have kept a lot of people away."

He nodded. "I just checked the radar on my phone. Looks like more snow."

"Yet, who knows—it could still veer off and miss us entirely. But if you don't want to be snowbound alone in your rental cabin, you're welcome to come out to my place."

"I need to pass, sorry."

This was the first invitation he'd turned down and she looked up at him in surprise. "Maybe another time then. You're welcome to join us for supper tomorrow."

"I'll actually be gone for a while. I need to book a flight to Dallas."

"Dallas?" Step by step, she'd been falling under his spell all over again, just as she had years ago. There was something about him that drew her like a magnet and made her think about a future with him.

But was all that charm and attention just a ruse? A way to distract her while his scheming aunt and her lawyers were working on his behalf?

With so few days left until the caseworker was supposed to visit, why would he leave now—unless it was to discuss plans to convince the family court judge about Ethan's custody?

She narrowed her eyes at him. "Why Dallas—and right now?"

"I just met with Devlin Stone and he gave me a lot to think about."

"Really?"

"He asked if I was interested in a job." Ethan's mouth lifted in a wry grin. "Second offer I've had this week."

Well, she hadn't expected *that*. Hannah frowned. "Both here in town?"

"Devlin's is, but he isn't in a rush for an answer. The other offer came out of the blue—an old friend with a security firm in Dallas, and he's in a real bind. He needs someone right away, so he wants me to come down to talk in person."

"Really." Was it a real job or just a good excuse for a fast departure to Texas?

"No idea what I'm going to do, but it feels good to have offers, anyway."

"Interesting timing," she murmured.

"Why do you say that?"

She thought about the growing feelings between them—on her part, anyway. All of the time they'd spent together these past weeks.

And now, just like thirteen years ago, he was planning to leave. At least this time she had some warning.

Mission accomplished, she thought bitterly. He hadn't been here for her. With his aunt's lawyers and his newly established relationships with the kids, he'd likely get exactly what he wanted.

"Aren't you concerned about being here when the caseworker comes? I thought that was one of the main reasons you were staying in town all this time," she snapped.

"No. The main reason was to finally get to know my niece and nephew. After losing their parents, they deserve better than some absentee uncle who never shows up." He cocked an eyebrow and studied Hannah for a long moment. "You don't believe I'm coming back, do you?"

"Why would I *ever* think that?" Hannah snorted. "The sad part is that the kids really do care for you, and I can't figure out what you're planning to do. Just take off and leave them feeling heartbroken? Or maybe you're going off to finagle a victory with a family court judge in Dallas."

"And that's what you think of me," he said flatly. "I thought we had more between us this time. Something really good." He rocked back on his heels. "Guess I was wrong."

"I guess we both were," she said stiffly.

"I *am* coming back, but believe what you want to, Hannah."

Emotion clogged Hannah's throat as he gave each of the kids a quick hug then headed off down the sidewalk without a backward glance.

"Hannah," Cole called out when he reached the front of the line. Feeling as if she were in a daze, Hannah numbly went to join him.

Pastor Mark smiled kindly and rested his palm on Maisie's head. "And who is this fine dog?"

"She's Maisie. She's my best friend, and she's old. Can you help her?"

Pastor Mark blinked. "I sure wish I could, but no one on earth can make her young again. We can pray that she stays healthy and strong, and has a long life, though."

Cole nodded, closing his eyes as the pastor spoke his words of prayer and blessing. Then he tugged at Mark's sleeve before he could turn to the next person in line. "We have another dog in the car. Someone was really mean to her and we're trying to make her well again. Can you pray for her, too?"

After the pastor's second prayer, Cole beamed up at Hannah. "He did it! He prayed for Maisie and Belle both!"

She gave him a quick hug. "Now we'd better scoot so we can get back home. The wind is really coming up and it's getting cold."

They hurried through the square toward the car, their shoulders hunched and chins tucked down into their collars against the biting wind.

When she spied the Subaru, Hannah stopped abruptly. A burly man was moving around the car, peering in the windows. At the back, he glanced around as if watching out for passers-by, then he bent and appeared to be studying the dog inside the cage.

"Who is that?" Molly said. Her voice filled with alarm. "Is he trying to take Belle?"

"The car is locked. Wait here for a second."

Other people were coming up behind them on the sidewalk and heading in the same direction, providing Hannah with an extra measure of confidence. Hooking her purse strap over a shoulder, she strode boldly up to her car, her finger poised over the panic button on her keychain and her cell phone in her other hand. "This is my car. What are you doing?"

He straightened and bared his teeth in a thin leer that displayed a missing tooth in front. Something about him made a shiver crawl down her spine.

"I was just admirin' that dog. No harm in that. Is it yours?"

"I don't care to discuss it."

"Well, it looks like a fine dog, and she's looks mighty familiar. We might need to talk again real soon." He backed away from the rear bumper. Took a long, hard look at the license plate. Then he spun on his heel and walked away.

Hannah watched him disappear down the road before she motioned for the kids to come. As soon as they piled in the car, they were asking questions.

"Who was he?"

"Why was he looking in the car?"

"Was he trying to steal something?"

"Was he after Belle?"

Hannah locked all of the doors and buckled her seat belt, then looked over her shoulder. "I don't have any answers for you, but he's gone now and we're going home. Buckle your seat belts."

All the way home she went over every facet of the stranger's appearance. Exactly what he'd said and done. Could he somehow trace her address via her license number? Police could, but he looked more like a lowlife troublemaker than anyone who had a happy relationship with the cops and could call in a favor.

Then again, what couldn't you find online these days? The old days of privacy and anonymity were long gone.

Her gaze strayed to the dashboard and the mail she'd tossed there after last checking her mailbox. Leaning over, she snagged the top envelope with her fingertip and took a look at it.

If that man had any thought of finding her, he would have no trouble at all, because her address had been in plain sight for anyone to see.

On Monday morning Connie knocked lightly on Hannah's office door at the clinic and smiled. "How are things going out in the country?"

"Really well—I hope. With just ten days until Christmas, Molly and Cole are excited about winter break, of course."

"Any special plans?"

"I promised them rental skis and lessons at the local ski park, and both kids have made some friends. Now Cole joined a church youth group, so both of the kids will have a nice connection there."

"I'm so glad to hear it. Your place must be perfect for them—all those animals."

Hannah nodded. "I hope so. Molly is talking about wanting to join the 4-H club in town, so she can take the dog project with Belle and go to the obedience classes. Apparently there's a dog show at the county fair."

"And Belle is that poor, neglected stray someone dumped in your yard?"

"Yes, though there've been no huge miracles just yet. Molly works with her every day, but Belle has a long way to go." Hannah gazed at the framed photograph on her desk of Molly with Belle and Cole with Maisie. "But, honestly, I think the dog has helped Molly just as much as Molly is helping her. It's given her something to focus on, instead of her problems, and she seems happier now."

"I sure hope everything goes well for you with the custody situation. Those kids were blessed when they were able to move here."

"I pray for them every day, wanting the best for them."

"And how is it going with that handsome soldier of yours?"

"He's not mine, that's for sure." Hannah swallowed hard, reining in her less charitable thoughts. She hadn't heard from him since Saturday evening. What did he deserve—her doubt or her trust?

Her doubt, if she clung to common sense and past experience. She probably wouldn't see him again until they were on opposite sides in a Dallas courtroom. Any fantasies she'd had about happily-ever-afters with Ethan had been a complete waste of time.

"Maybe that's something to just give over to God, too," Connie said gently.

"You're right, of course. I should be trusting, not worrying. But it's so hard to just let go. I worry every day about what will happen with the custody hearing."

"I still think you two should get together." Connie winked. "That would be an easy solution."

"Right. But I'm not even sure where he's going to settle down. Beth's husband talked to him about a job here in Wisconsin, and he had an offer from a company in Dallas. Last I heard, he was flying down for an interview."

"Is shared custody a possibility? Like people arrange after divorce?"

"The last thing either of us wants is such an unsettled life for these kids. Back and forth, summers and holidays, wrenching them away from their friends. The caseworkers say the court would not approve of that, in any case."

Connie's shoulders slumped in defeat. "So there is going to be a really hard decision coming up."

Hannah nodded. "The caseworker will be coming for her thirty-day home visit any day now. We were also supposed to have one at sixty and ninety days, but now I wonder if I'll get that much time."

"Oh, honey—I'm sorry."

"Yeah. Christmas is my favorite time of the year, but this could be the worst one of my life."

A piece of paper fluttered from Connie's fingertips to the floor and she bent to pick it up. "I almost forgot. I came down to give you this. New admission in Room 202 on the hospital side. She came into the ER late last night, and this morning she's asking to see you."

"I've got three pediatric appointments this morning starting at nine. I'll go see her when I go to the long-term-care unit after that."

Connie rolled her eyes. "The nurses would probably appreciate it if you could slip over there now. This is an older lady and she's being difficult. I believe they're hoping you can calm her down."

"Is she someone we know?"

"Unfortunately, I'm afraid you know her rather well. It's Gladys Rexworth."

Chapter Seventeen

Hannah knocked lightly on the door of Room 202. "It's Hannah Dorchester. Can I come in?"

"Please do. I want to get this over with."

She sounded as imperious as ever and Hannah could only imagine what the woman was upset about now. The food. The comfort of her bed. The size of her private room. Or, most likely, her old grievances that were never going to be forgotten as long as the woman breathed.

Hannah walked in and stood at the foot of her bed. "Mrs. Rexworth."

Gladys made a sharp, dismissive motion with her hand. "I suppose you've seen my chart and know why I'm here."

There was certainly a lot of equipment in there. Two IV poles. A monitor tracing her respirations and cardiac rhythm. A discrete catheter tube trailing out from under the blankets to a bag hanging at the side of her bed.

"Actually, no. You're with a different medical group now."

"Surely you people look anyway—just to snoop."

Hannah exhaled slowly. "Strict privacy laws prevent that. Unless I'm asked to be involved in your care by the medical staff—or by you—I cannot access your chart. No one can share information about patients outside of these walls, either. So you needn't worry. Your secrets are safe."

"I doubt that very much." Gladys glowered at her. "I thought you might be planning to stop by and crow about your little victory, and I figured I'd get it over with."

Hannah drew a blank. "Victory? Do you mean the inspection of my rescue?"

Gladys drew herself up in bed. "I have no idea what you're talking about."

But Hannah knew that wasn't true.

The woman's lips compressed in a grim line and she continued. "Never let it be said that I am too proud to admit a mistake. I guess you *might* have been right about my meds."

"If you're being honest, then I will be, too. There was no 'might' about it."

"Yet I'd gotten along just *fine* for all those years."

"I wasn't sure why someone had written all of those prescriptions for you. Maybe you got them from several sources. But I could not, with good judgment and concern for your safety, renew them, and no doctor in our practice would do so, either. If I remember correctly, there were some powerful sedatives and pain meds that posed serious interaction problems. And the doses were far too high."

"My arthritis and back pain are beyond bearing. I

had to have them to just get out of bed, but no one seems to understand that."

"Did your new doctor agree with you?"

Gladys sniffed. "No. I assumed you people found out who he was when my records were transferred, and you warned him."

"So you've been doing well on safer options?"

"I couldn't end up bed-bound with pain, so I did some research online and started asking friends who travel. I discovered that when I vacationed I could get what I needed from those storefront pharmacies in Mexico, and some of it online."

Hannah rocked back on her heels, appalled. "So you've been treating yourself without medical supervision. And your doctor probably didn't know, so he couldn't have known about possible drug interactions whenever he prescribed something else."

Gladys managed a small, stiff nod. "Which, I'm afraid, is why I ended up in the ER last night. If the EMTs hadn't come so quickly, they say I would have died."

Gladys had been one of the most difficult patients Hannah had ever dealt with, but never had she wished the woman would be harmed by her own, wrong-headed opinions.

"I'm very sorry. I hope your recovery will be swift, Gladys." Hannah glanced at the clock on the wall. "If there isn't anything else—"

"Wait."

Hannah moved back to the foot of her bed. "Yes?"

The woman's jaw worked, as if her words tasted sour on her tongue. "I was foolish to risk my health. I... I should have listened to you. And I realize that because of my pride I've only caused trouble for myself—it takes an hour's drive to visit my doctor, now. So I wonder if the Aspen Creek Clinic would have me back."

"I'll ask the doctors, but I expect we would. Just think about it for a while, and let us know. It would be easy enough to have your records transferred."

Hannah shook her head in disbelief as she headed back to the clinic. Apparently, Gladys rarely experienced opposition, because she'd angrily retaliated for years over that medication issue.

She'd bad-mouthed the Aspen Creek Clinic, the physicians and Hannah in particular. And Hannah had no doubt that she'd been the one behind the ongoing, anonymous complaints about the animal rescue.

She'd offered no admission of guilt or apology for that.

But the fact that she'd actually admitted she was wrong was so unbelievable—on par with a blizzard in July—that Hannah was still reeling when she reached her office.

Nothing would surprise her after this.

There'd been no word from Ethan since their argument Saturday evening. Finally unable to stand the uncertainty, she'd driven past his rental cabin on Wednesday, but his truck was still gone and the lights were out. Now it was already Saturday afternoon, and his silent message was perfectly clear.

He was done with Aspen Creek, done with her. And she should count herself blessed for having avoided becoming even more deeply involved with a man she couldn't trust. So why did it feel as if a part of her heart had been torn away?

Because she was a foolish, foolish woman. One who had loved him all those years ago and apparently had never stopped.

After dropping Cole and Molly off at church for a youth group Christmas party, Hannah stopped by the feed store for more pellets for Penelope and hurried home to work on the house, thankful that Trevor's parents had offered to bring the kids home afterward.

There'd been no word from the caseworker about her home visit, but with Christmas Eve next Thursday, it could be any day now. Would the woman expect a spotless kitchen? Would she grill the kids on every aspect of their lives? If one of them complained about their chores, or the school, or their friends, would that torpedo any chance that they could stay here?

Hannah had no idea and the looming visit made her feel as jittery as if she'd had way too much espresso.

And maybe none of her efforts would even matter.

But it was all too believable that Ethan was down in Dallas, meeting with his aunt's lawyers and planning his next move once the Wisconsin home visit was completed.

She slowed the vehicle to turn into her driveway. An unfamiliar, battered pickup, its tailgate rusted to fragile lace, stood parked in front of her house. The cacophony of dogs barking inside the house was deafening, even out there.

She frowned. Who could be here now—and where was the driver? No one had called about seeing one of the animals.

A feeling of unease swept through her, yet she could hardly call the sheriff's office because an unfamiliar vehicle was there. Maybe the driver was lost. Maybe this was a mom, shepherding her child through yet another school fund-raiser sale and they were looking for her out back.

Shoving her cell phone into her jacket pocket, she eased out of her car…and froze. The burly man she'd seen looking into her car in town came around the corner of the garage. He was carrying a leash.

She swallowed hard and squared her shoulders. "Can I help you?"

He gave her a derisive glance then braced his hands on the garage door and stood on tiptoe to peer into the high, narrow windows of the garage. "I'm here for my dog. Where is she?"

Hannah had no doubt that he'd tried all the doors, hoping to break in. "You are trespassing. As the rescue center website states, appointments are always necessary, and you don't have one."

"I don't need an appointment to pick up my own dog," he snarled.

Slowly pulling out her cell phone, she pressed the speed dial number for 9-1-1 and held the phone to her ear. "I've got a situation here—an angry, aggressive man, and I need a deputy. No idea who this guy is. Yes—that's right…48193 Spruce."

"Wasted call, lady. No sheriff can keep me from claiming my own dog."

"I don't know what dog you're talking about. Did you check the website? Do you have the dog's number?"

"You had the dog in your car in town last Saturday. Remember?"

"If that's true, why didn't you say something then?"

"I don't believe in making a scene."

Not where there were witnesses. "So you decided to skulk out here when nobody was home."

"I could have you arrested for theft. Hand her over."

"And I've got the photographs and vet bills—so you could be arrested for animal abuse. Actually, my vet has her own copies of everything, and said she's turning it all over to the sheriff's office this week."

He cast an edgy glance toward the road, where she could already hear the sound of an approaching car. So maybe he wasn't so eager to visit with a deputy, after all.

He pulled his truck door open, but hesitated and started straight toward her. "Don't make me have to come back, lady. You'll never know when. Maybe some night you and those kids will be sleeping, all peaceful like, and you suddenly see—"

He outweighed her by a good hundred pounds and he was a lot taller. But she hadn't studied and taught self-defense for nothing, and his forward momentum was just what she needed.

Landing a swift, full-force kick to his groin, she grabbed his wrist when he buckled and twisted it high behind his back as he fell. Then she had him nailed to the ground, groaning and gasping, with her knee on his spine and his arm wrenched in a painful position he could not escape.

She leaned close to his ear. "Just another inch and you'll need rotator cuff surgery or, maybe, you'll never use this arm again. I won't care either way, believe me.

Not after you threatened my kids. So if I were you, I would never, ever, come back."

At the sound of a car door, she looked over her shoulder to welcome the deputy.

But it wasn't a patrol car parked behind her Subaru and that sure wasn't a deputy. The pale tan car sported a round county decal on the door and the woman staring at her held a big notebook, not a weapon. And she'd been close enough to hear Hannah's every word.

The woman's frightened gaze darted between Hannah and the man on the ground, then she looked toward the wail of a siren flying up the road.

Before he hauled the intruder away, the deputy questioned everyone, including the social worker. The entire process took over an hour.

After the deputy left, Hannah gave the social worker—Liz Anderson—a tour of the house and yard, and had shown her the temporary animal pens in the garage. Now the two of them were sitting in Hannah's kitchen.

Liz sat hunched over a mug of coffee she was gripping with both shaking hands. "Does this sort of thing happen…um, often, with your animal rescue?"

"First time ever," Hannah said firmly. "I'm still mystified about why that man was so aggressive and so desperate to get the dog back."

"But she was his, right?"

"He did know about the position of several scars, but he'd abused and neglected her horribly. I now think someone finally nabbed her from his property and brought her here, hoping to save her from a horrible situation. I'll do everything in my power to make sure she ends up in a loving home."

Liz slanted a troubled look at her. "You seem to lead a very exciting and hectic life."

"No, not really. I have a good career and I take in animals who need to find a good home. But now that Molly and Cole are here, they are my primary focus. I'm thrilled to have the chance to give them the home they deserve. I hope you'll see them settling in better each time you come."

Liz bit her lower lip. "I'm so glad we are in agreement about them having a loving and stable home, but I'm afraid there has been a misunderstanding. Did you not receive a letter from the family court in Dallas?"

Hannah suddenly felt faint. "A letter?"

"The attorneys representing Mr. Williams have discussed Molly and Cole on a number of occasions, and the court agreed— to drag out this process through the next ninety days is not in the children's best interest. The plan is to finalize the custody issue by December thirty-first."

"And do you foresee the result?" Hannah's voice sounded dull and faraway, even to her own ears.

"Frankly, I can't say. I do know split custody—as with a divorce—is not even on the table, nor will it be."

"I see." So Ethan had betrayed her yet again—just as she'd feared. There probably hadn't been a job interview at all. Had he flown to Texas to meet with those attorneys this past week to make sure his plan was firmly in place?

"It's not a done deal yet, of course," Liz added in a soothing tone. "But, don't worry. No matter what happens, the children will still be here with you through Christmas and, even if they go back to Texas, I'm sure you'll be able to visit."

Chapter Eighteen

Ethan wearily drove back to Aspen Creek from the airport on Christmas Eve Day, rehearsing the words he planned to say when he reached Hannah's house.

He'd been praying a lot lately and now he started praying again—wanting Hannah to be at home so they could work things out once and for all. Fearing that she would be there and would shut the door in his face. Or that she wouldn't hear him through.

Her car was in the drive. *Thank you, Lord.*

He strode up to the door, knocked and let himself in. Molly and Cole were at the base of the Christmas tree, shaking presents and stacking them back with the rest.

Cole spied him first. "You're back!" he squealed, rushing over for a hug. "We were afraid you wouldn't come! And guess what? A big box came from Texas today, and it was all of our special Christmas ornaments! Great-Aunt Cynthia sent them. So we put them all on the tree. Isn't it pretty?"

"It sure is, buddy."

Molly ran over, too, more reserved at her age, but she

looked up at him with shining eyes and hugged him. "I'm so glad you're here, Uncle Ethan! Hannah will be happy—she's been really sad since you've been gone. She's out feeding the animals, if you want to see her."

Sad? He suspected she was more angry than sad, but allowed himself a small glimmer of hope.

"I've missed you guys so much." Ethan brushed a kiss against her forehead.

Molly stepped back and gave him an accusing look. "Then how come you left for so long?"

"I didn't plan to. But things got really complicated and it all took longer than I thought. Can you kids stay in here for a while? Hannah and I need to talk. Privately."

"But then you're staying, right? It's Christmas Eve, you know."

"I wouldn't miss it for the world." Ethan tousled Cole's hair then headed for the garage with long strides.

The moment he walked in and closed the door behind him, Hannah turned around with a smile. Then the light faded from her eyes. "You're back."

"I wish I'd been here."

"I'm sure you had all sorts of business to attend to in Texas," she said flatly. "A job interview, wasn't it?"

"That was why I went, yes."

"And you decided to take the job?"

"Devlin offered me a job here. And I've been offered the job in Dallas, as well." He gave a short, self-deprecating laugh. "But I haven't decided. Yet."

Hannah folded her arms over her chest. "Nice to have options, anyway."

"Funny—until I came up here, my only career goal was to get back into active duty. But that obviously isn't in the cards. Not with my injuries. Not given what I want to do with the rest of my life."

"So you've sorted out your future, then."

"Not entirely. I went to visit my aunt to see how she's doing with her broken hip, and things went south after that."

"Really." The troubled look in her eyes betrayed her, despite her nonchalant tone.

"Hannah, I can imagine what you're thinking, but I didn't go to Texas trying to wrangle the court into giving me custody. I discovered my aunt was trying to do that all by herself and I had to stop it."

She froze. "And how did that go?"

"She thought she was doing the right thing, but the legal mess she created with her lawyers had become a tangle of legal issues that took days to work through."

"And now you've gotten it worked out to your satisfaction?" Hannah said coldly. "As you can see, I'm not wealthy enough to fight you all in court."

"That won't be necessary." He pulled an envelope from his pocket and handed it to her. "A bill for a safe-deposit box rented by Rob and Dee was forwarded to my aunt. She went to that bank to cancel the box rental and clear out the contents, and found this letter. It was written by my brother a few days after Molly was born and saved all these years. He probably just forgot about it."

Hannah skimmed the letter then read it again more slowly, her hands shaking.

Dear Ethan,
If you're reading this, something must have hap-

*pened to Dee and me. I want you to be our ex-
ecutor, and to take Molly and any other kids we
might have.*

*I trust you, and no one else, to do the right
thing and raise them right. You and I sure know
how tough it is to have neglectful, irresponsible
parents. I pray my kids will have a far better life.
Rob*

"So you've got what you want," she said bitterly.
"Proof that your brother wanted you to take his children
if anything ever happened to Dee and him. There's no
way I can fight this."

"But I can't believe he still meant it at the time he
died. You were just twenty and in college when Molly
was born. I was in the army and had an income, so I'm
sure that's why he named me guardian back then. But
now—with the life I've led all over the globe, and you,
with a great job and your roots so firmly planted here?
He and Dee would have chosen you in a heartbeat. It's
just a shame they never thought to write it down."

She searched his face, tears glittering in her eyes.
"So what are you saying?"

He tore Rob's letter in two and then rested his hands
on her shoulders. "I've told my interfering aunt, her attorneys and the court that I am not interested in con-
testing custody. I've signed documents to that effect."

"Oh, Ethan." A tear spilled down Hannah's cheek.
"I'm sorry for the things I've said. For doubting you."

"I admit I first came up here wanting to gain full
custody. I thought I owed it to Rob to raise his kids
right," Ethan admitted. "But I was wrong. You're won-

derful with them. You're everything they need to grow up happy and strong, and no matter what happens between you and me, that bond should not be threatened."

"So what happens now?" She swallowed hard. "Are you leaving?"

"I'd like to start over with you. I want us to forget our ill-fated, crazy beginning back when we were too young to know what we really wanted. I want a chance to see where we can go—the two of us—without all the drama of child custody issues to tear us apart."

She rested a hand at the side of his cheek. "I'd like that, too."

"But it's going to take time, I know," he added. "And you were right—I'm going to join a support group— finally. And I'm going to start counseling. I don't want to be living half a life anymore. I want to be worthy of you."

She slid her hand behind his neck and drew him close for a sweet, lingering kiss. "It all sounds wonderful, Ethan."

He tipped his head. "About that heart of yours, I still want to win it. I hope to be a part of your life until these kids have children of their own and we're in rocking chairs watching them grow. So, what do you think? Are we too old to go steady?"

Her tears started in earnest now and she started to laugh. "I think you won my heart years ago and never let it go, so maybe we should set our sights a little higher. But, yes—that sounds perfect to me. And what a wonderful Christmas gift!"

Epilogue

"Are you sure this is going to work?" Keeley whispered, eyeing Molly and Cole.

Dressed in a white, eyelet-lace dress, Molly held Belle's leash tight as she smoothed the big, white bow on the dog's collar.

Cole, in a pale blue Oxford shirt and tie, fidgeted next to them, holding on to Maisie. Maisie's bow was already askew and Cole's tie wasn't straight, but getting two nervous kids and two dogs ready for this moment had been an accomplishment in itself.

What a journey these past six months had been.

"I think everything is absolutely perfect." Hannah smiled at her old friend. "I just can't believe we're all here for a day I never thought would happen."

Late-afternoon sunshine filtered through the massive oaks and maples, scattering golden coins of light over the small gathering of friends already seated in rows of white chairs, listening to the soaring notes of a violin and harp.

Everyone was here who mattered to her and her heart swelled at the joy of this moment.

A few yards away Ethan finished talking to Devlin, then he came over to join Hannah and Keeley. "No second thoughts?" he teased as he tucked Hannah's arm around his.

"Never." She reached up to curve a hand behind his head and drew him into a lingering kiss. "I couldn't be happier."

The music changed to Pachelbel's Canon in D and Molly sent Hannah a worried glance. "N-now?"

Hannah smiled and nodded, then watched the children proceed up the short, grassy aisle to the flower-bedecked lattice archway where Pastor Mark stood waiting.

At the front, Molly turned to the left and Cole to the right, their dogs obediently sitting next to them.

"They were perfect," Hannah breathed. "I'm so proud of them!"

She looked up at Ethan and their gazes met, locked.

Ethan now worked for Devlin, and the two were planning to turn the business into a partnership. Someone had made a significant donation toward building a new animal shelter in town just last week—probably Gladys, out of sheer guilt for being so difficult in the past.

But, best of all, the child custody issues were all in the past and by next month Ethan and Hannah would be the children's adoptive parents.

Ethan smiled down at her. "Just last Christmas, I never would've guessed this day could be possible. But, Hannah, you've made me the happiest guy on earth."

He drew her into a warm embrace and a kiss that told

her just how much he meant it—one that sent tingles of joy clear to her toes.

And then they walked arm in arm to the pastor and their new beginning as husband and wife.

* * * * *

Recipe

Super Easy Roll-Out Cookies

This recipe remains easy to work with, even after rolling it out a number of times. It's great for making cookies with children because the dough is very easy to handle.

Preheat oven to 350°F.

Cream together:
1 cup shortening
(don't substitute butter or margarine)
1½ cups sugar

Add to creamed mixture and mix well:
2 eggs
1 tsp. vanilla
2 tbsp. milk

Add the following dry ingredients:
4 cups flour
1½ tsp. cream of tartar
1 tsp. baking soda
½ tsp. salt

Optional: *1 tsp. cinnamon and/or 1 tsp. nutmeg*

Roll out the dough and cut out with cookie cutters. Place on greased cookie sheet, at least an inch apart.

Decorate with colored sugars, sprinkles and/or red hots before baking, or frost after they are baked and cooled.

Bake for 8-10 minutes, until golden.

Yield will depend on the size of your cookie cutters.

WE HOPE YOU ENJOYED
THIS BOOK FROM

LOVE INSPIRED
INSPIRATIONAL ROMANCE

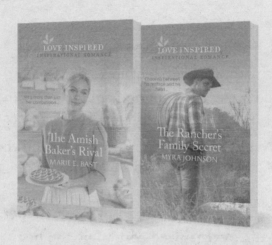

Uplifting stories of faith, forgiveness and hope.

Fall in love with stories where faith helps
guide you through life's challenges, and discover
the promise of a new beginning.

6 NEW BOOKS AVAILABLE EVERY MONTH!

LIHALO2021

LOVE INSPIRED

Stories to uplift and inspire

Fall in love with Love Inspired—
inspirational and uplifting stories of faith
and hope. Find strength and comfort in
the bonds of friendship and community.
Revel in the warmth of possibility and the
promise of new beginnings.

Sign up for the Love Inspired newsletter
at **LoveInspired.com** to be the first
to find out about upcoming titles,
special promotions and exclusive content.

CONNECT WITH US AT:

Facebook.com/LoveInspiredBooks

Twitter.com/LoveInspiredBks